# MAPMAKERS

## AND THE

## ENCHANTED MOUNTAIN

Also by Cameron Chittock and Amanda Castillo
*Mapmakers and the Lost Magic*

# MAPMAKERS

## AND THE ENCHANTED MOUNTAIN

Written by
**CAMERON CHITTOCK**

Illustrated by
**AMANDA CASTILLO**

Colored by
Sara Calhoun

RH GRAPHIC
New York

*Mapmakers and the Enchanted Mountain* was written with pencil and paper before being transferred to a Word document. It was drawn and colored digitally in Photoshop and lettered with the artist's own handwritten font.

Text copyright © 2023 by Cameron Chittock
Cover art and interior illustrations copyright © 2023 by Amanda Castillo

All rights reserved. Published in the United States by RH Graphic, an imprint of Random House Children's Books, a division of Penguin Random House LLC, New York.

RH Graphic with the book design is a trademark of Penguin Random House LLC.

Visit us on the web! RHKidsGraphic.com • @RHKidsGraphic

Educators and librarians, for a variety of teaching tools, visit us at RHTeachersLibrarians.com

Library of Congress Cataloging-in-Publication Data is available upon request.
ISBN 978-0-593-17290-2 (paperback) — ISBN 978-0-593-17291-9 (hardcover)
ISBN 978-0-593-17292-6 (library binding) — ISBN 978-0-593-17293-3 (ebook)

Designed by Patrick Crotty
Coloring by Sara Calhoun
Title design by Walter Parenton

MANUFACTURED IN CHINA
10 9 8 7 6 5 4 3 2 1
First Edition

**A comic on every bookshelf.**

For Rowe
—C.C.

For Mama Li, whose love for our family and roots is
always an inspiration. Mahal kita magpakailanman.
—A.C.

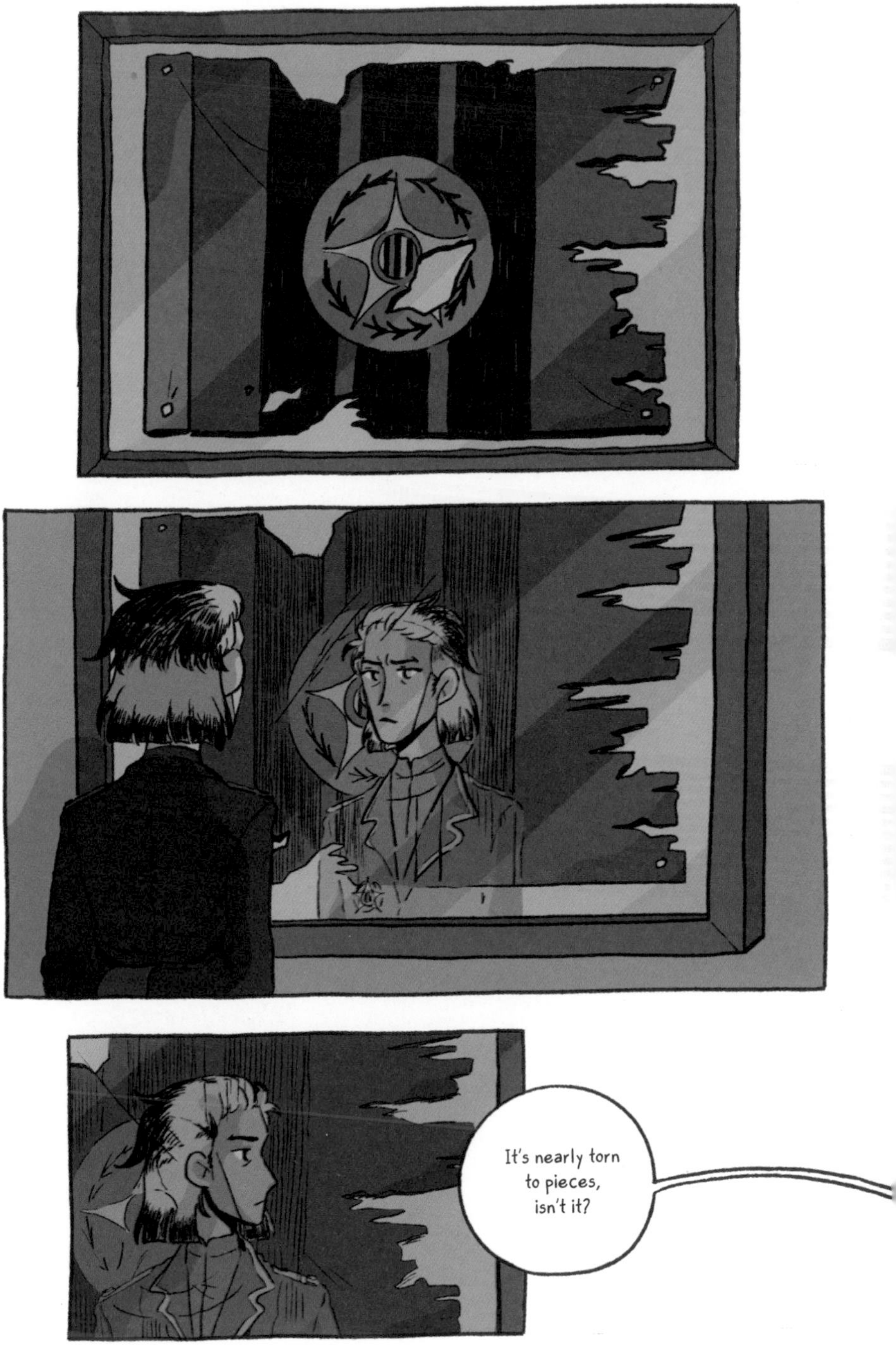
It's nearly torn to pieces, isn't it?

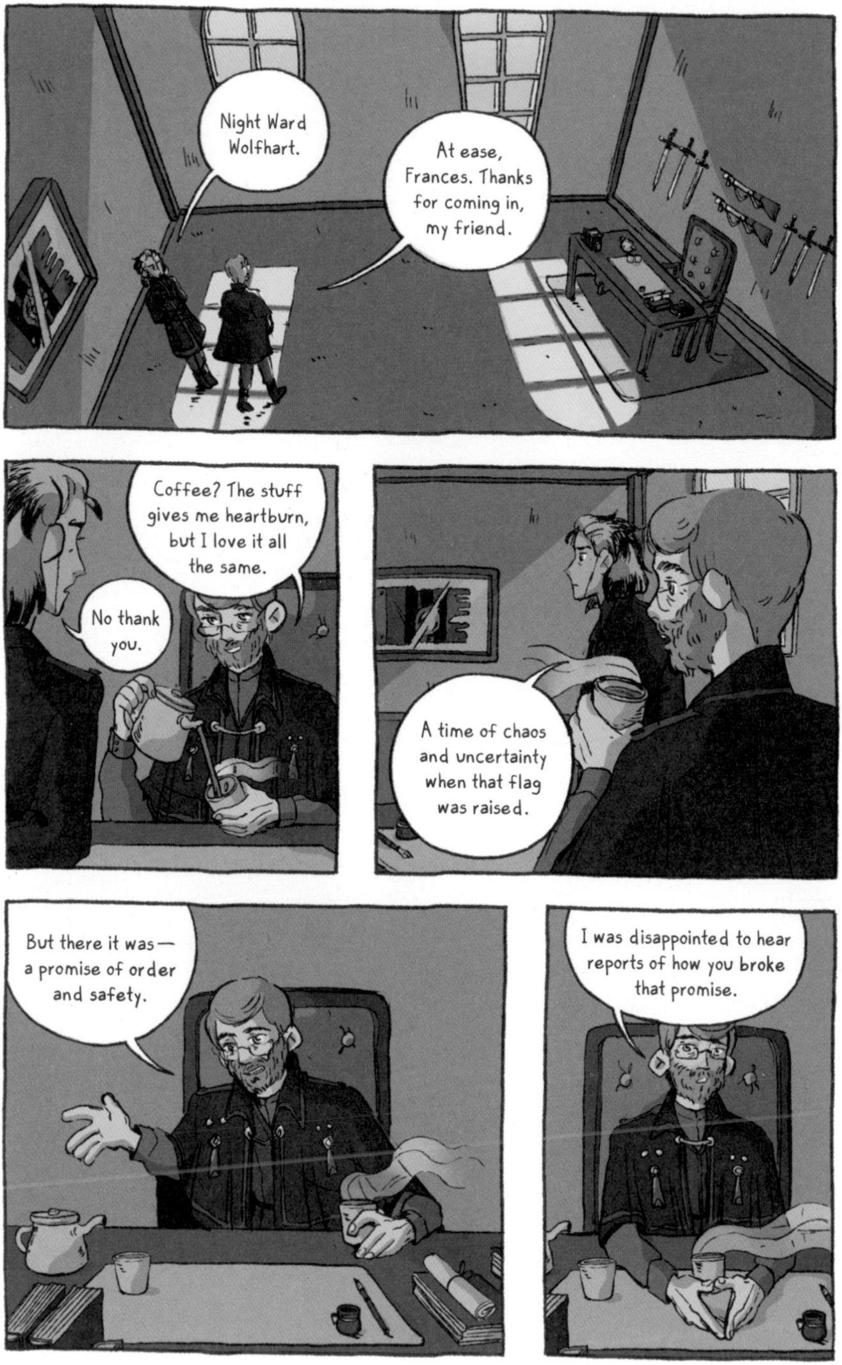
Night Ward Wolfhart.
At ease, Frances. Thanks for coming in, my friend.
Coffee? The stuff gives me heartburn, but I love it all the same.
No thank you.
A time of chaos and uncertainty when that flag was raised.
But there it was— a promise of order and safety.
I was disappointed to hear reports of how you broke that promise.

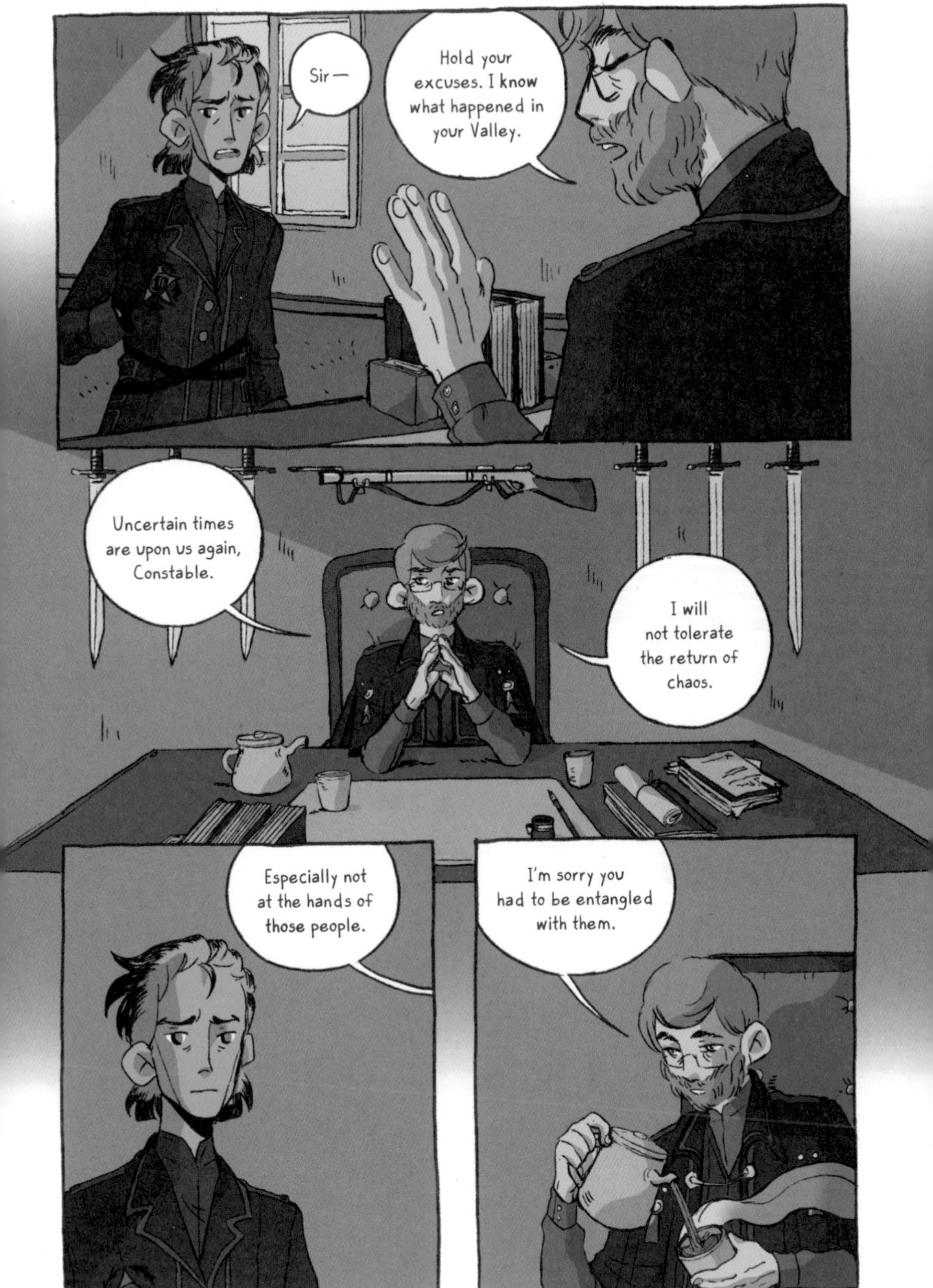
Sir—
Hold your excuses. I know what happened in your Valley.
Uncertain times are upon us again, Constable.
I will not tolerate the return of chaos.
Especially not at the hands of those people.
I'm sorry you had to be entangled with them.

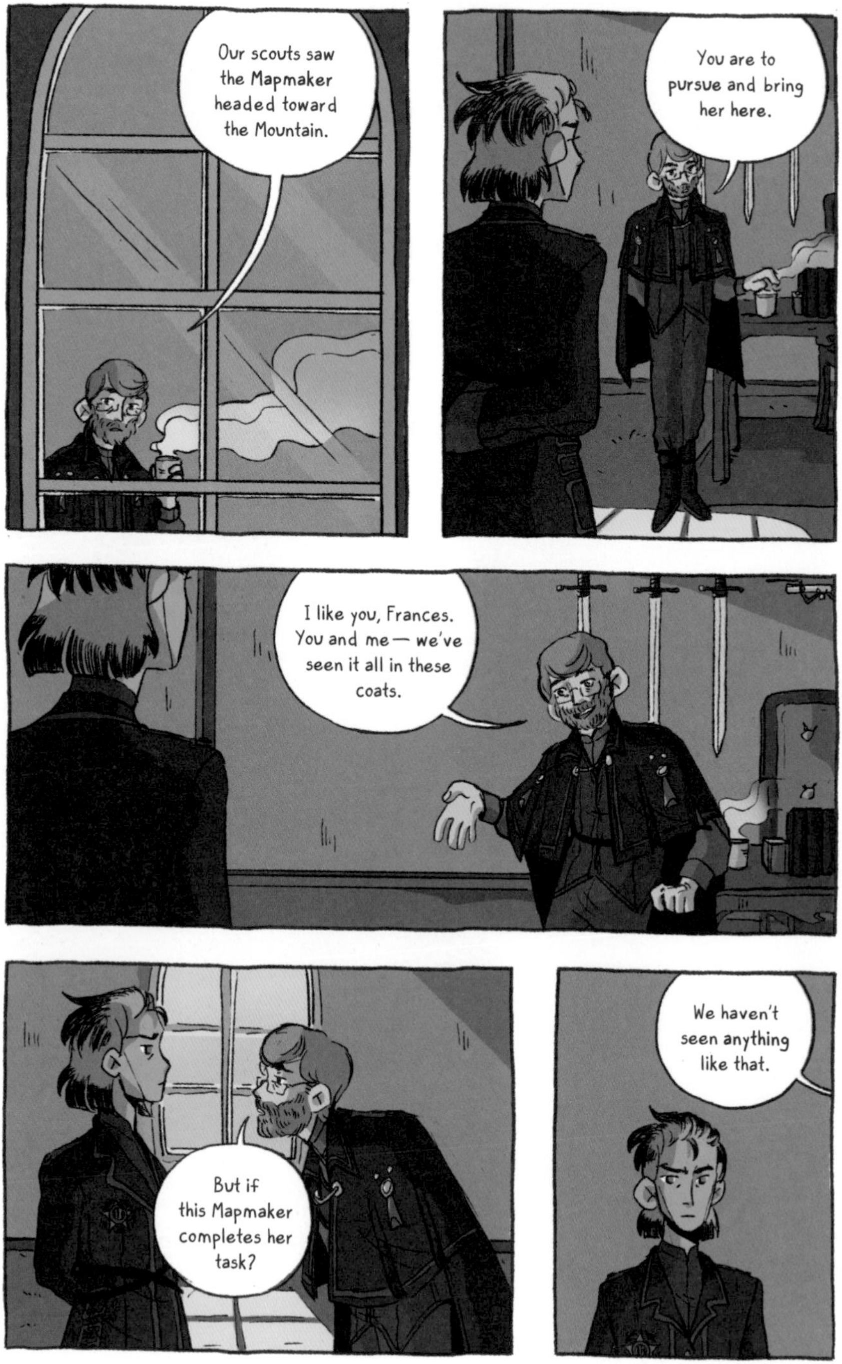
Our scouts saw the Mapmaker headed toward the Mountain.
You are to pursue and bring her here.
I like you, Frances. You and me— we've seen it all in these coats.
But if this Mapmaker completes her task?
We haven't seen anything like that.

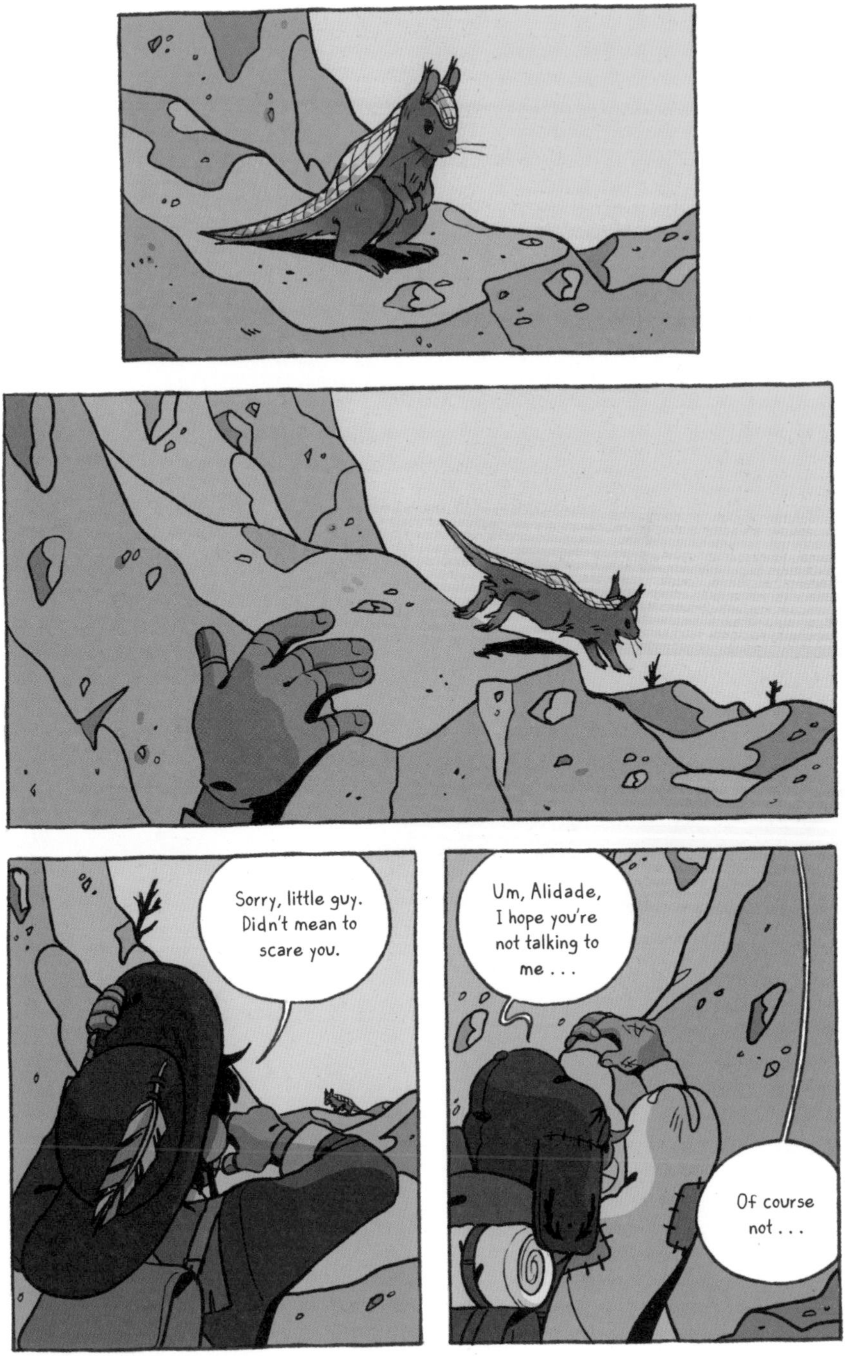
Sorry, little guy. Didn't mean to scare you.
Um, Alidade, I hope you're not talking to me . . .
Of course not . . .

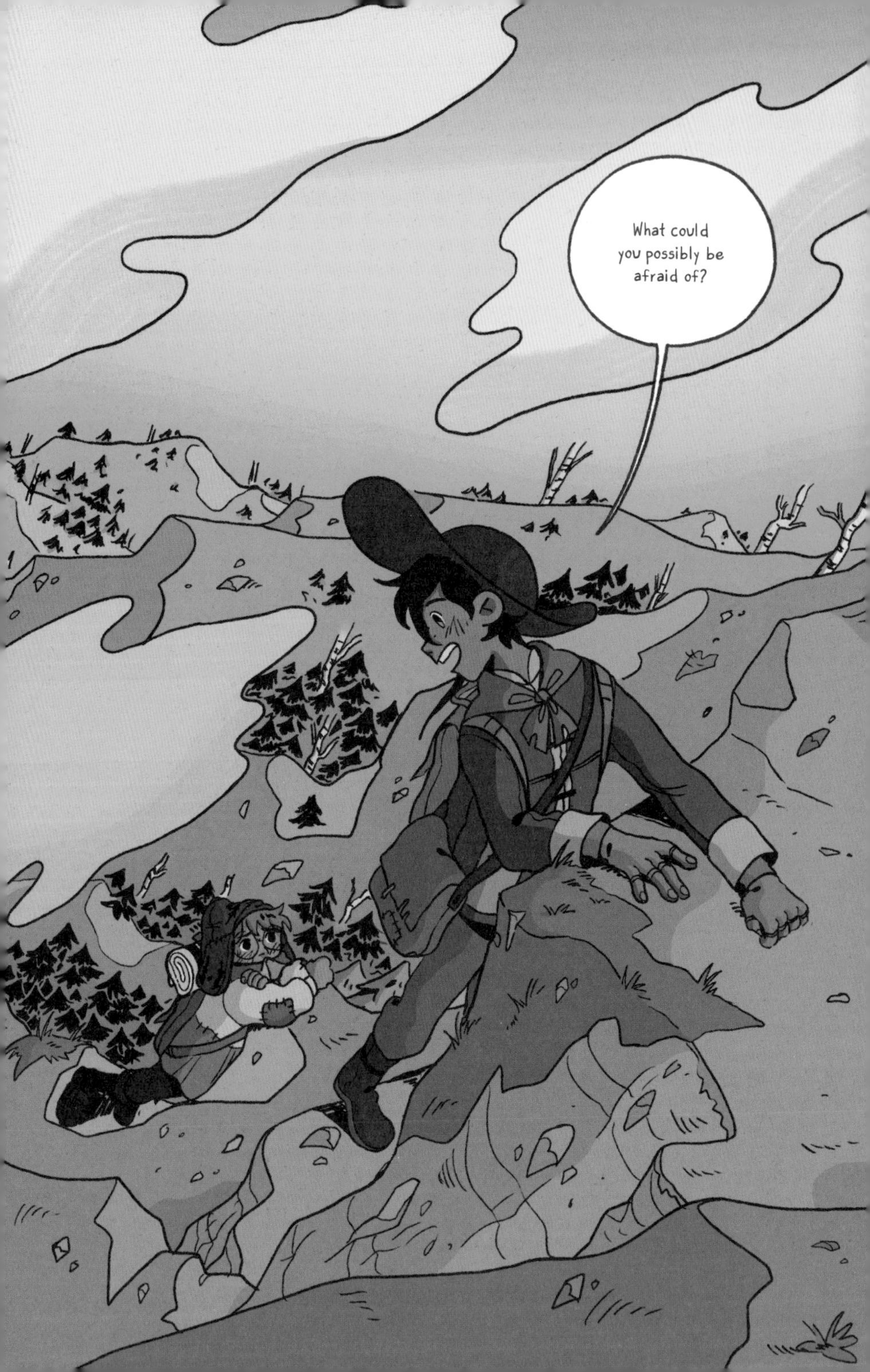
What could you possibly be afraid of?

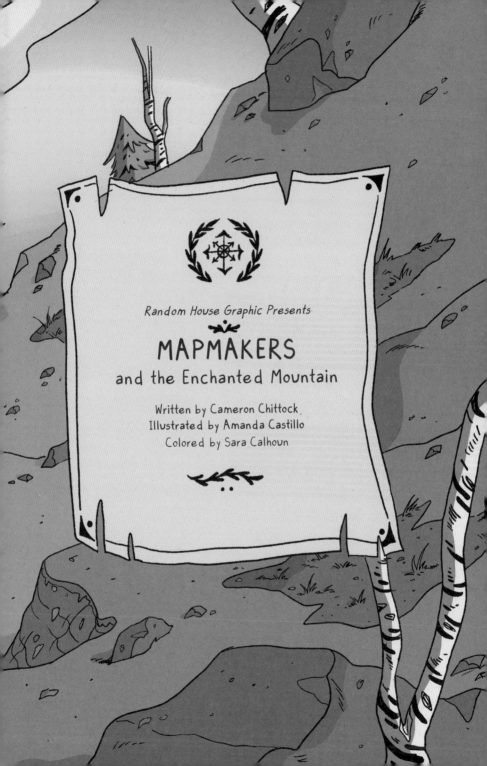

Random House Graphic Presents

# MAPMAKERS
## and the Enchanted Mountain

Written by Cameron Chittock
Illustrated by Amanda Castillo
Colored by Sara Calhoun

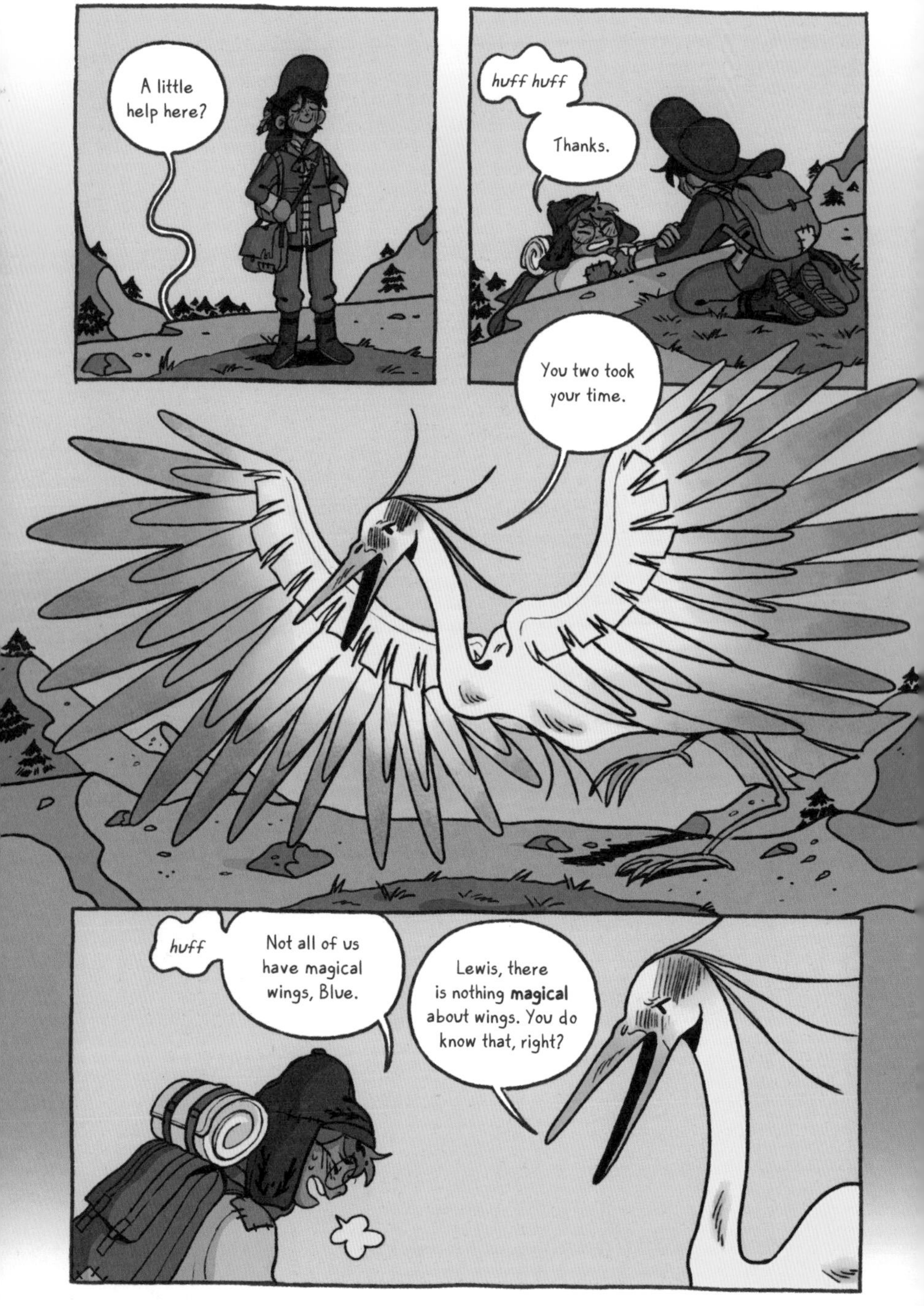
A little help here?
huff huff
Thanks.
You two took your time.
huff
Not all of us have magical wings, Blue.
Lewis, there is nothing **magical** about wings. You do know that, right?

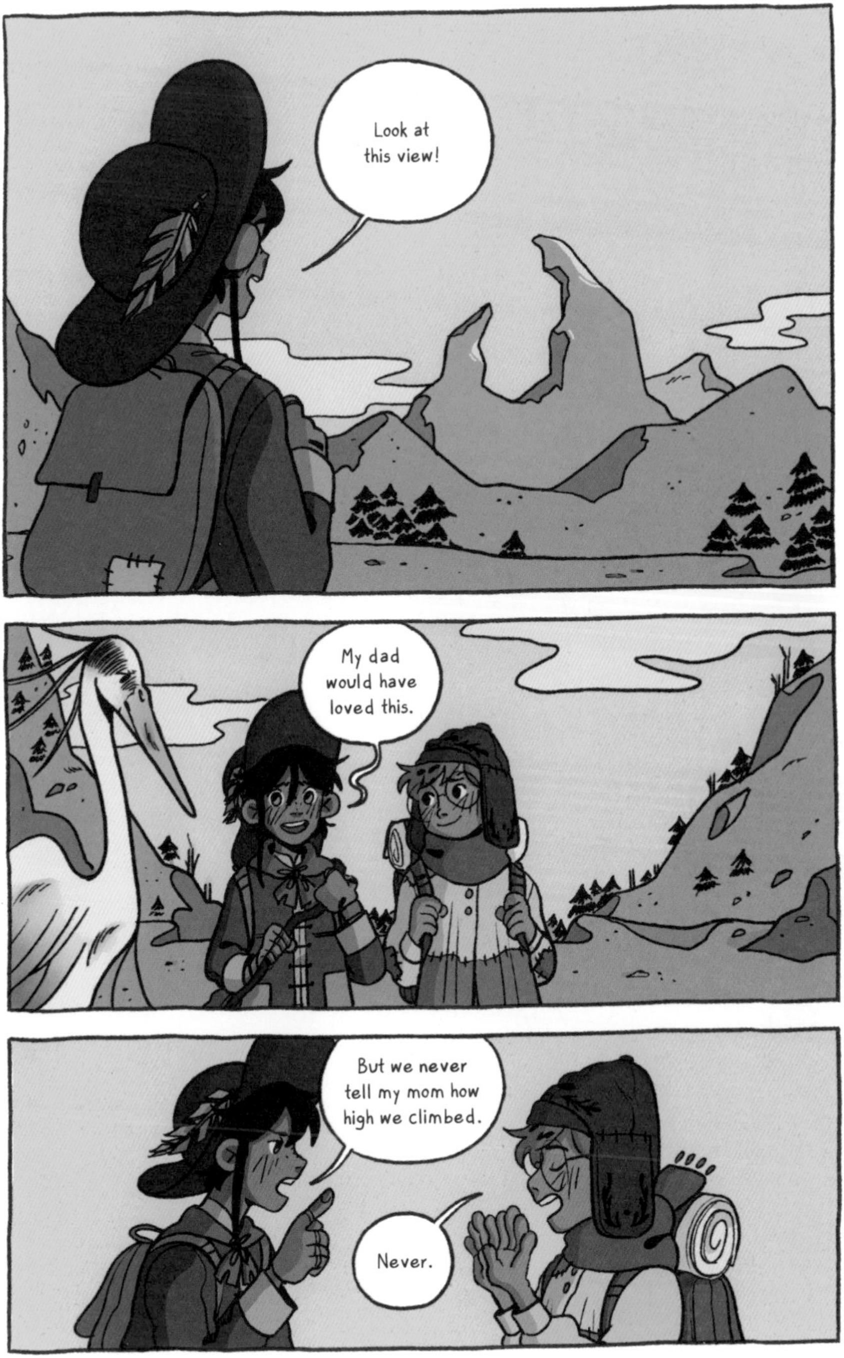
Look at this view!
My dad would have loved this.
But we never tell my mom how high we climbed.
Never.

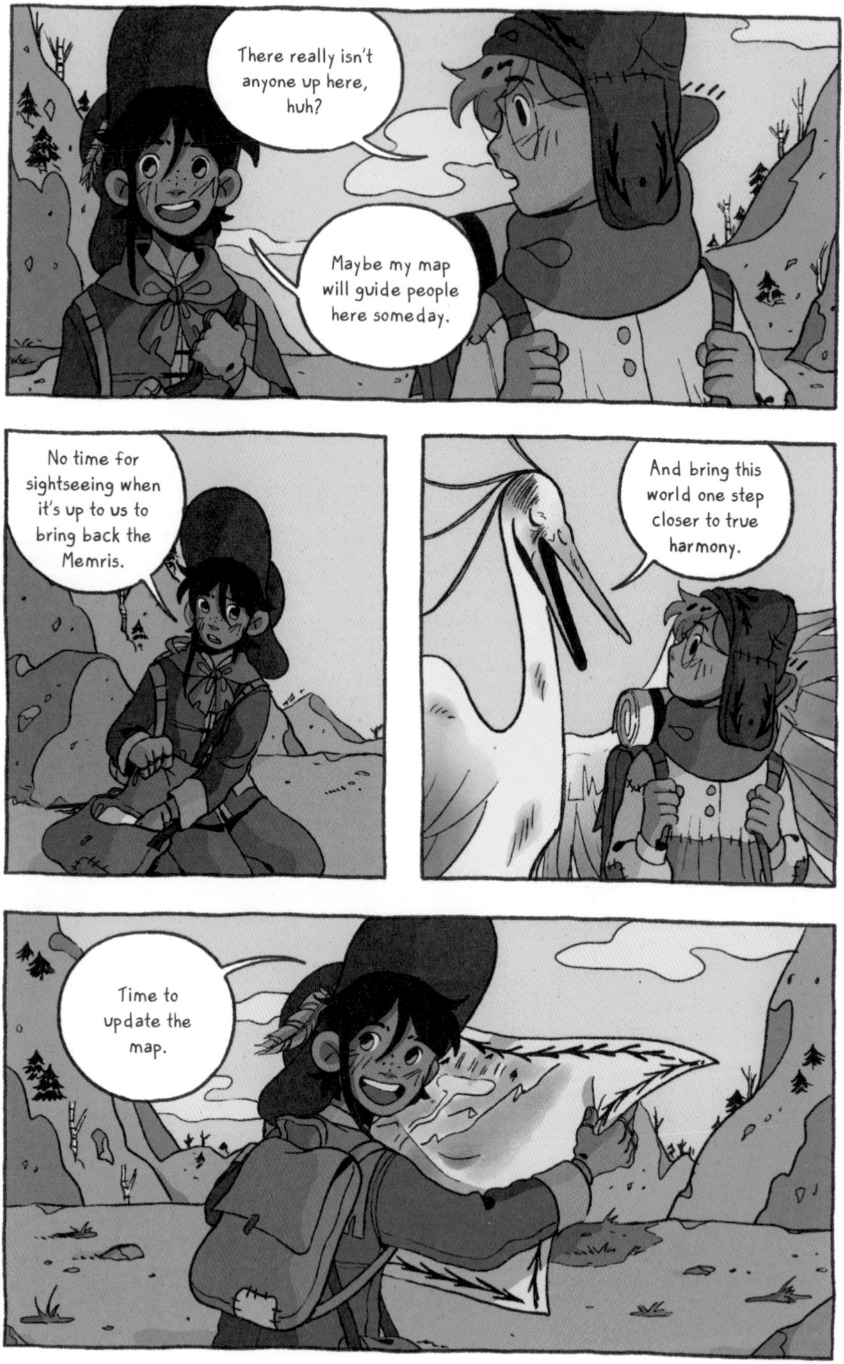
There really isn't anyone up here, huh?
Maybe my map will guide people here someday.
No time for sightseeing when it's up to us to bring back the Memris.
And bring this world one step closer to true harmony.
Time to update the map.

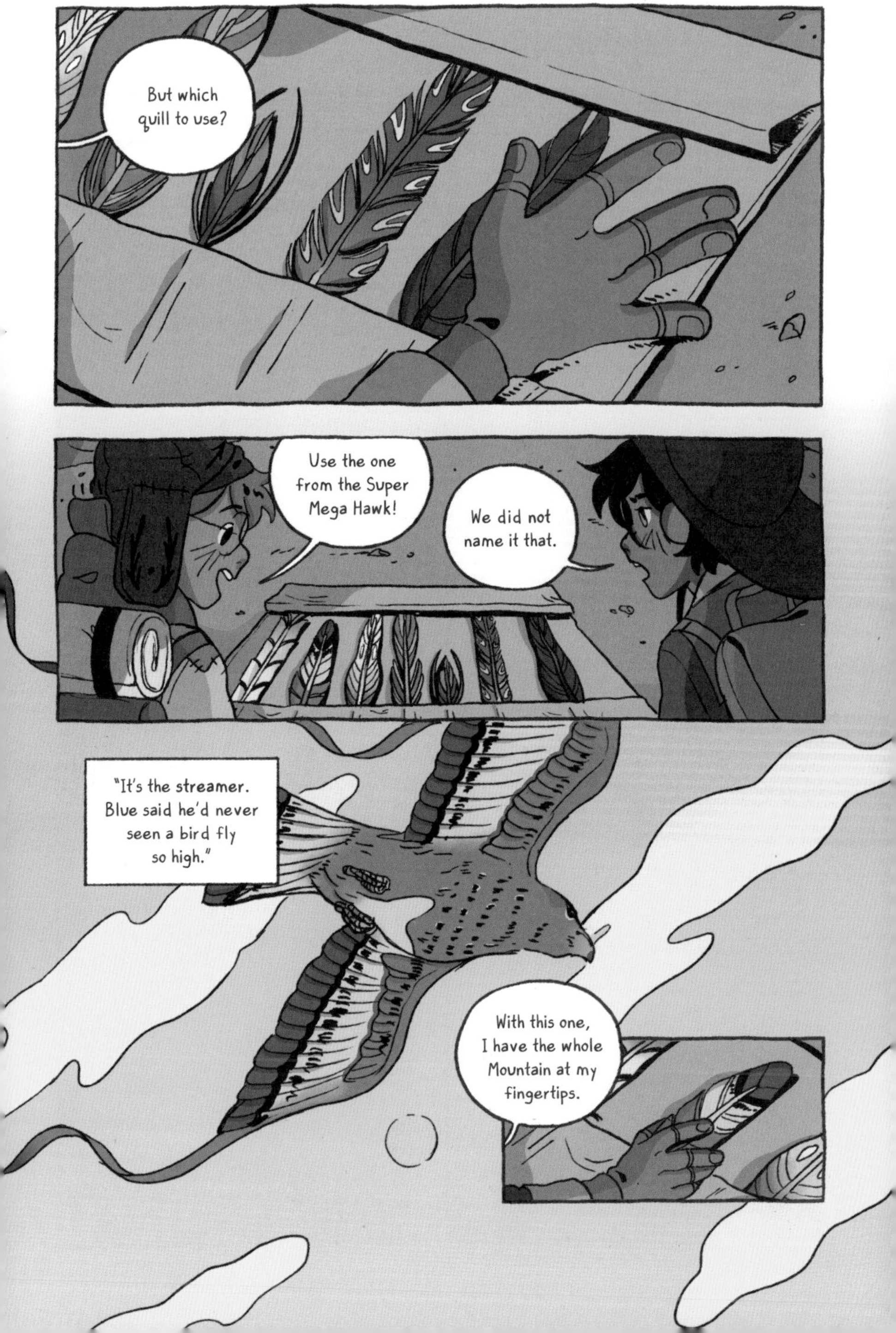
But which quill to use?
Use the one from the Super Mega Hawk!
We did not name it that.
"It's the streamer. Blue said he'd never seen a bird fly so high."
With this one, I have the whole Mountain at my fingertips.

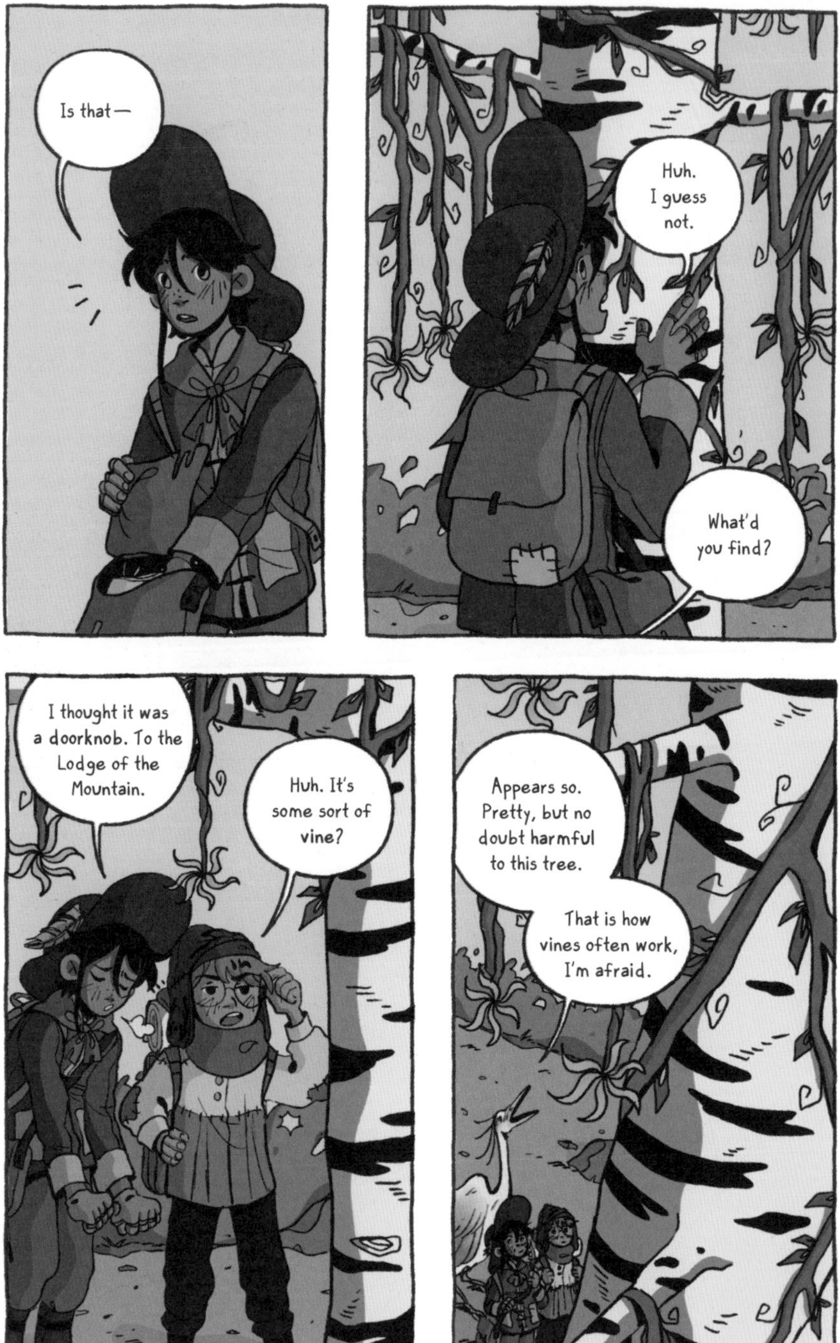
Is that—
Huh. I guess not.
What'd you find?
I thought it was a doorknob. To the Lodge of the Mountain.
Huh. It's some sort of vine?
Appears so. Pretty, but no doubt harmful to this tree.
That is how vines often work, I'm afraid.

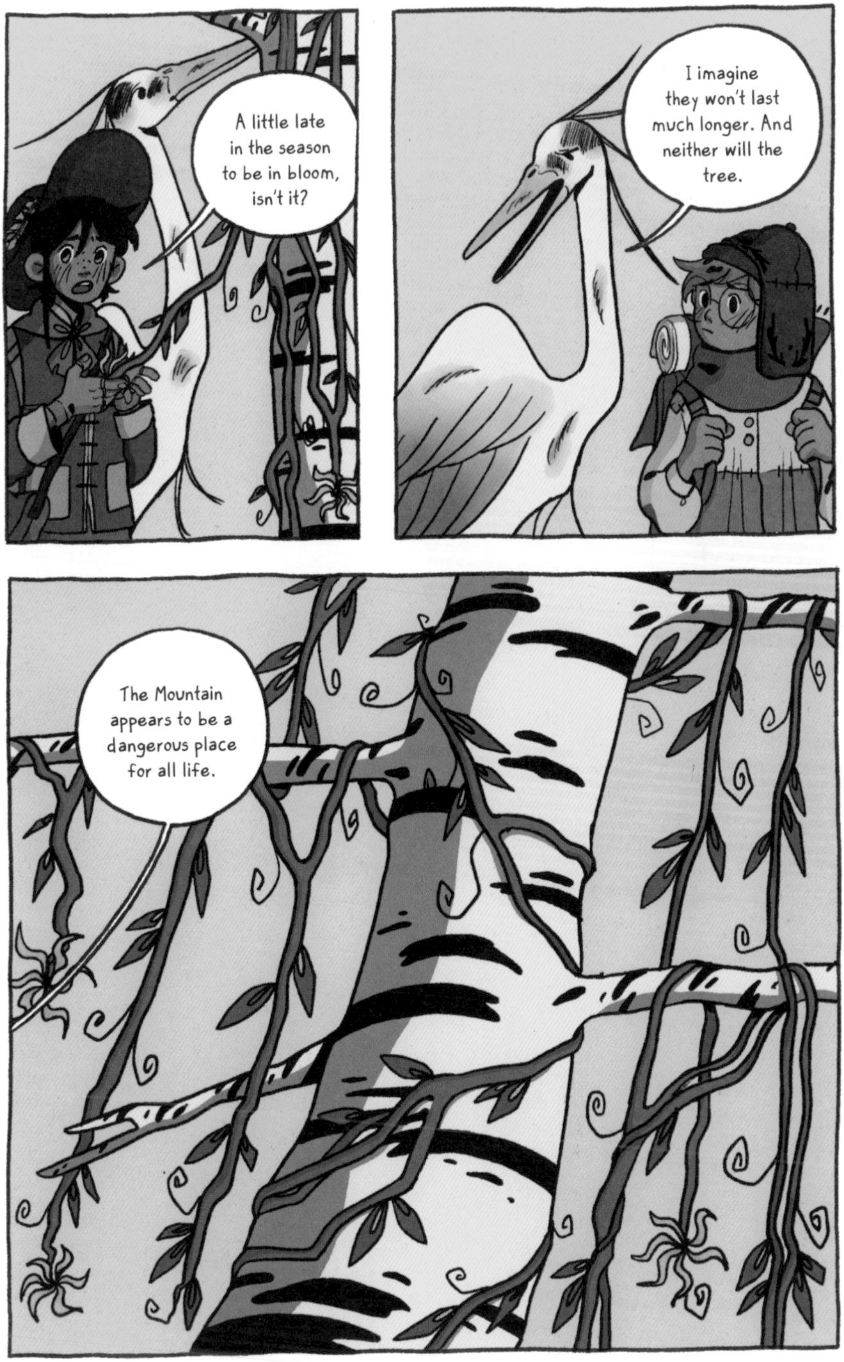
A little late in the season to be in bloom, isn't it?
I imagine they won't last much longer. And neither will the tree.
The Mountain appears to be a dangerous place for all life.

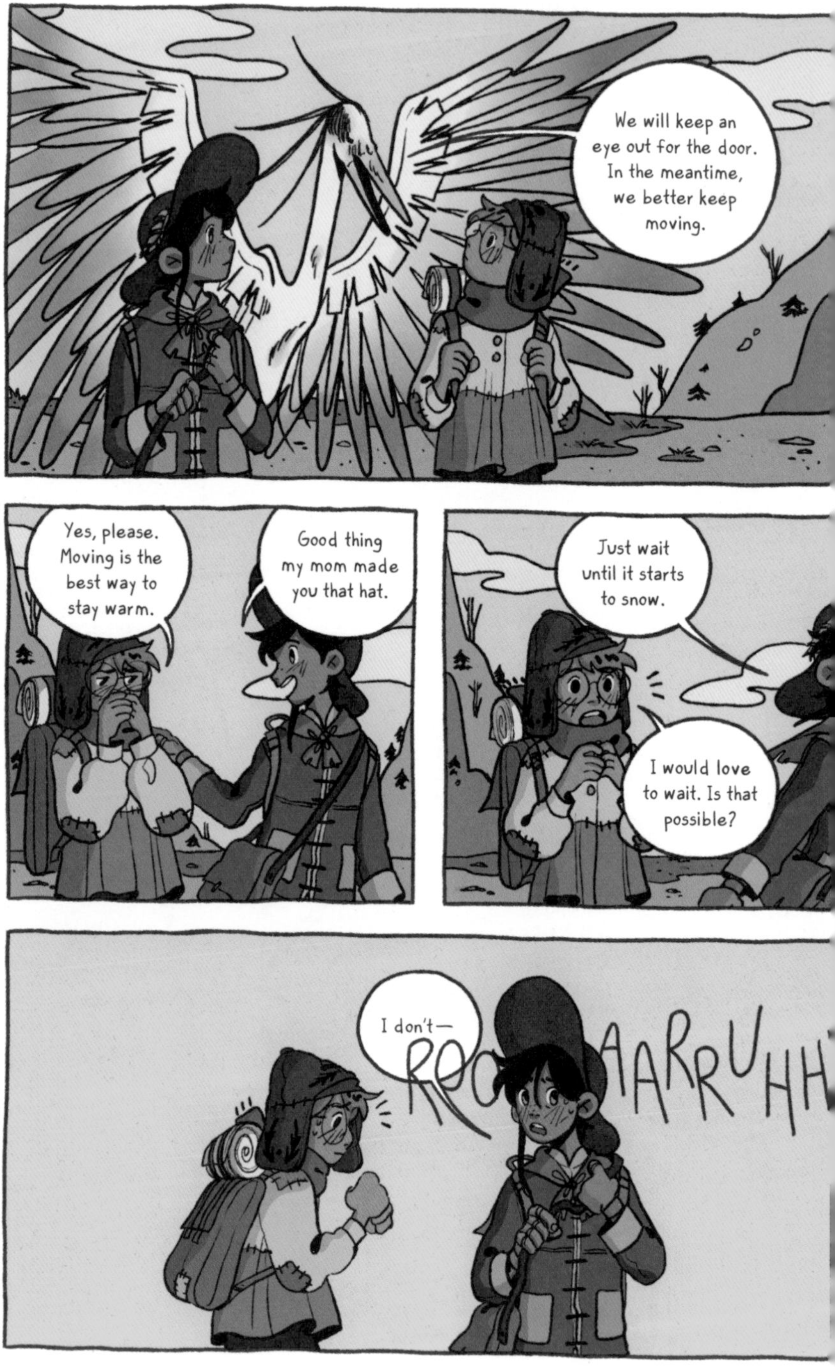
We will keep an eye out for the door. In the meantime, we better keep moving.
Yes, please. Moving is the best way to stay warm.
Good thing my mom made you that hat.
Just wait until it starts to snow.
I would love to wait. Is that possible?
I don't—
ROOAARRUHH

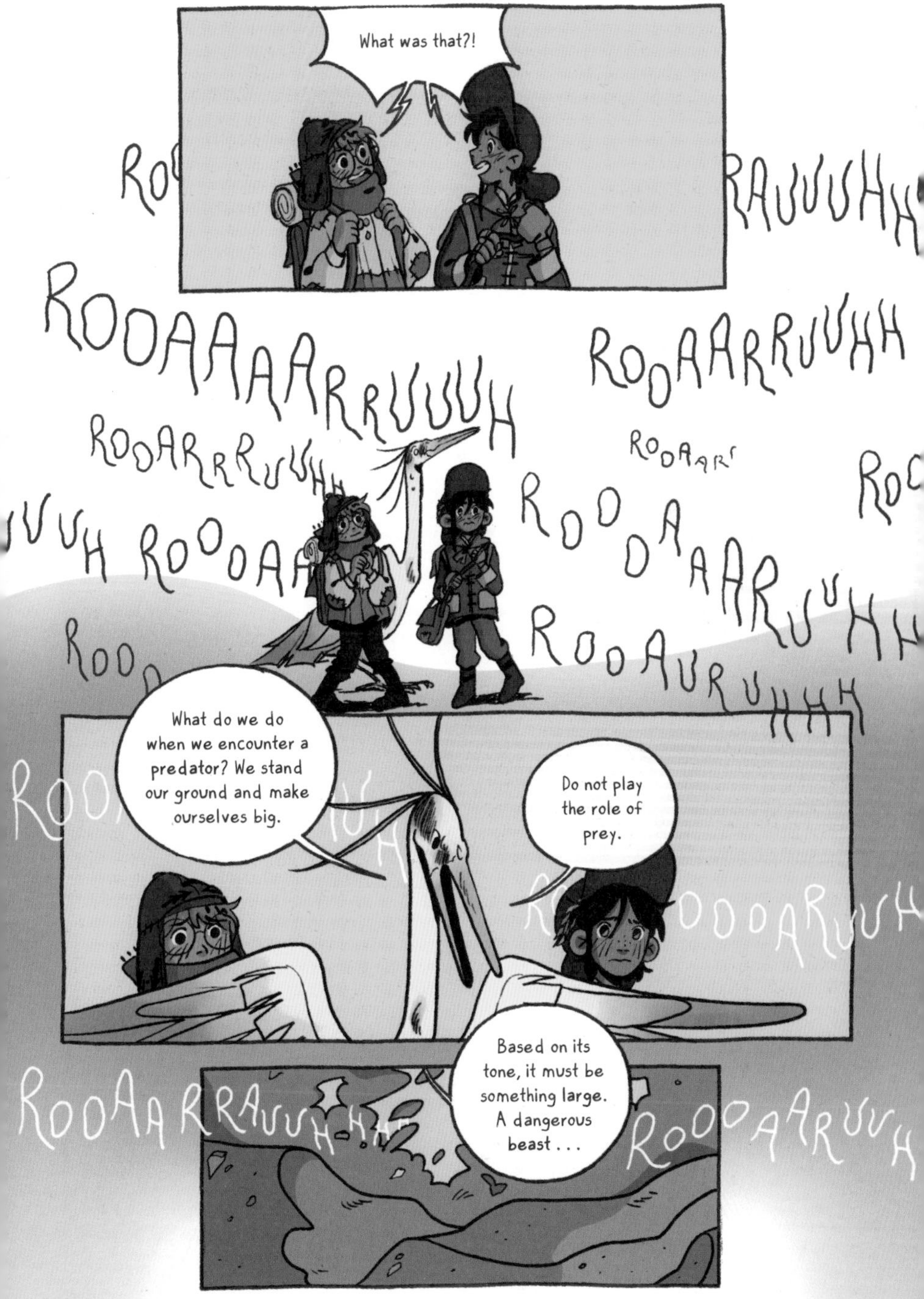
What was that?!
ROO
RAUUUHH
ROOAAAARRUUUH
ROOAARRUUHH
ROOARRRUUHH
ROOAAR
ROOOAAARRUUHH
UUH ROOOA
ROOAURUHHH
ROOO
What do we do when we encounter a predator? We stand our ground and make ourselves big.
Do not play the role of prey.
ROOOOARUUH
Based on its tone, it must be something large. A dangerous beast . . .
ROOAARRAUUH-HA
ROOOAARUUH

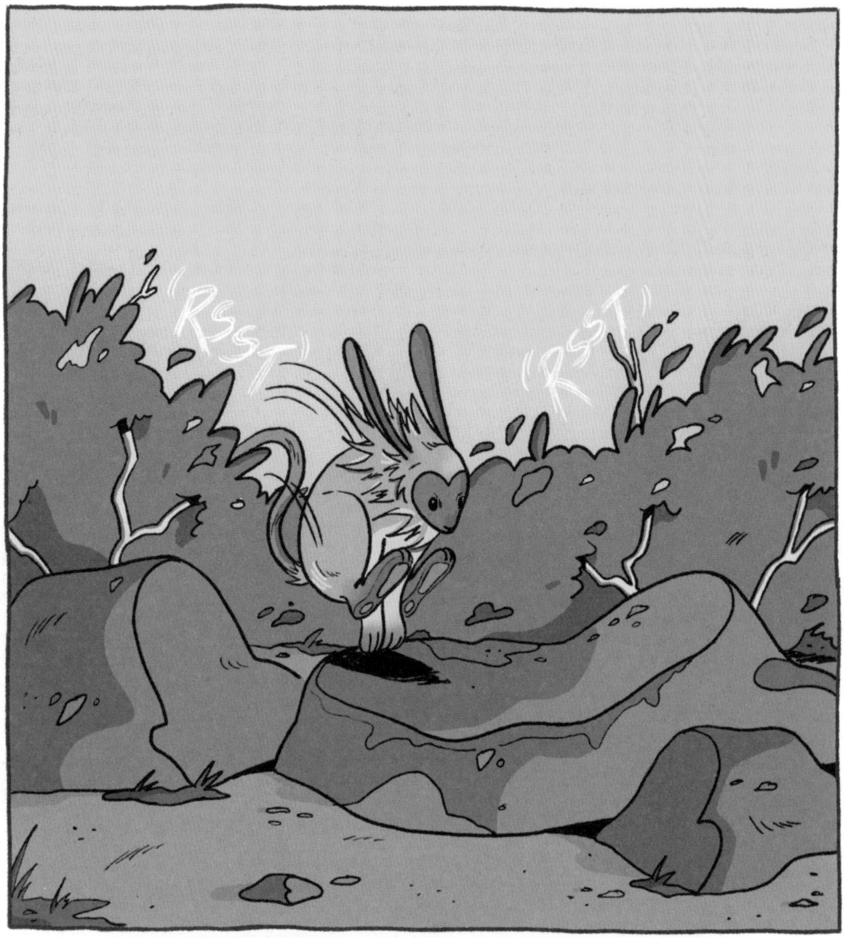
(RSST)
(RSST)

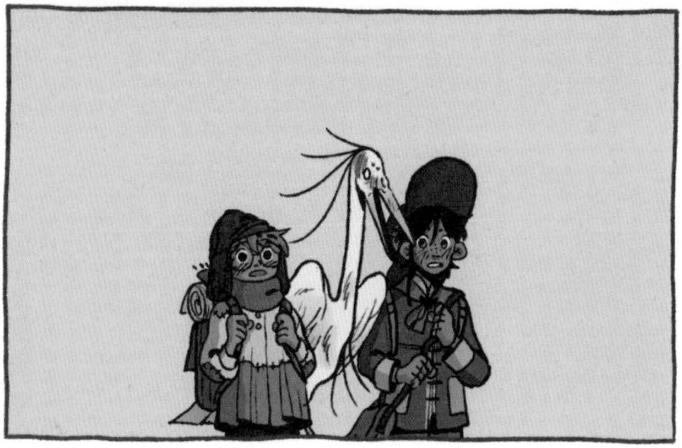

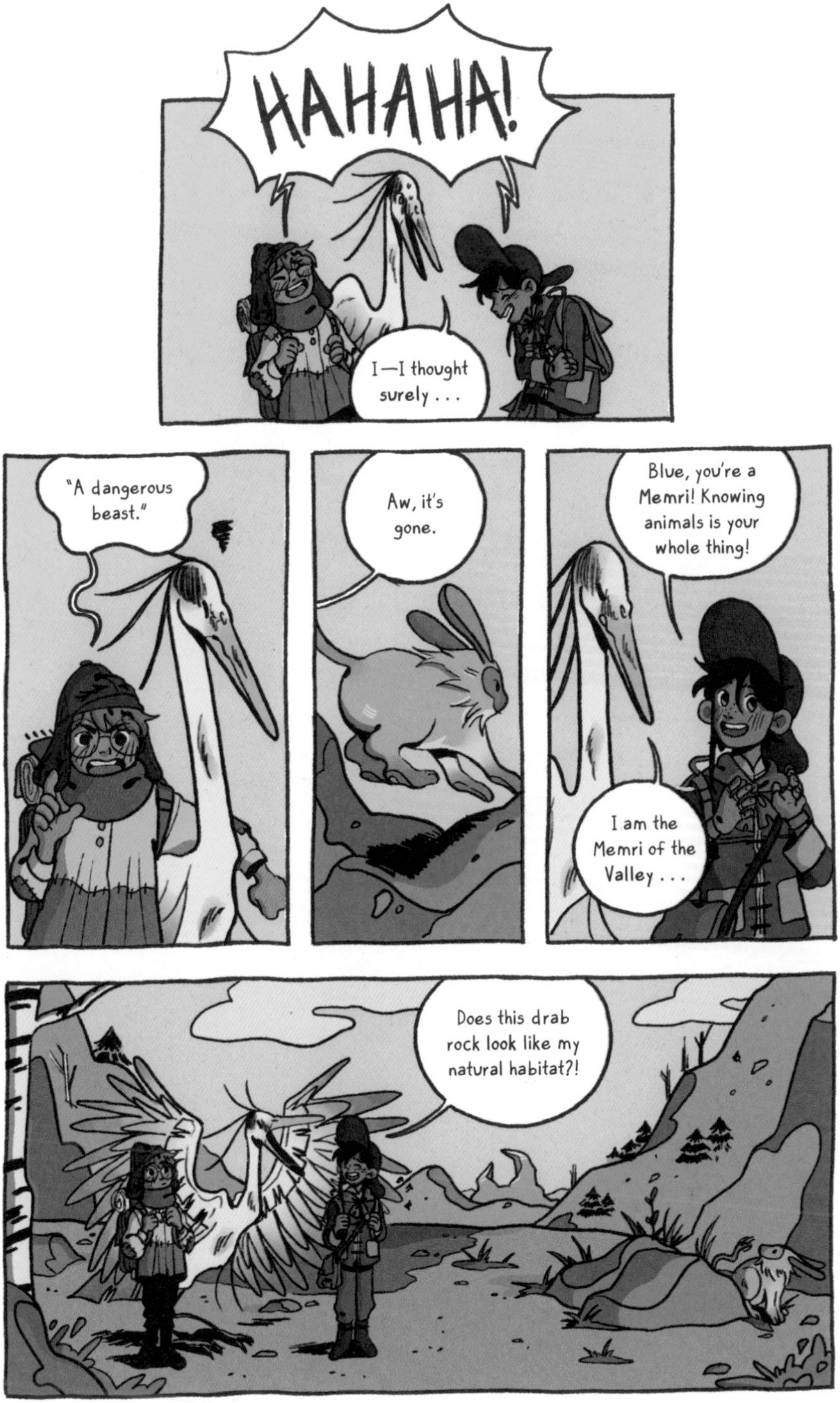
HAHAHA!
I—I thought surely . . .
"A dangerous beast."
Aw, it's gone.
Blue, you're a Memri! Knowing animals is your whole thing!
I am the Memri of the Valley . . .
Does this drab rock look like my natural habitat?!

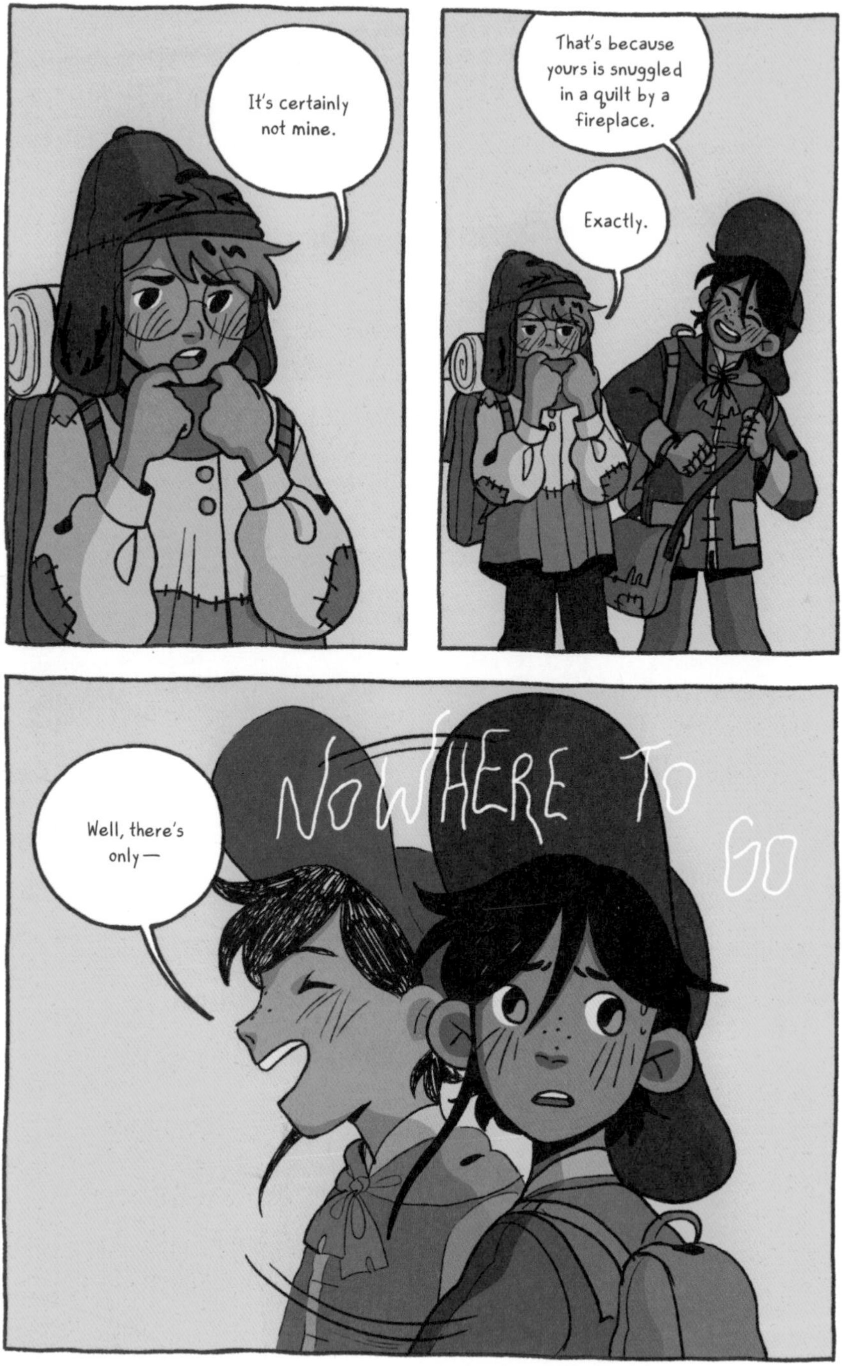
It's certainly not mine.
That's because yours is snuggled in a quilt by a fireplace.
Exactly.
Well, there's only—
NOWHERE TO GO

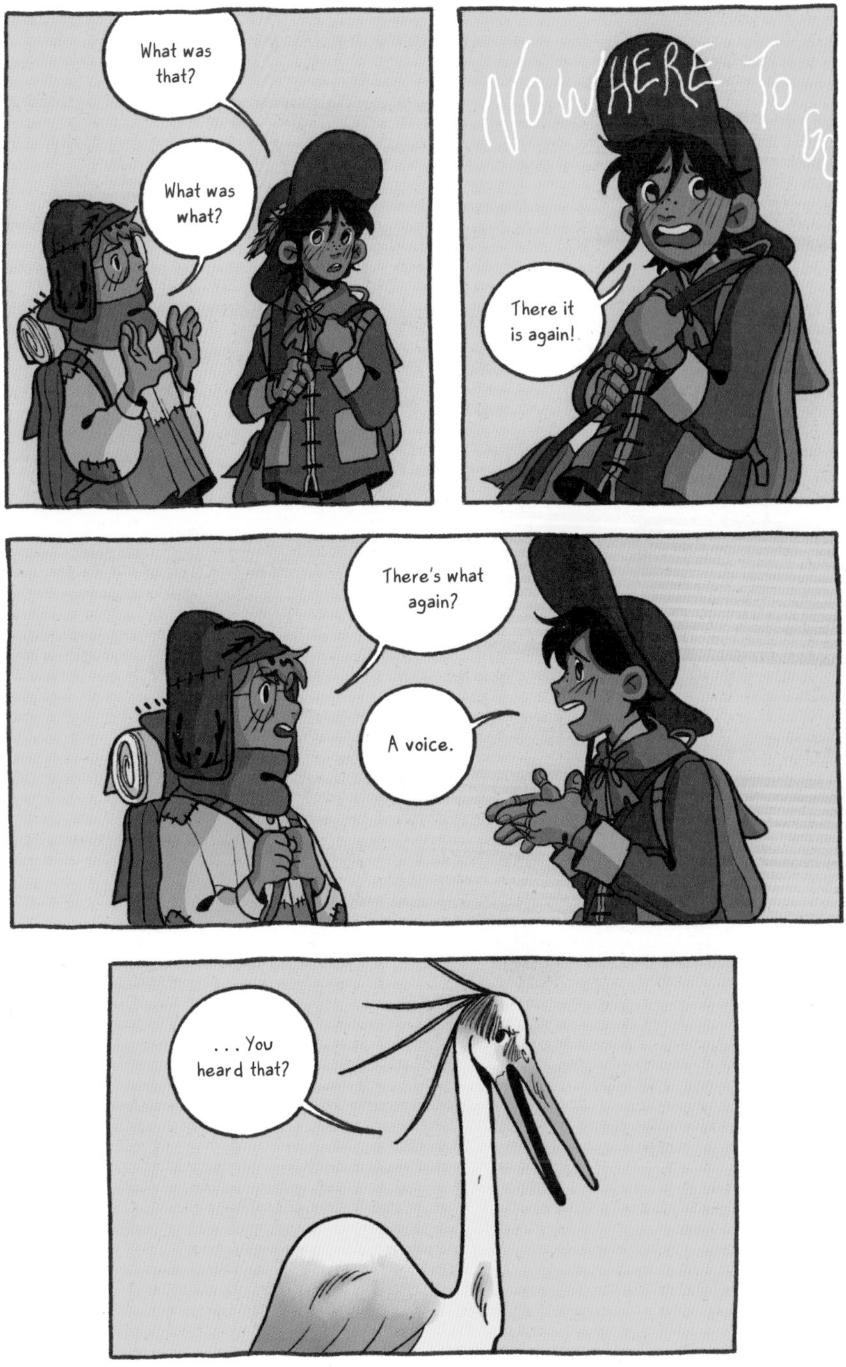
What was that?
What was what?
NOWHERE TO GO
There it is again!
There's what again?
A voice.
. . . You heard that?

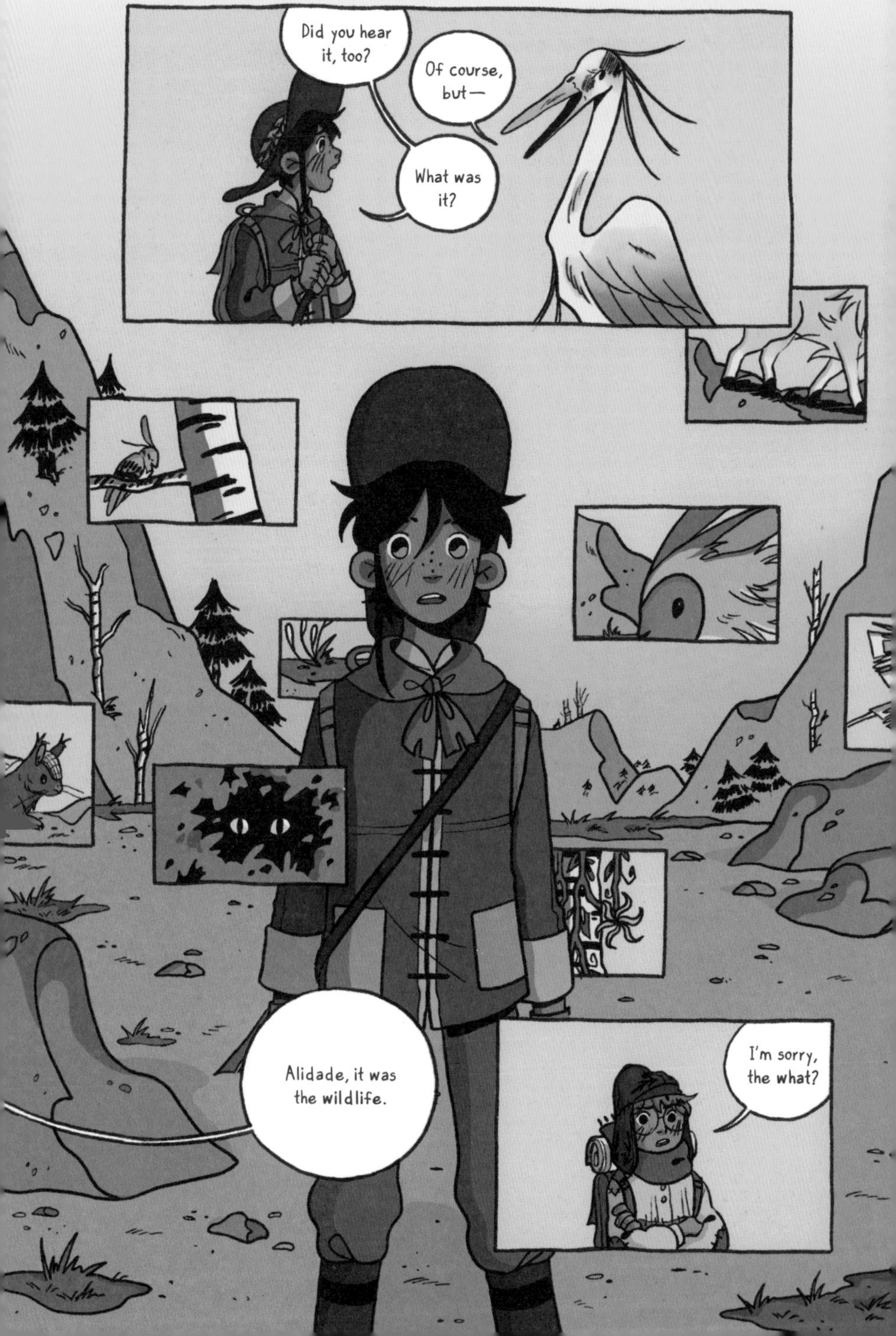
Did you hear it, too?
Of course, but—
What was it?
Alidade, it was the wildlife.
I'm sorry, the what?

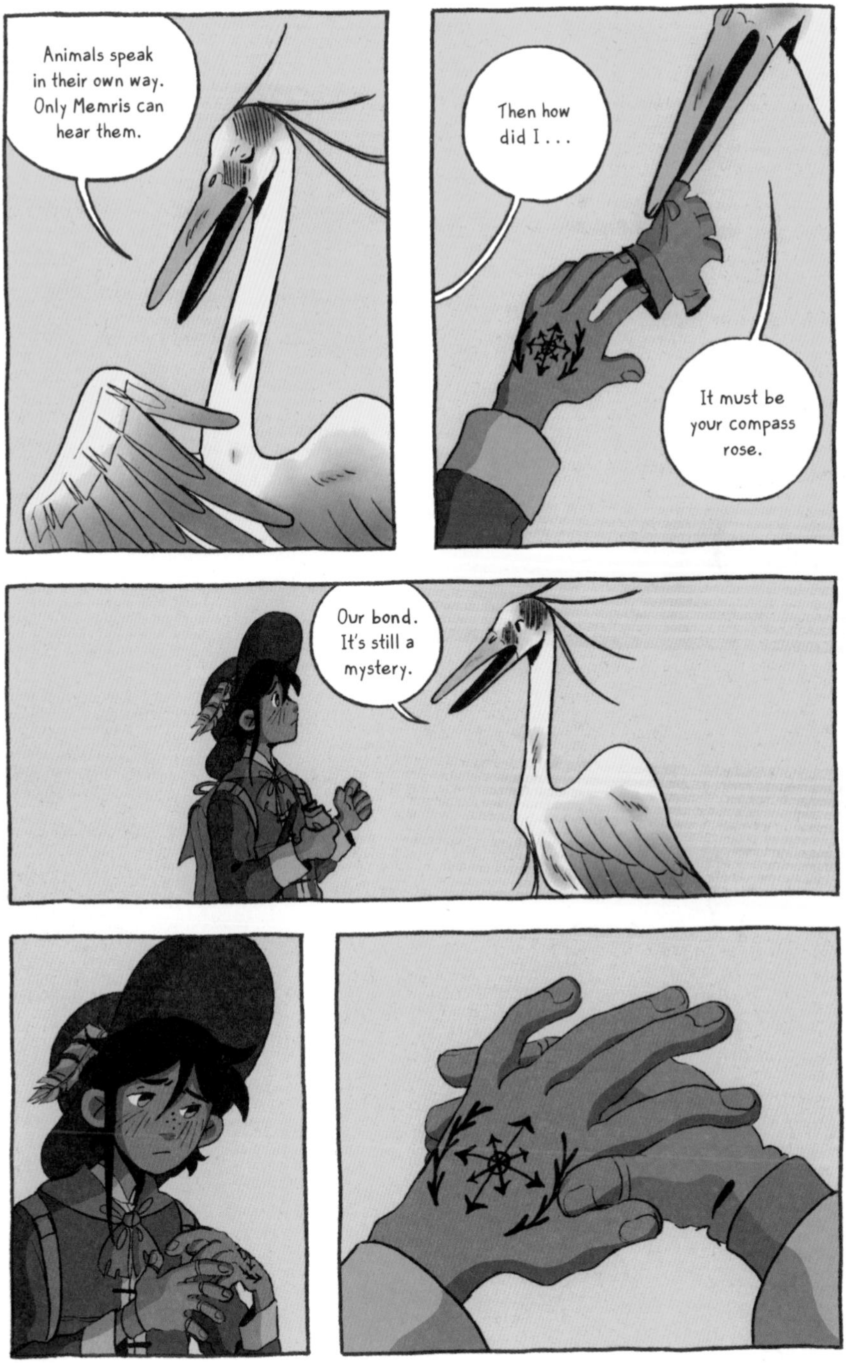
Animals speak in their own way. Only Memris can hear them.
Then how did I . . .
It must be your compass rose.
Our bond. It's still a mystery.

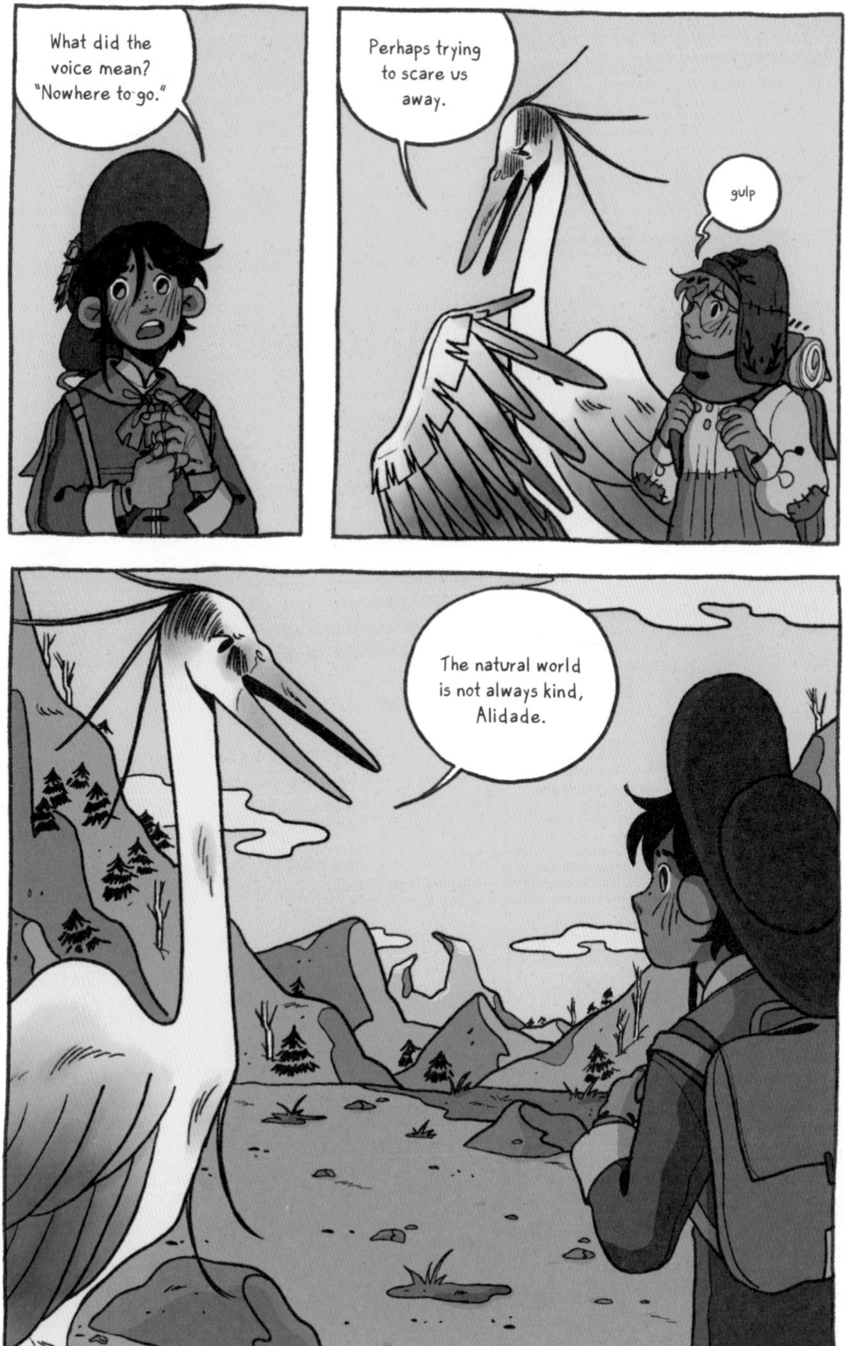
What did the voice mean? "Nowhere to go."
Perhaps trying to scare us away.
gulp
The natural world is not always kind, Alidade.

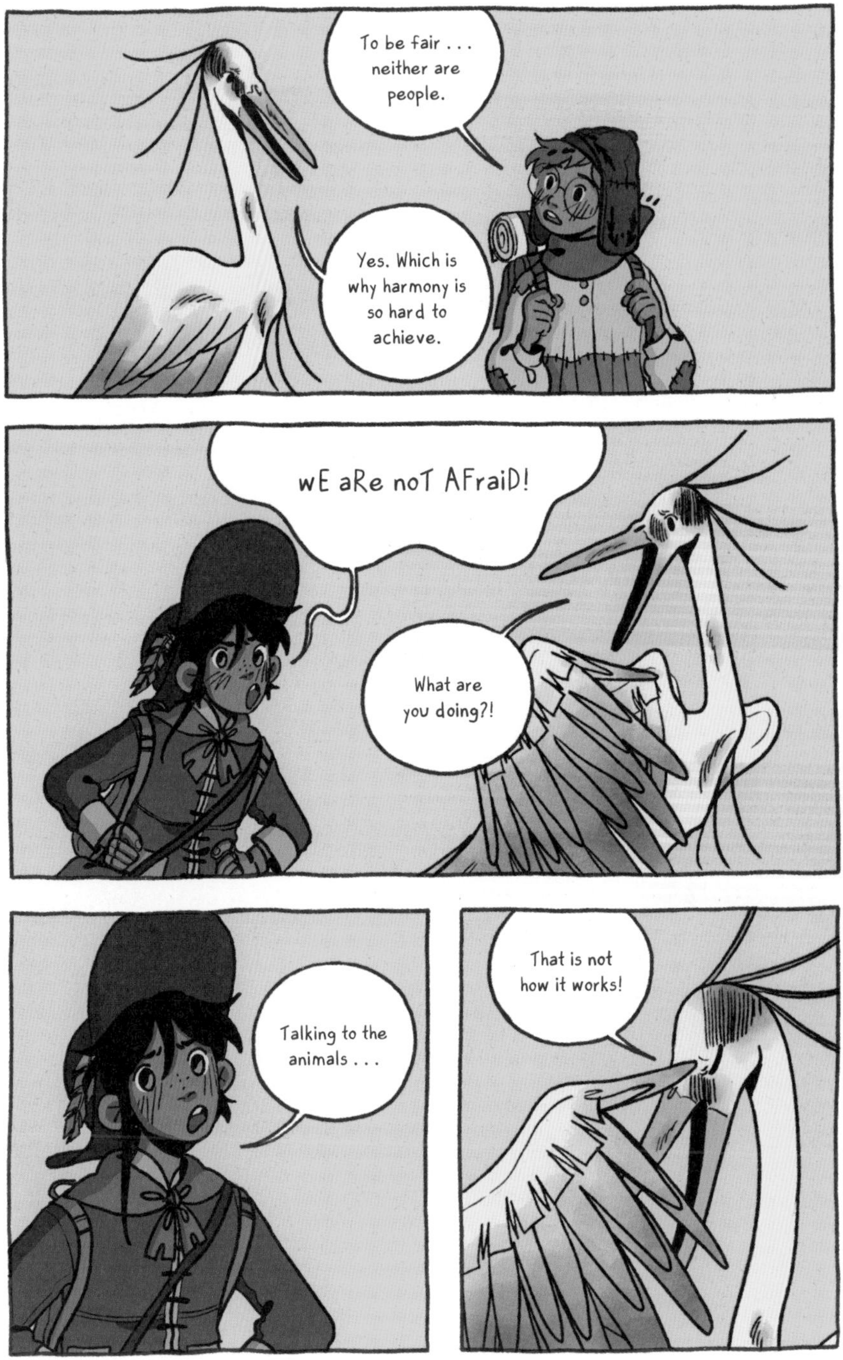
To be fair . . . neither are people.
Yes. Which is why harmony is so hard to achieve.
wE aRe noT AFraiD!
What are you doing?!
Talking to the animals . . .
That is not how it works!

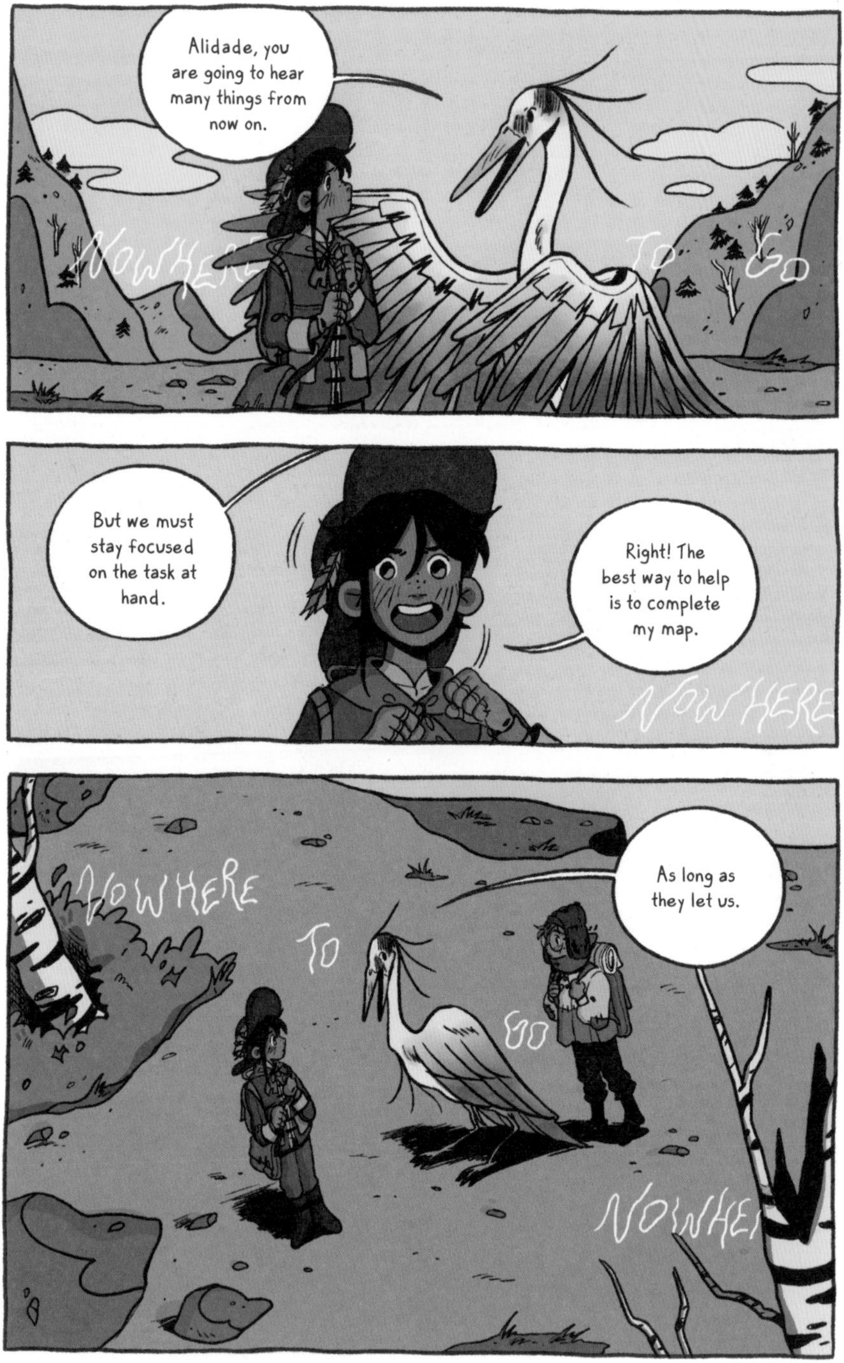
Alidade, you are going to hear many things from now on.
NOWHERE TO GO
But we must stay focused on the task at hand.
Right! The best way to help is to complete my map.
NOWHERE
NOWHERE TO GO
As long as they let us.

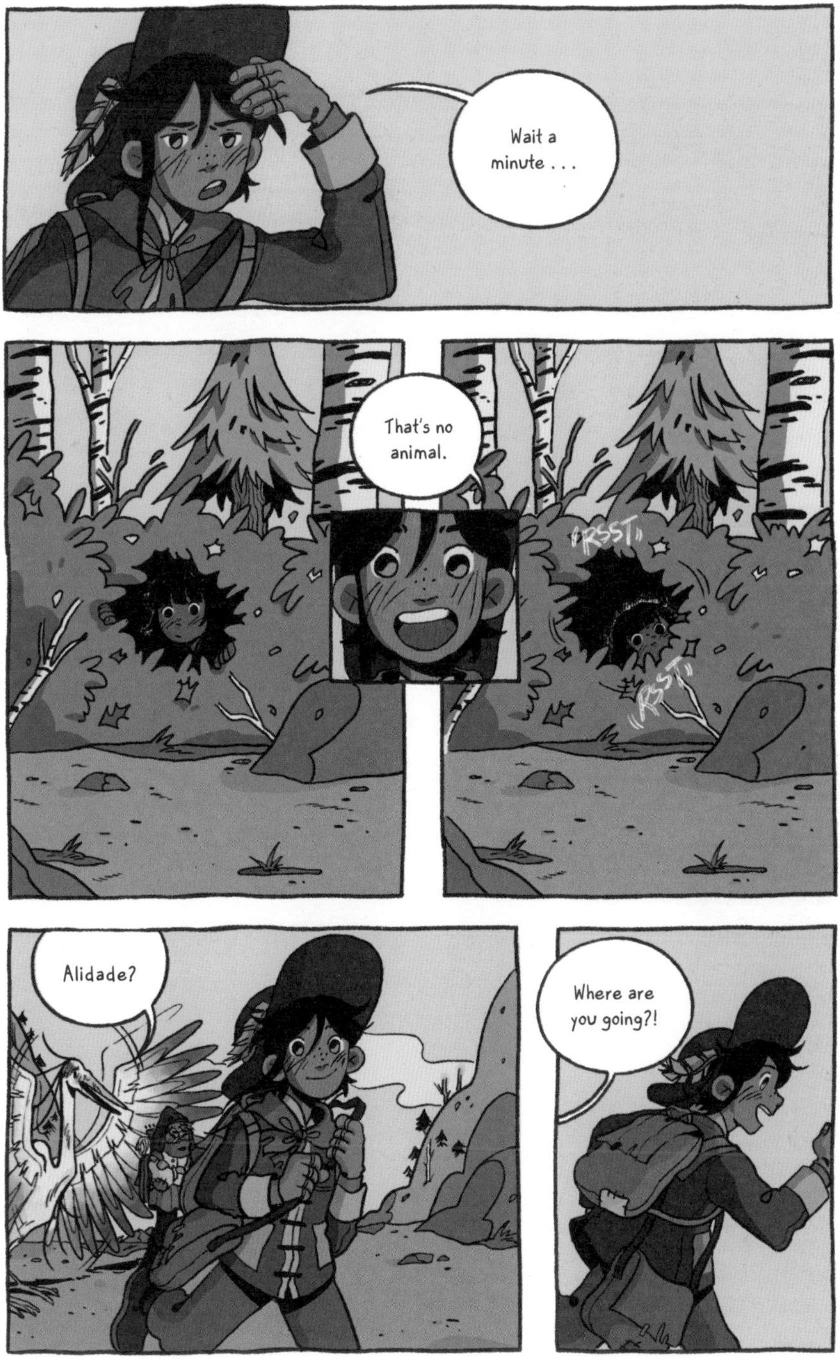
Wait a minute . . .
That's no animal.
RSST
RSST
Alidade?
Where are you going?!

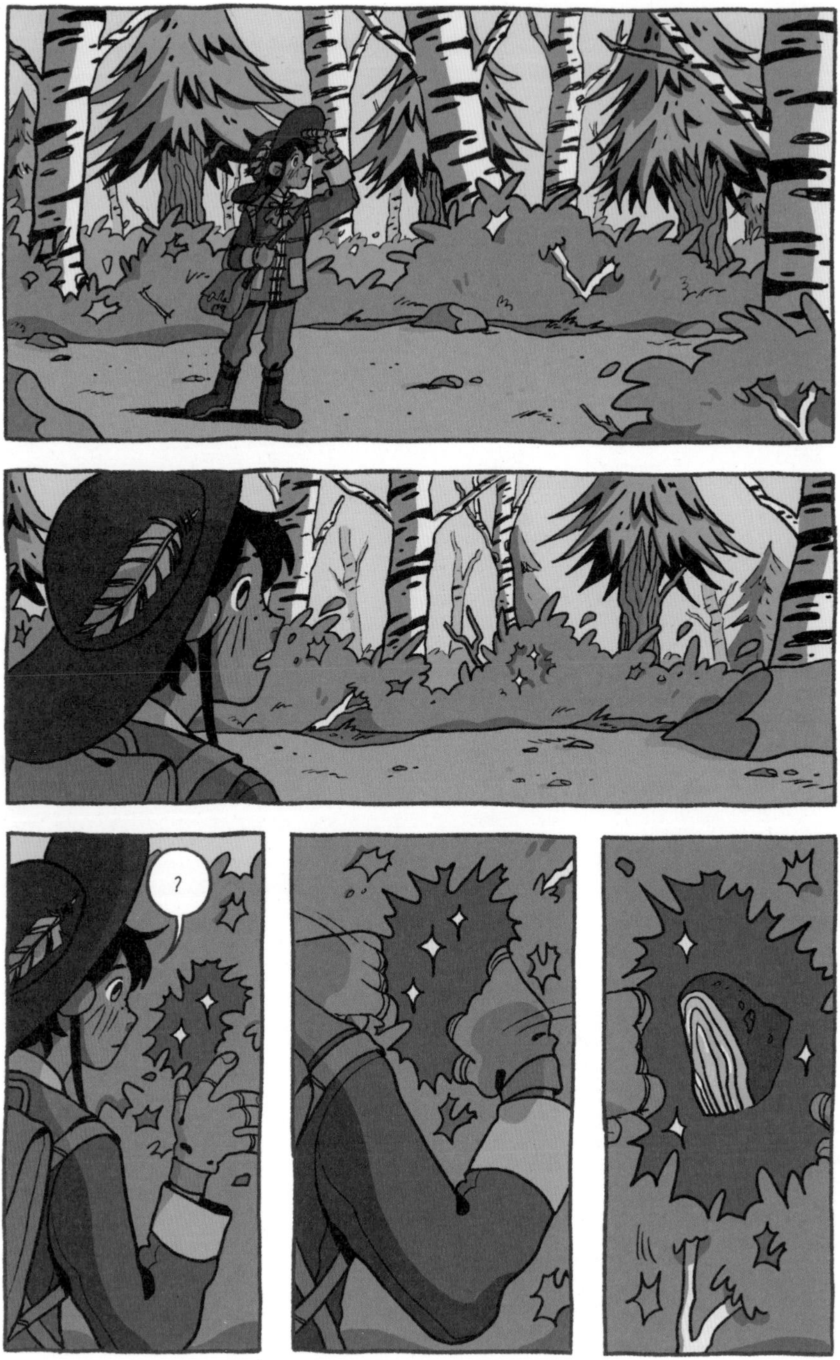
?

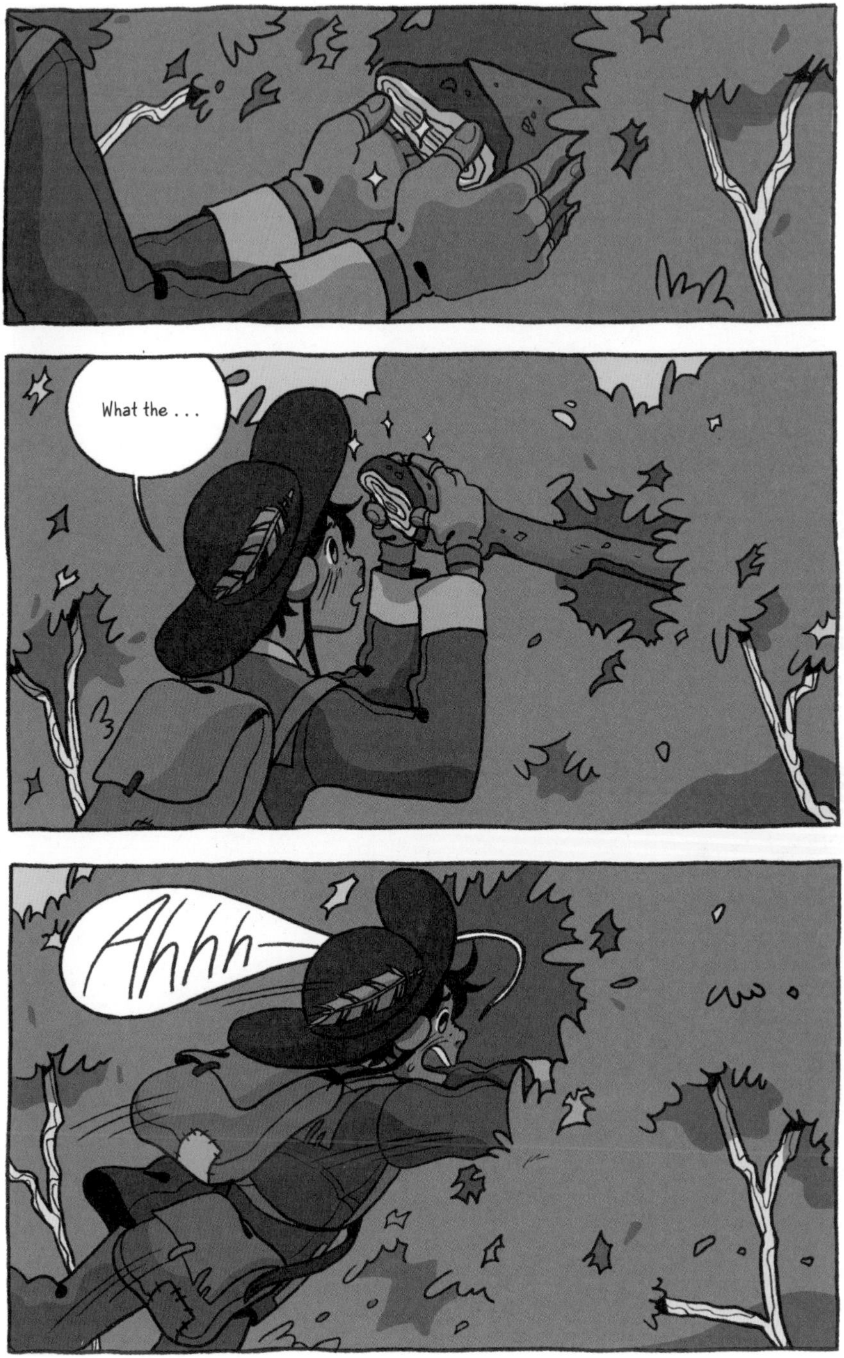
What the . . .
Ahhh—

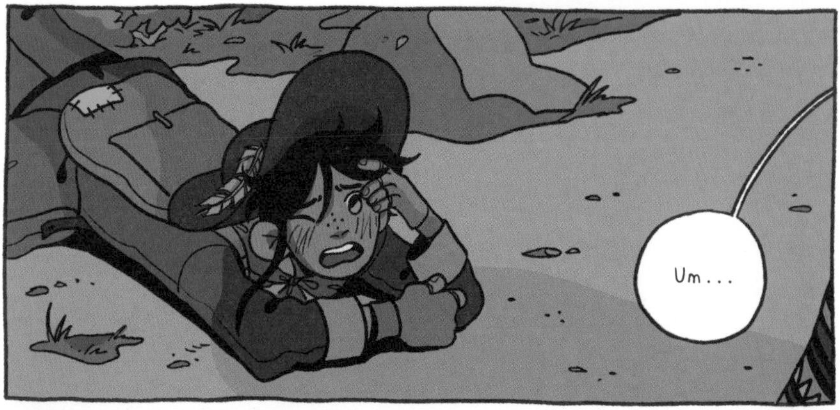
Um...

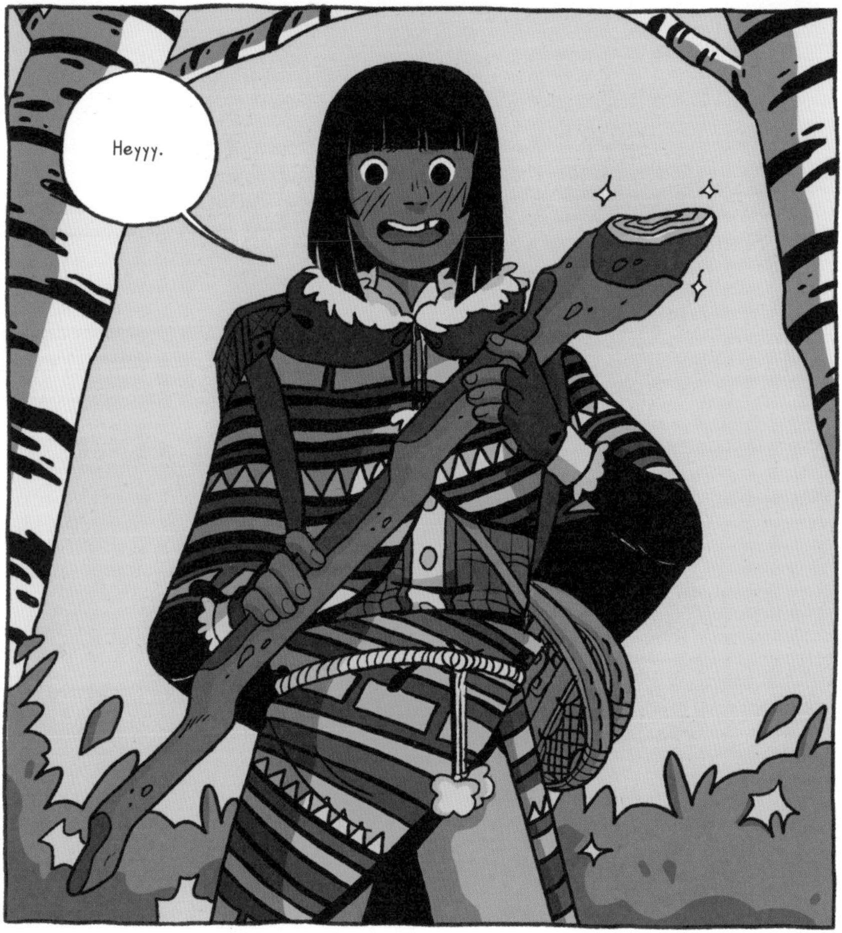
Heyyy.

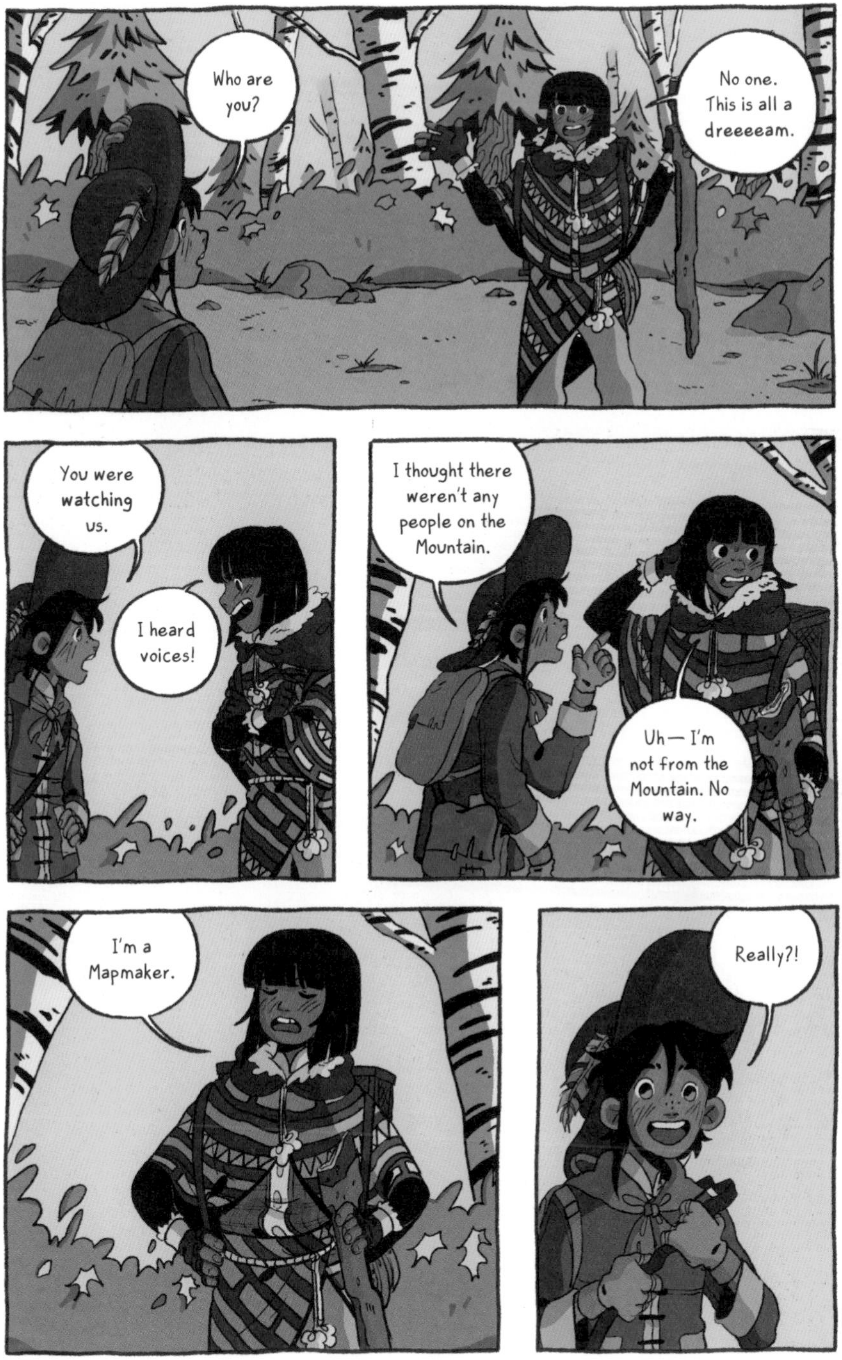
Who are you?
No one. This is all a dreeeeam.
You were watching us.
I heard voices!
I thought there weren't any people on the Mountain.
Uh— I'm not from the Mountain. No way.
I'm a Mapmaker.
Really?!

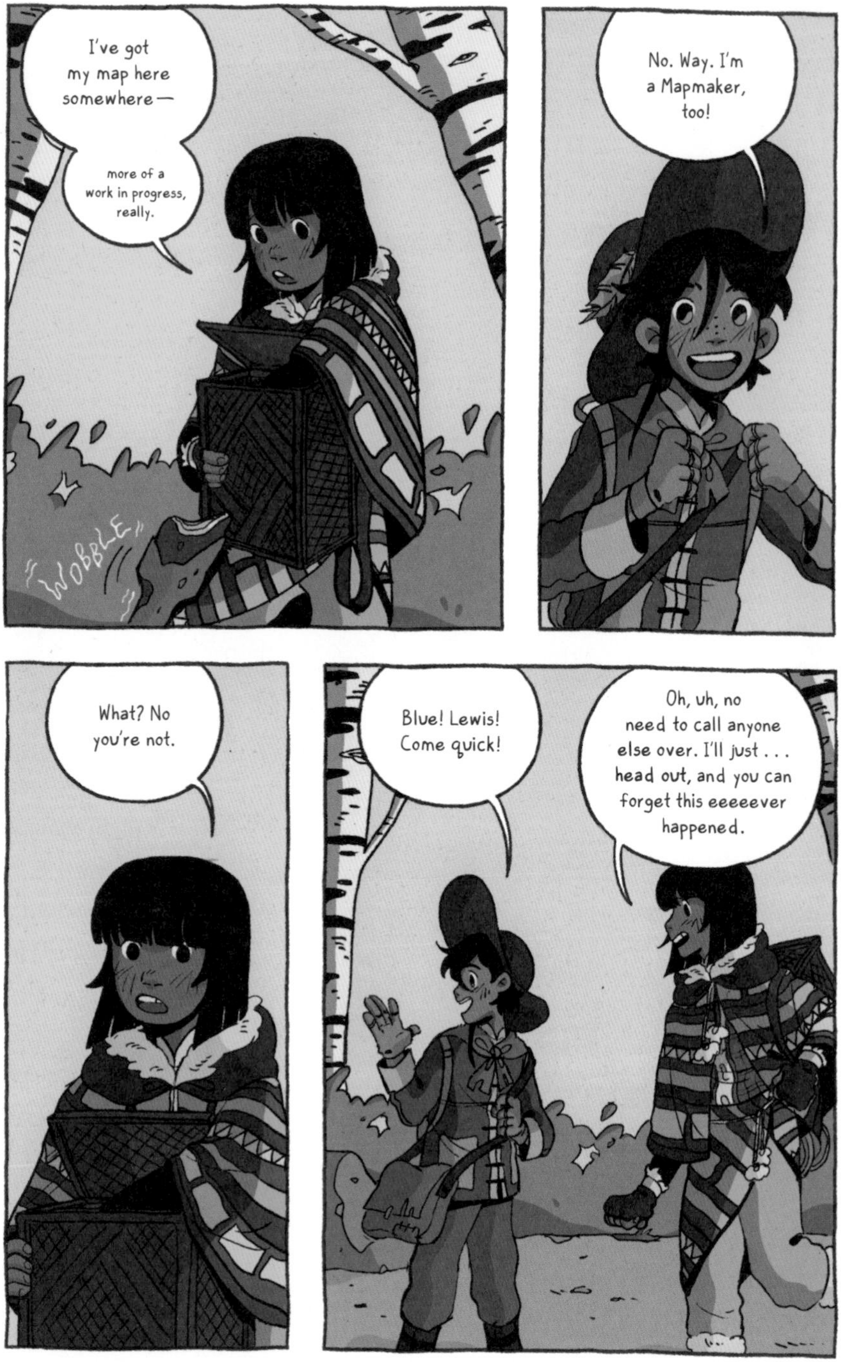
I've got my map here somewhere—
more of a work in progress, really.
WOBBLE
No. Way. I'm a Mapmaker, too!
What? No you're not.
Blue! Lewis! Come quick!
Oh, uh, no need to call anyone else over. I'll just . . . head out, and you can forget this eeeeever happened.

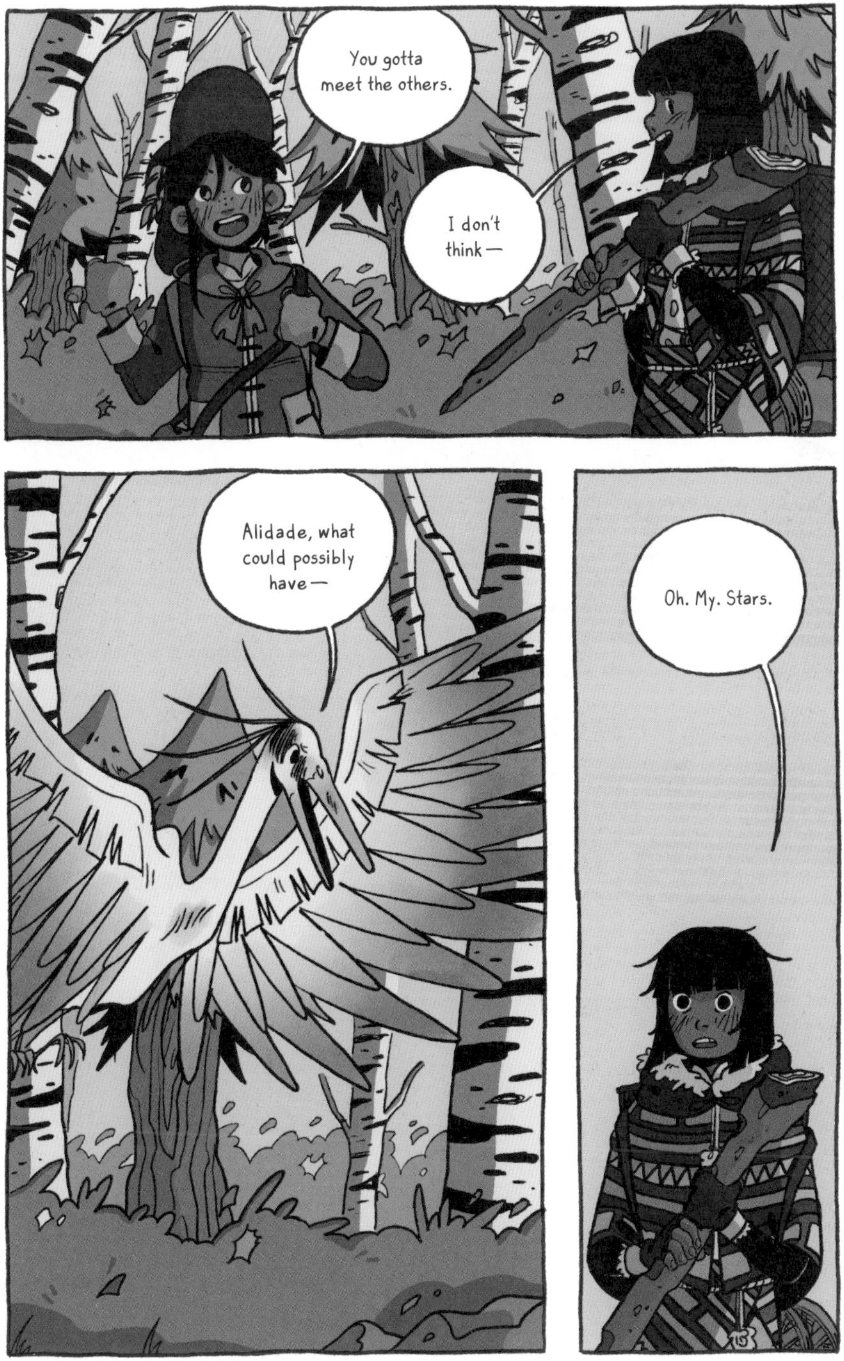
You gotta meet the others.
I don't think—
Alidade, what could possibly have—
Oh. My. Stars.

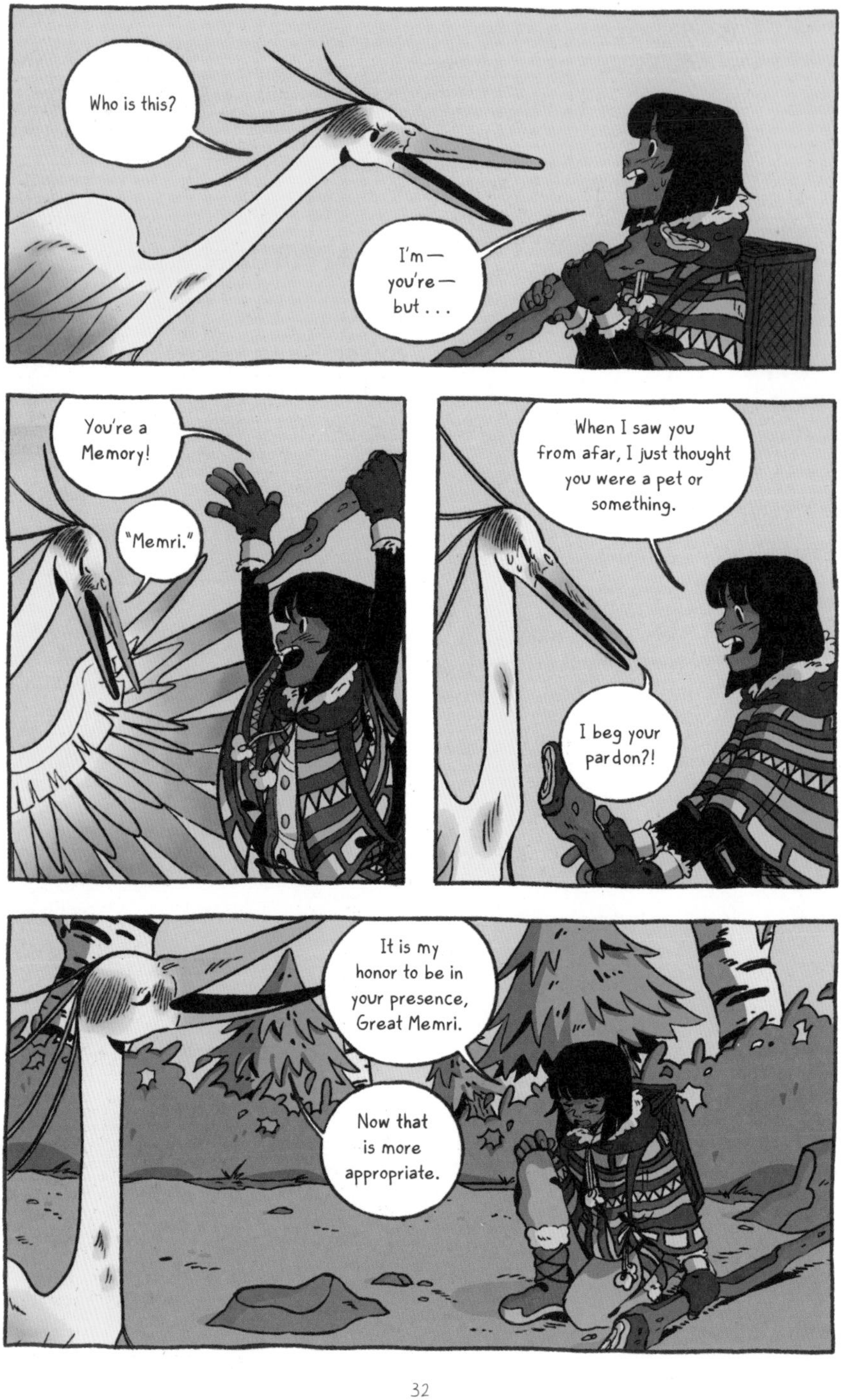
Who is this?
I'm— you're— but . . .
You're a Memory!
"Memri."
When I saw you from afar, I just thought you were a pet or something.
I beg your pardon?!
It is my honor to be in your presence, Great Memri.
Now that is more appropriate.

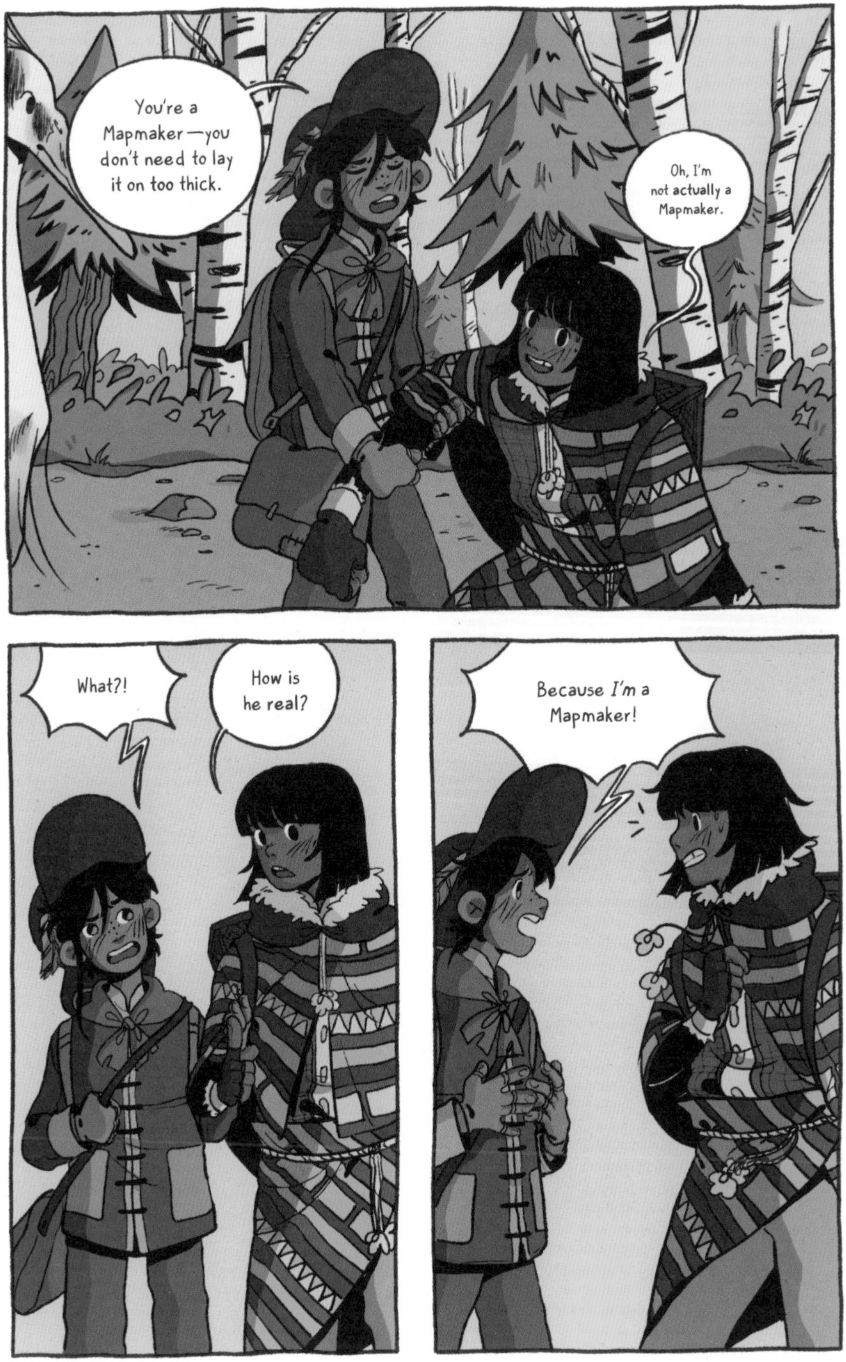
You're a Mapmaker—you don't need to lay it on too thick.
Oh, I'm not actually a Mapmaker.
What?!
How is he real?
Because *I'm* a Mapmaker!

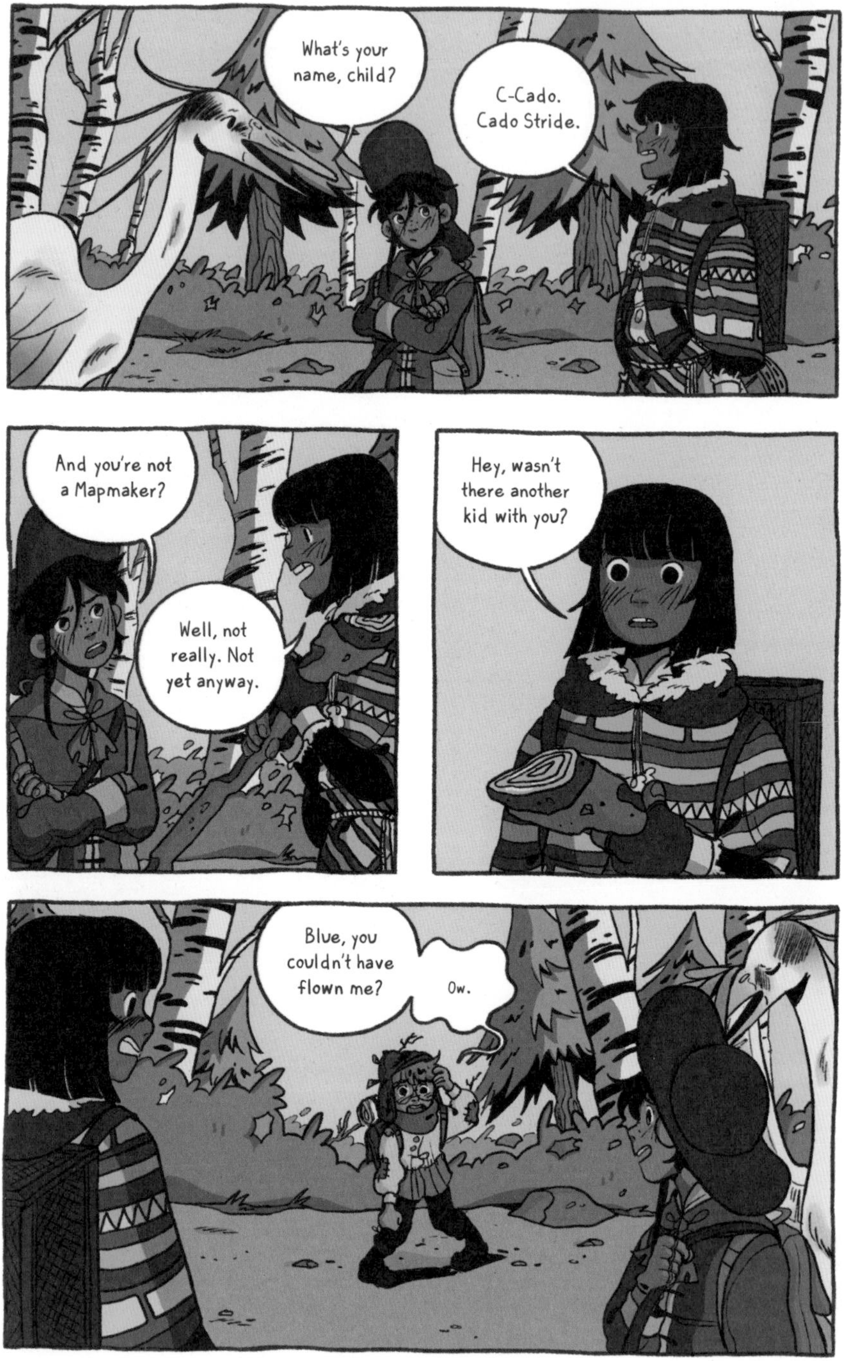
What's your name, child?
C-Cado. Cado Stride.
And you're not a Mapmaker?
Well, not really. Not yet anyway.
Hey, wasn't there another kid with you?
Blue, you couldn't have flown me?
Ow.

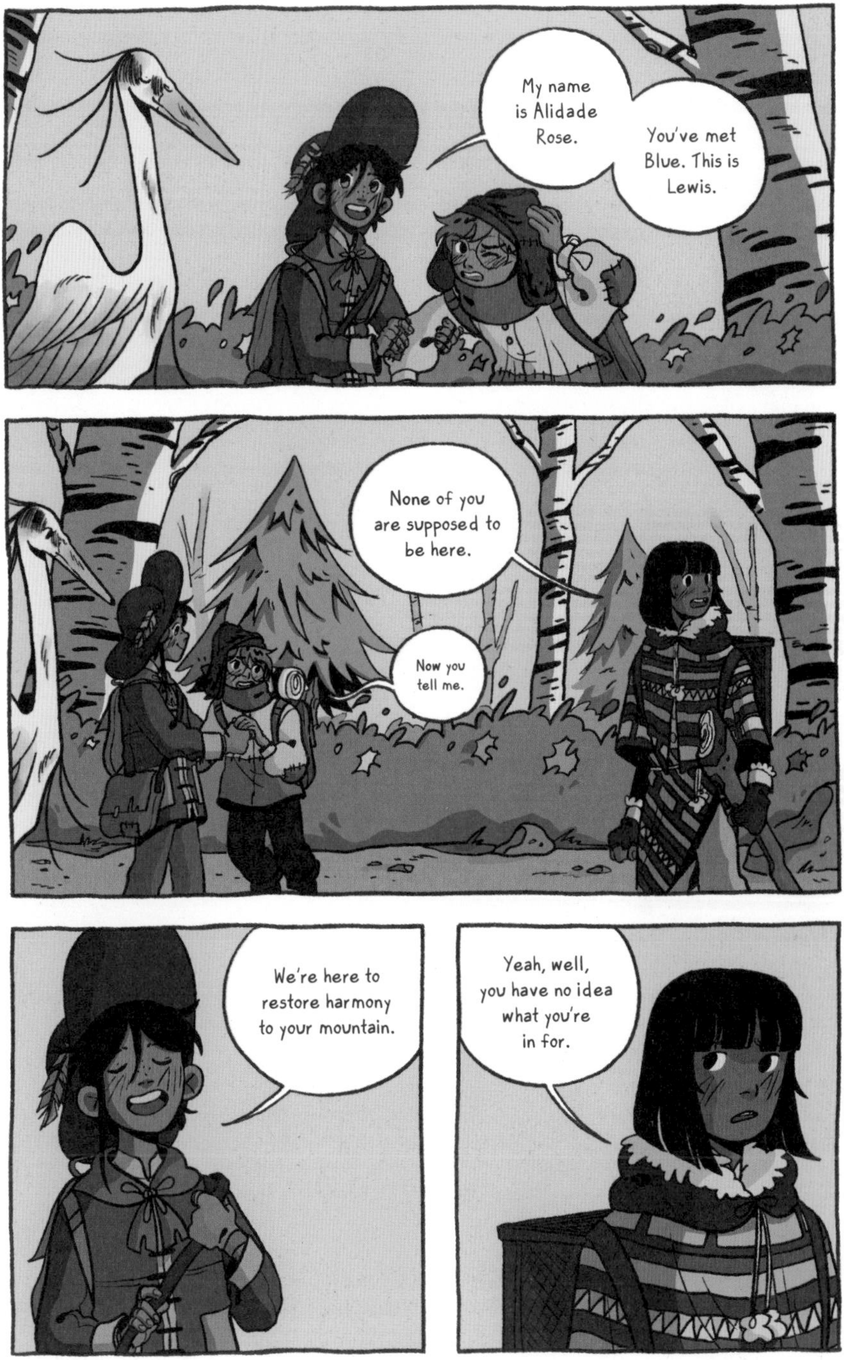
My name is Alidade Rose.
You've met Blue. This is Lewis.
None of you are supposed to be here.
Now you tell me.
We're here to restore harmony to your mountain.
Yeah, well, you have no idea what you're in for.

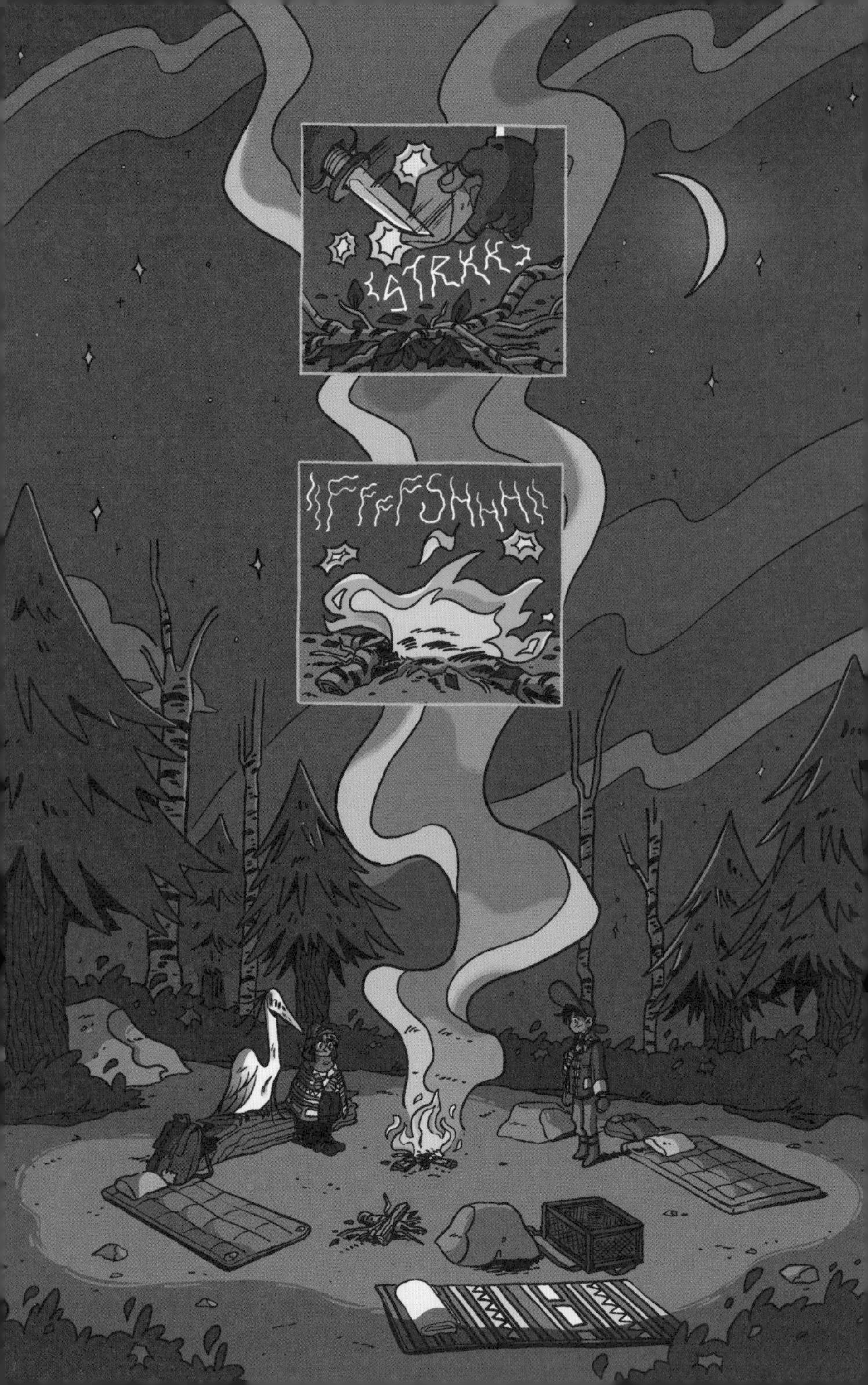
STRKK
FFFFSHHH

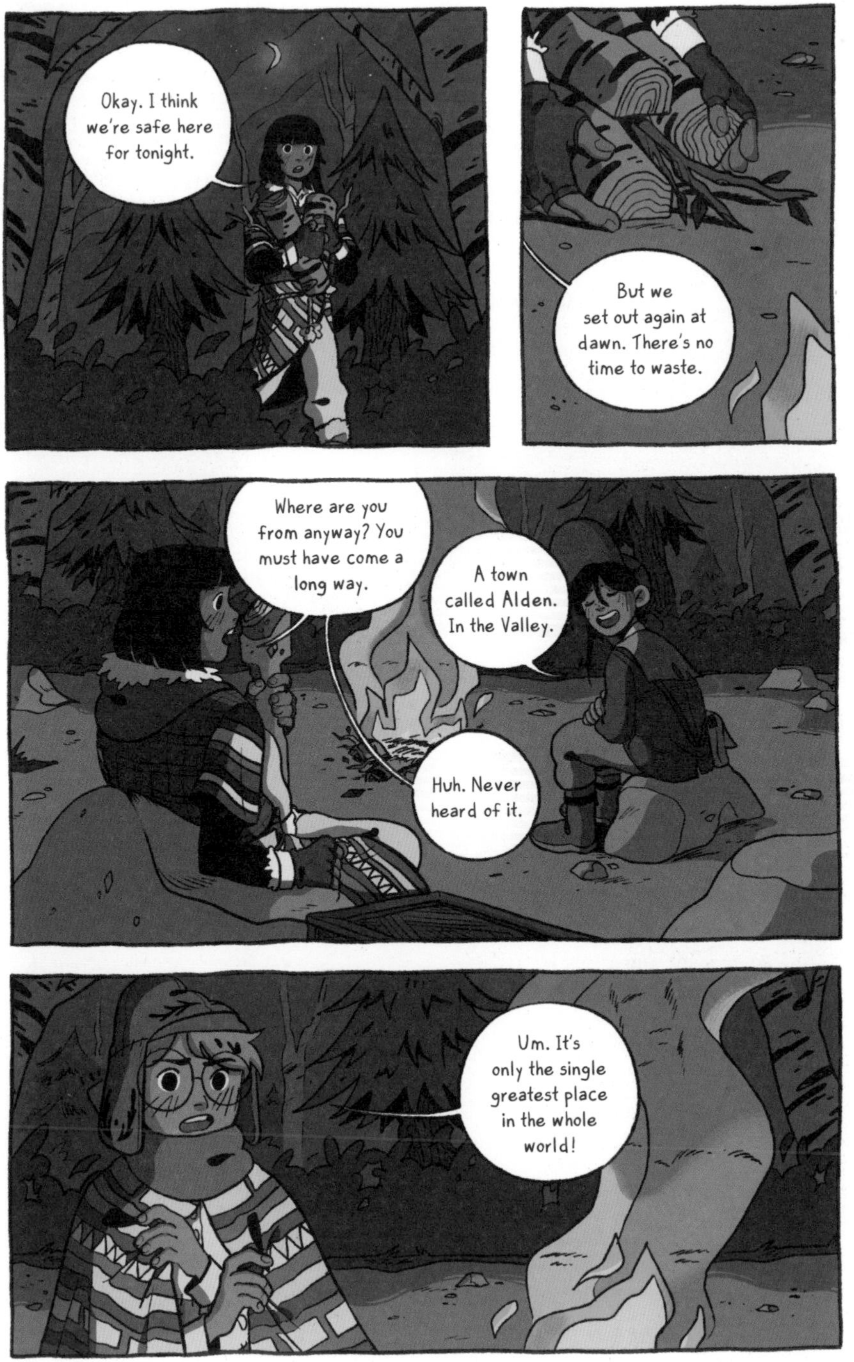
Okay. I think we're safe here for tonight.
But we set out again at dawn. There's no time to waste.
Where are you from anyway? You must have come a long way.
A town called Alden. In the Valley.
Huh. Never heard of it.
Um. It's only the single greatest place in the whole world!

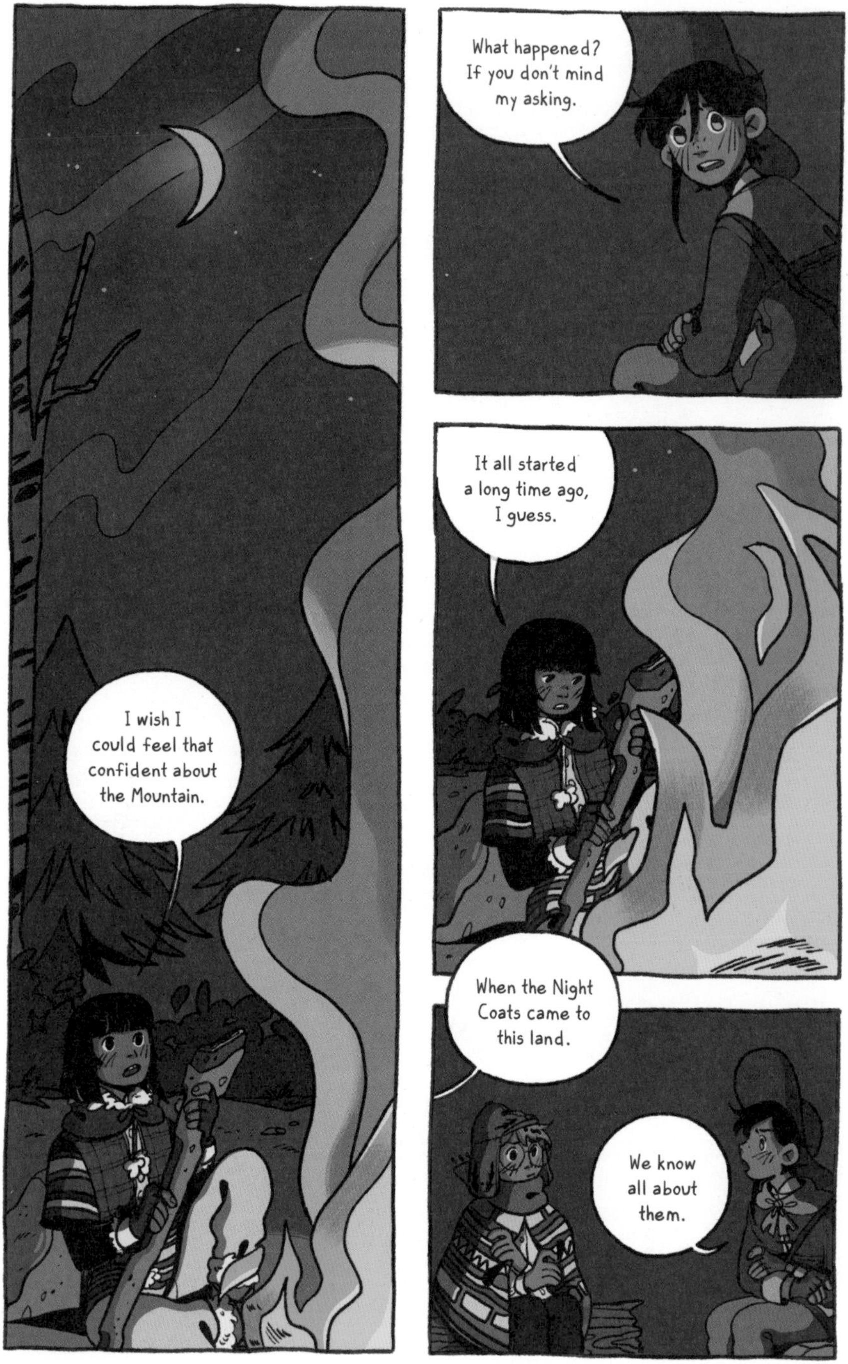
I wish I could feel that confident about the Mountain.
What happened? If you don't mind my asking.
It all started a long time ago, I guess.
When the Night Coats came to this land.
We know all about them.

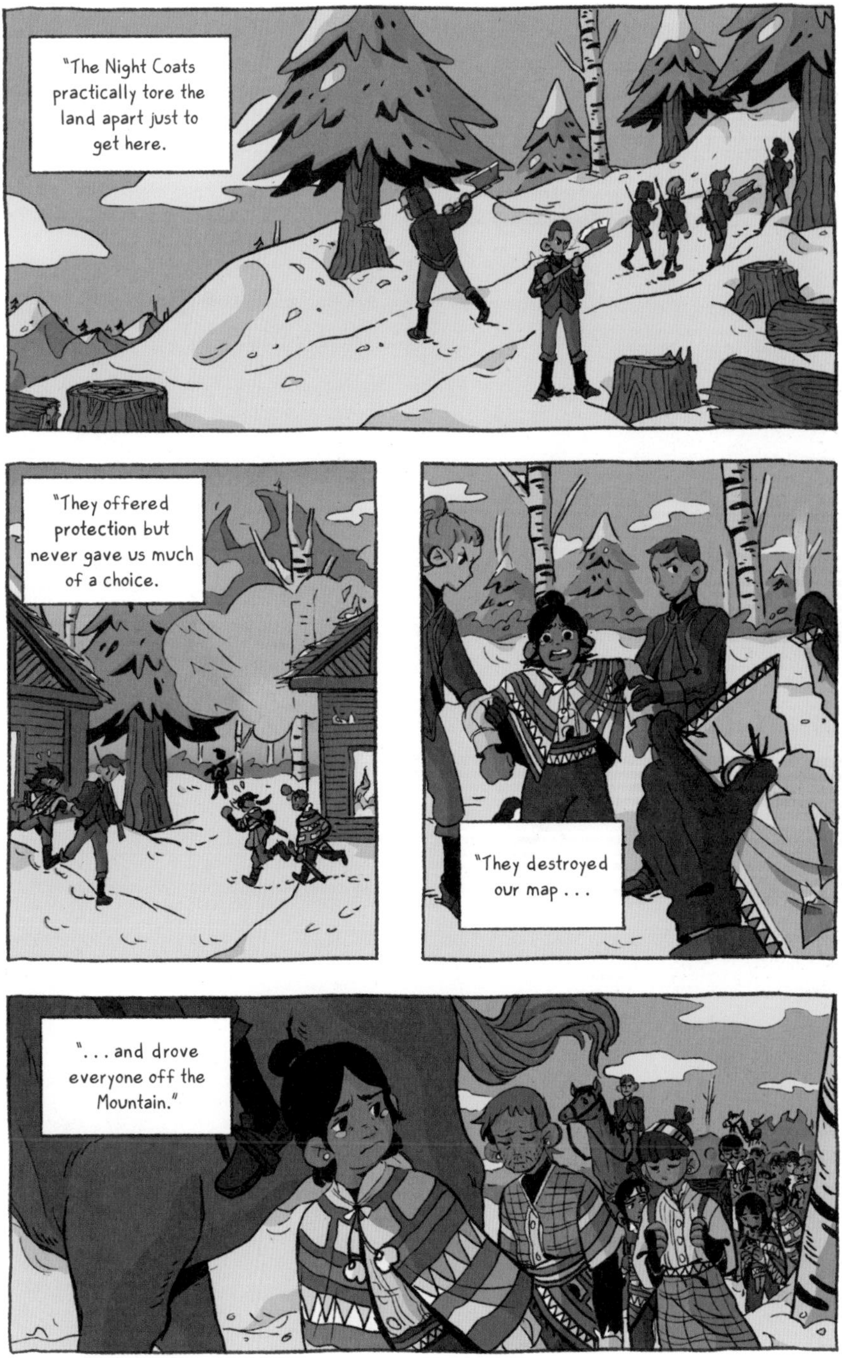
"The Night Coats practically tore the land apart just to get here.
"They offered protection but never gave us much of a choice.
"They destroyed our map . . .
". . . and drove everyone off the Mountain."

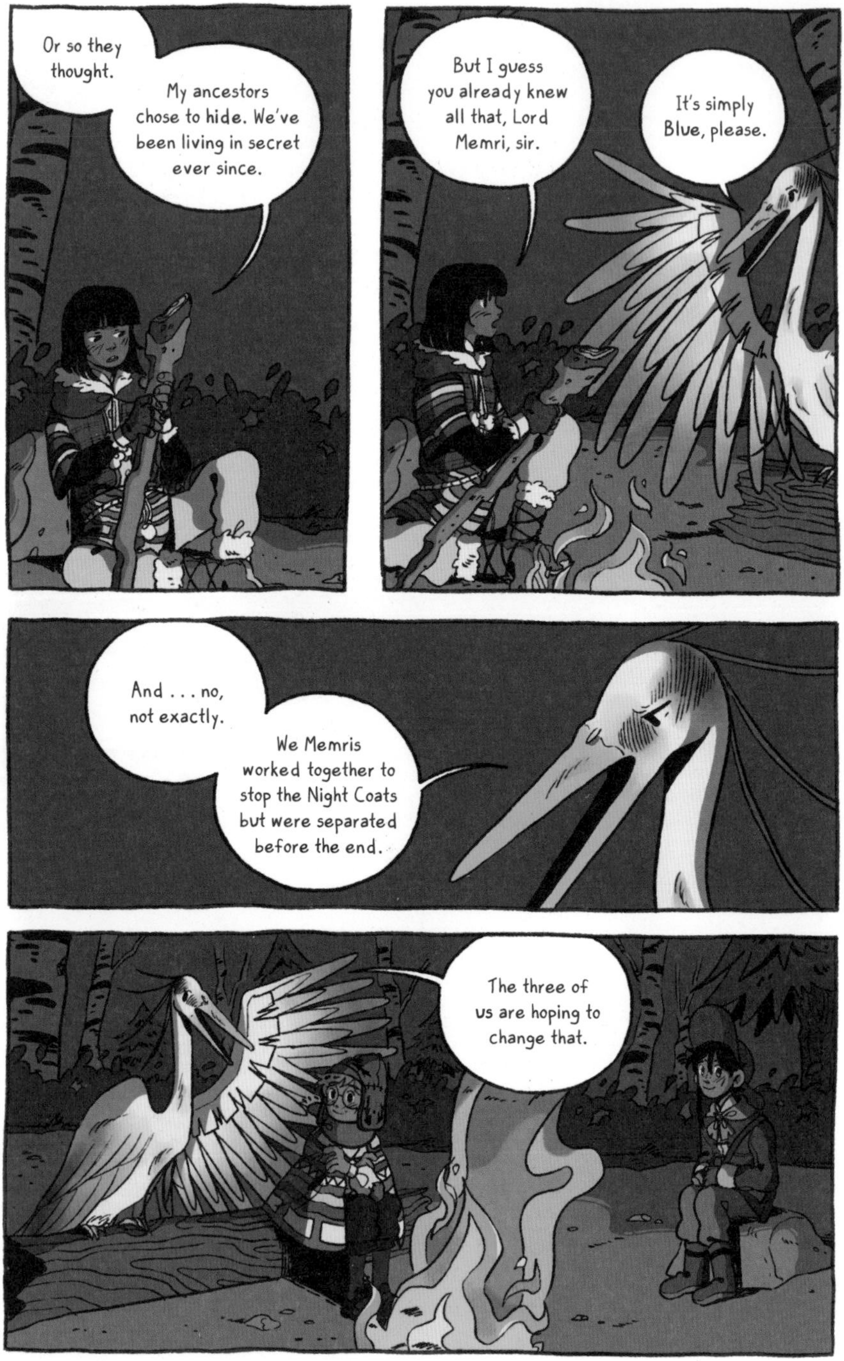
Or so they thought.
My ancestors chose to hide. We've been living in secret ever since.
But I guess you already knew all that, Lord Memri, sir.
It's simply Blue, please.
And . . . no, not exactly.
We Memris worked together to stop the Night Coats but were separated before the end.
The three of us are hoping to change that.

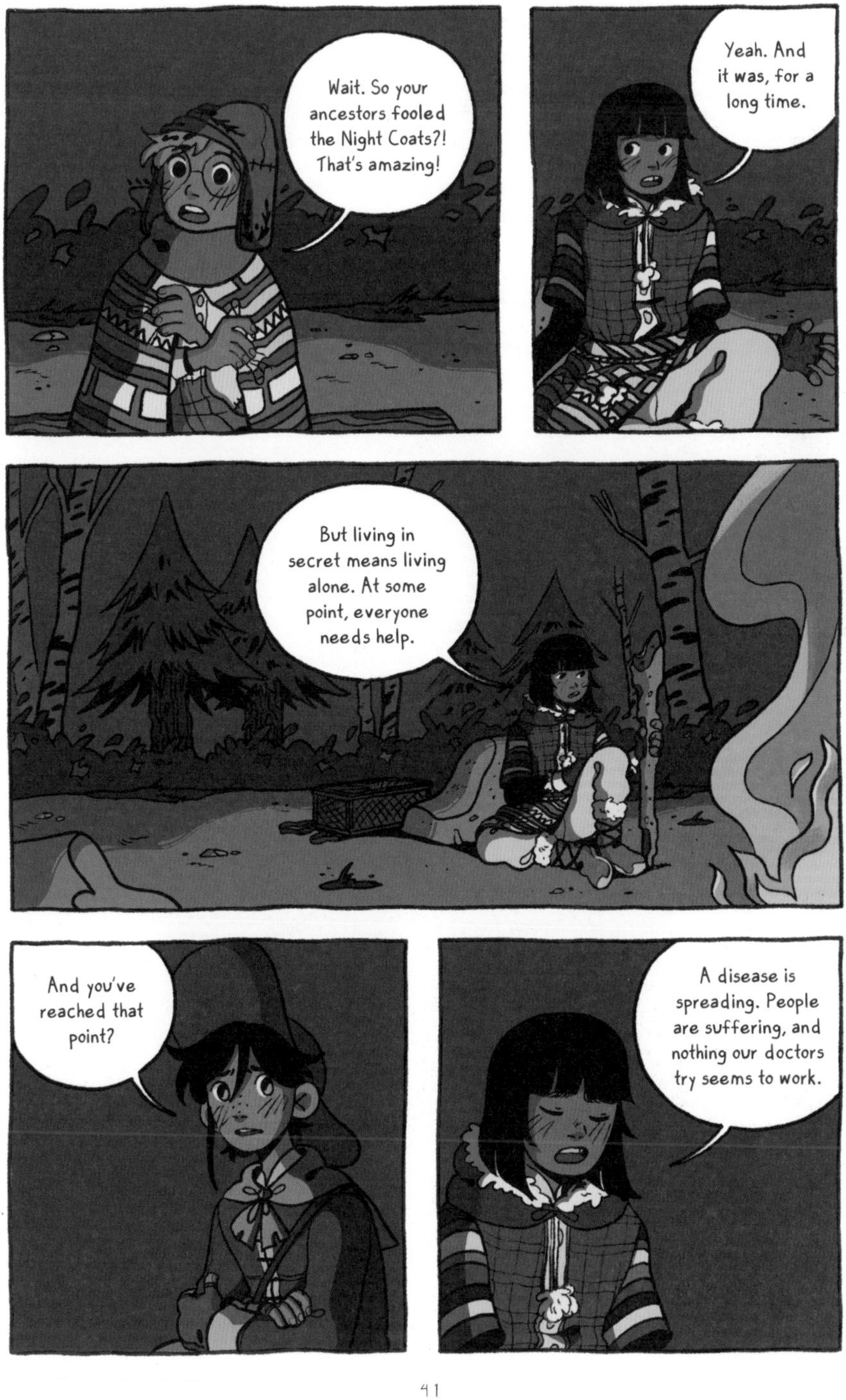
Wait. So your ancestors fooled the Night Coats?! That's amazing!
Yeah. And it was, for a long time.
But living in secret means living alone. At some point, everyone needs help.
And you've reached that point?
A disease is spreading. People are suffering, and nothing our doctors try seems to work.

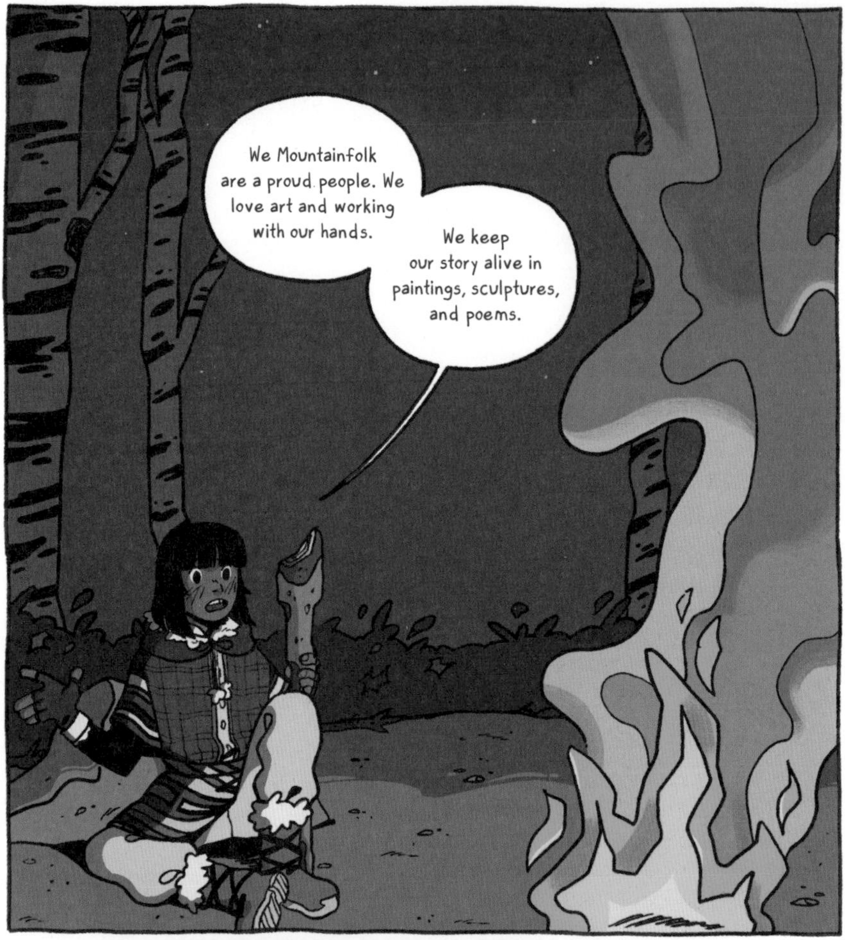
We Mountainfolk are a proud people. We love art and working with our hands.
We keep our story alive in paintings, sculptures, and poems.

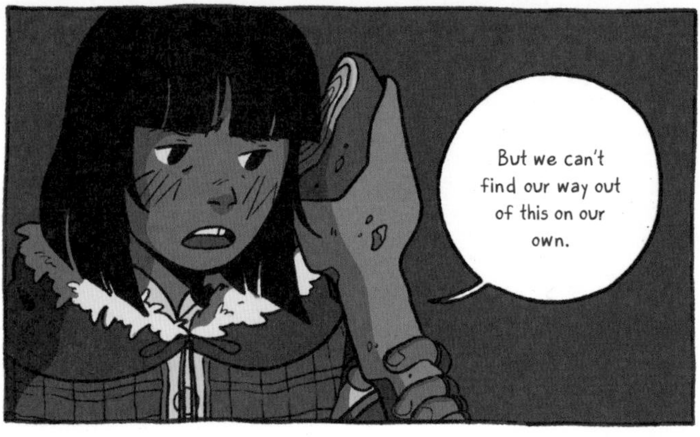
But we can't find our way out of this on our own.

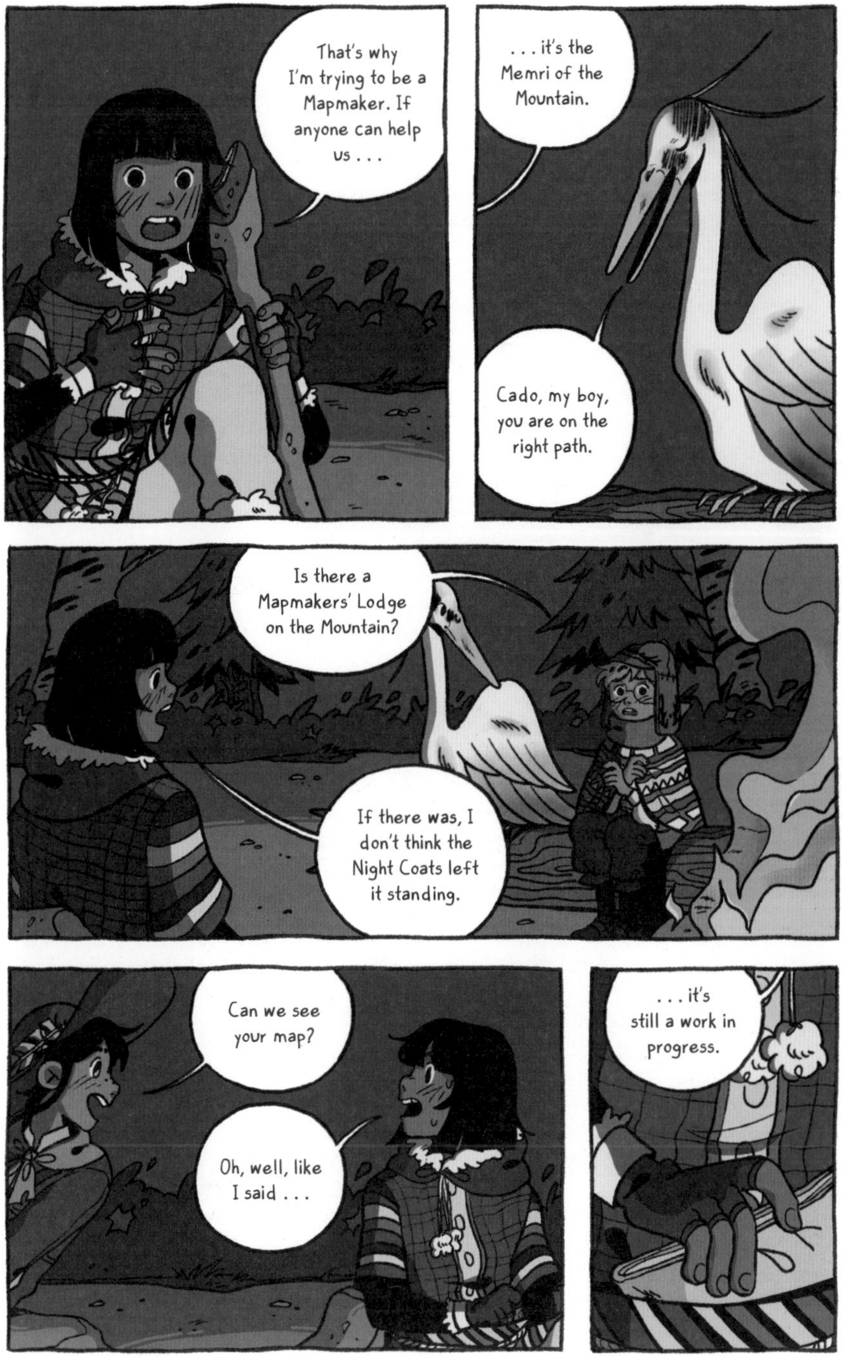
That's why I'm trying to be a Mapmaker. If anyone can help us . . .
. . . it's the Memri of the Mountain.
Cado, my boy, you are on the right path.
Is there a Mapmakers' Lodge on the Mountain?
If there was, I don't think the Night Coats left it standing.
Can we see your map?
Oh, well, like I said . . .
. . . it's still a work in progress.

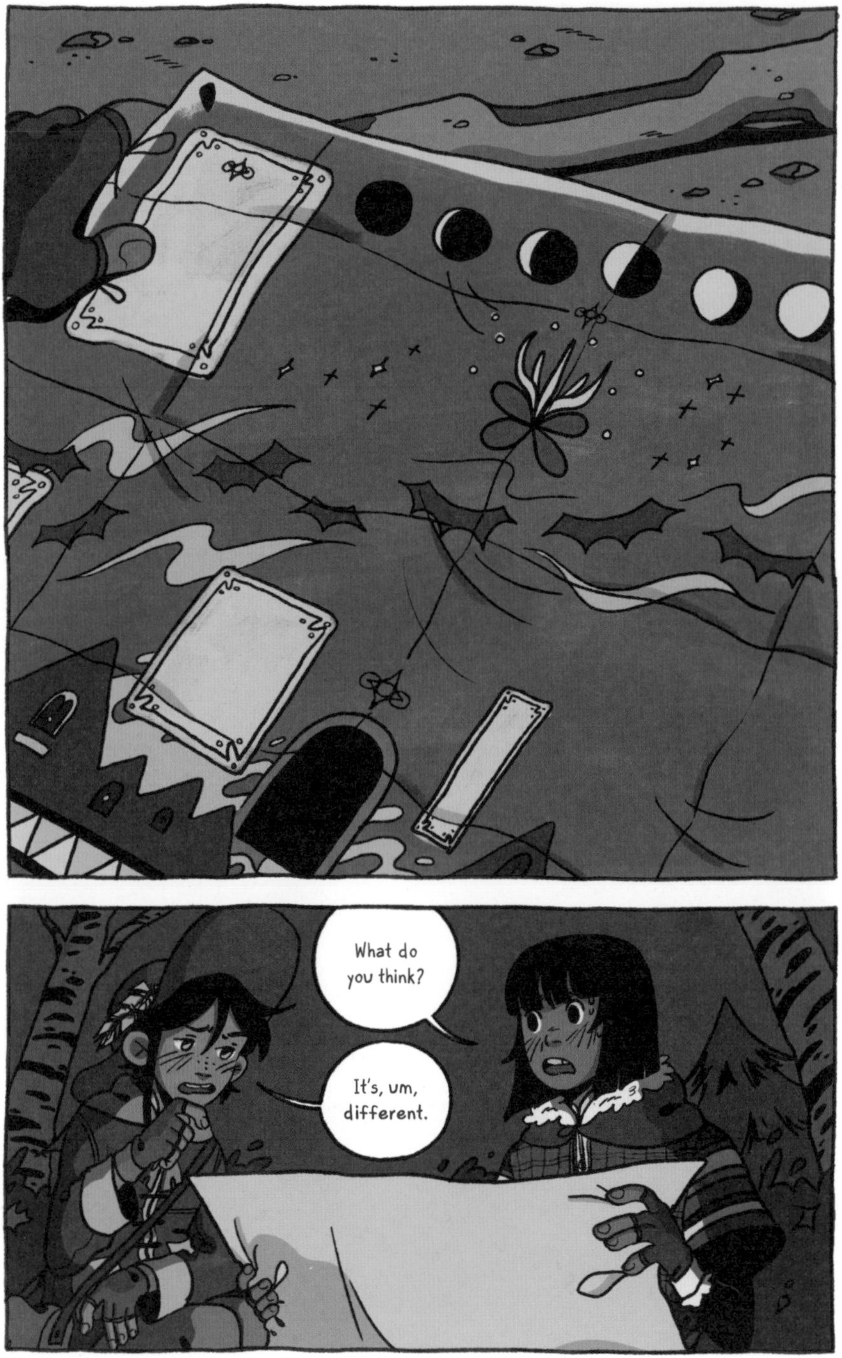
What do you think?
It's, um, different.

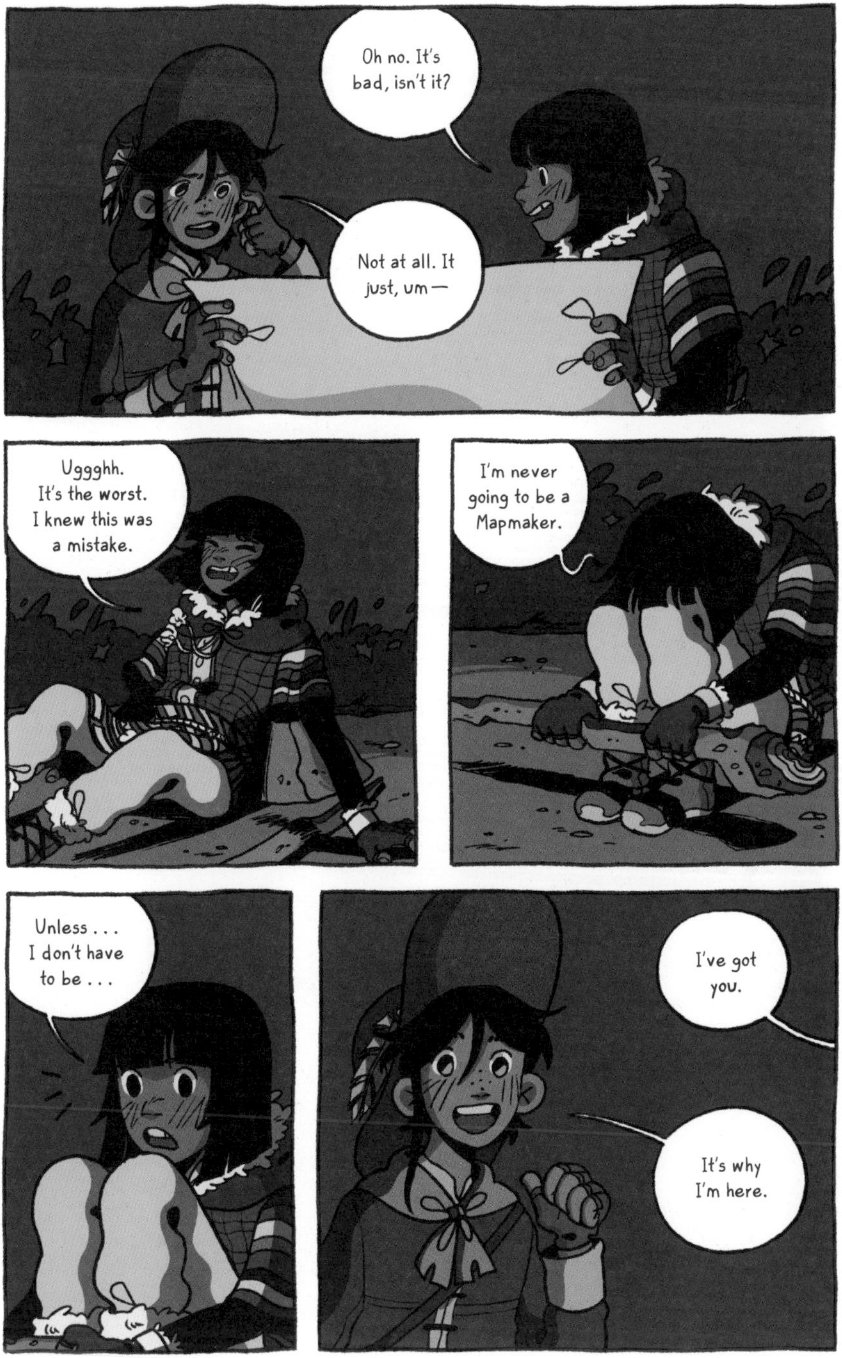
Oh no. It's bad, isn't it?
Not at all. It just, um—
Uggghh. It's the worst. I knew this was a mistake.
I'm never going to be a Mapmaker.
Unless . . . I don't have to be . . .
I've got you.
It's why I'm here.

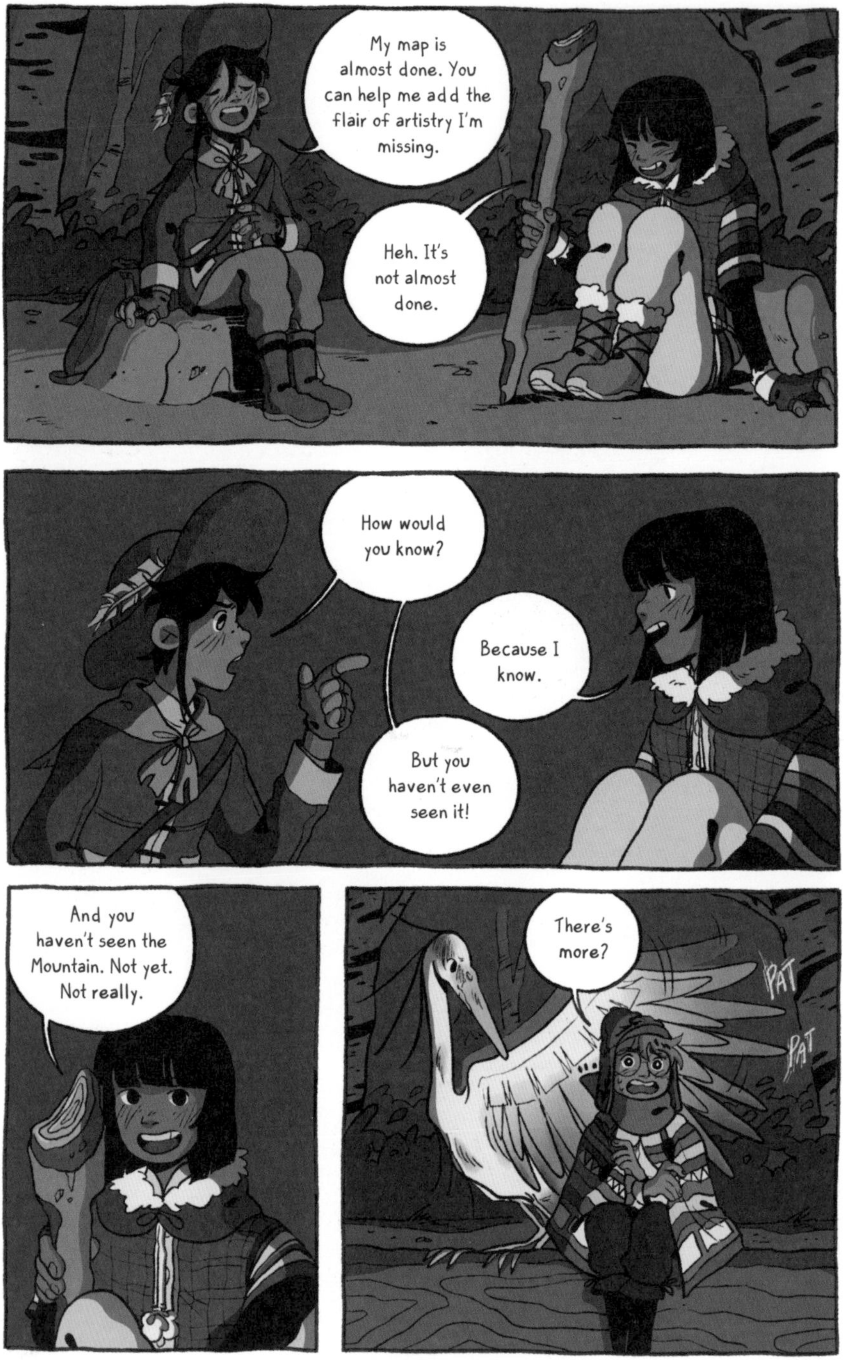
My map is almost done. You can help me add the flair of artistry I'm missing.
Heh. It's not almost done.
How would you know?
Because I know.
But you haven't even seen it!
And you haven't seen the Mountain. Not yet. Not really.
There's more?
PAT
PAT

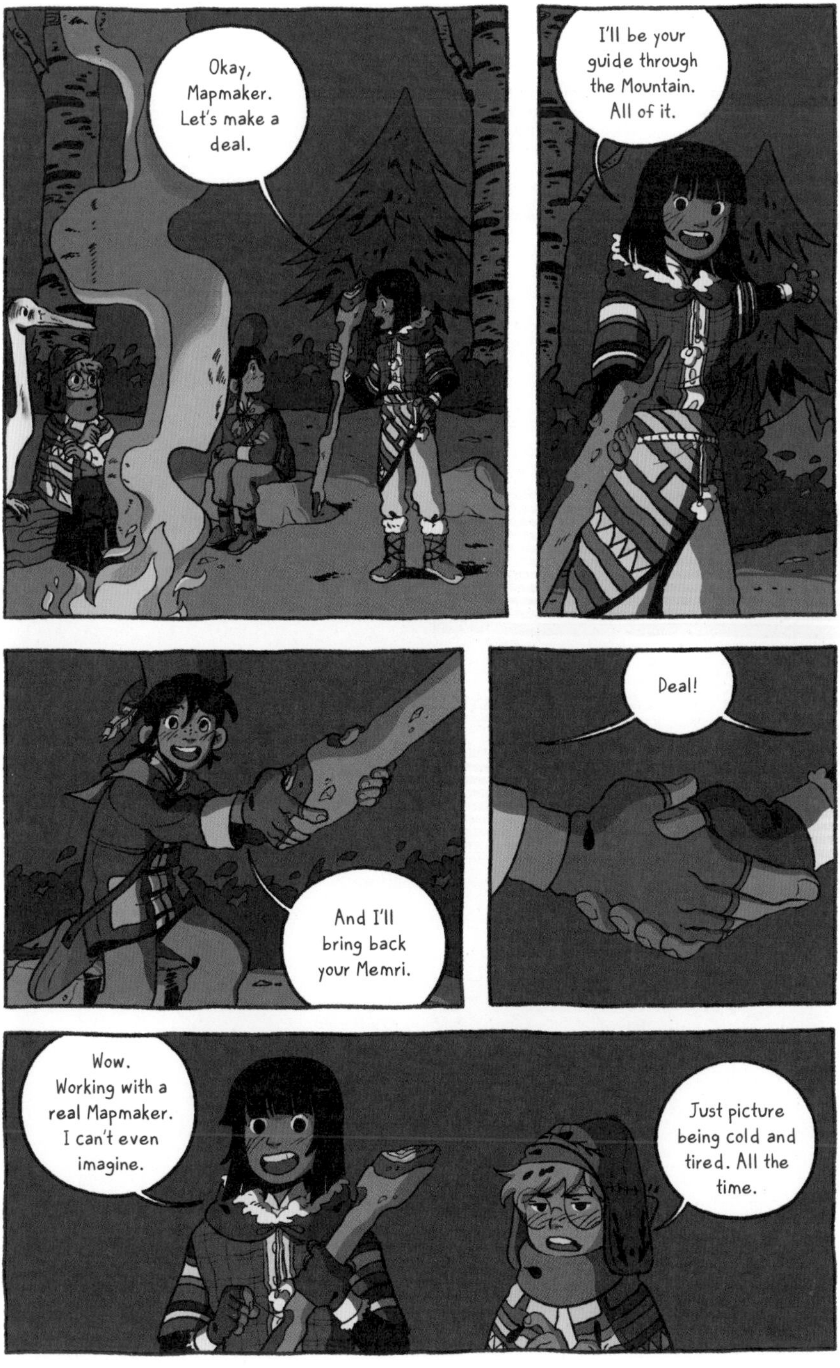
Okay, Mapmaker. Let's make a deal.
I'll be your guide through the Mountain. All of it.
And I'll bring back your Memri.
Deal!
Wow. Working with a real Mapmaker. I can't even imagine.
Just picture being cold and tired. All the time.

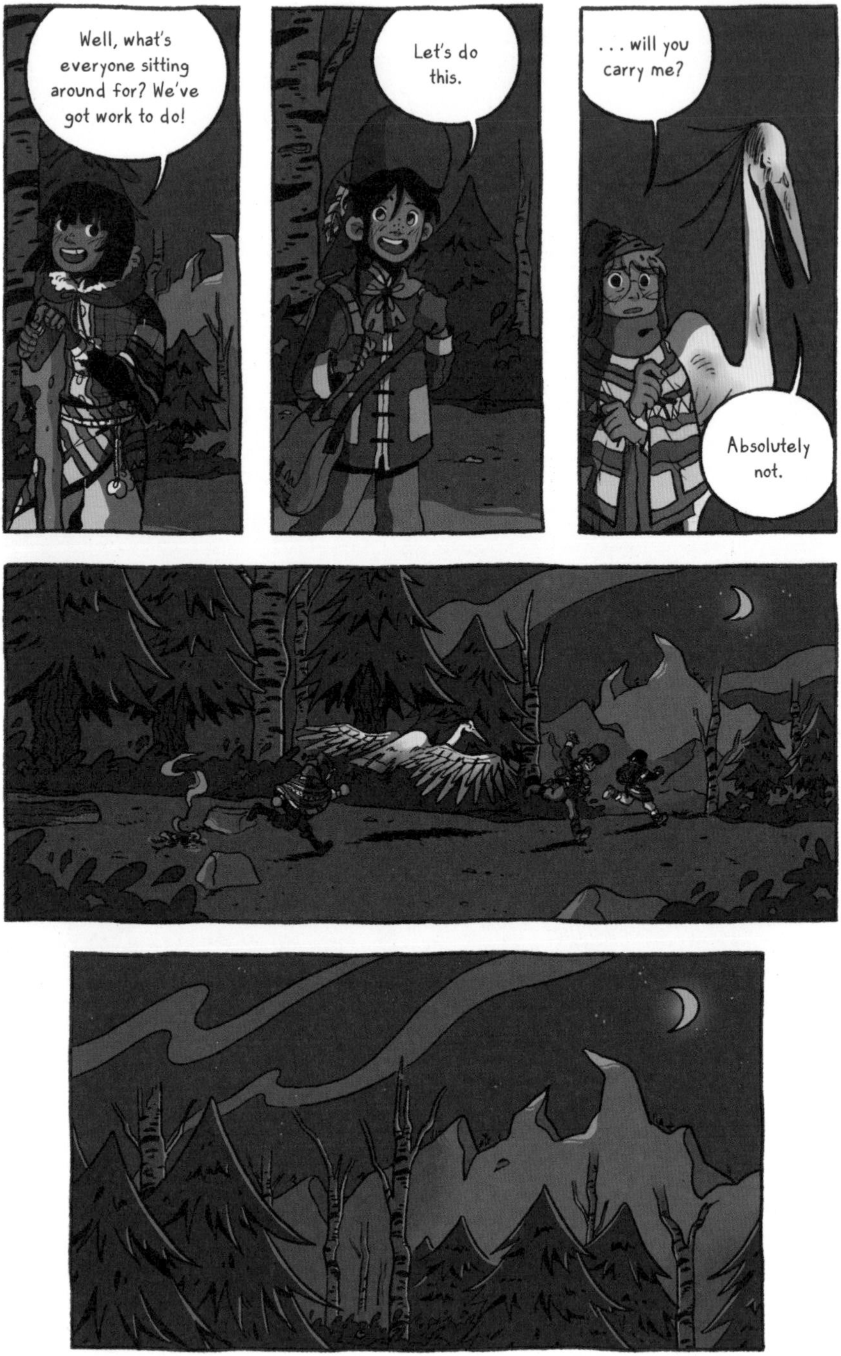
Well, what's everyone sitting around for? We've got work to do!
Let's do this.
. . . will you carry me?
Absolutely not.

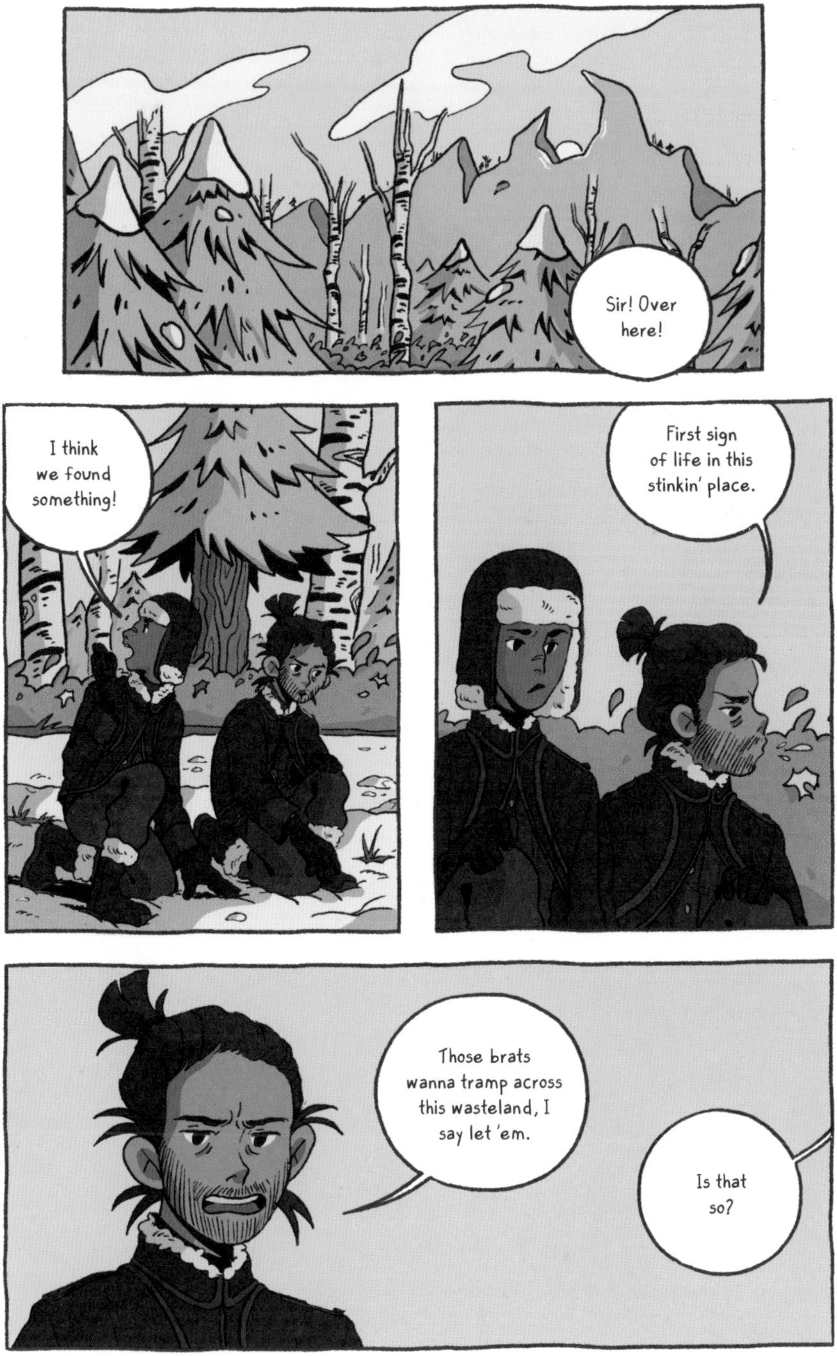
Sir! Over here!
I think we found something!
First sign of life in this stinkin' place.
Those brats wanna tramp across this wasteland, I say let 'em.
Is that so?

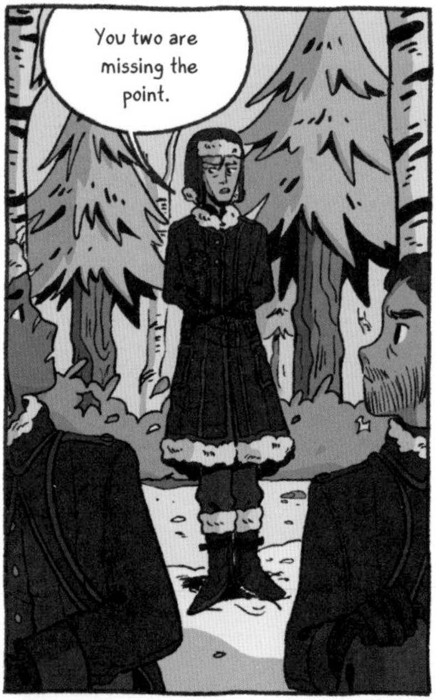
You two are missing the point.

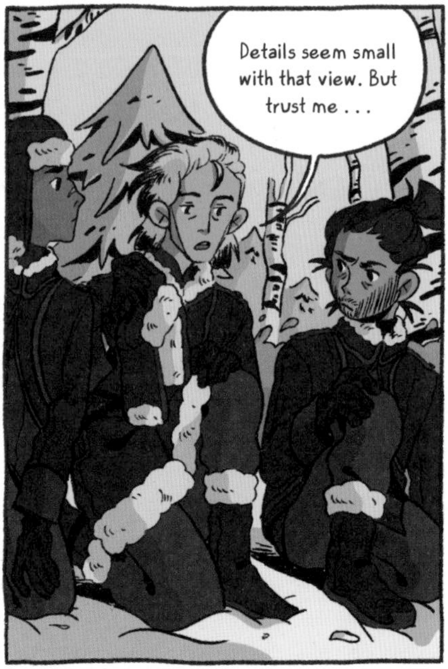
Details seem small with that view. But trust me . . .

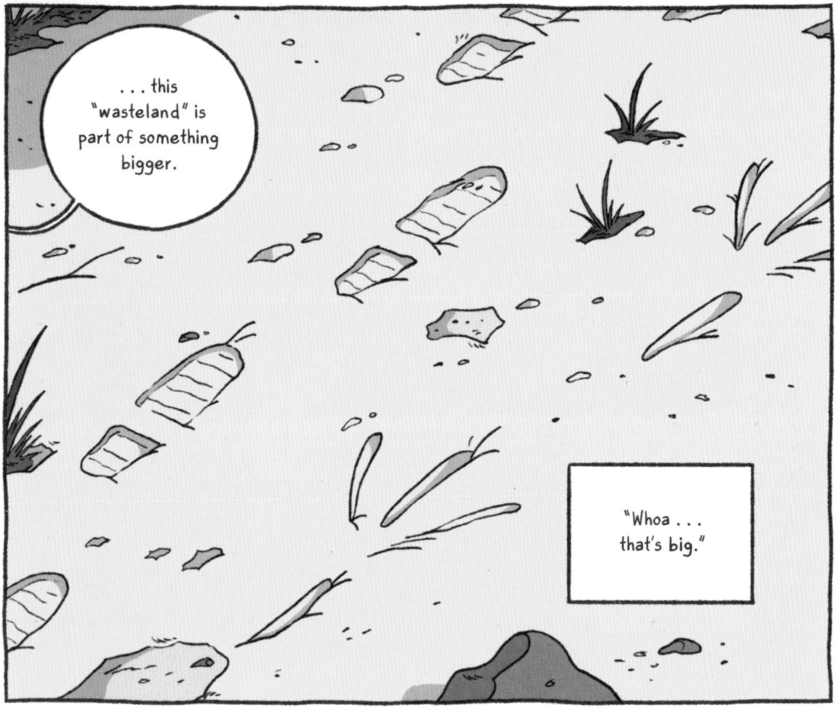
. . . this "wasteland" is part of something bigger.
"Whoa . . . that's big."

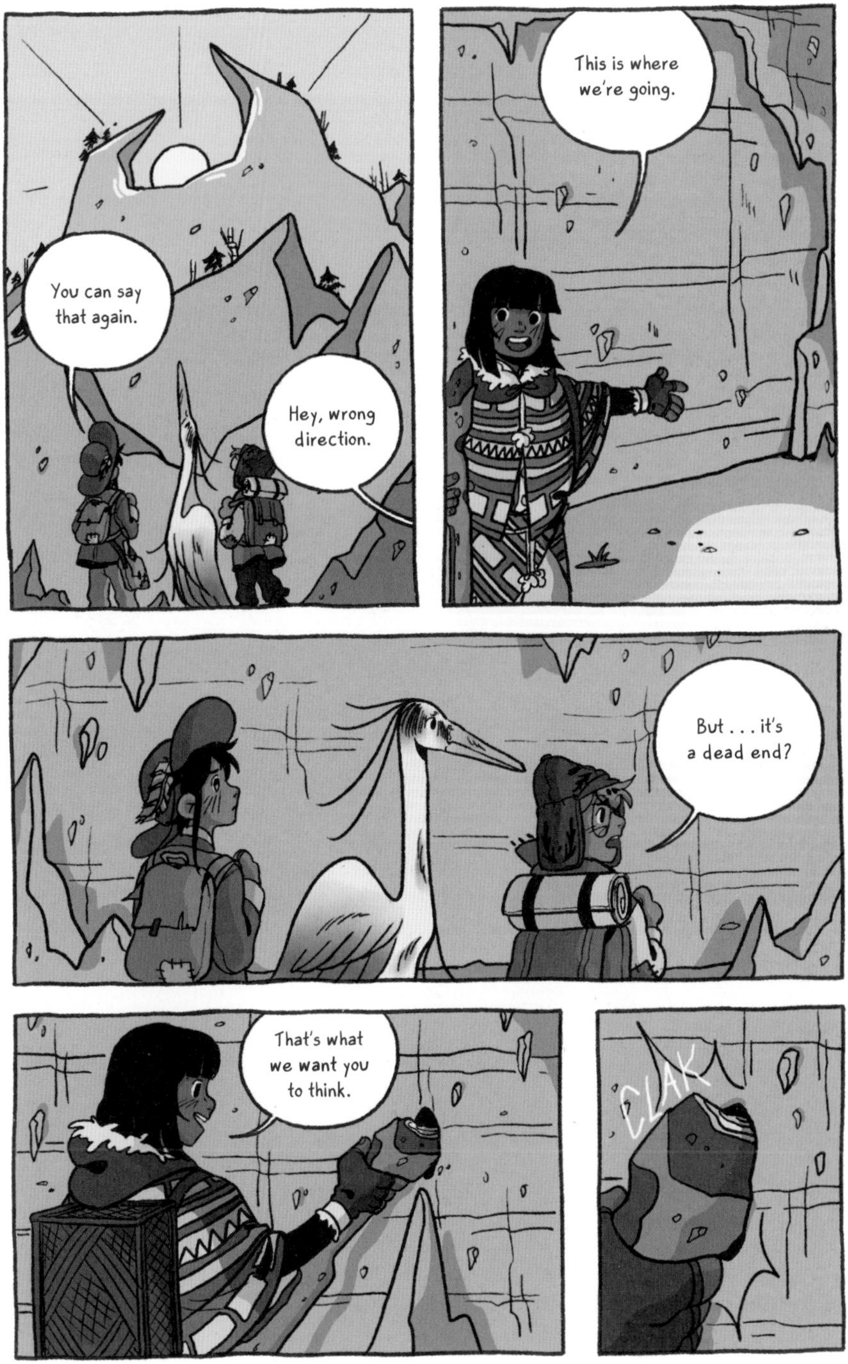
You can say that again.
Hey, wrong direction.
This is where we're going.
But . . . it's a dead end?
That's what we want you to think.
CLAK

SHUUUUURRRN

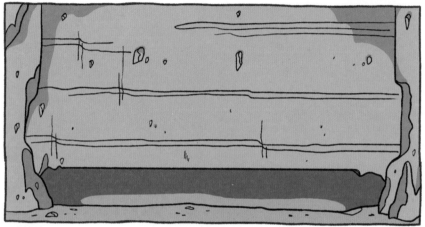

When you said you all hid . . . you meant in a cave . . .

That's one way to put it, I guess.

How do we get in? We crawl?

Yup.

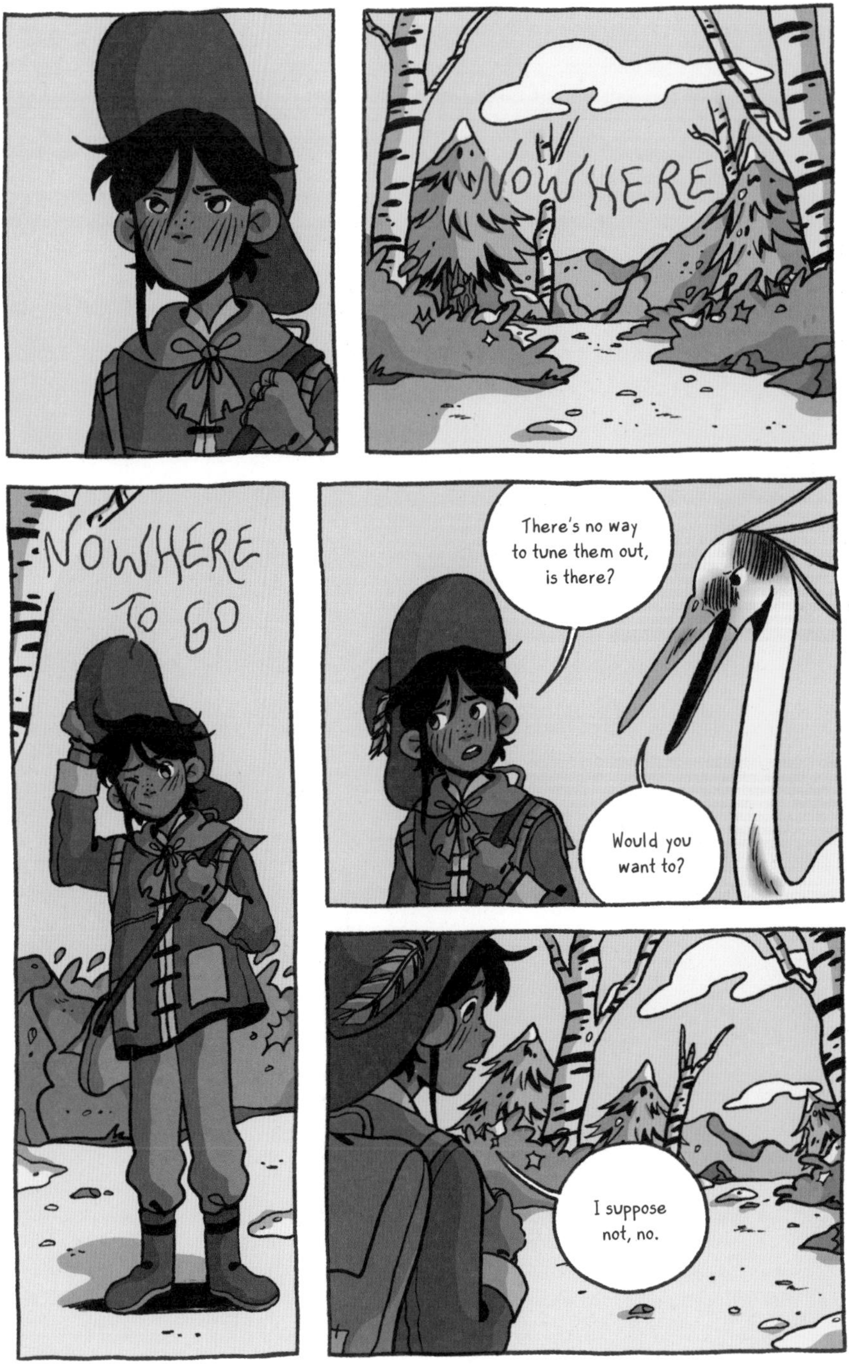
NOWHERE
NOWHERE
TO GO
There's no way to tune them out, is there?
Would you want to?
I suppose not, no.

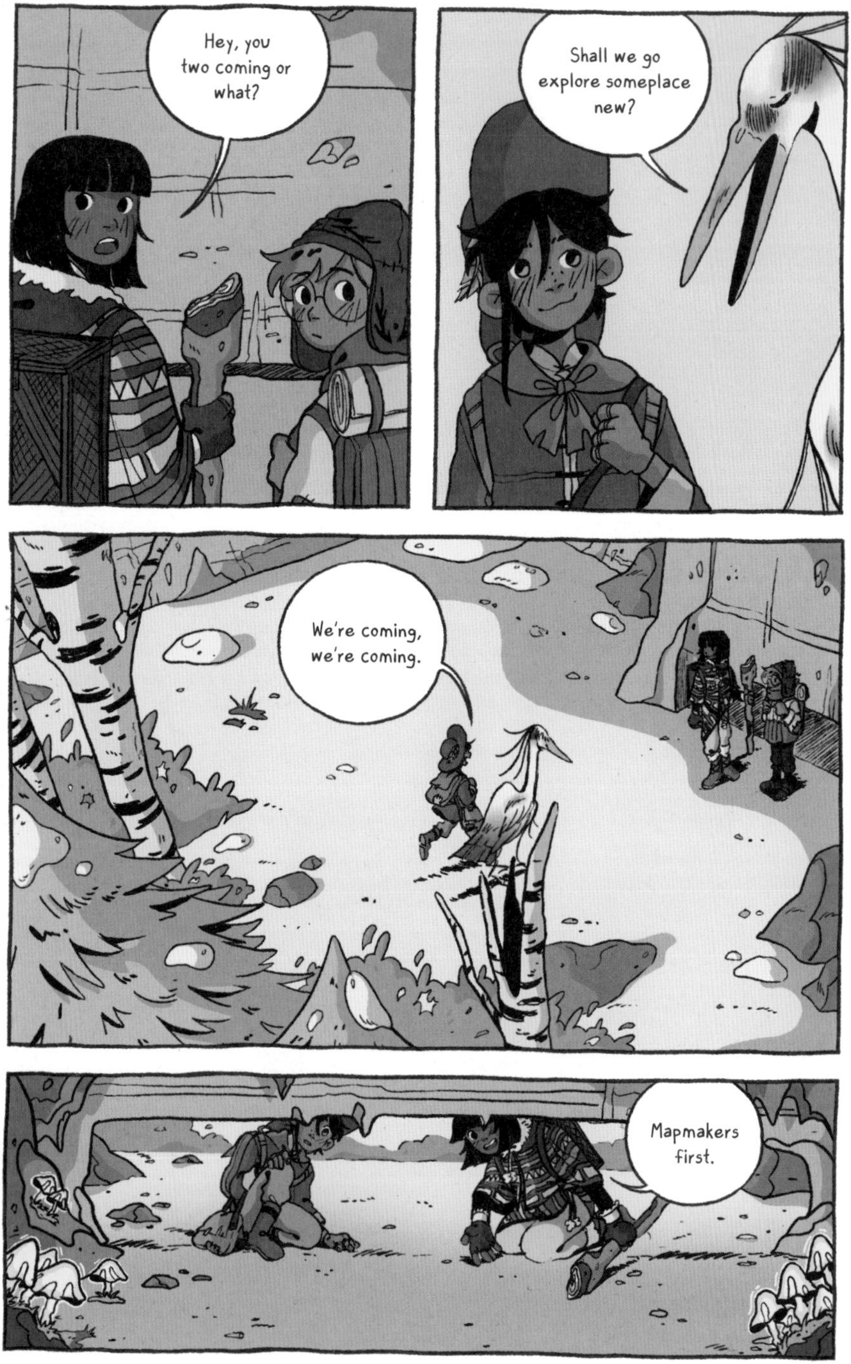
Hey, you two coming or what?
Shall we go explore someplace new?
We're coming, we're coming.
Mapmakers first.

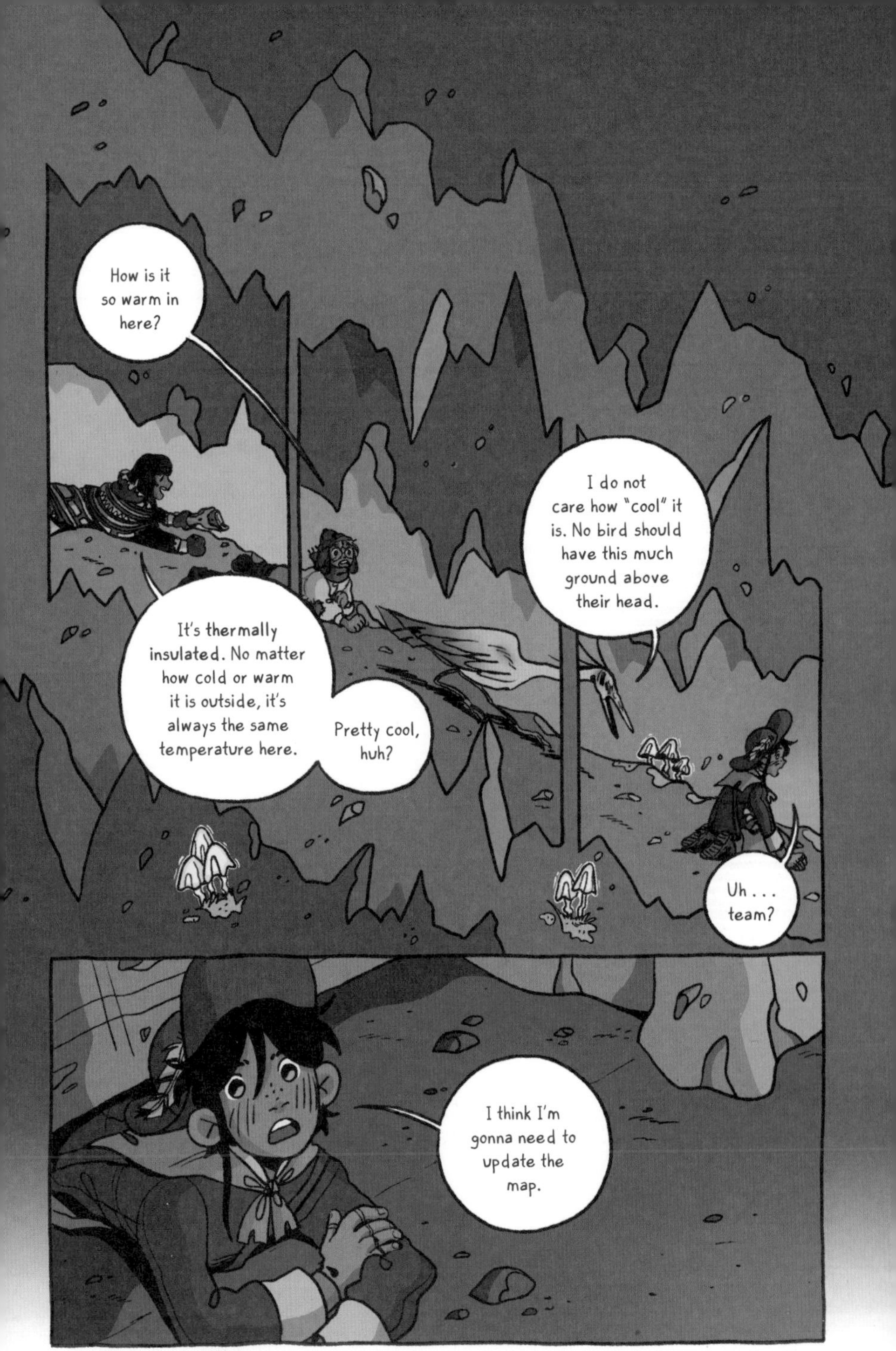
How is it so warm in here?
It's thermally insulated. No matter how cold or warm it is outside, it's always the same temperature here.
Pretty cool, huh?
I do not care how "cool" it is. No bird should have this much ground above their head.
Uh . . . team?
I think I'm gonna need to update the map.

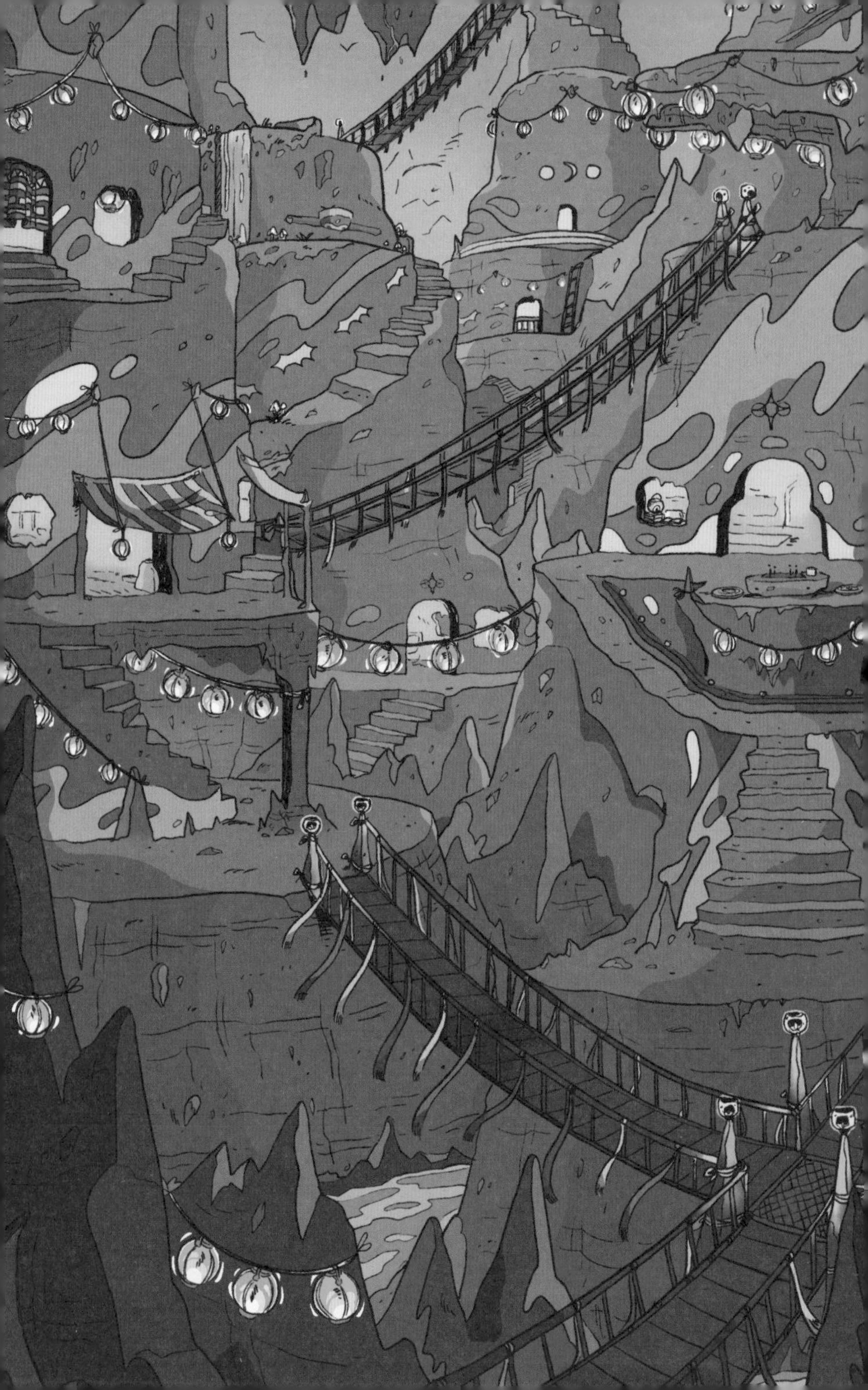

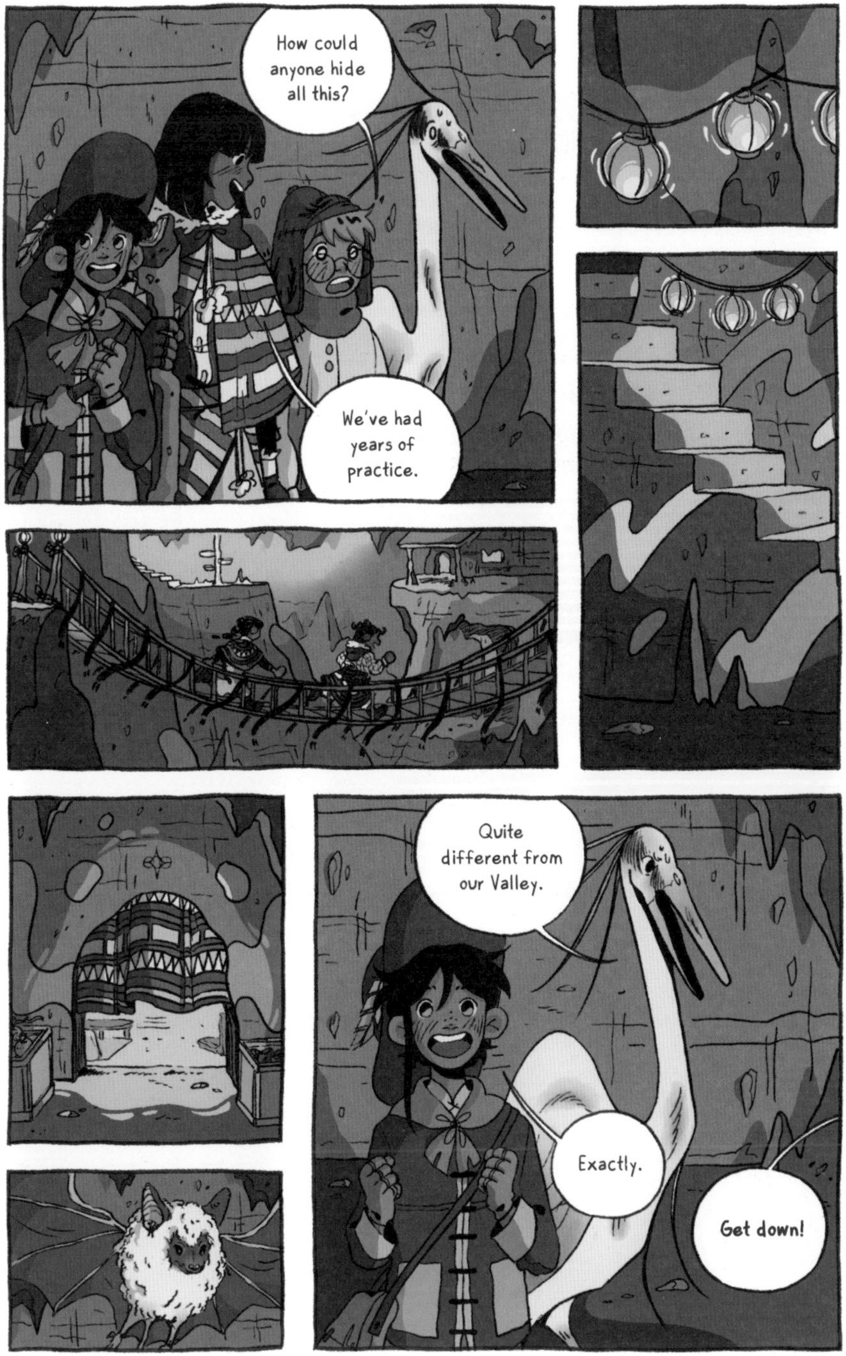
How could anyone hide all this?
We've had years of practice.
Quite different from our Valley.
Exactly.
Get down!

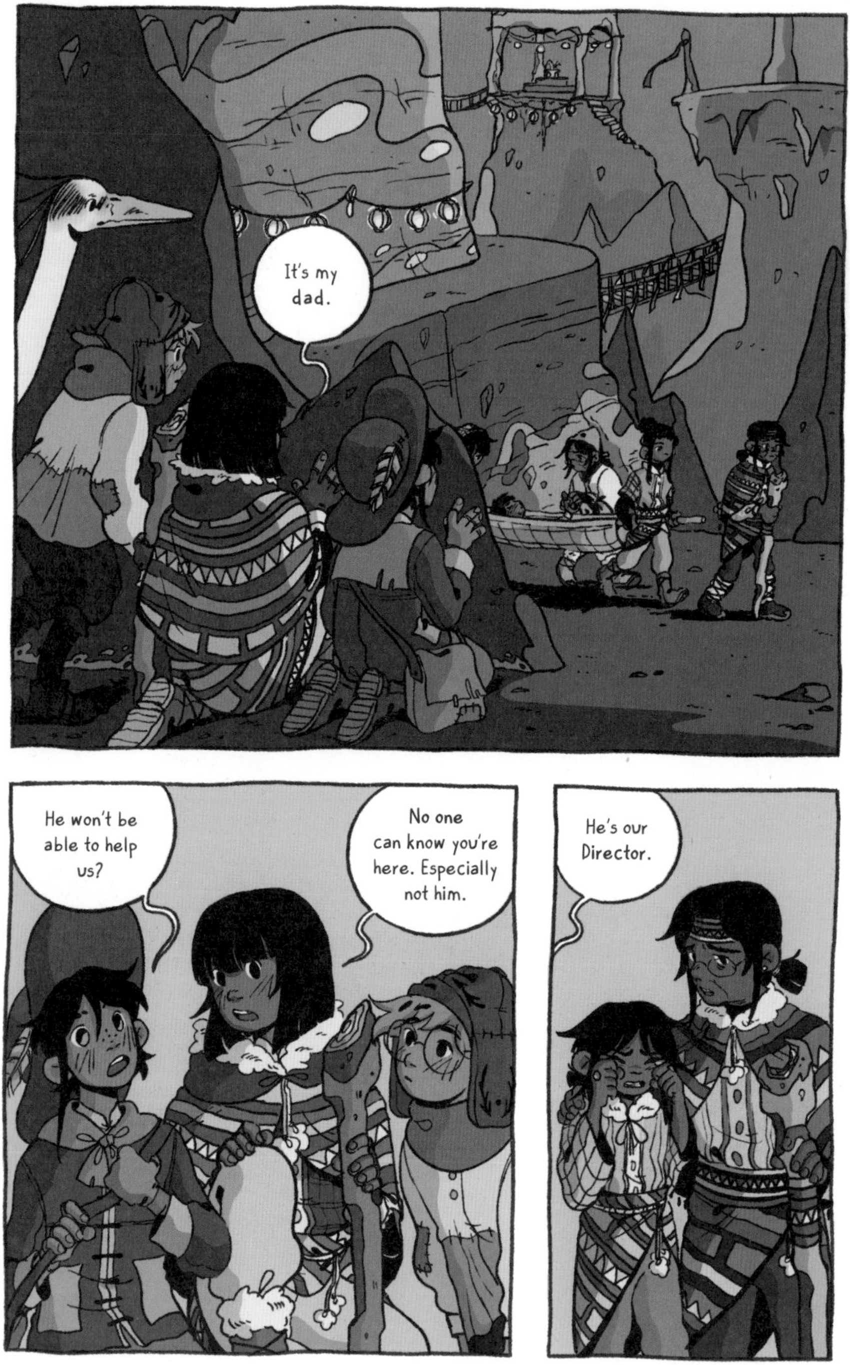
It's my dad.
He won't be able to help us?
No one can know you're here. Especially not him.
He's our Director.

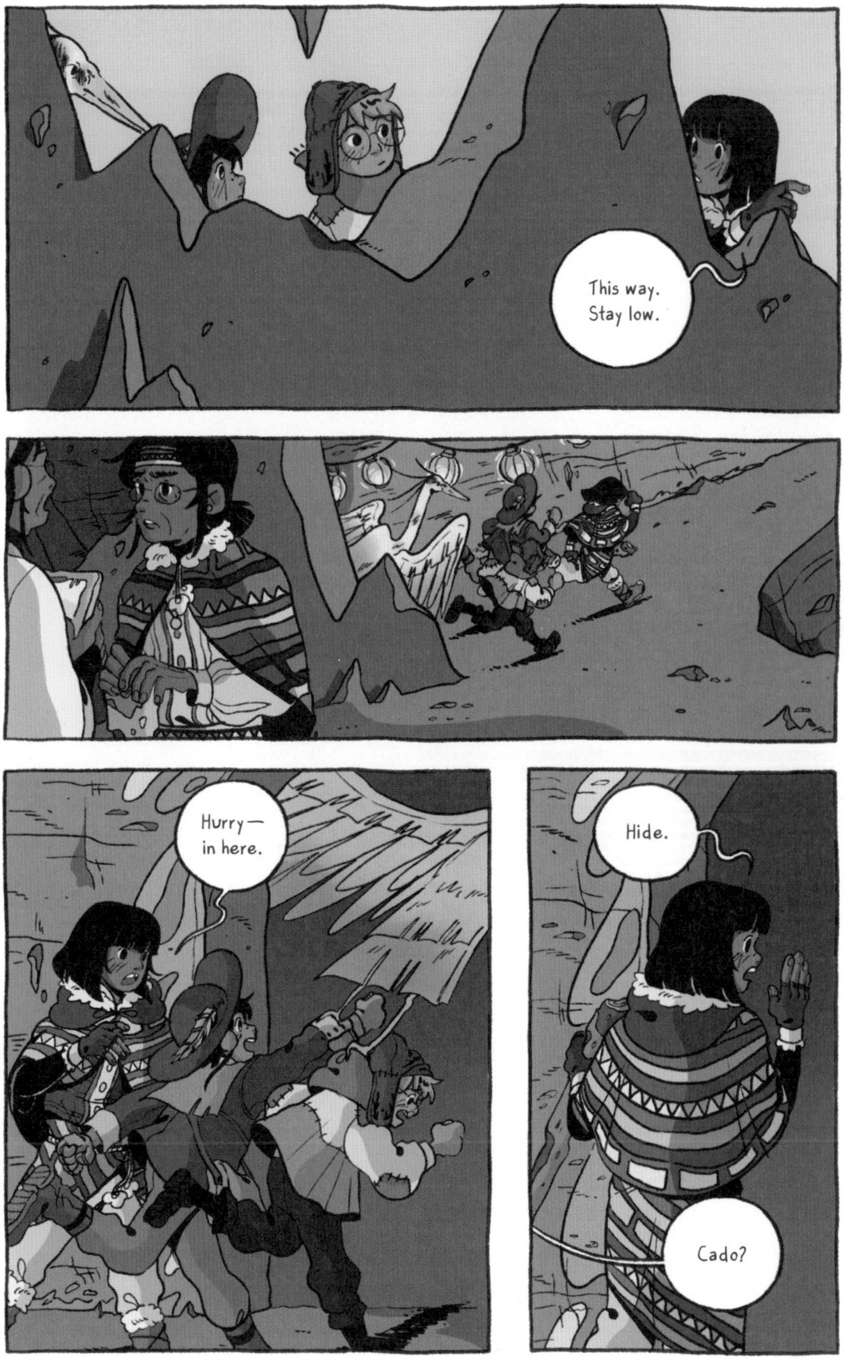
This way.
Stay low.
Hurry—
in here.
Hide.
Cado?

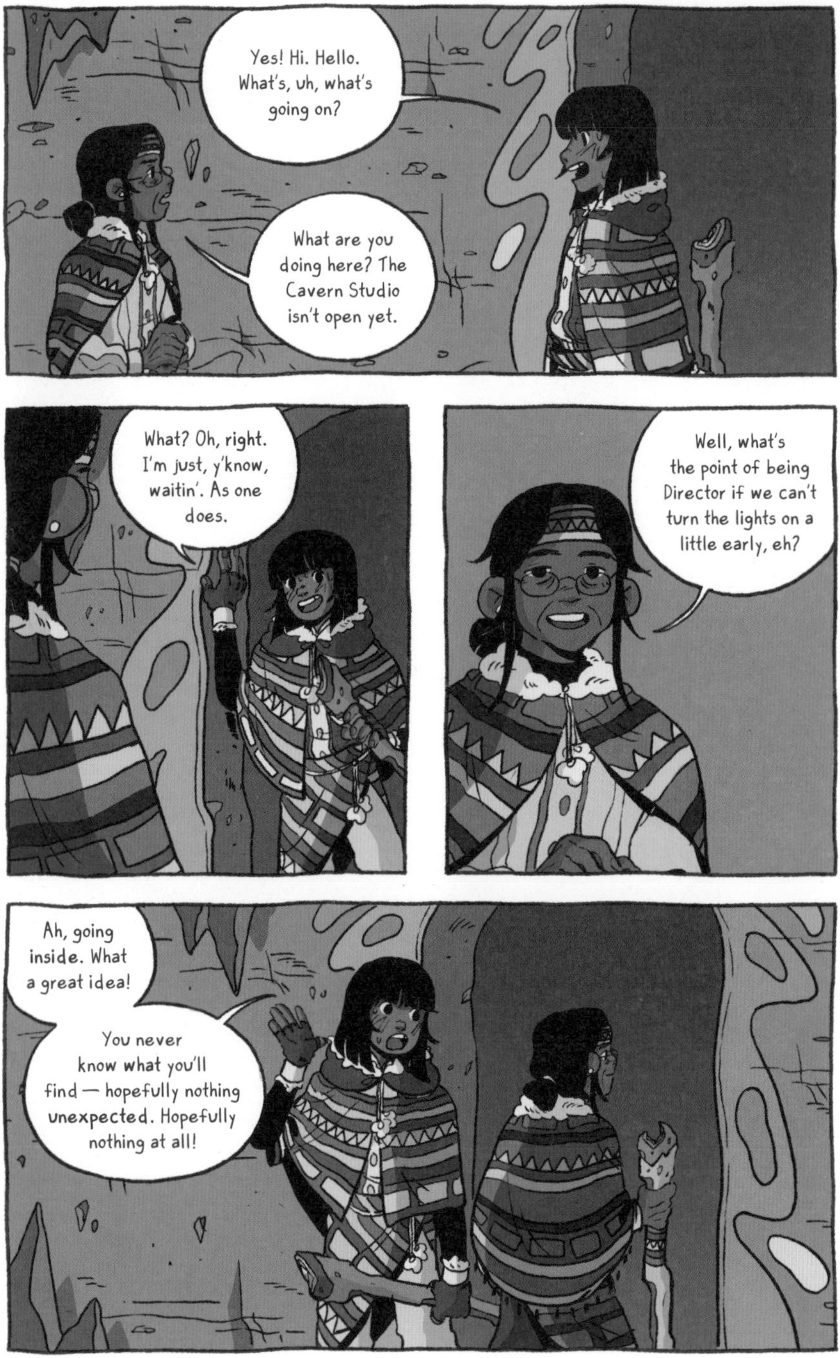
Yes! Hi. Hello. What's, uh, what's going on?
What are you doing here? The Cavern Studio isn't open yet.
What? Oh, right. I'm just, y'know, waitin'. As one does.
Well, what's the point of being Director if we can't turn the lights on a little early, eh?
Ah, going inside. What a great idea!
You never know what you'll find — hopefully nothing unexpected. Hopefully nothing at all!

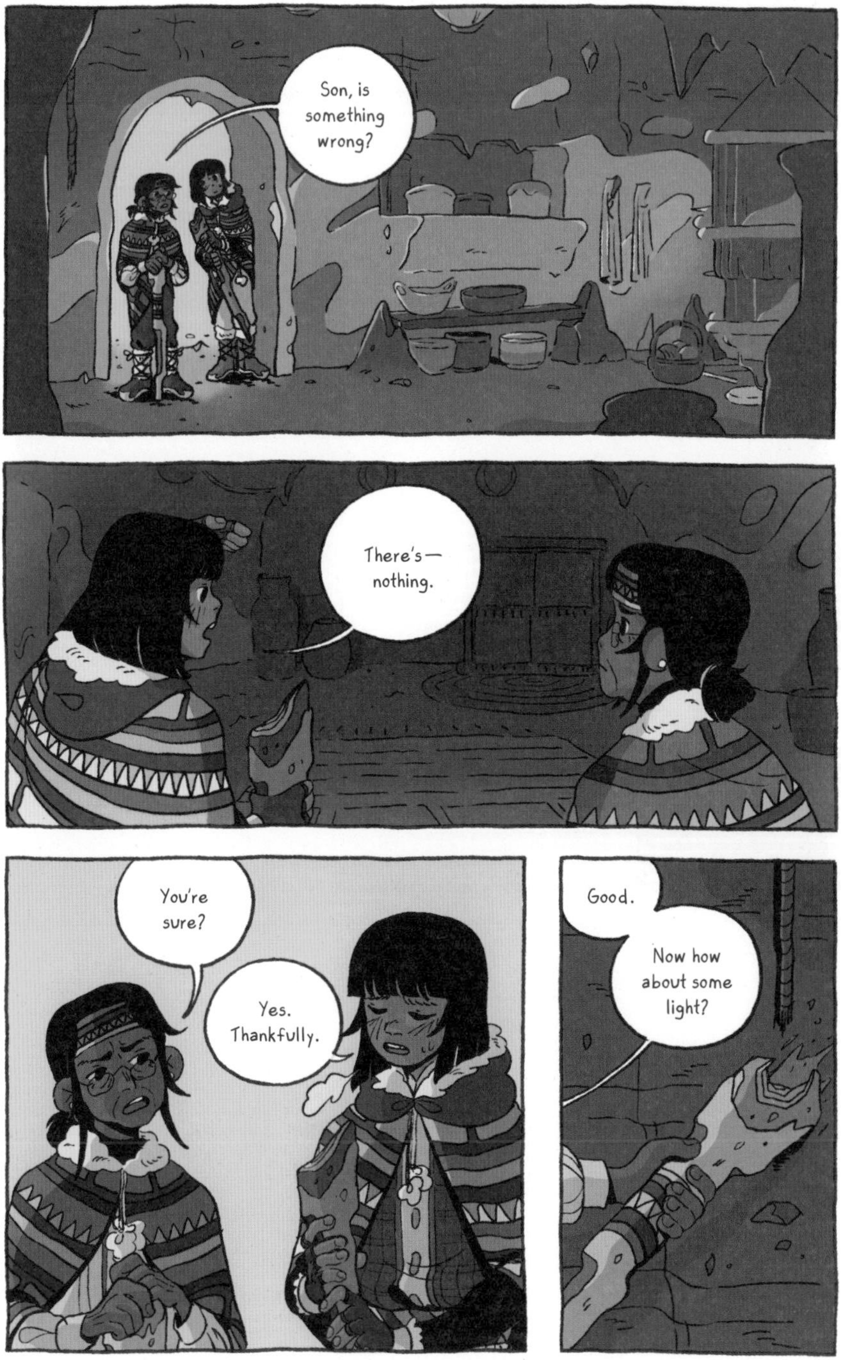
Son, is something wrong?
There's— nothing.
You're sure?
Yes. Thankfully.
Good.
Now how about some light?

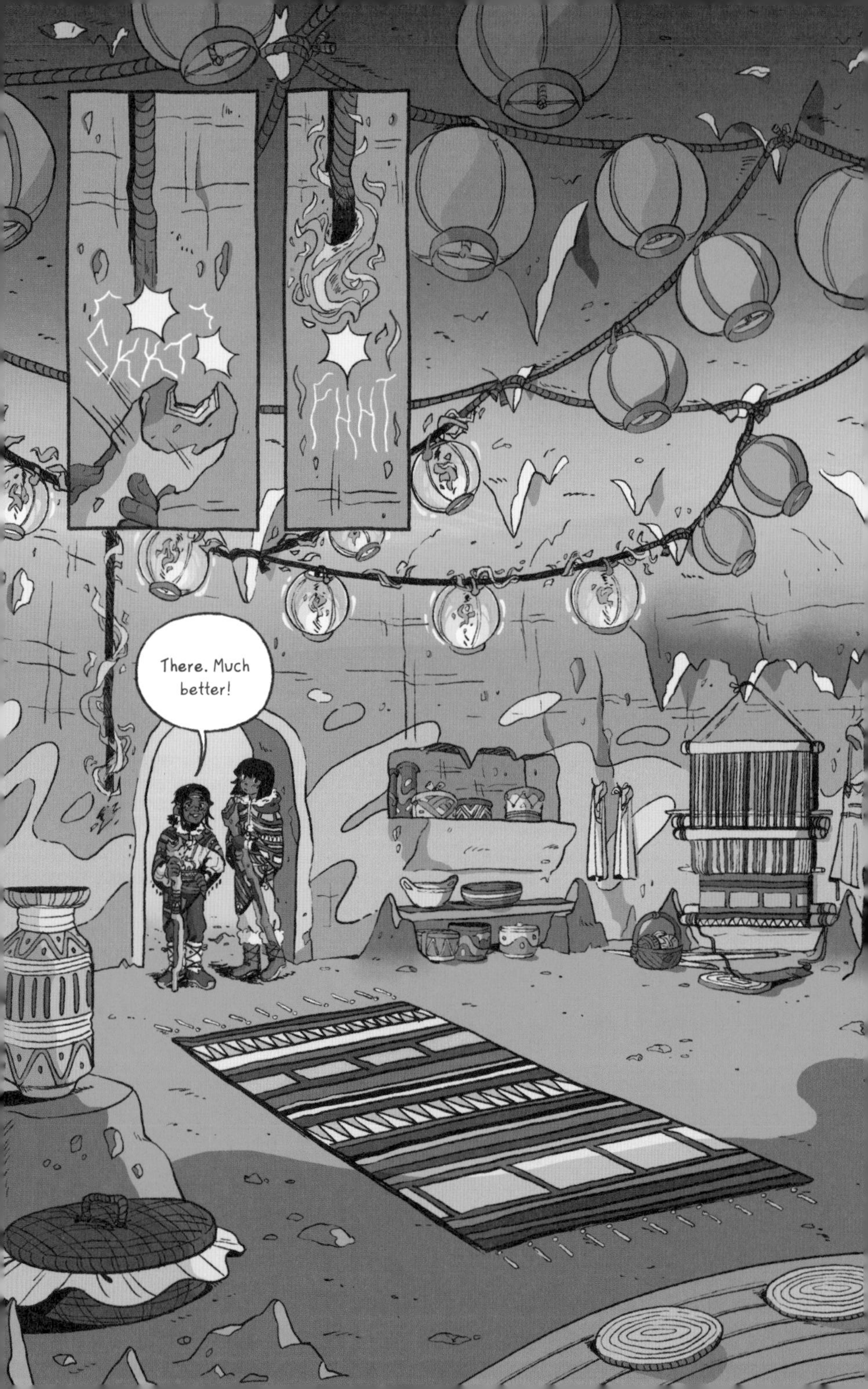
SKKT
FHHT
There. Much better!

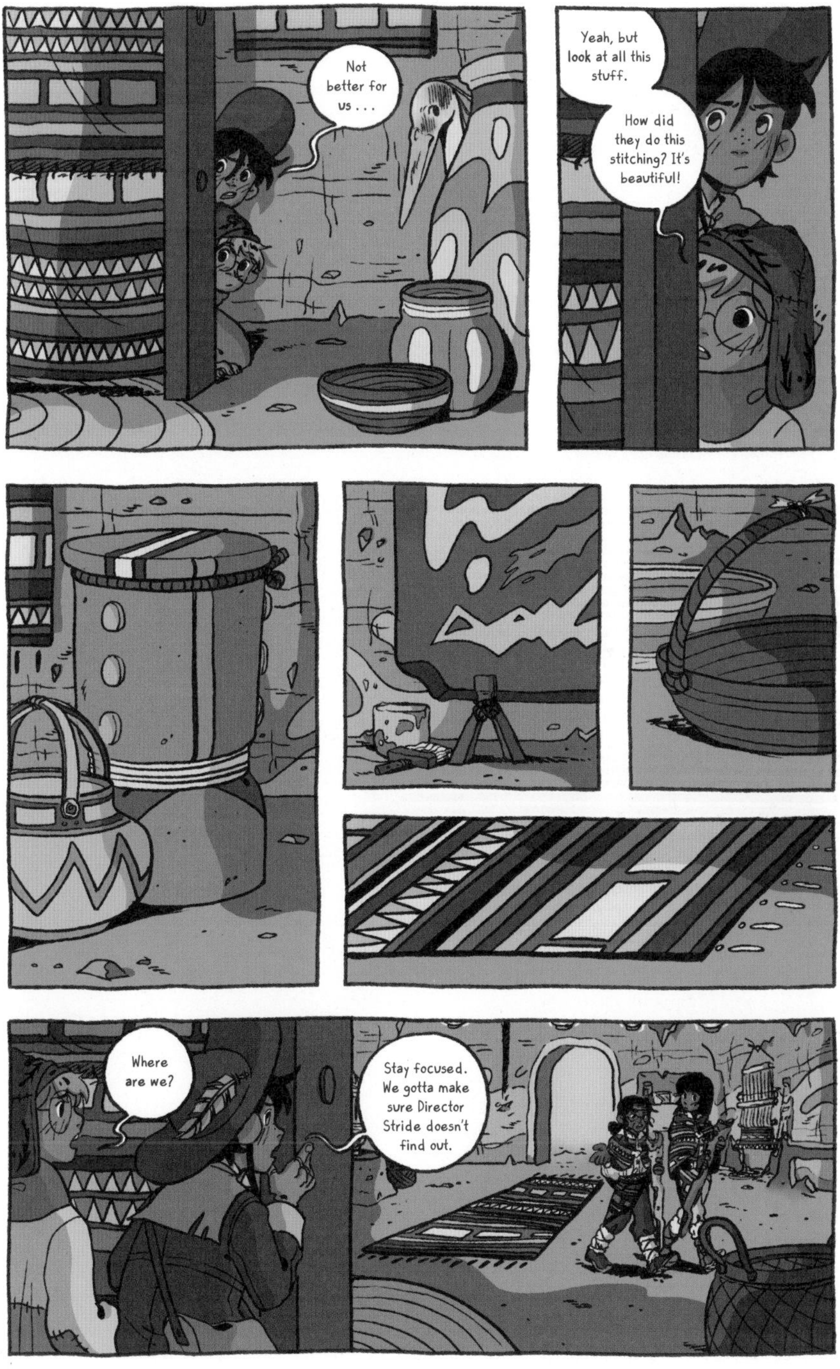

Not better for us . . .
Yeah, but look at all this stuff.
How did they do this stitching? It's beautiful!
Where are we?
Stay focused. We gotta make sure Director Stride doesn't find out.

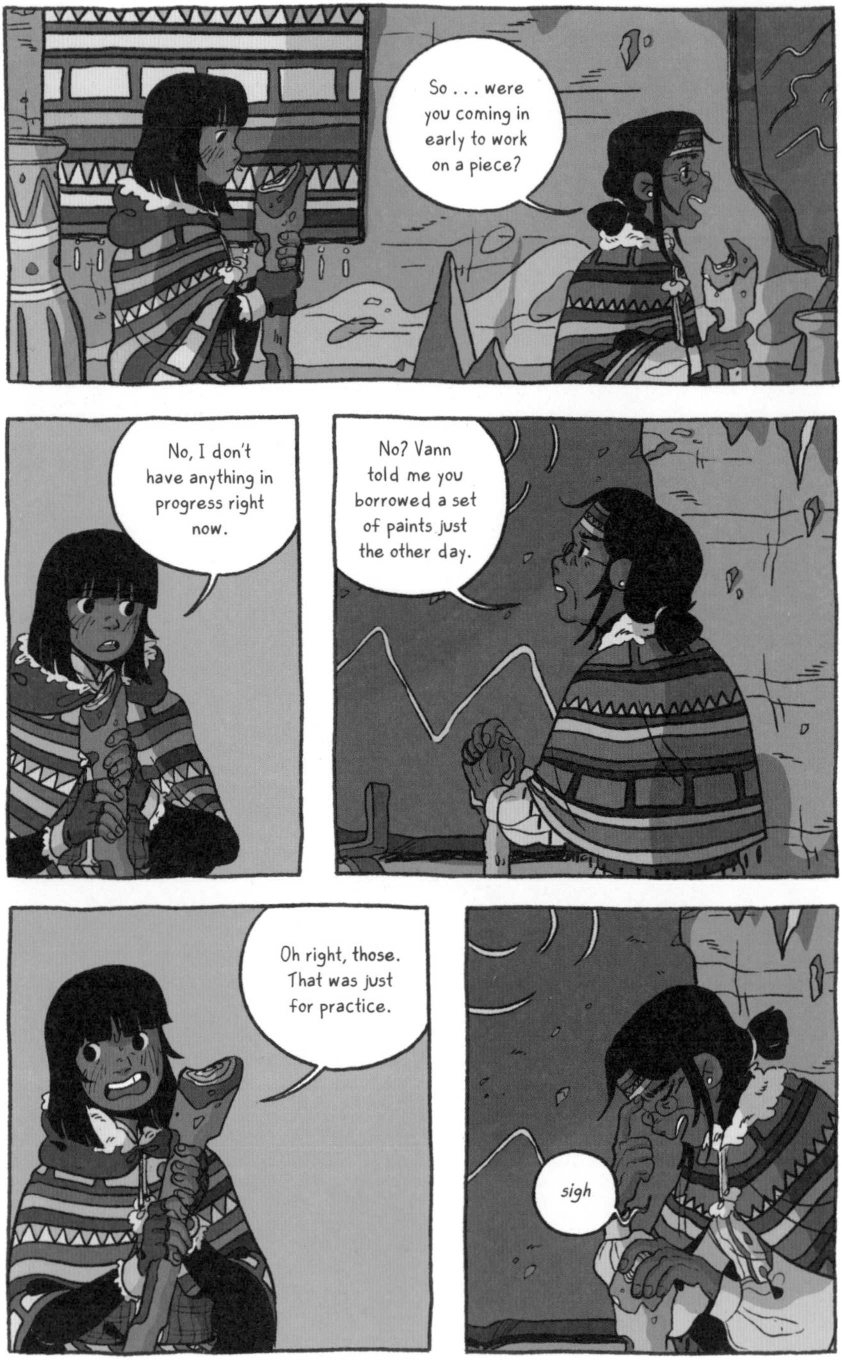
So . . . were you coming in early to work on a piece?
No, I don't have anything in progress right now.
No? Vann told me you borrowed a set of paints just the other day.
Oh right, those. That was just for practice.
sigh

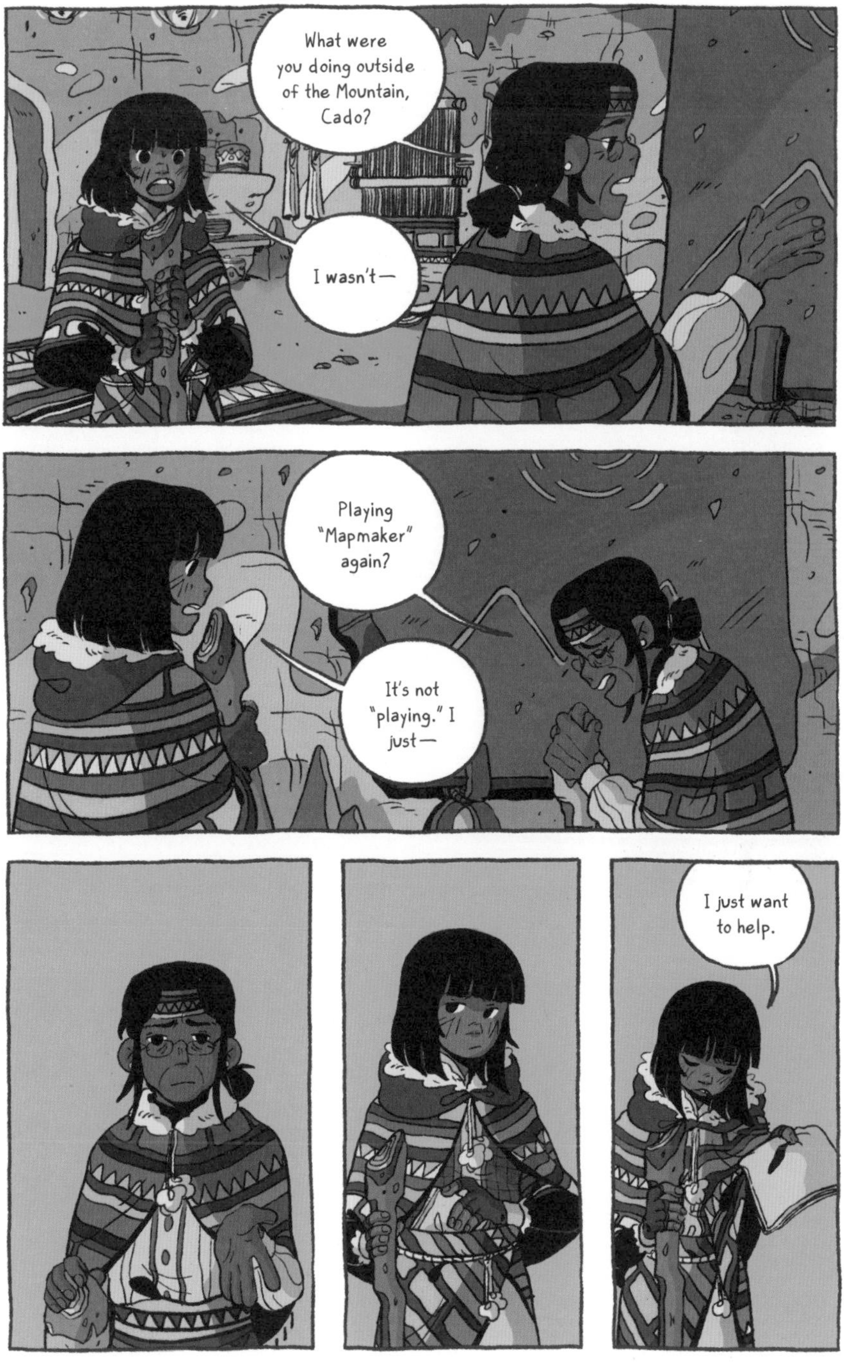
What were you doing outside of the Mountain, Cado?
I wasn't—
Playing "Mapmaker" again?
It's not "playing." I just—
I just want to help.

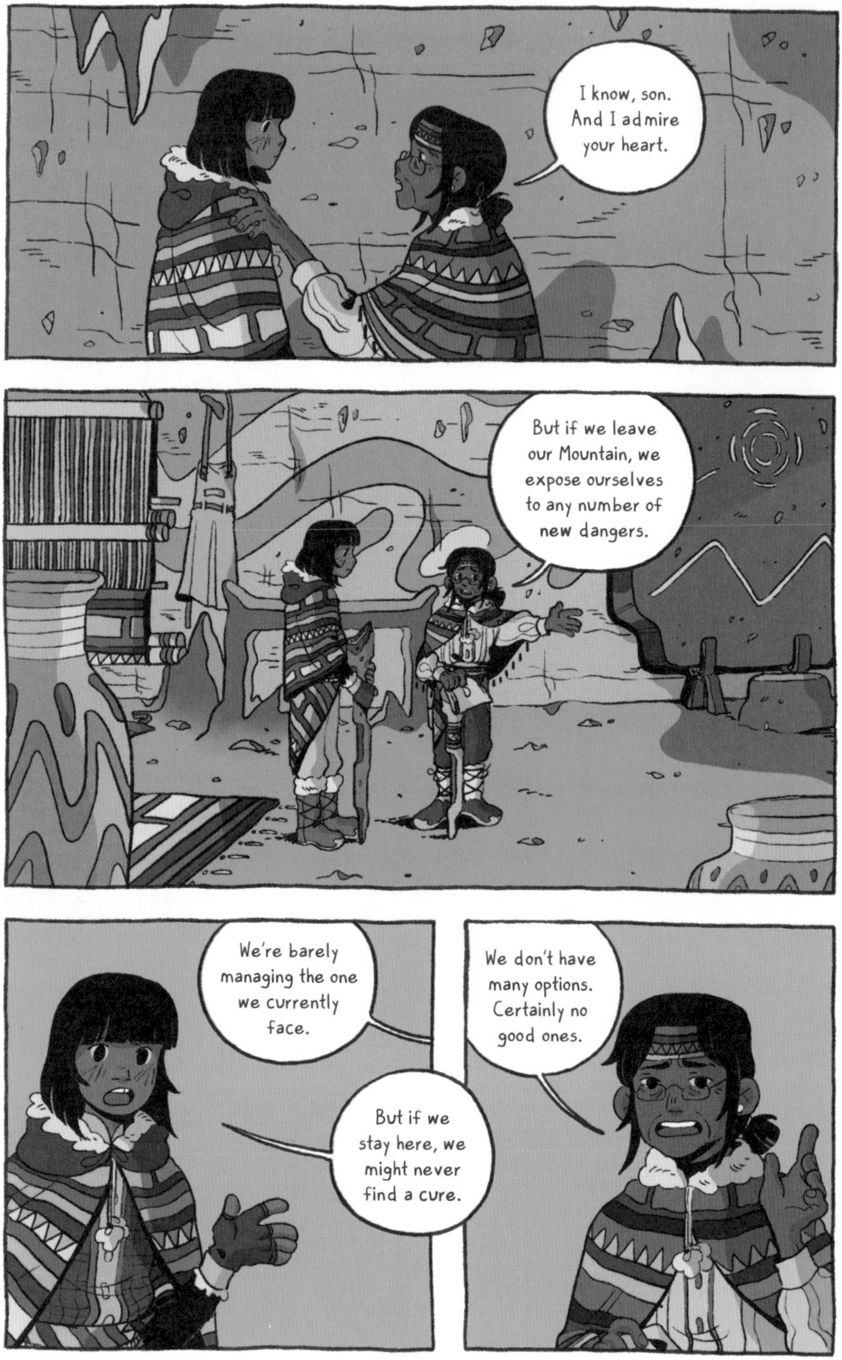
I know, son. And I admire your heart.
But if we leave our Mountain, we expose ourselves to any number of new dangers.
We're barely managing the one we currently face.
But if we stay here, we might never find a cure.
We don't have many options. Certainly no good ones.

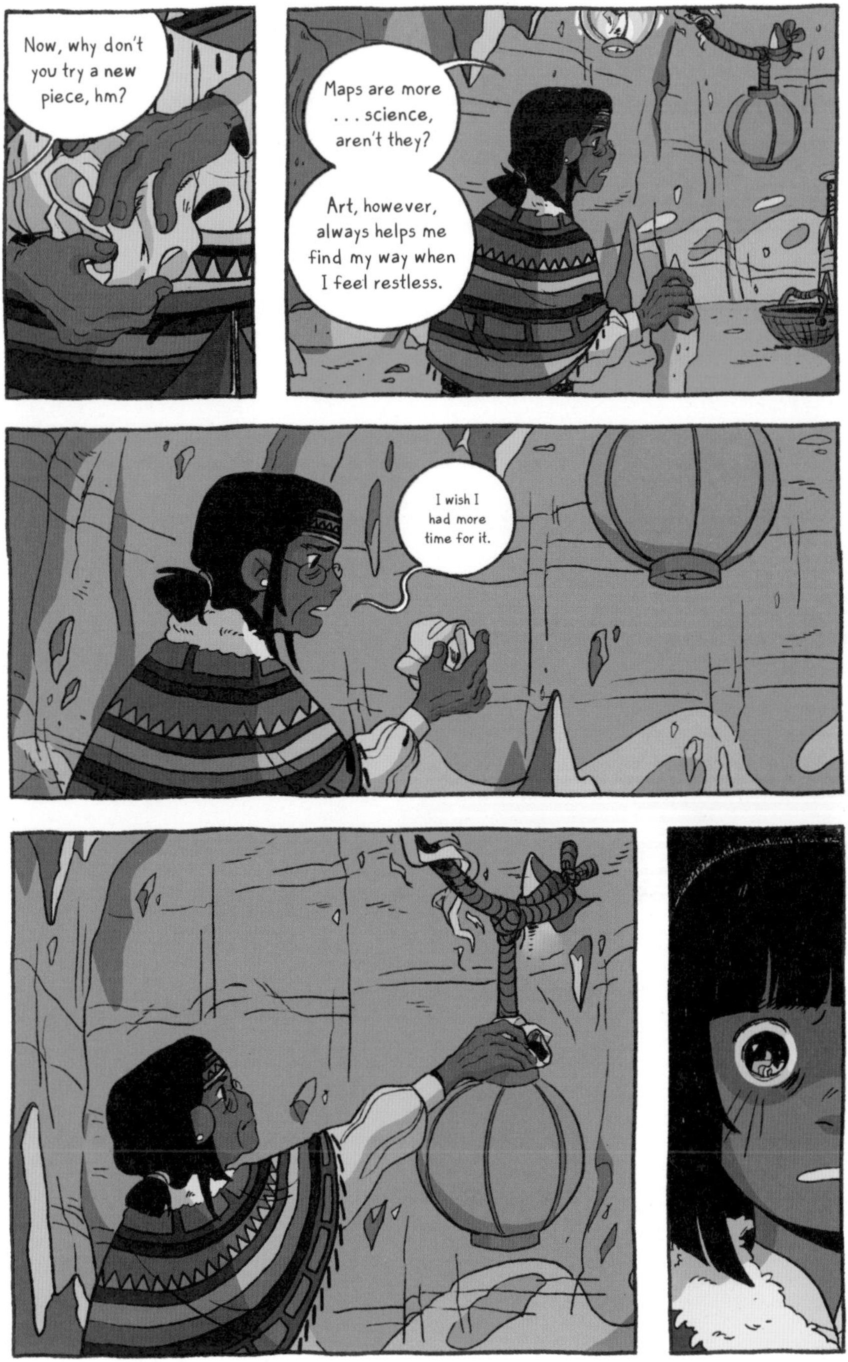
Now, why don't you try a new piece, hm?
Maps are more . . . science, aren't they?
Art, however, always helps me find my way when I feel restless.
I wish I had more time for it.

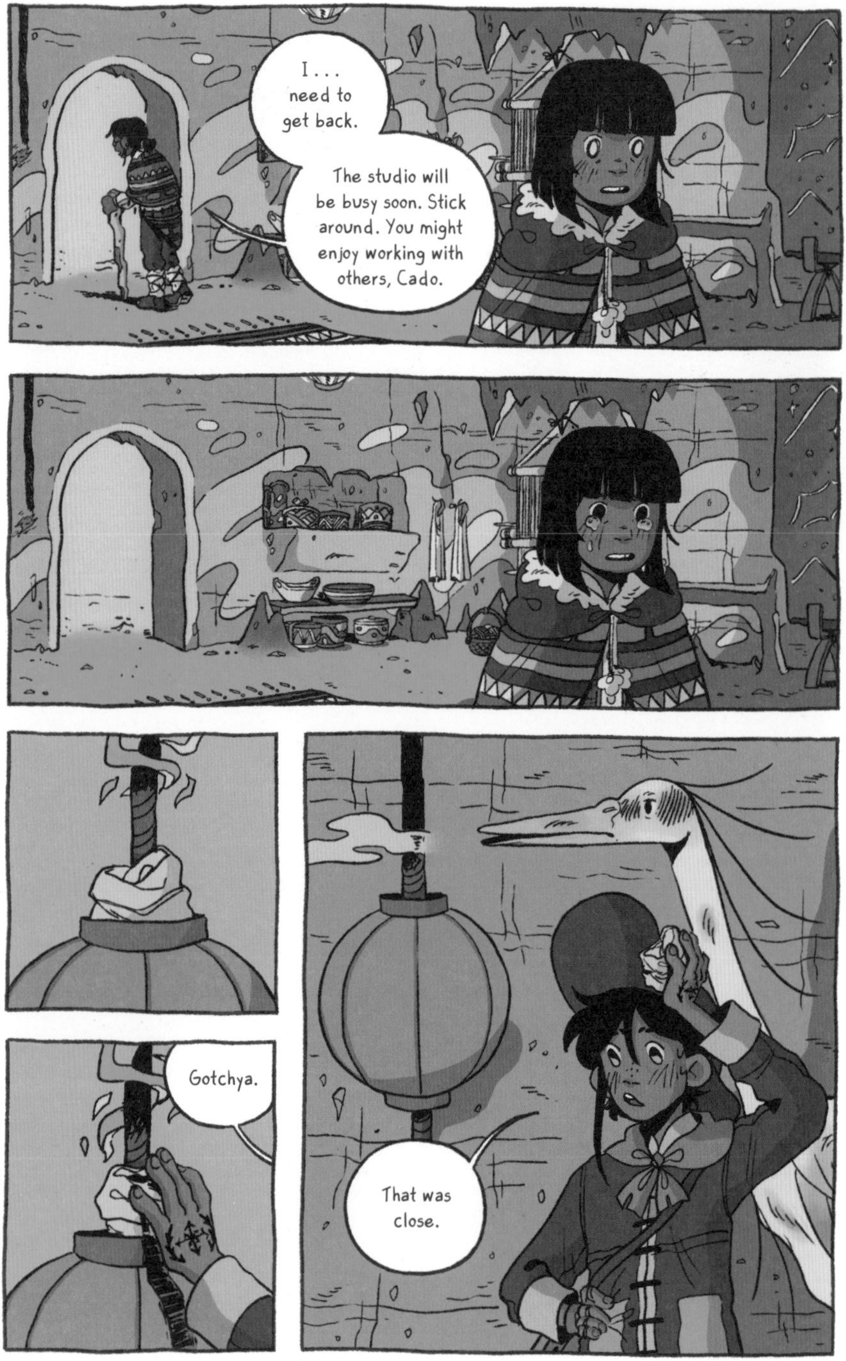
I . . . need to get back.
The studio will be busy soon. Stick around. You might enjoy working with others, Cado.
Gotchya.
That was close.

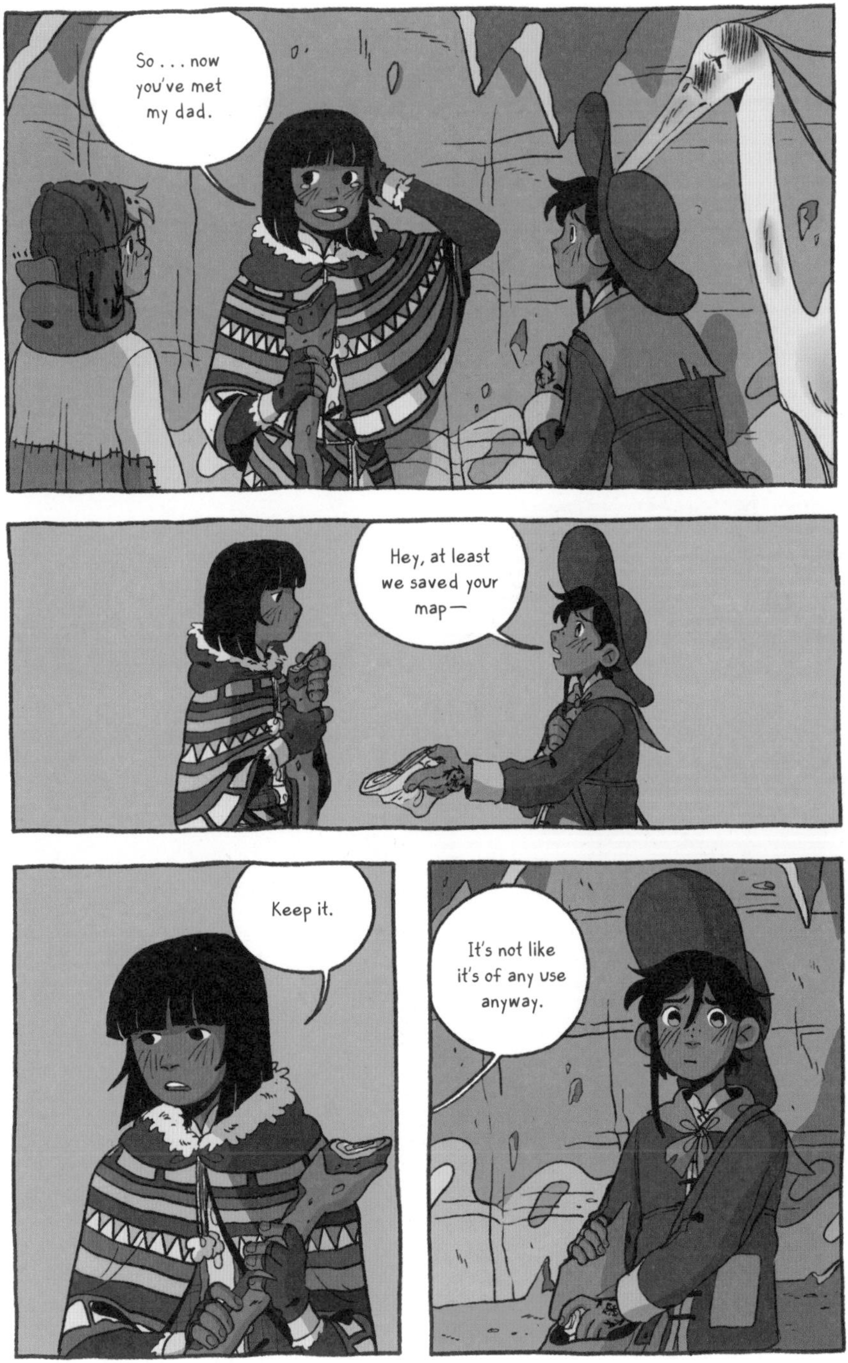
So . . . now you've met my dad.
Hey, at least we saved your map—
Keep it.
It's not like it's of any use anyway.

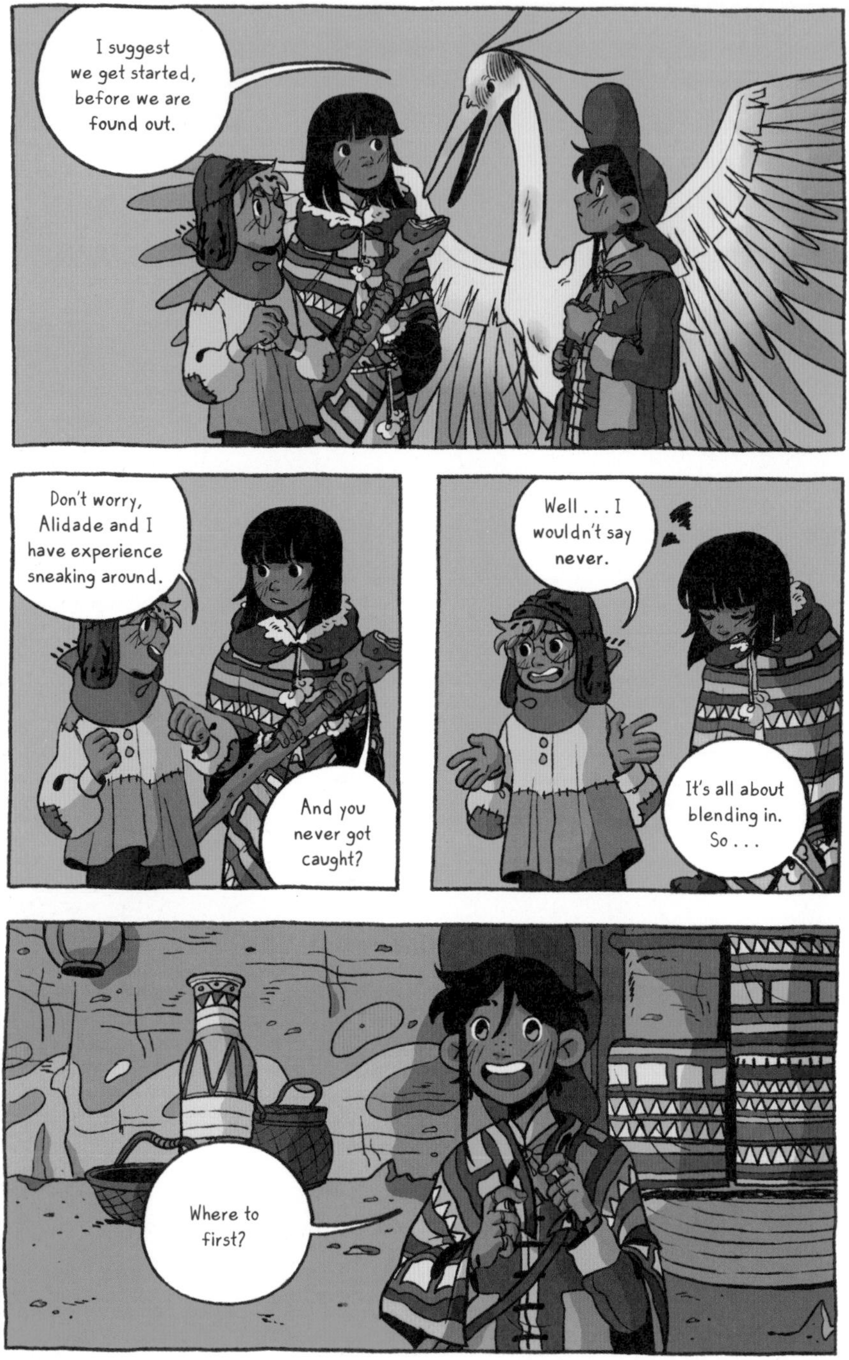
I suggest we get started, before we are found out.
Don't worry, Alidade and I have experience sneaking around.
And you never got caught?
Well . . . I wouldn't say never.
It's all about blending in. So . . .
Where to first?

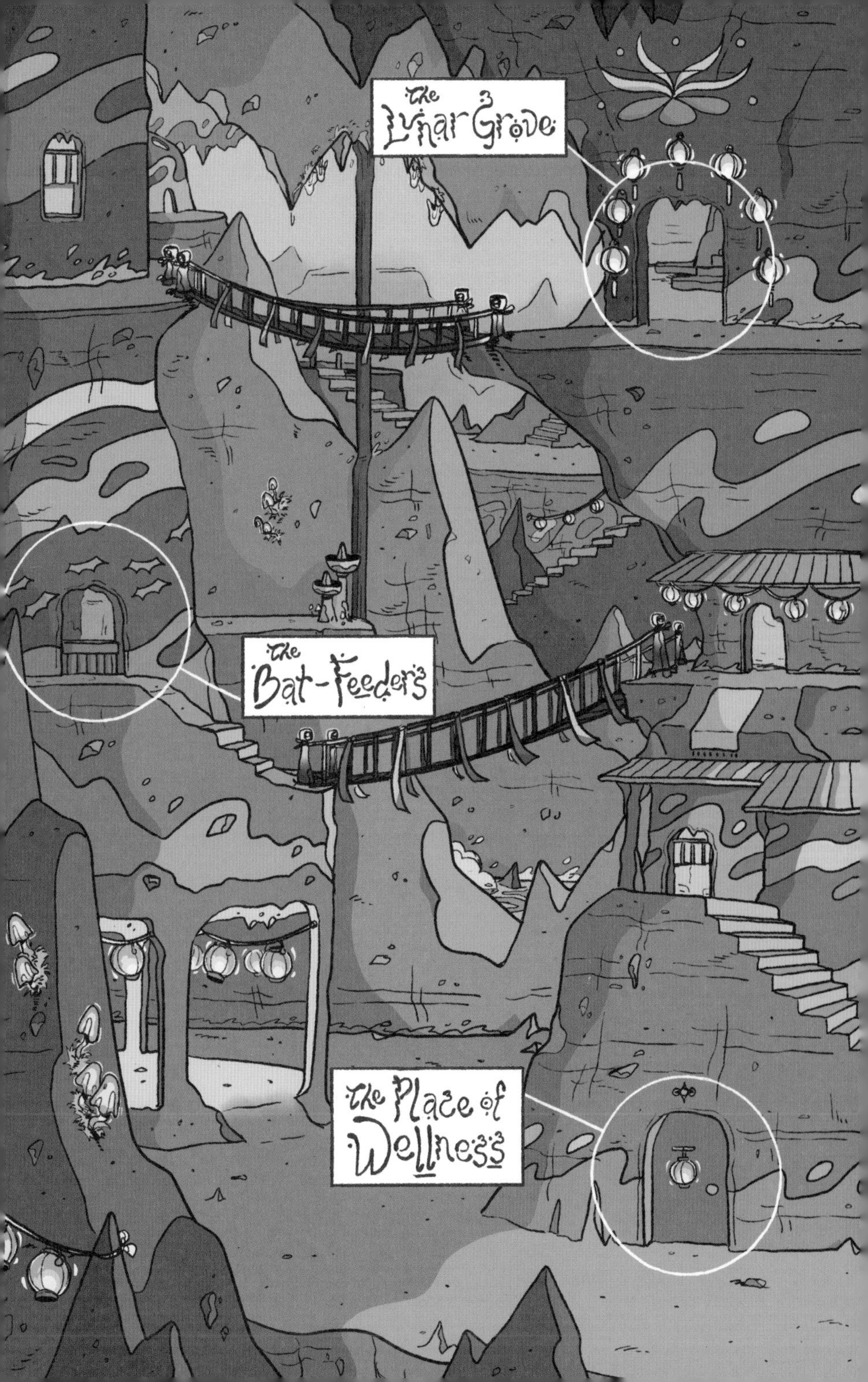
The Lunar Grove
The Bat-Feeders
The Place of Wellness

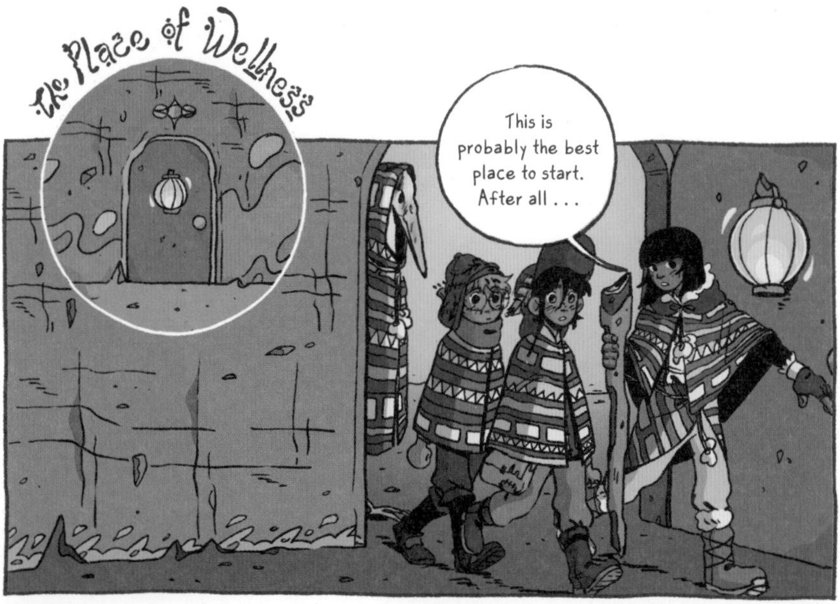
The Place of Wellness
This is probably the best place to start. After all . . .

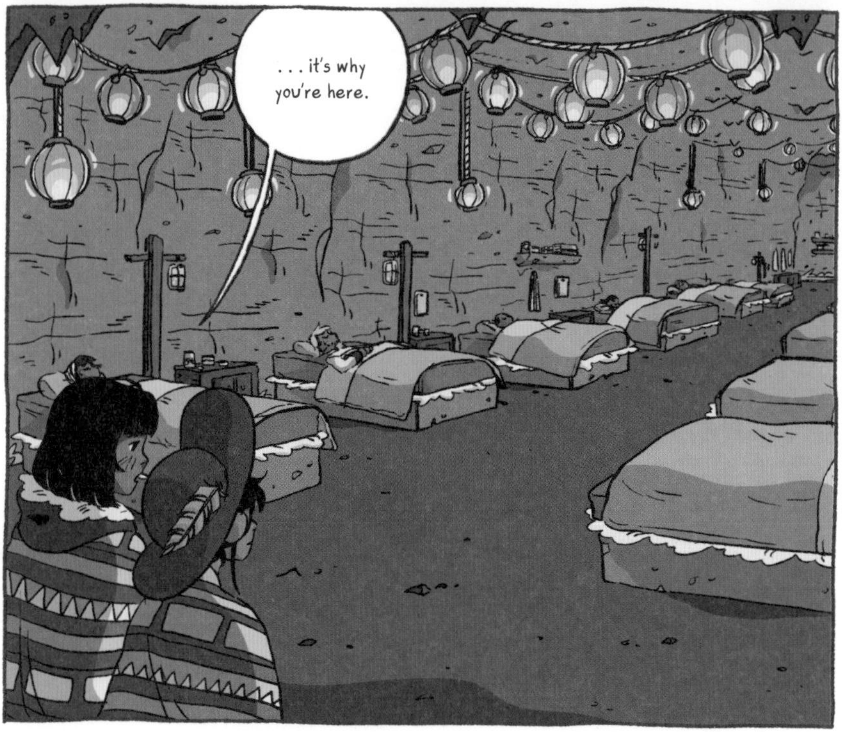
. . . it's why you're here.

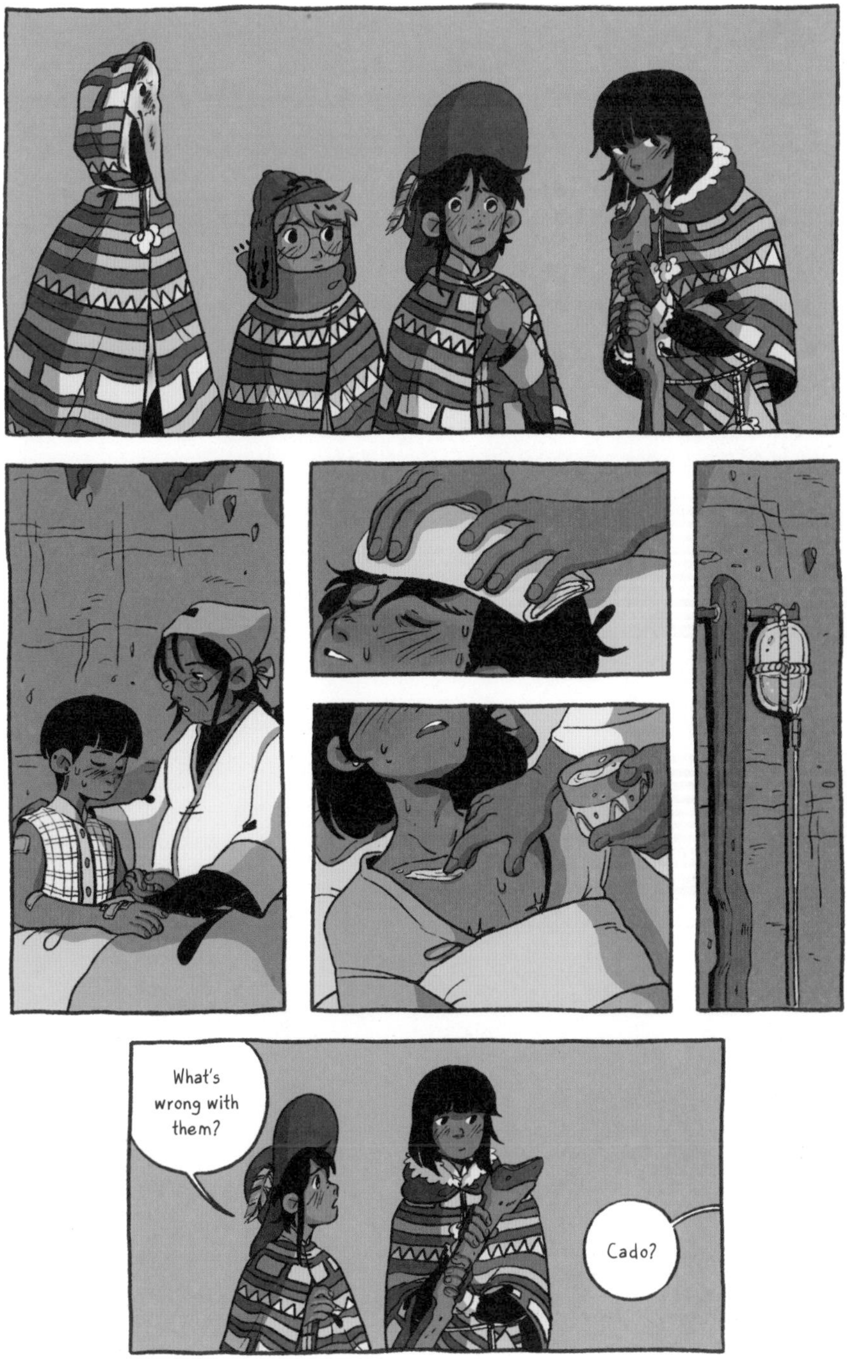
What's wrong with them?
Cado?

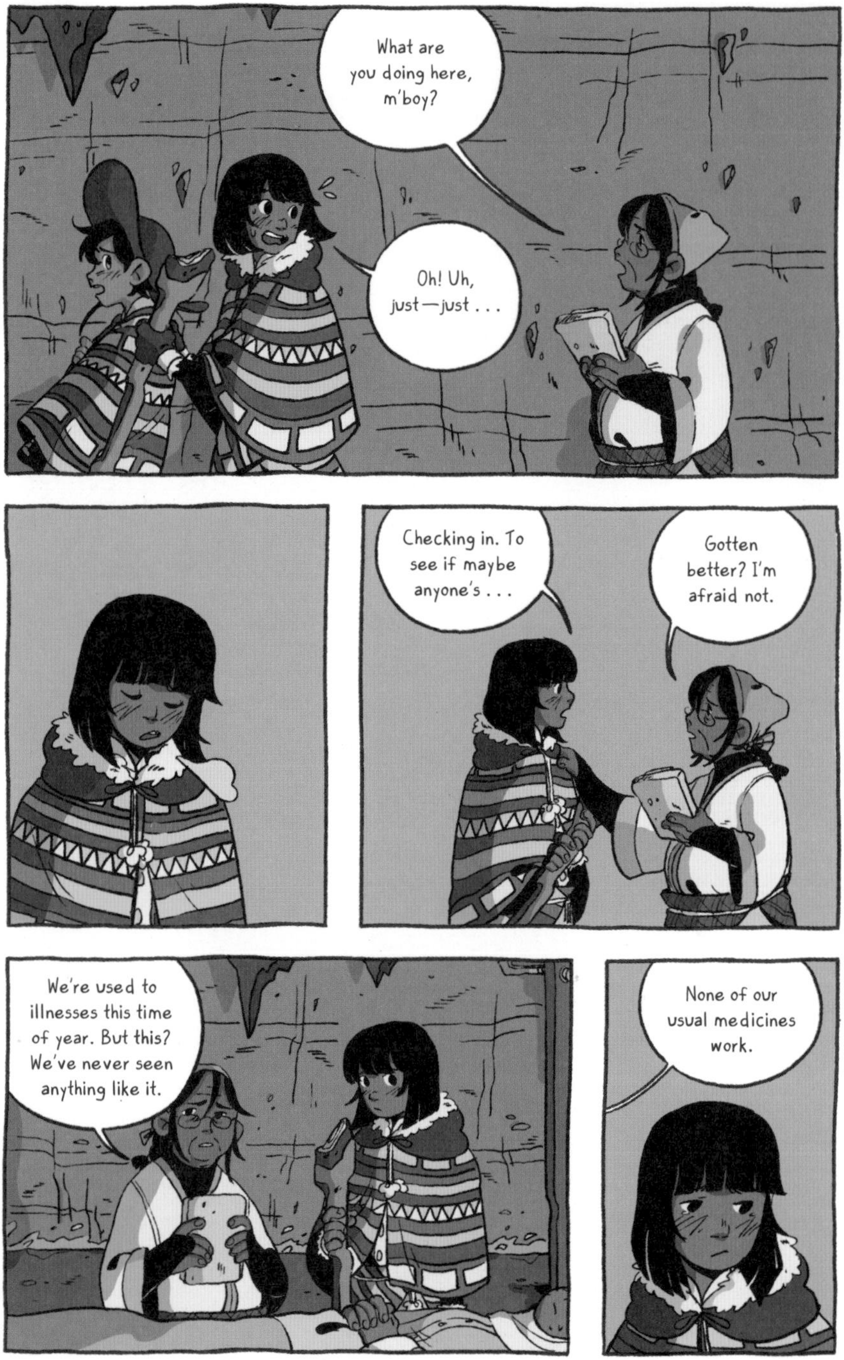
What are you doing here, m'boy?
Oh! Uh, just—just . . .
Checking in. To see if maybe anyone's . . .
Gotten better? I'm afraid not.
We're used to illnesses this time of year. But this? We've never seen anything like it.
None of our usual medicines work.

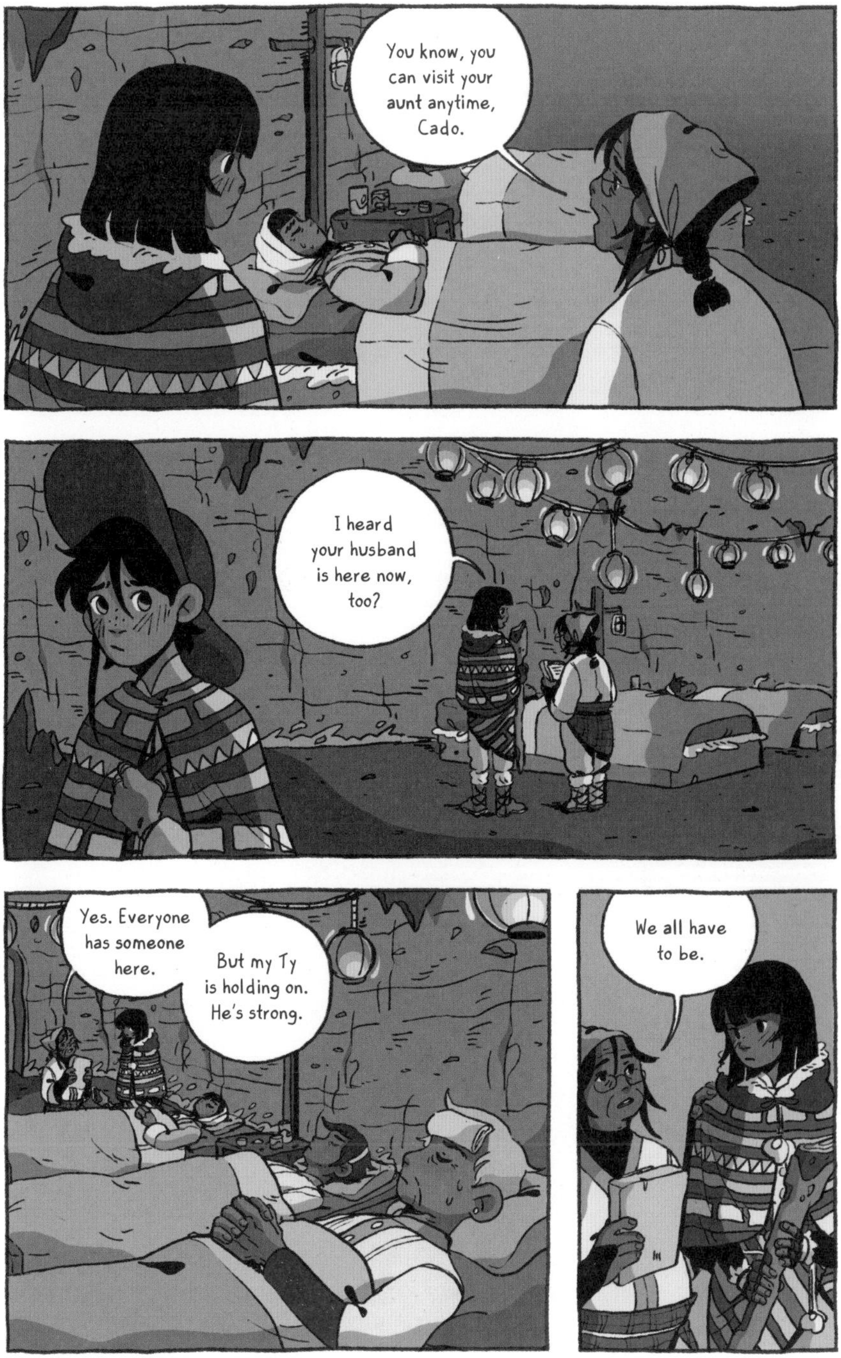
You know, you can visit your aunt anytime, Cado.
I heard your husband is here now, too?
Yes. Everyone has someone here.
But my Ty is holding on. He's strong.
We all have to be.

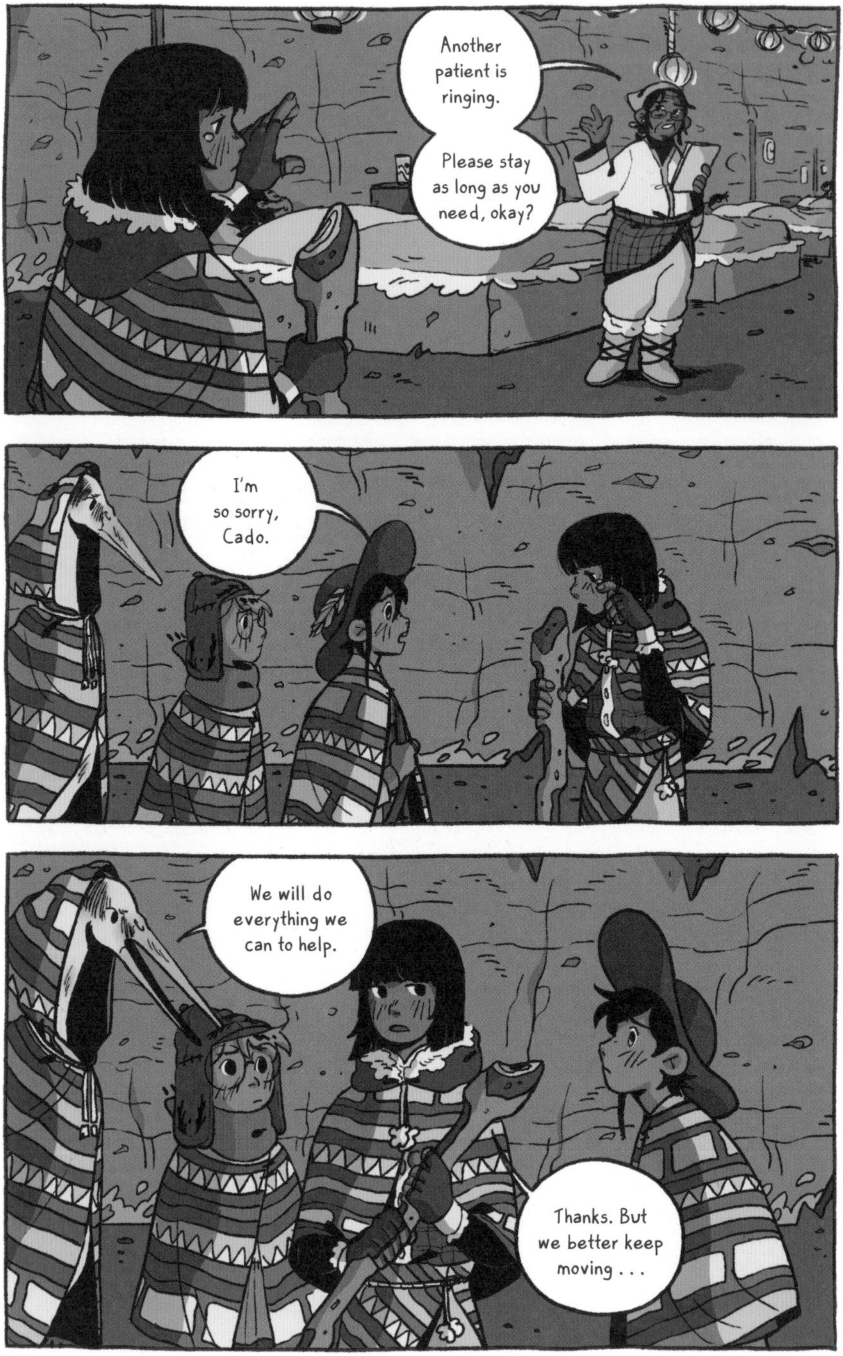
Another patient is ringing.
Please stay as long as you need, okay?
I'm so sorry, Cado.
We will do everything we can to help.
Thanks. But we better keep moving . . .

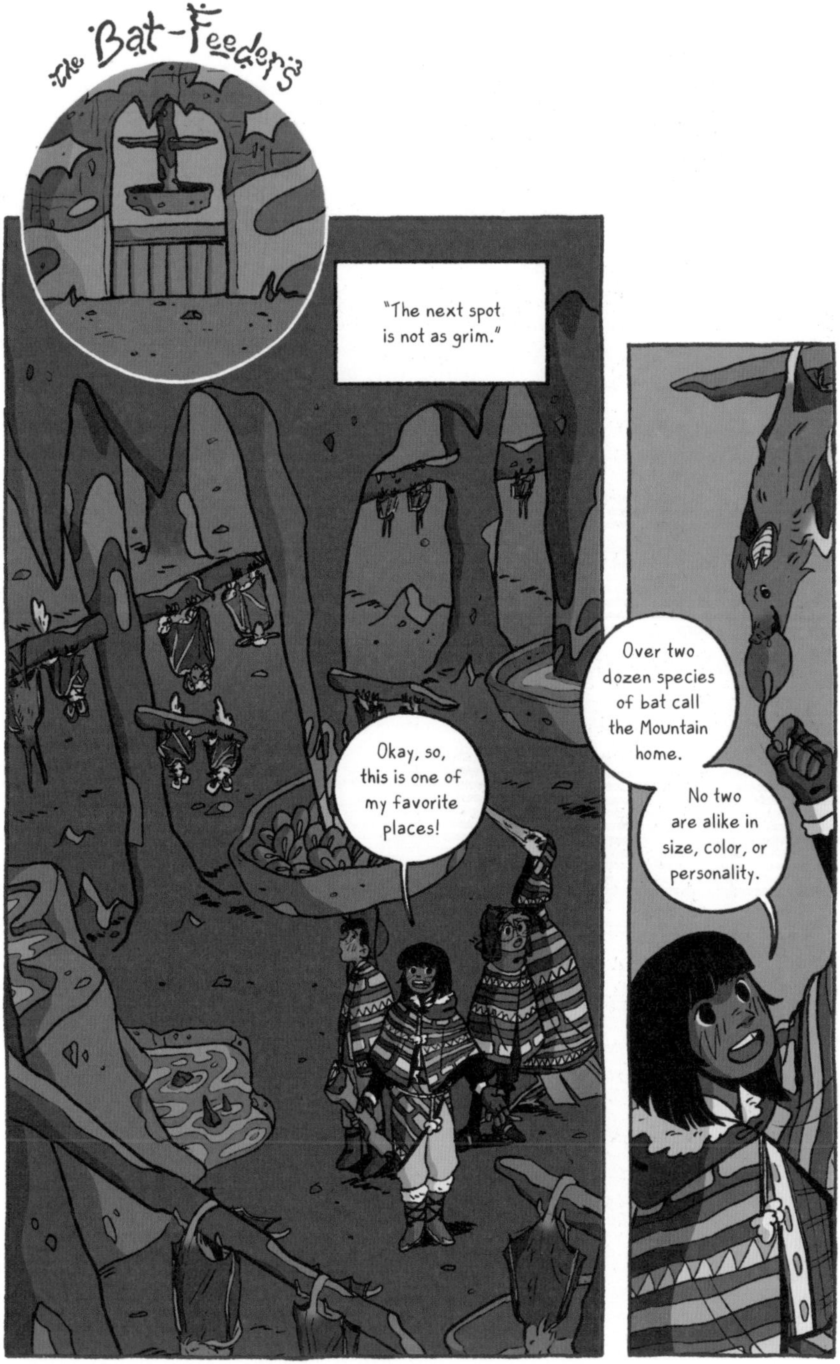
the Bat-Feeders
"The next spot is not as grim."
Okay, so, this is one of my favorite places!
Over two dozen species of bat call the Mountain home.
No two are alike in size, color, or personality.

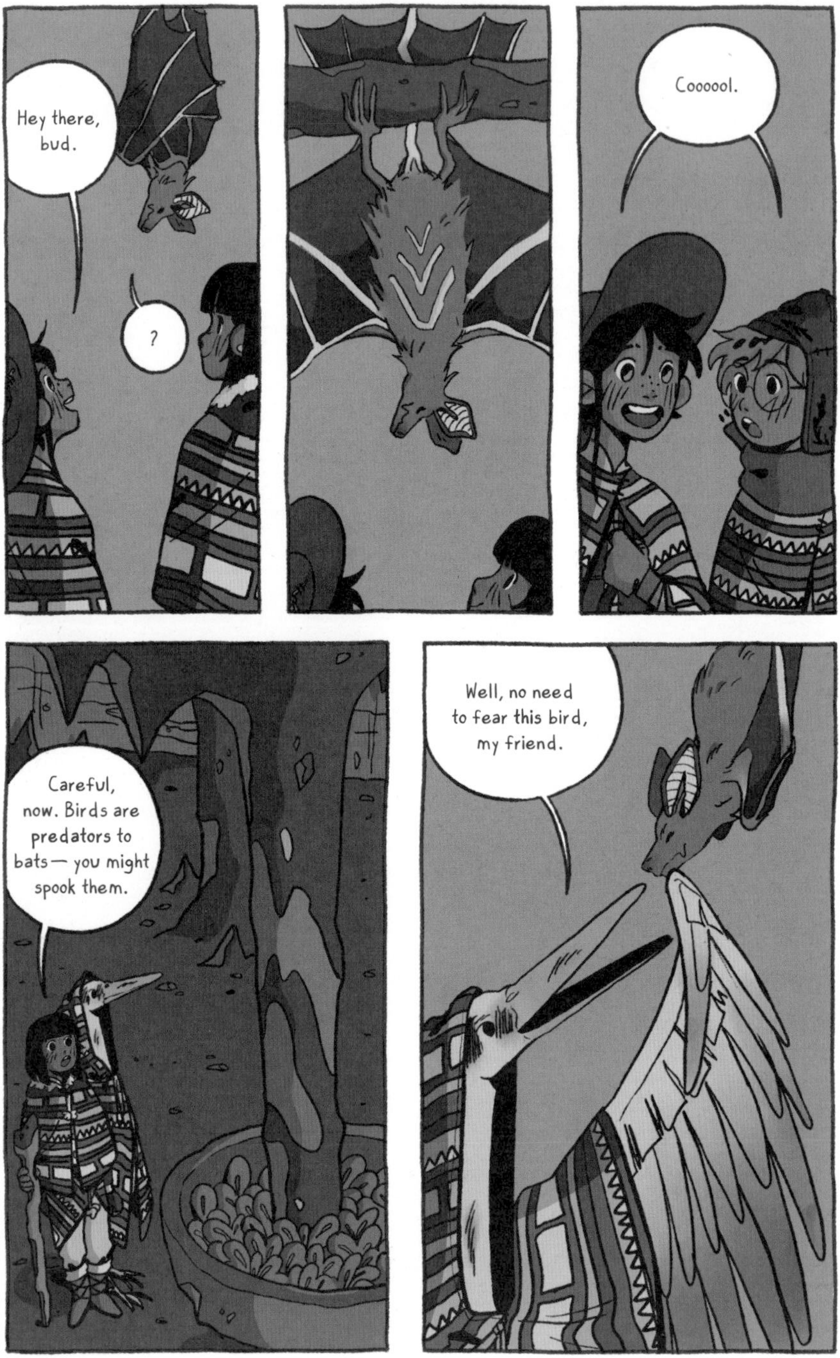

Hey there, bud.
?
Coooool.
Careful, now. Birds are predators to bats— you might spook them.
Well, no need to fear this bird, my friend.

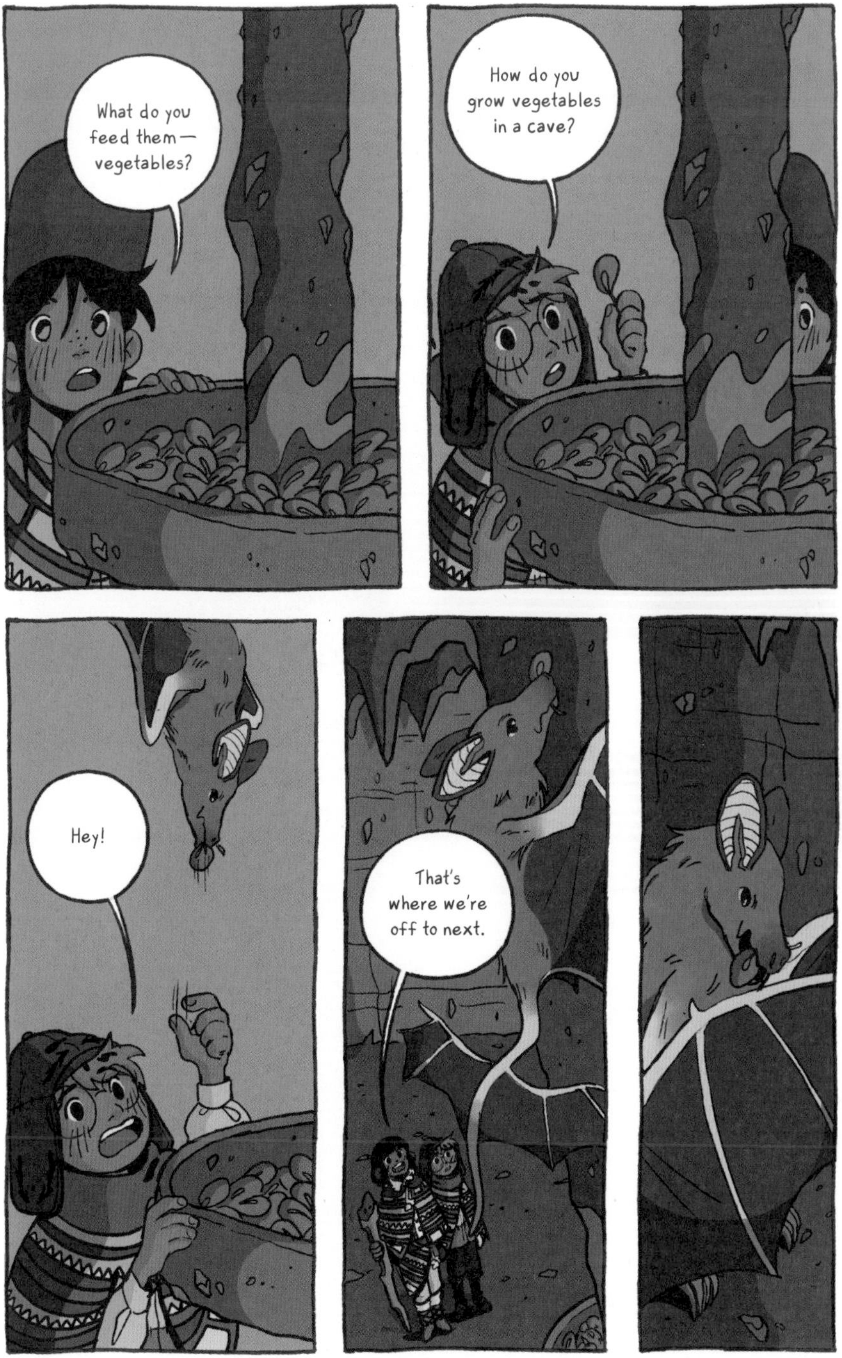
What do you feed them—vegetables?
How do you grow vegetables in a cave?
Hey!
That's where we're off to next.

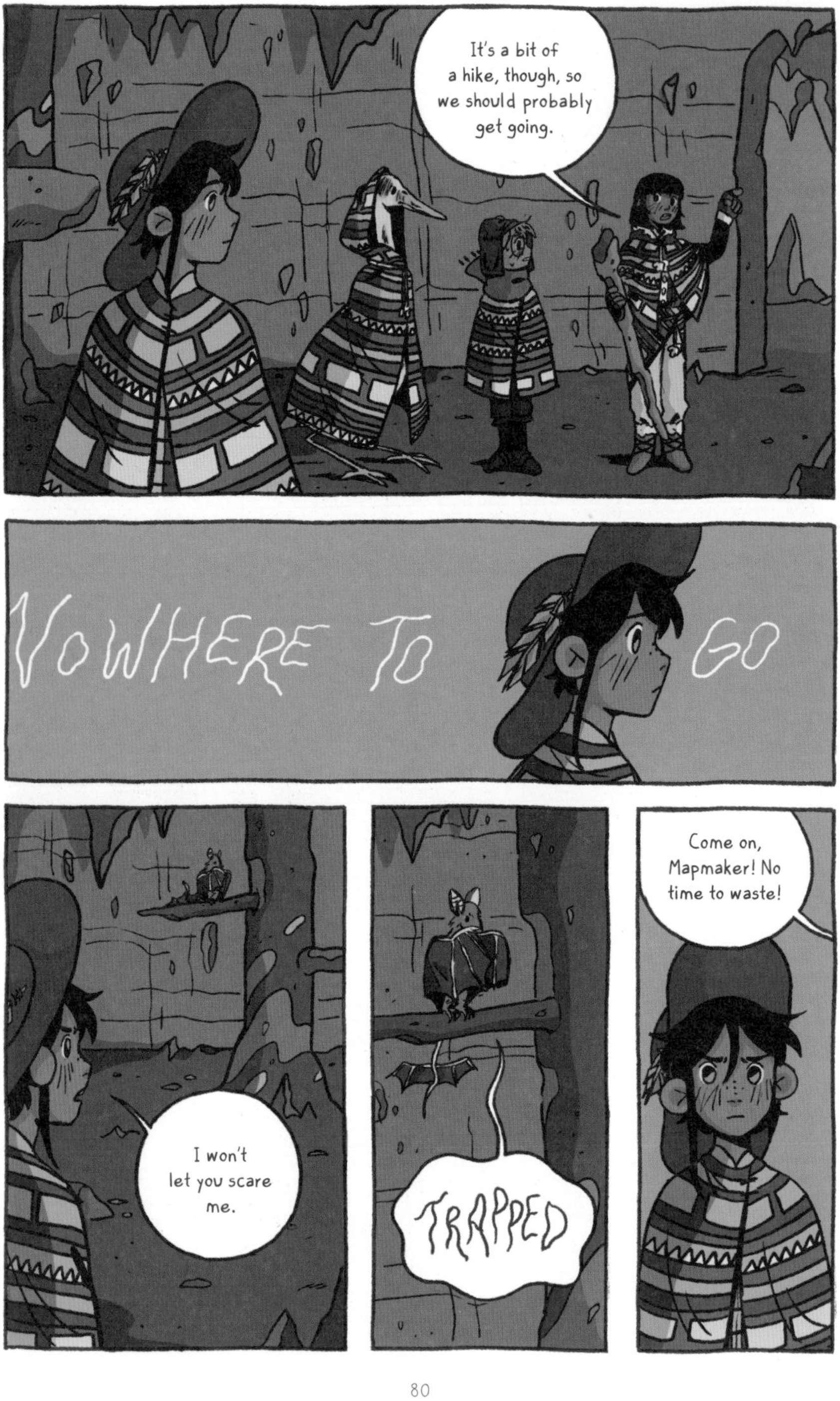
It's a bit of a hike, though, so we should probably get going.
NOWHERE TO GO
I won't let you scare me.
TRAPPED
Come on, Mapmaker! No time to waste!

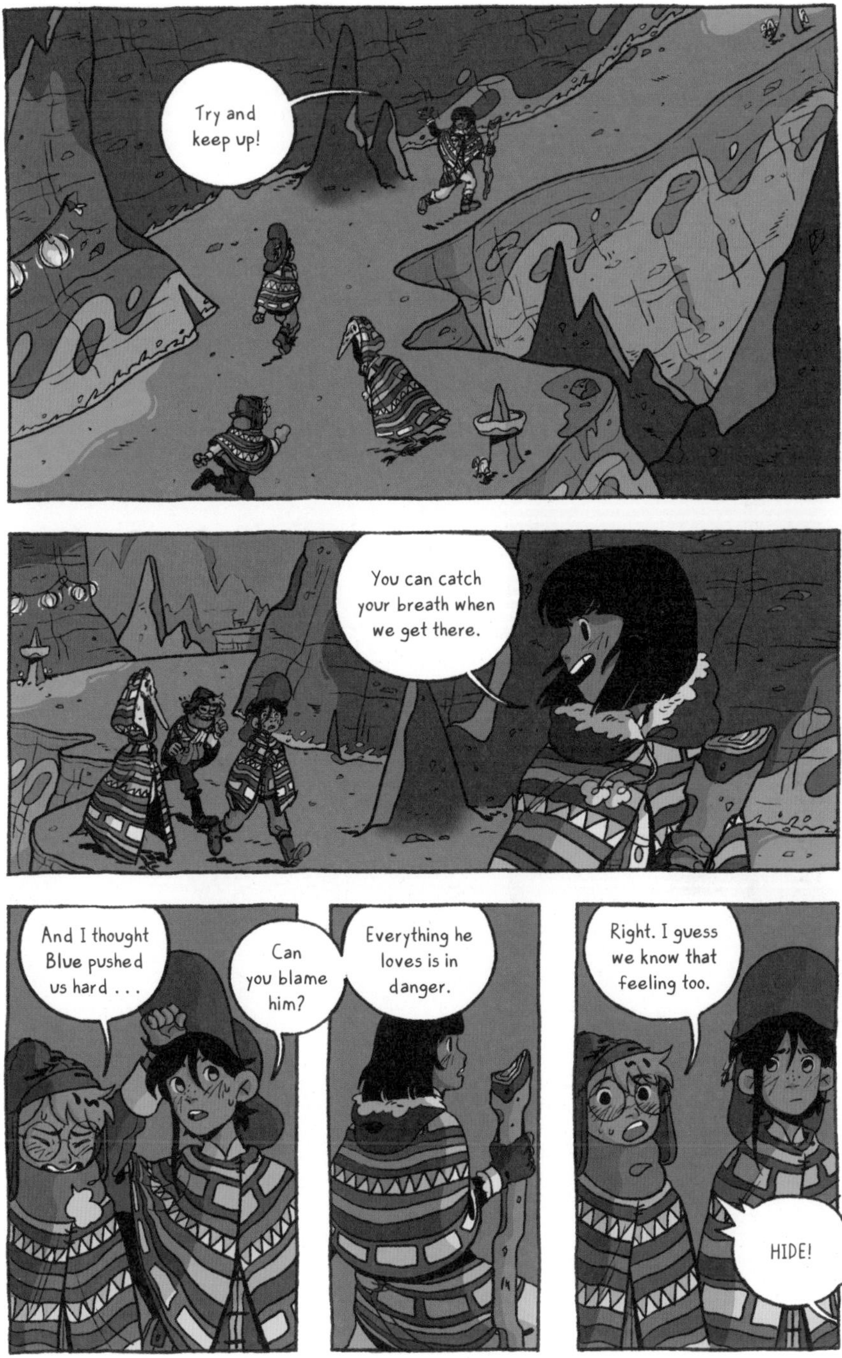
Try and keep up!
You can catch your breath when we get there.
And I thought Blue pushed us hard . . .
Can you blame him?
Everything he loves is in danger.
Right. I guess we know that feeling too.
HIDE!

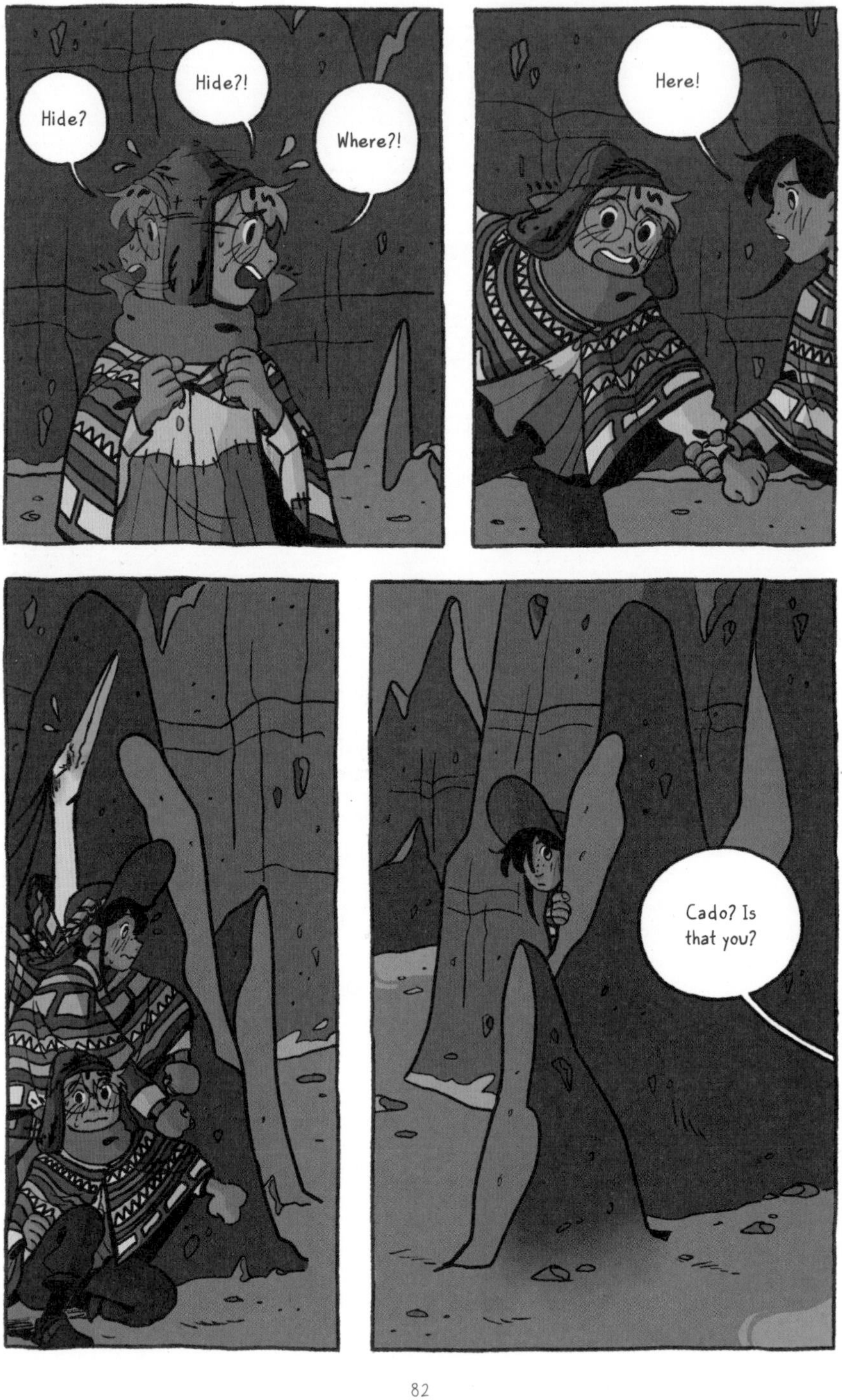
Hide?
Hide?!
Where?!
Here!
Cado? Is that you?

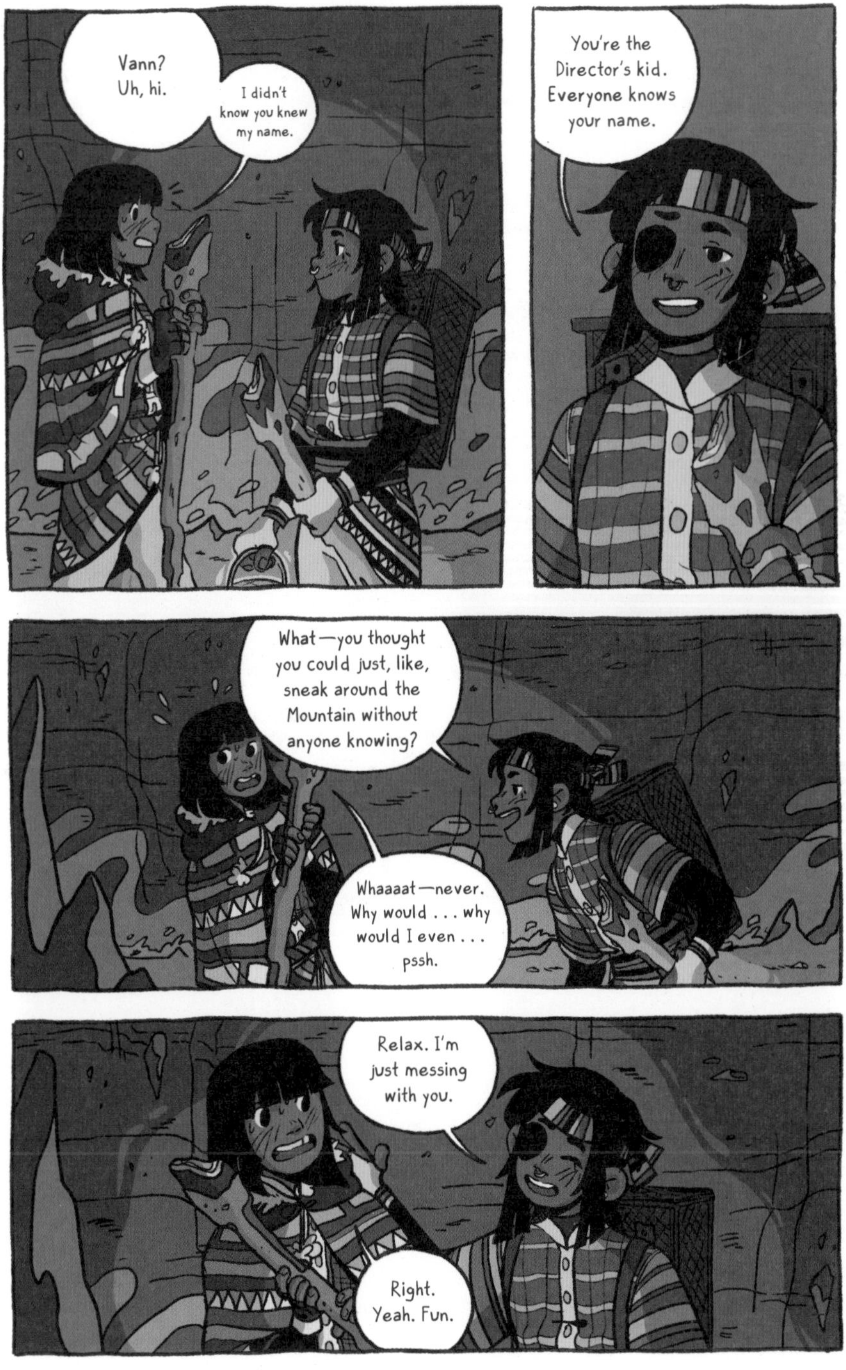
Vann?
Uh, hi.
I didn't know you knew my name.
You're the Director's kid. Everyone knows your name.
What—you thought you could just, like, sneak around the Mountain without anyone knowing?
Whaaaat—never. Why would . . . why would I even . . . pssh.
Relax. I'm just messing with you.
Right. Yeah. Fun.

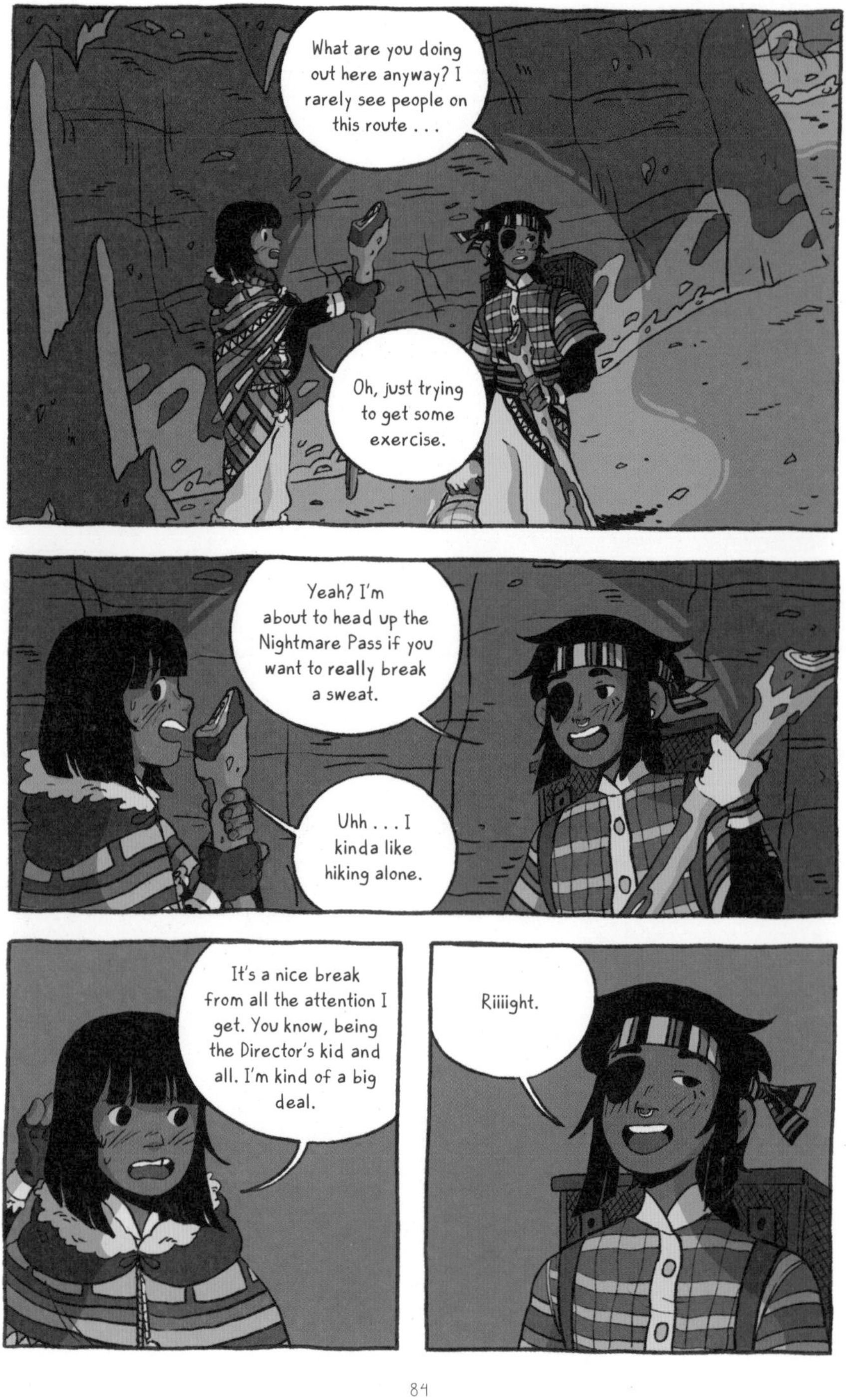
What are you doing out here anyway? I rarely see people on this route . . .
Oh, just trying to get some exercise.
Yeah? I'm about to head up the Nightmare Pass if you want to really break a sweat.
Uhh . . . I kinda like hiking alone.
It's a nice break from all the attention I get. You know, being the Director's kid and all. I'm kind of a big deal.
Riiiight.

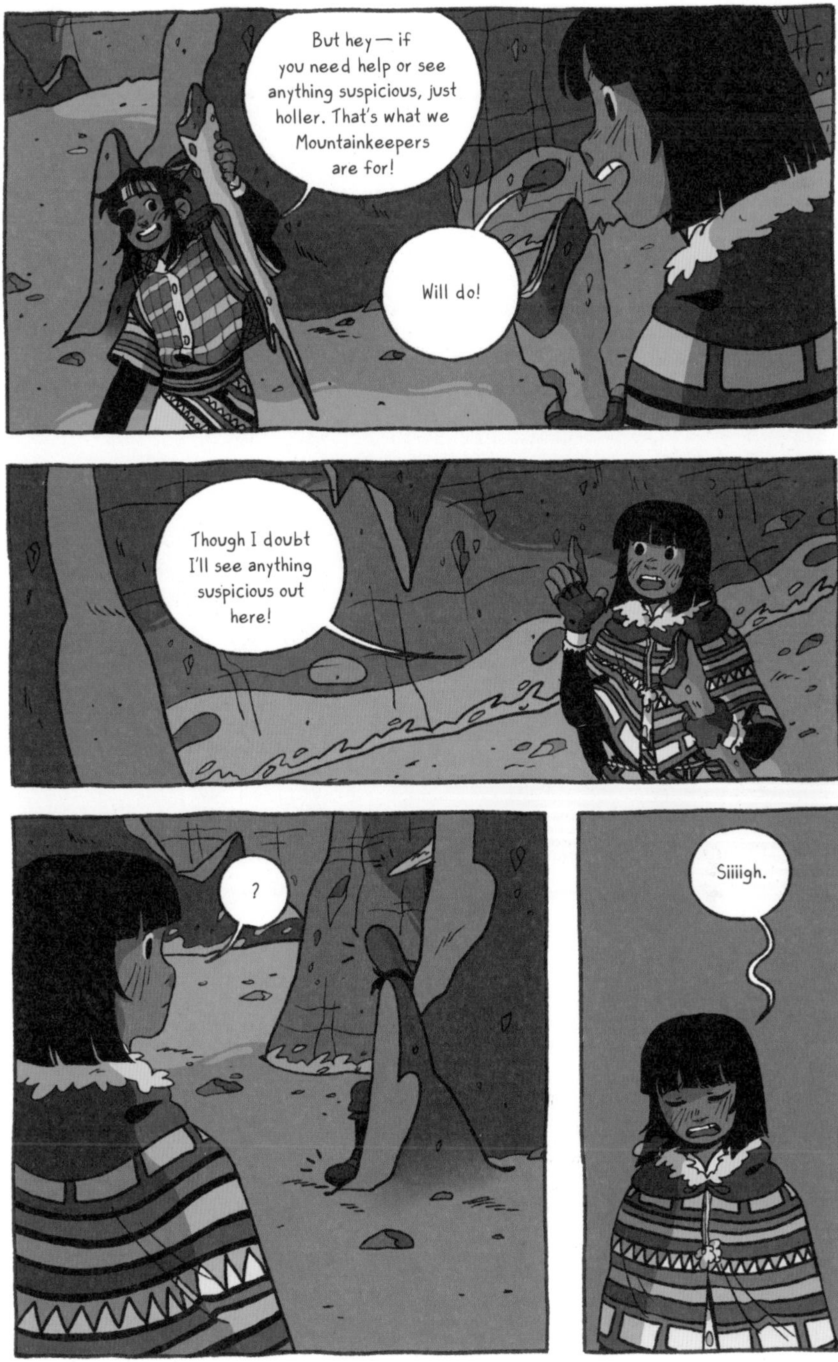
But hey — if you need help or see anything suspicious, just holler. That's what we Mountainkeepers are for!
Will do!
Though I doubt I'll see anything suspicious out here!
?
Siiiigh.

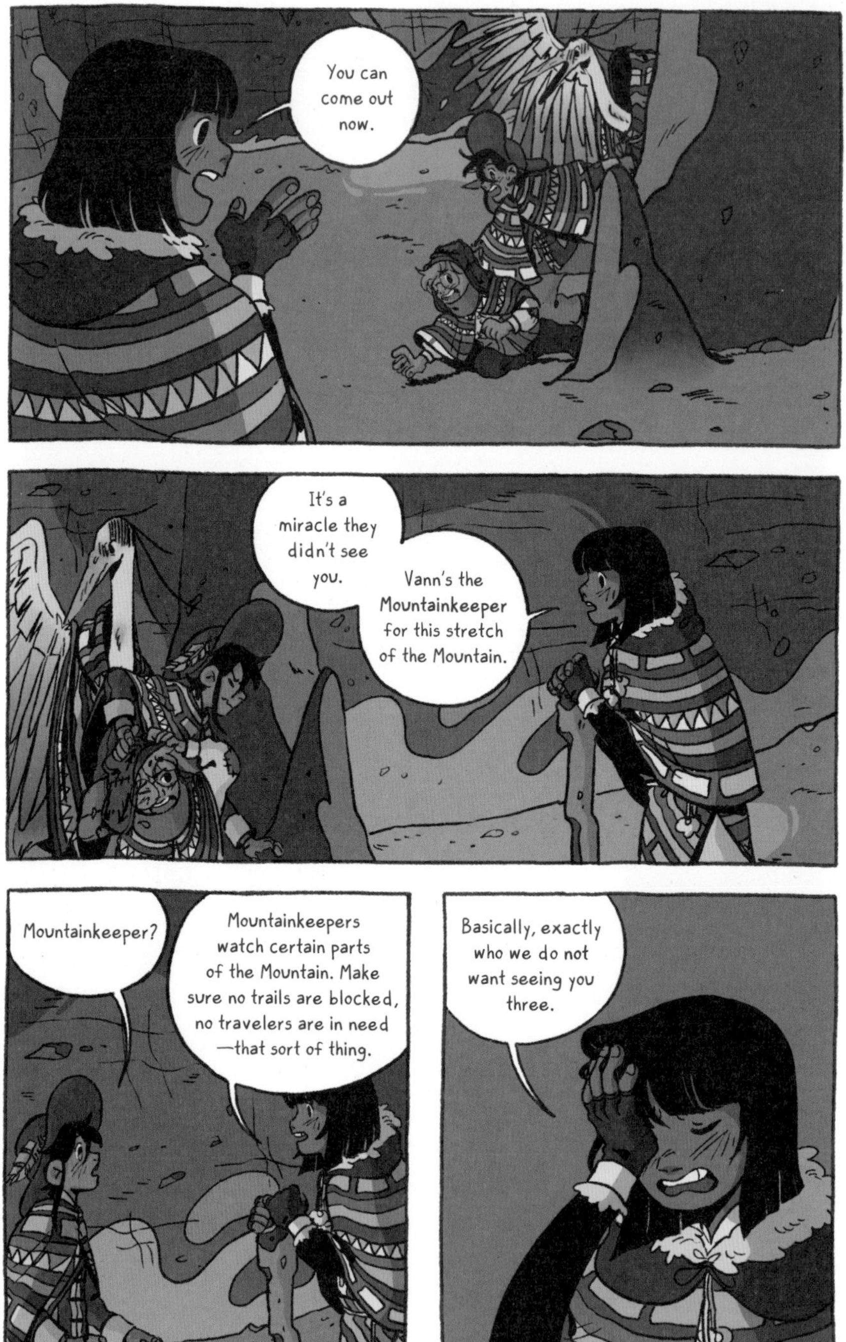
You can come out now.
It's a miracle they didn't see you.
Vann's the Mountainkeeper for this stretch of the Mountain.
Mountainkeeper?
Mountainkeepers watch certain parts of the Mountain. Make sure no trails are blocked, no travelers are in need —that sort of thing.
Basically, exactly who we do not want seeing you three.

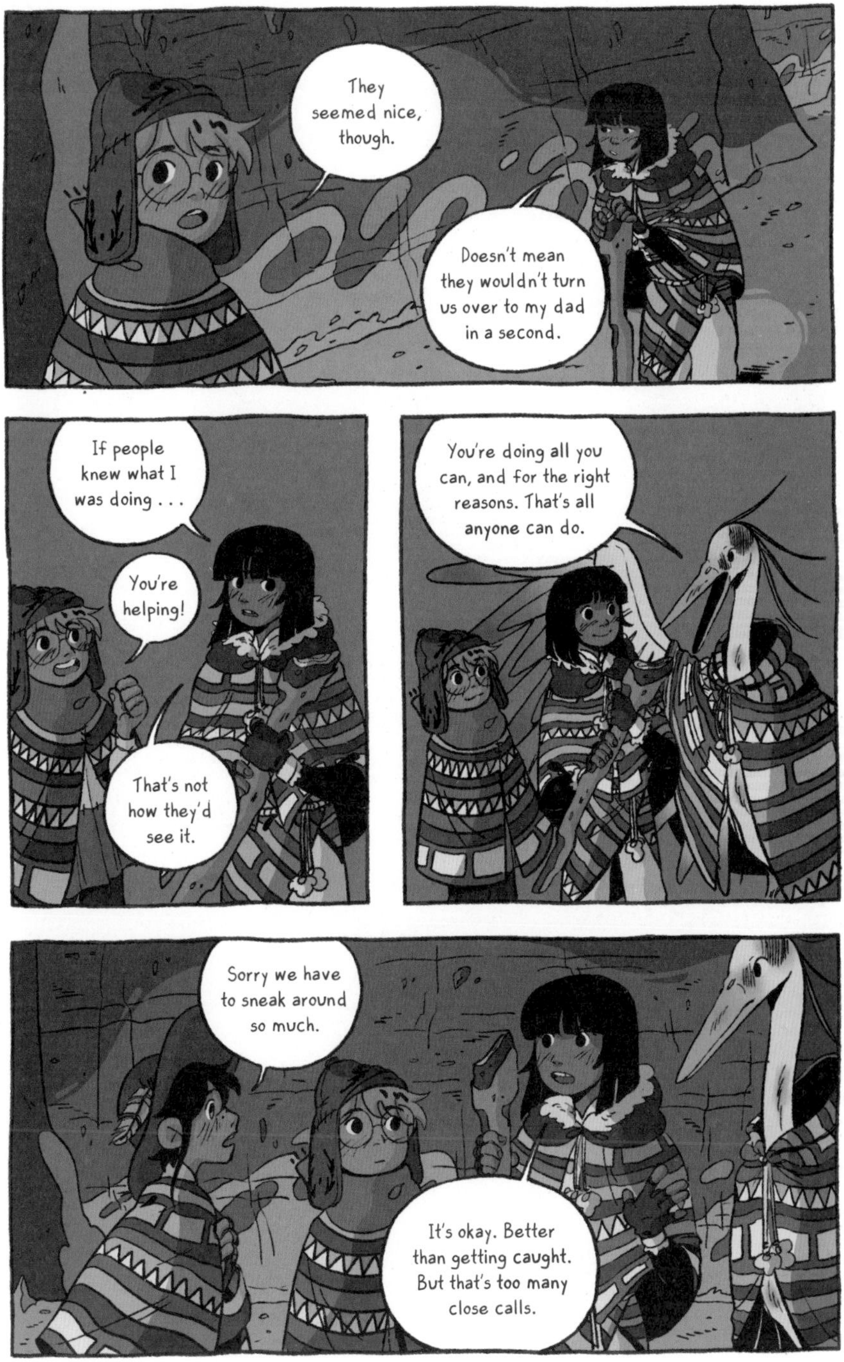
They seemed nice, though.
Doesn't mean they wouldn't turn us over to my dad in a second.
If people knew what I was doing . . .
You're helping!
That's not how they'd see it.
You're doing all you can, and for the right reasons. That's all anyone can do.
Sorry we have to sneak around so much.
It's okay. Better than getting caught. But that's too many close calls.

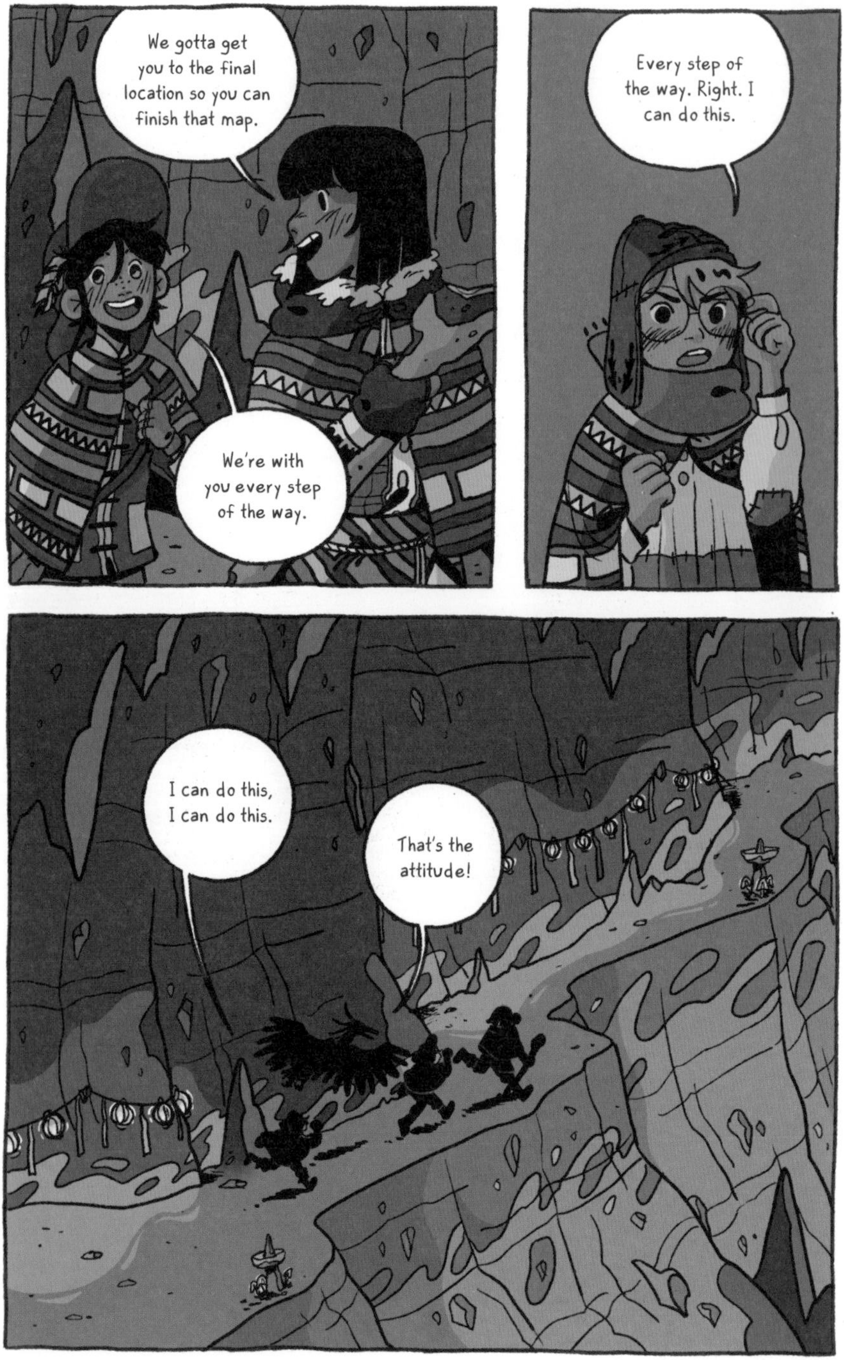
We gotta get you to the final location so you can finish that map.
We're with you every step of the way.
Every step of the way. Right. I can do this.
I can do this, I can do this.
That's the attitude!

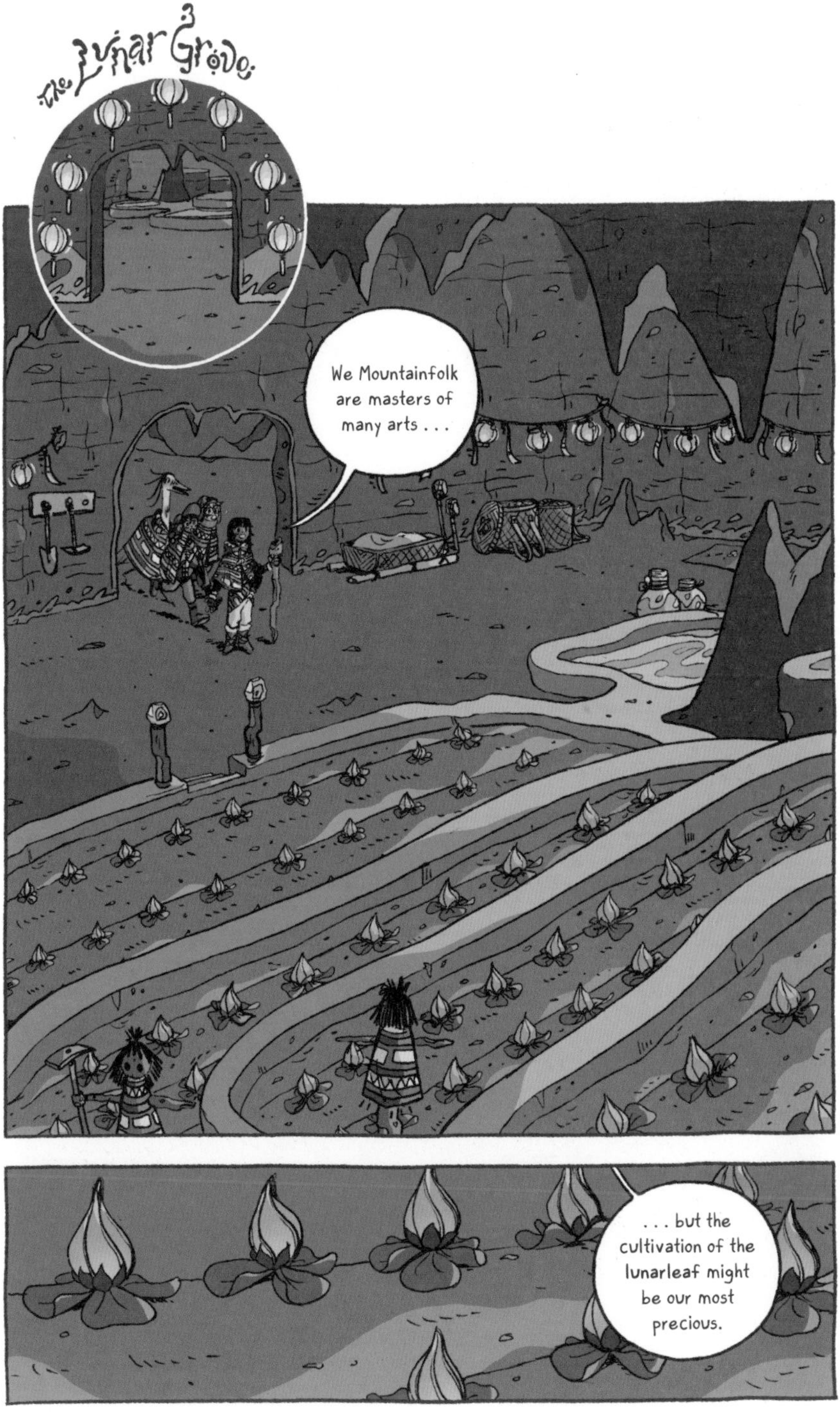
The Lunar Grove
We Mountainfolk are masters of many arts . . .
. . . but the cultivation of the lunarleaf might be our most precious.

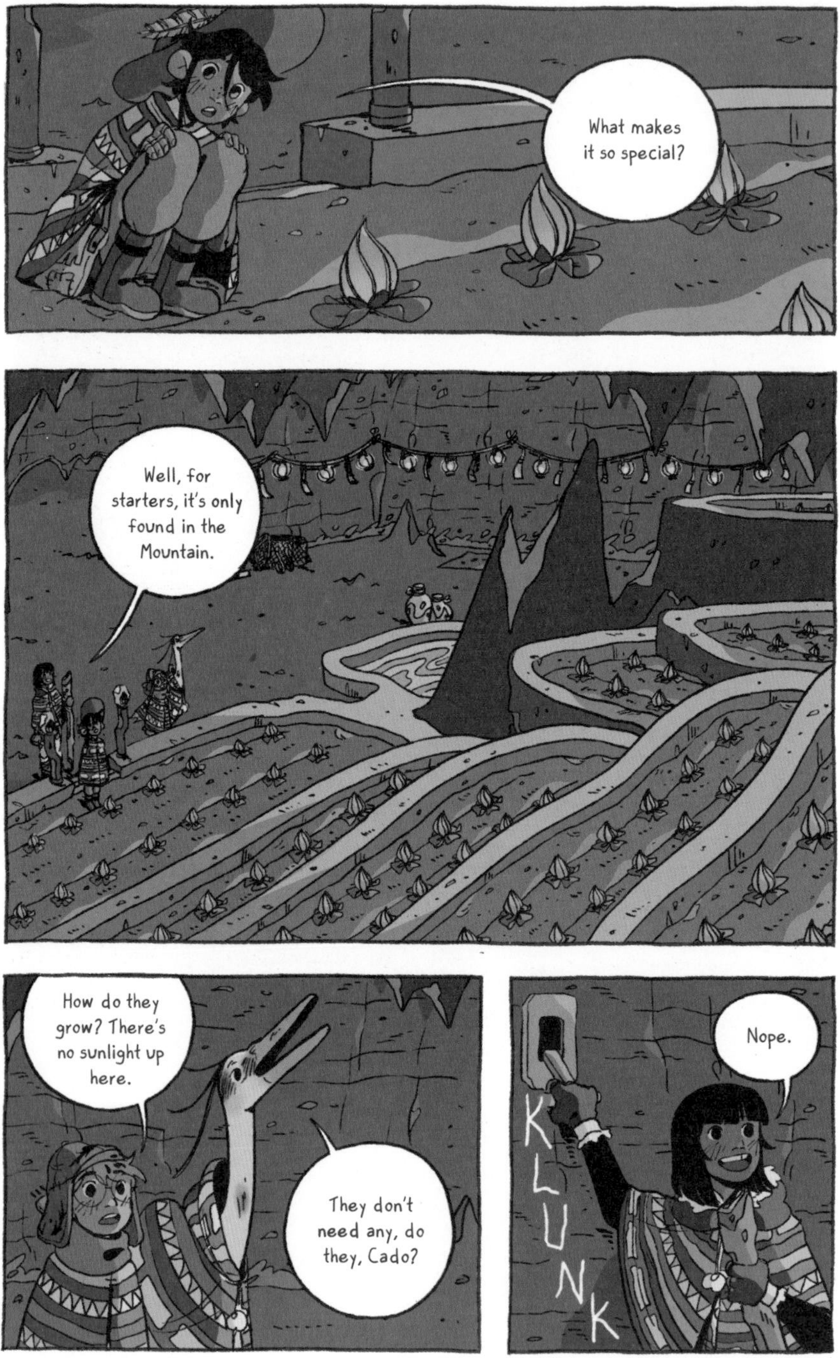

What makes it so special?
Well, for starters, it's only found in the Mountain.
How do they grow? There's no sunlight up here.
They don't need any, do they, Cado?
KLUNK
Nope.

CREAK

CREAK

CREAK

It won't be long until the sun goes down, and that's when we really open the windows.

Ahh . . .

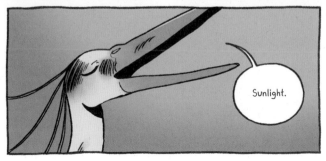

Sunlight.

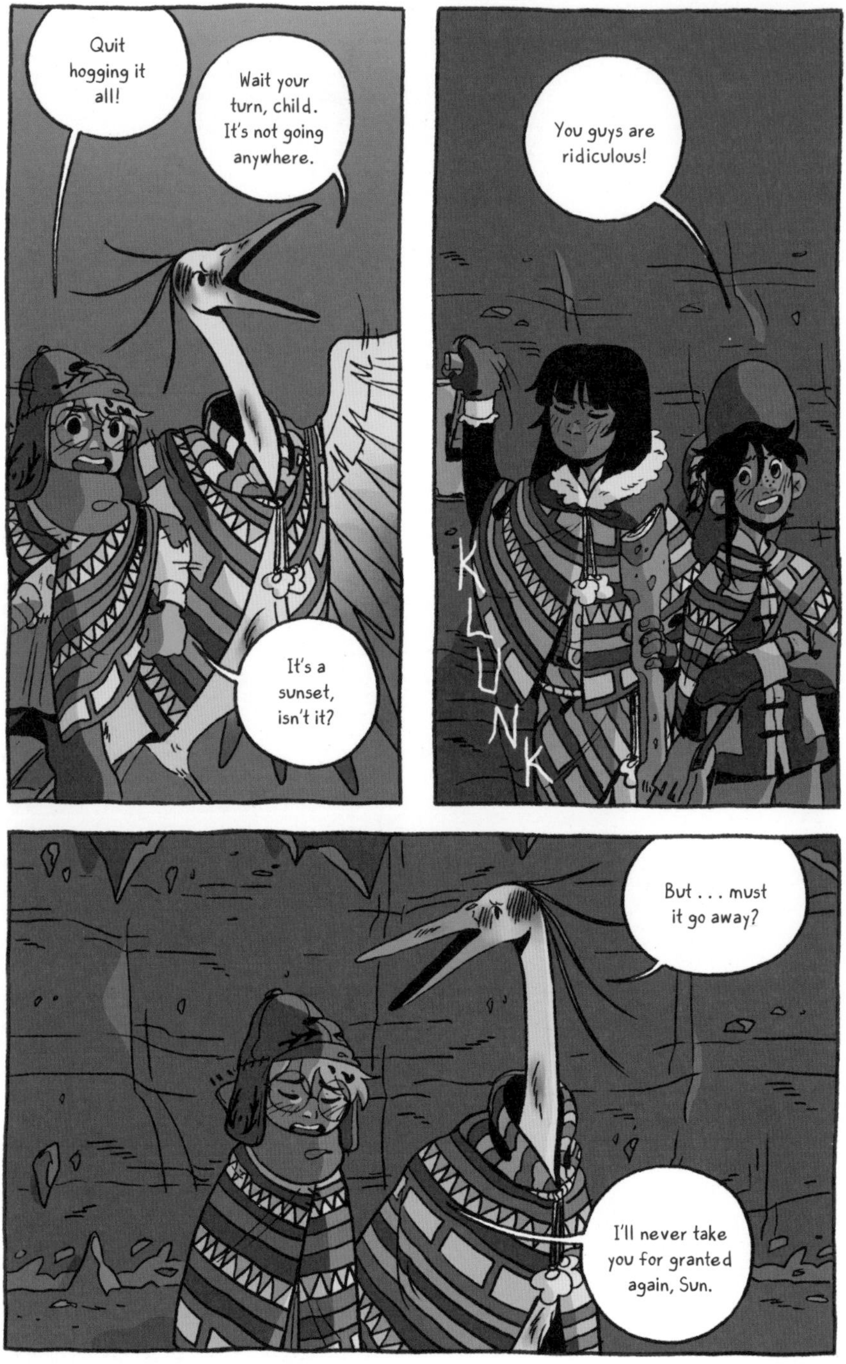
Quit hogging it all!
Wait your turn, child. It's not going anywhere.
It's a sunset, isn't it?
You guys are ridiculous!
KLUNK
But . . . must it go away?
I'll never take you for granted again, Sun.

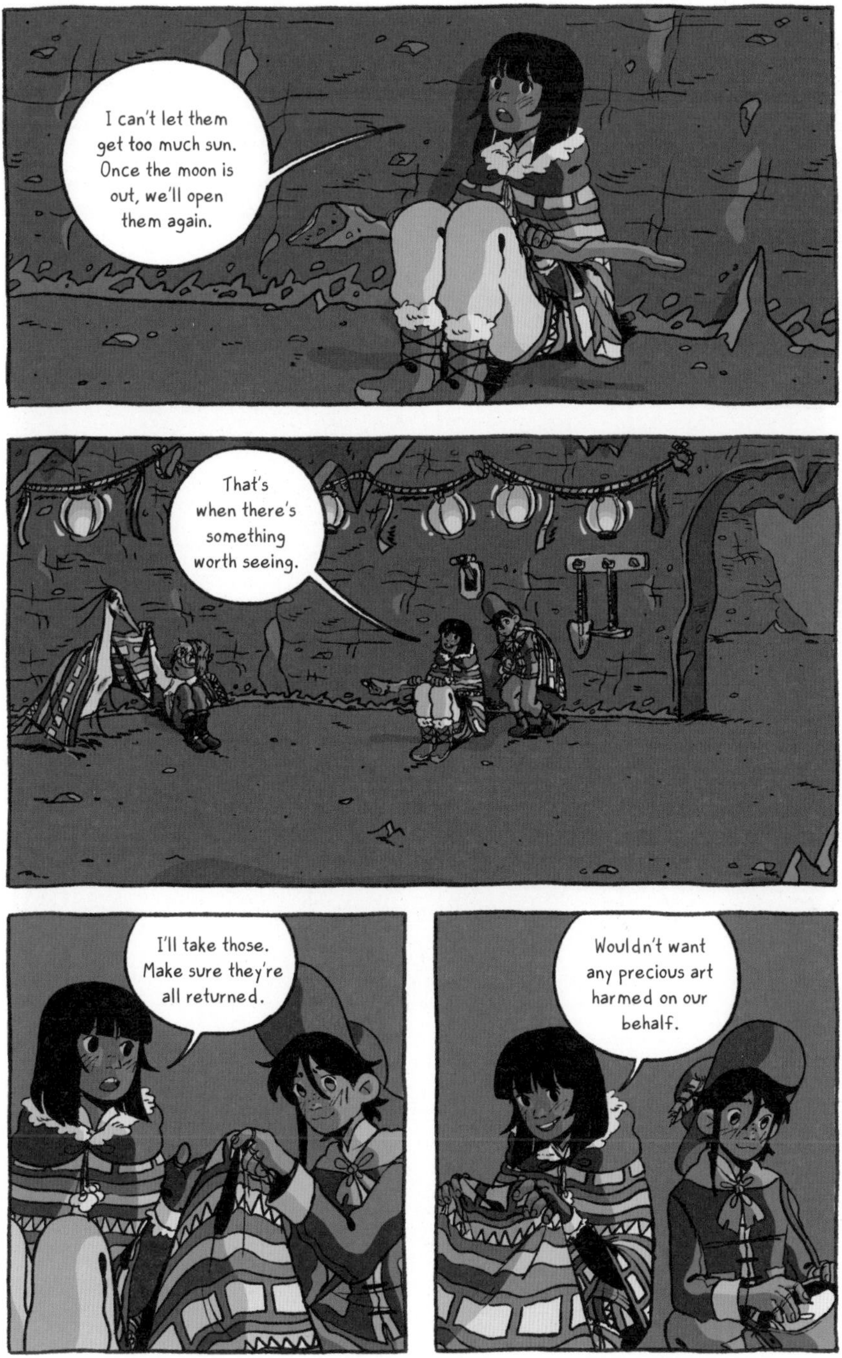
I can't let them get too much sun. Once the moon is out, we'll open them again.
That's when there's something worth seeing.
I'll take those. Make sure they're all returned.
Wouldn't want any precious art harmed on our behalf.

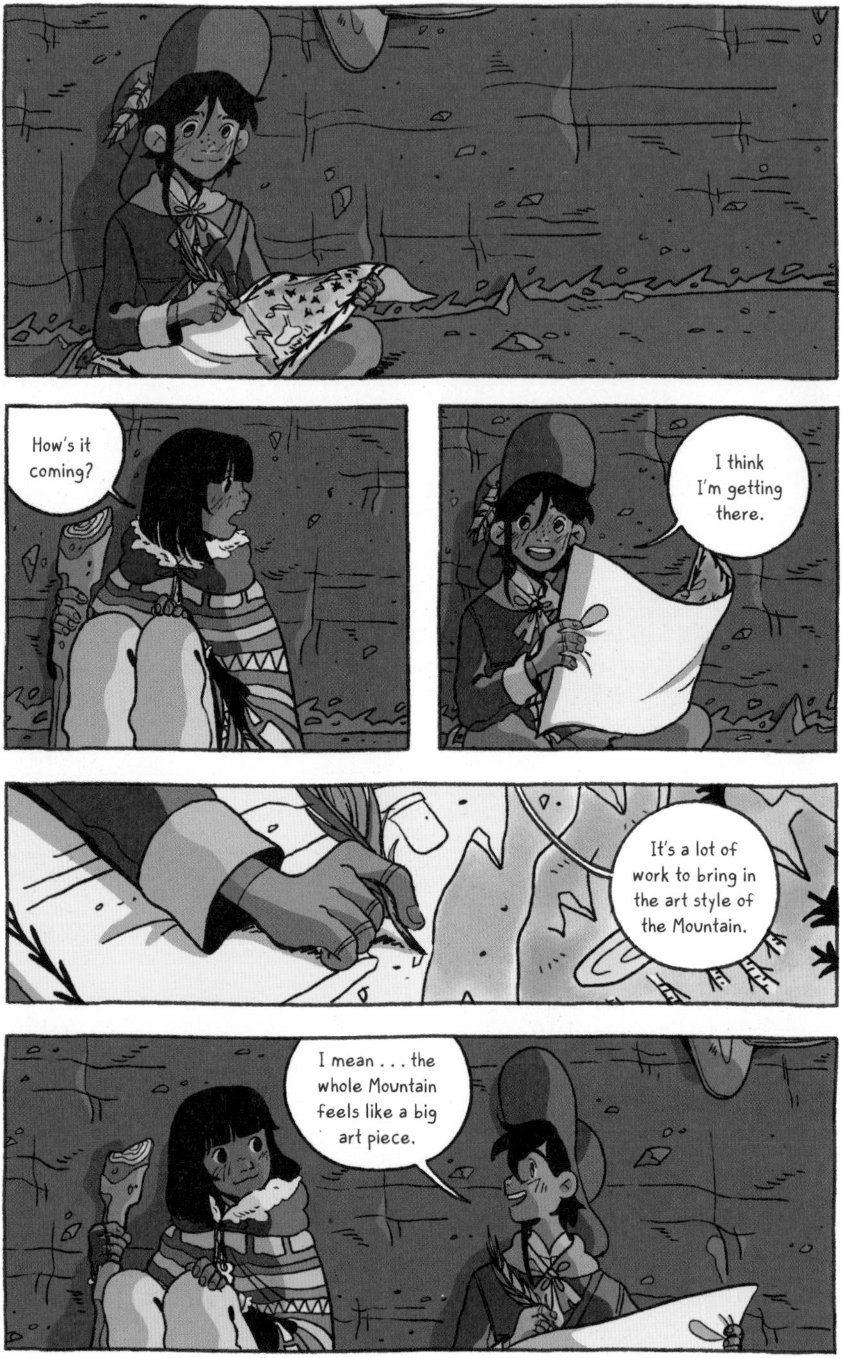
How's it coming?
I think I'm getting there.
It's a lot of work to bring in the art style of the Mountain.
I mean . . . the whole Mountain feels like a big art piece.

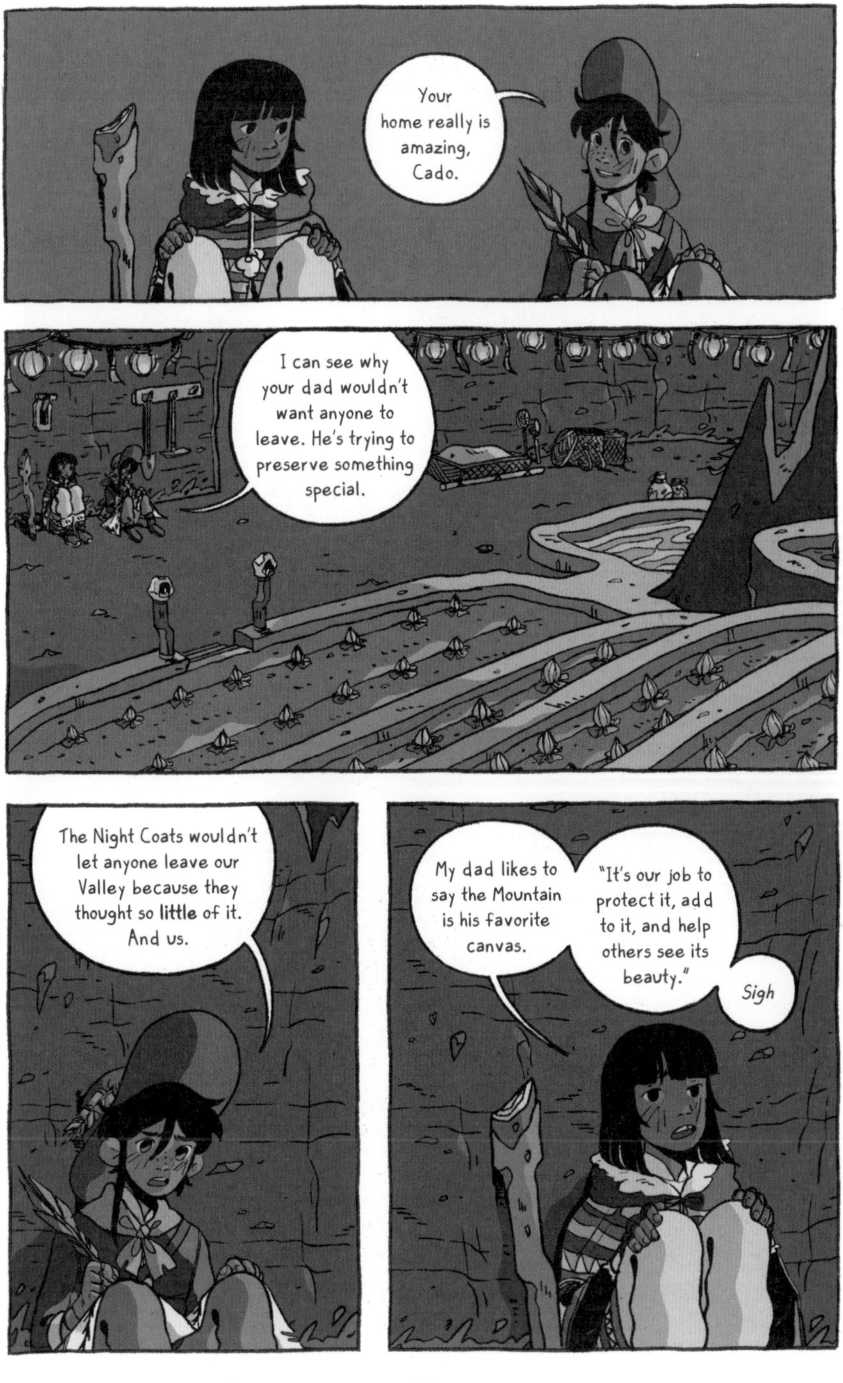
Your home really is amazing, Cado.
I can see why your dad wouldn't want anyone to leave. He's trying to preserve something special.
The Night Coats wouldn't let anyone leave our Valley because they thought so **little** of it. And us.
My dad likes to say the Mountain is his favorite canvas.
"It's our job to protect it, add to it, and help others see its beauty."
*Sigh*

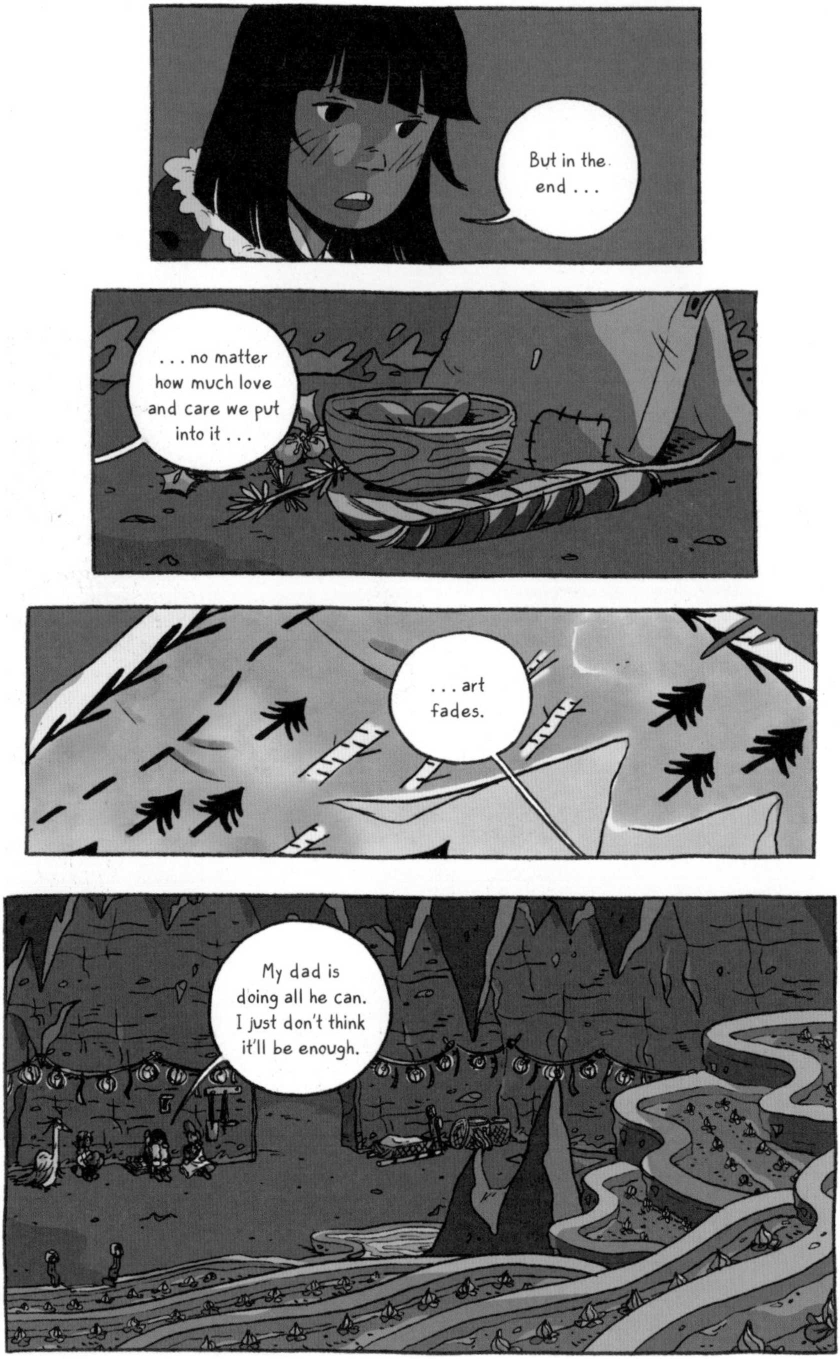
But in the end . . .
. . . no matter how much love and care we put into it . . .
. . . art fades.
My dad is doing all he can. I just don't think it'll be enough.

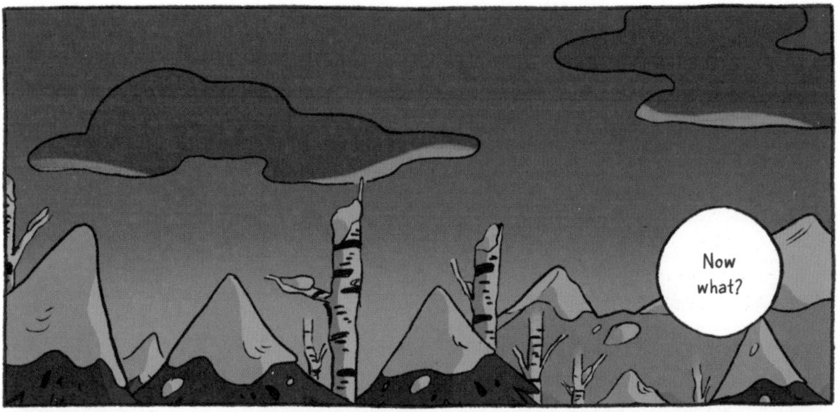
Now what?

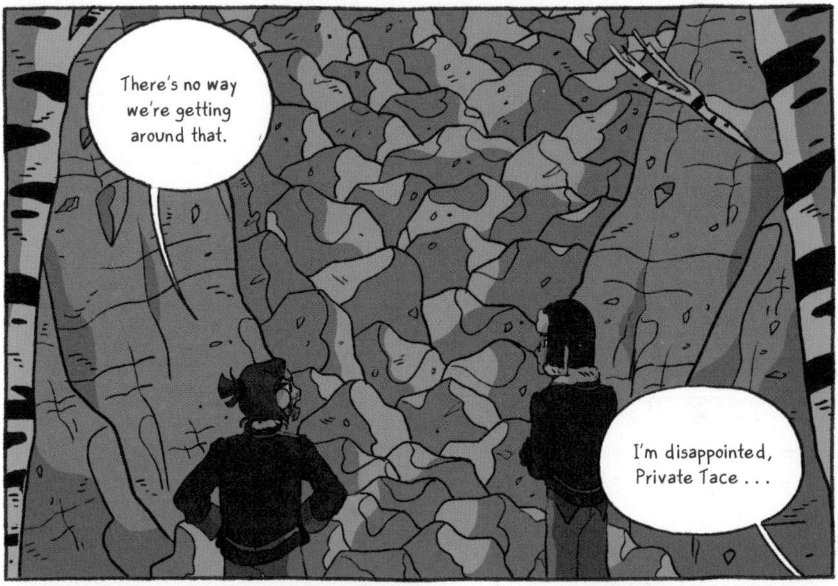
There's no way we're getting around that.
I'm disappointed, Private Tace . . .

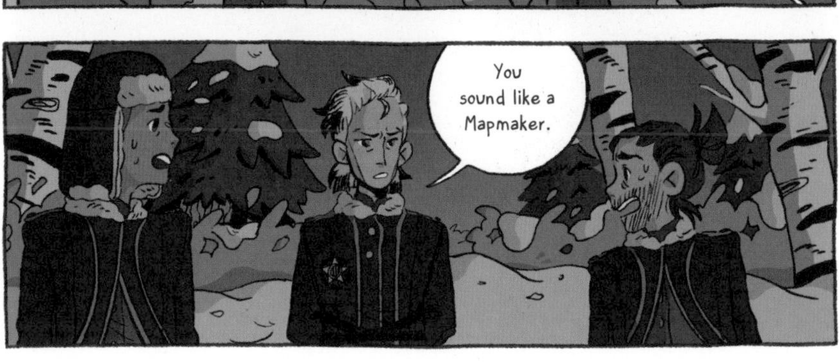
You sound like a Mapmaker.

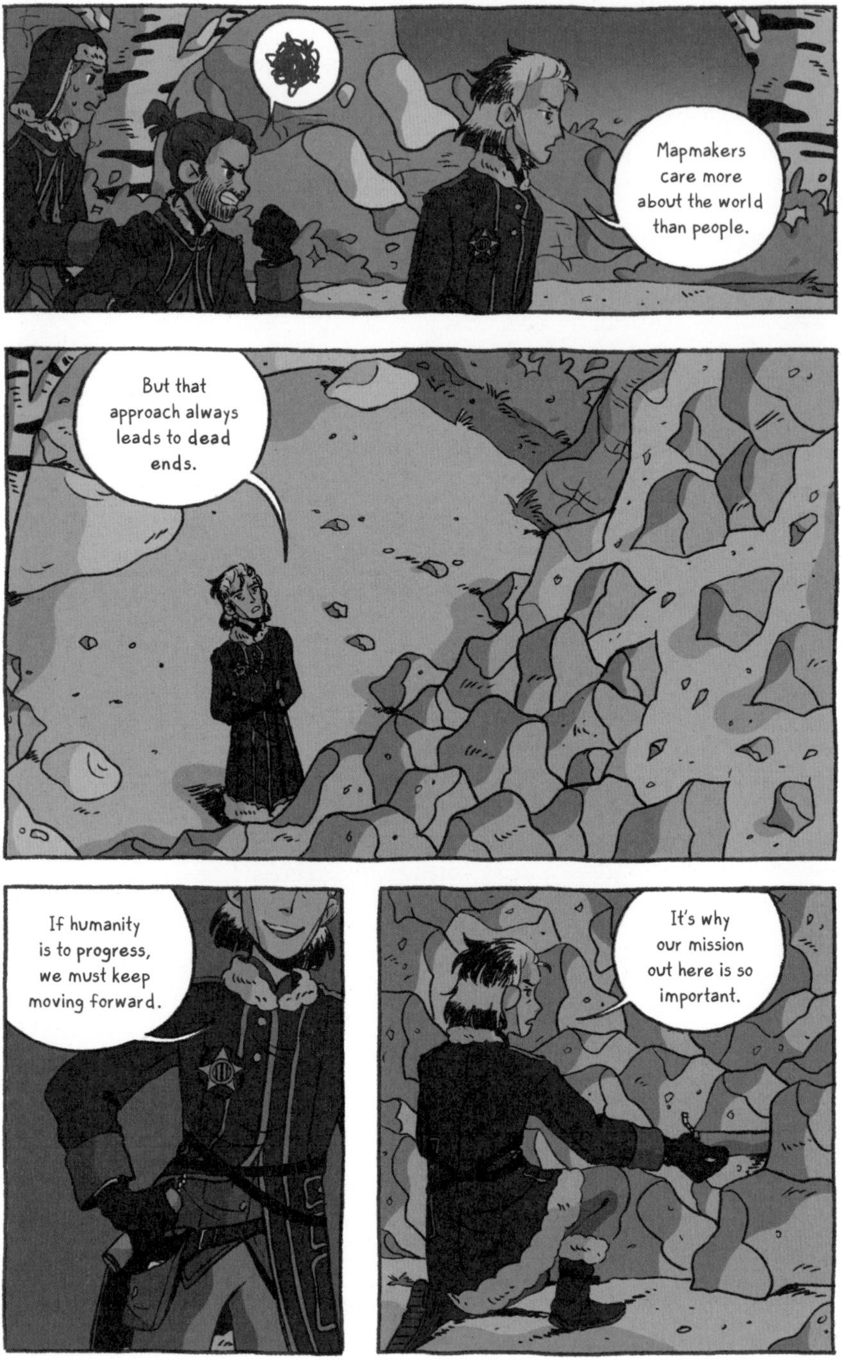
Mapmakers care more about the world than people.
But that approach always leads to dead ends.
If humanity is to progress, we must keep moving forward.
It's why our mission out here is so important.

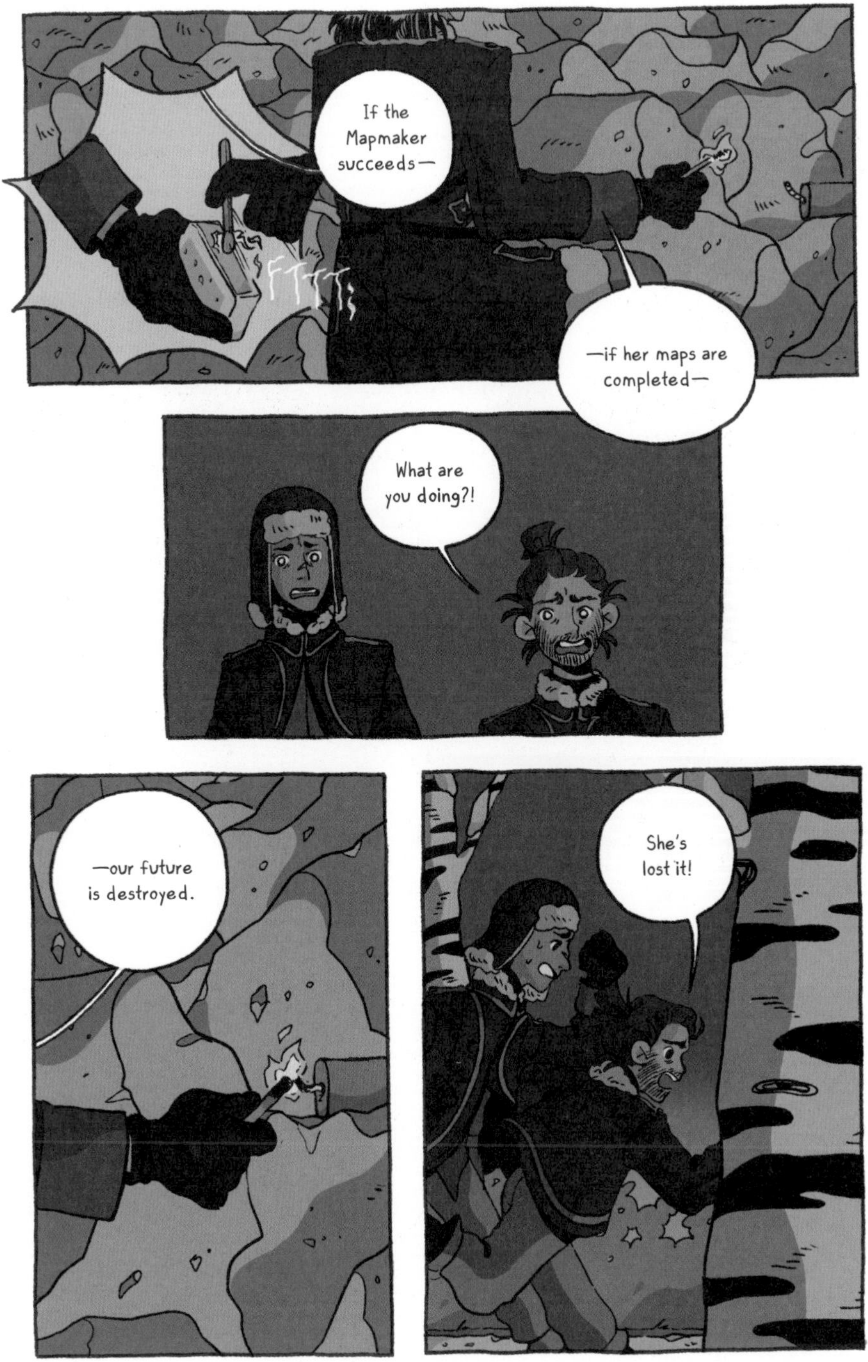
If the Mapmaker succeeds—
FTTTT
—if her maps are completed—
What are you doing?!
—our future is destroyed.
She's lost it!

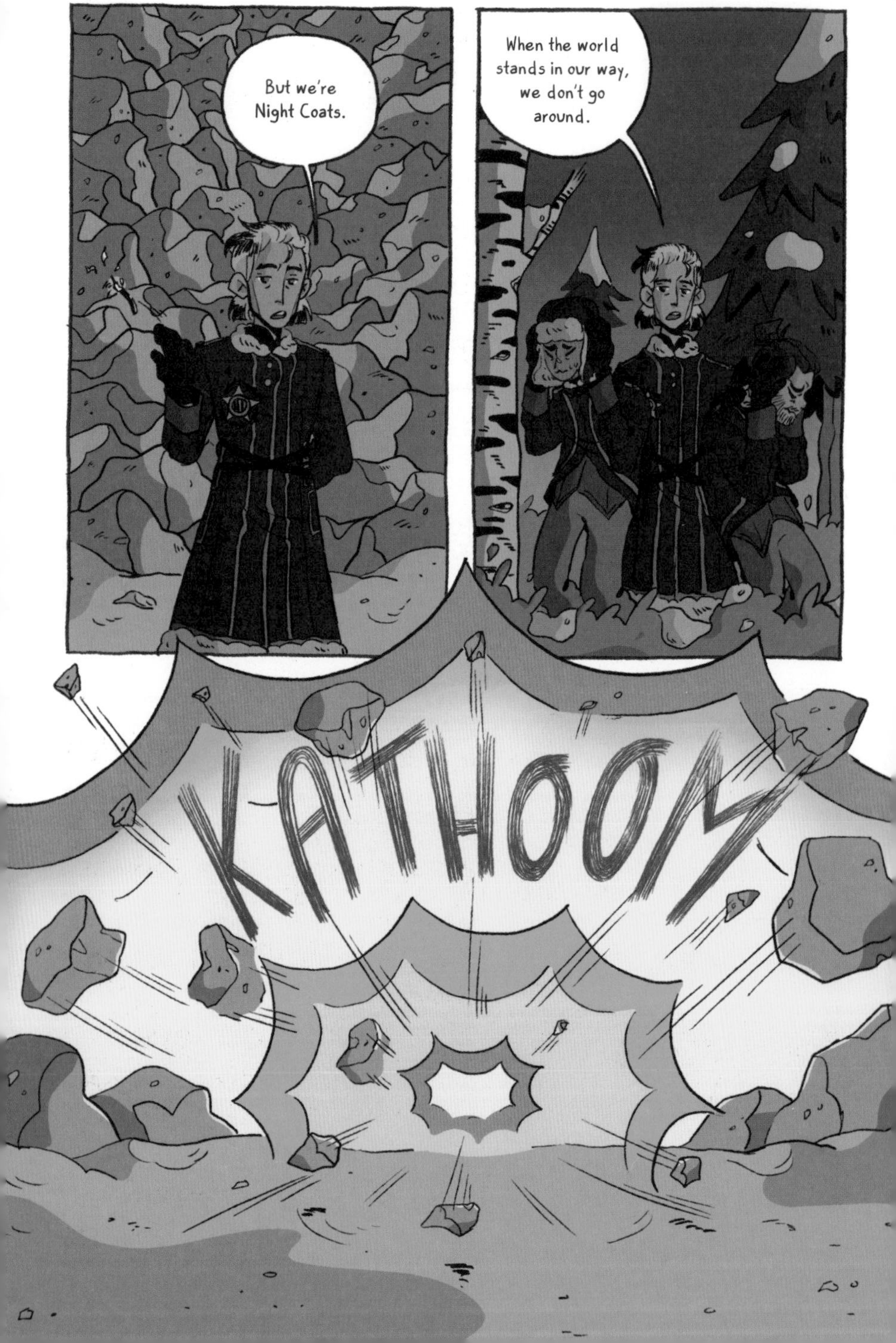

But we're Night Coats.
When the world stands in our way, we don't go around.
KATHOOM

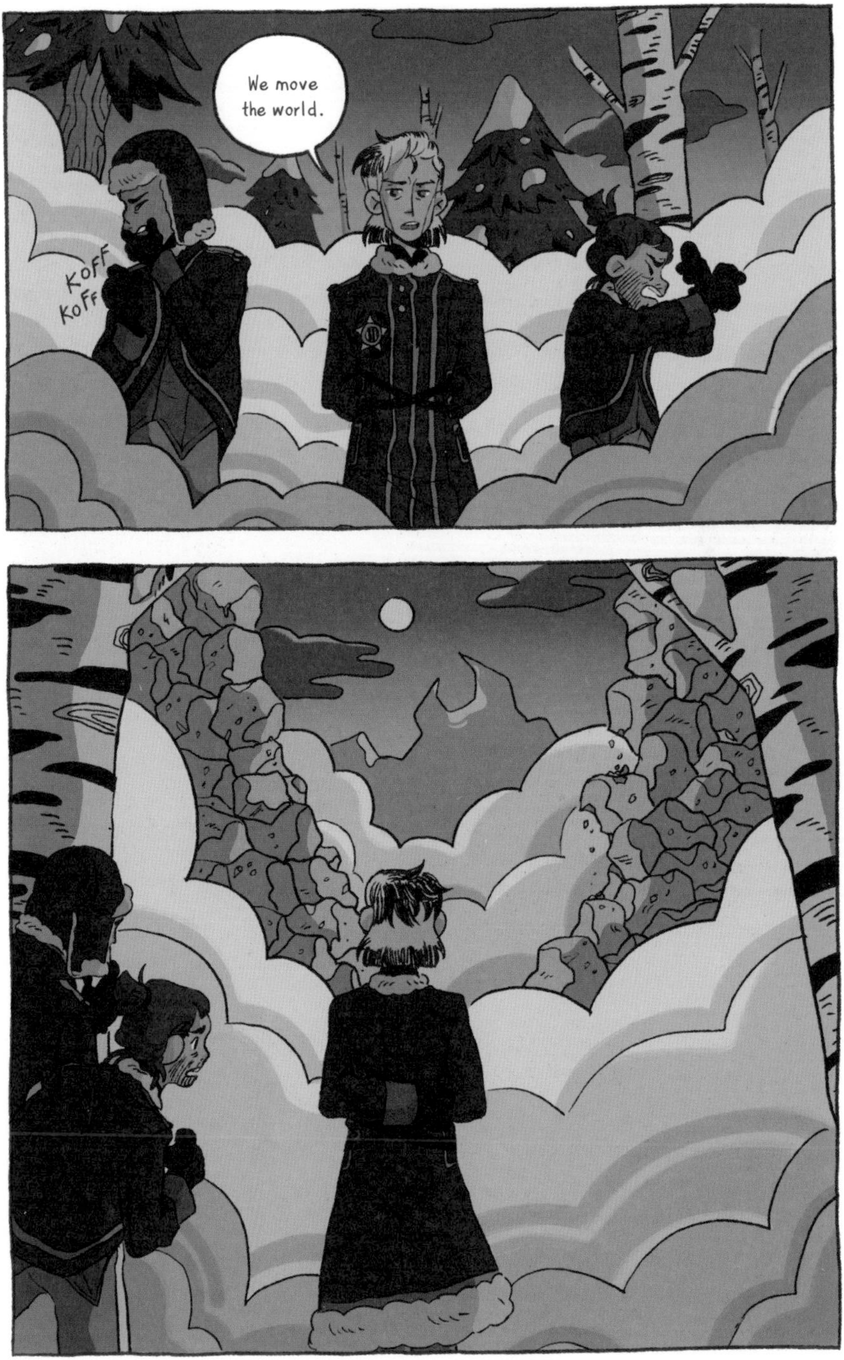
We move the world.
KOFF KOFF

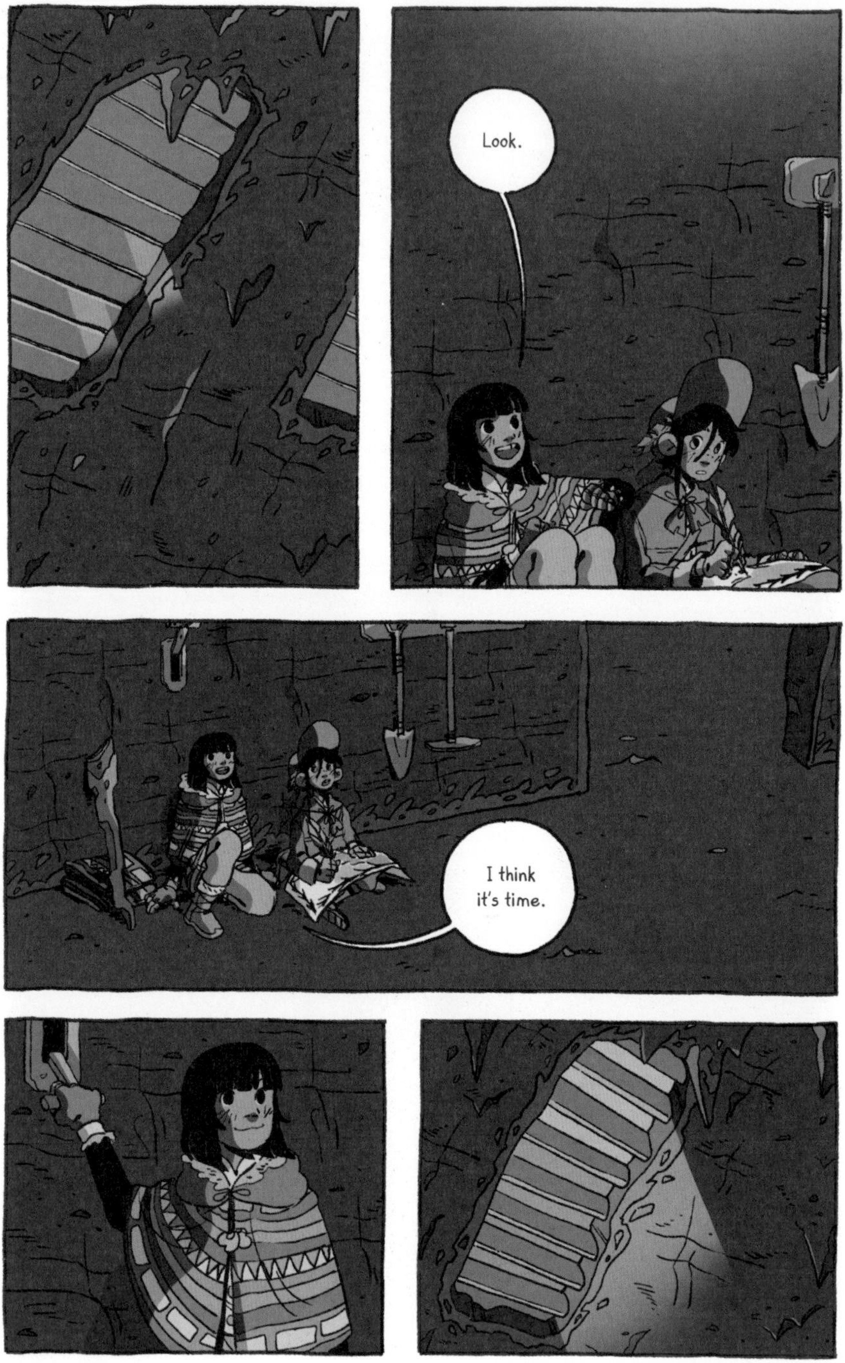
Look.
I think it's time.

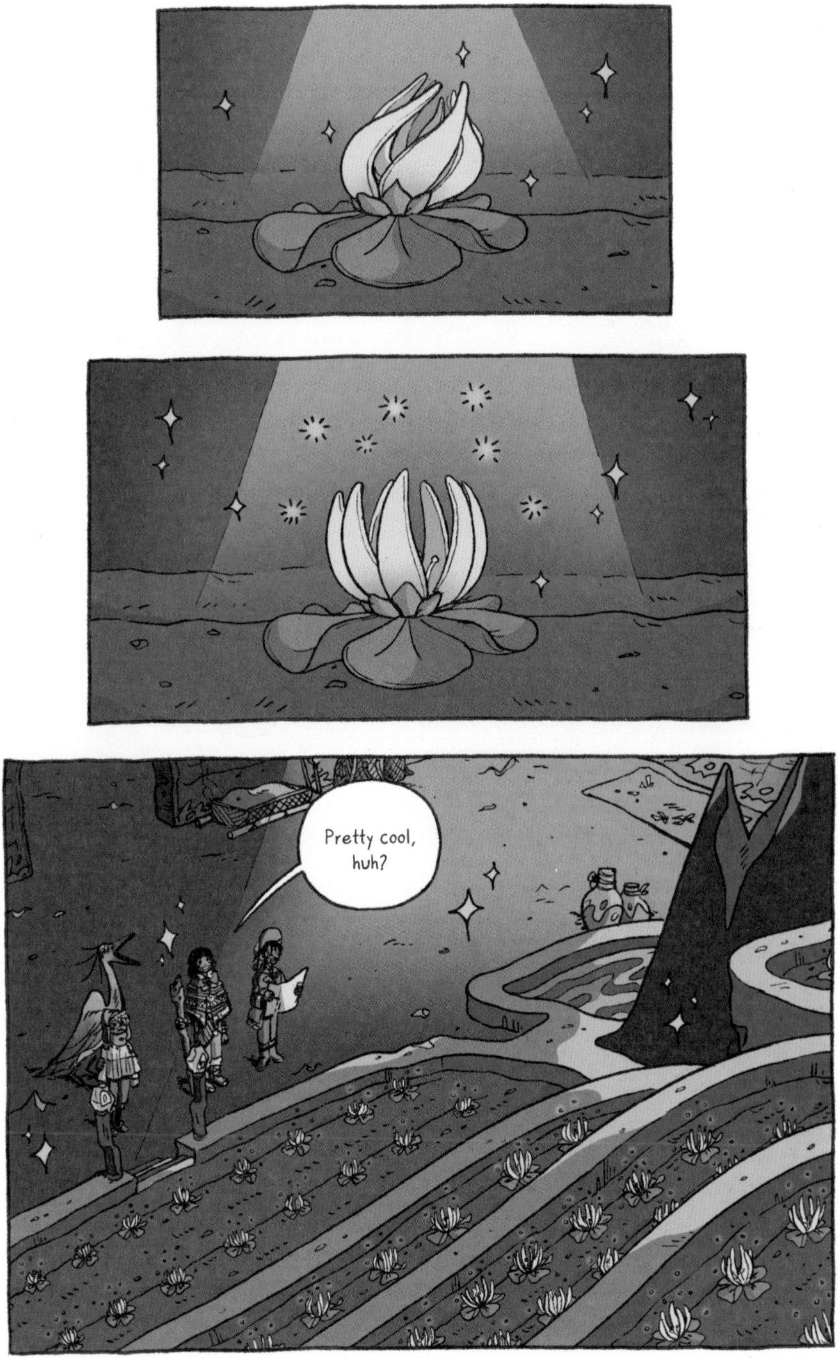
Pretty cool,
huh?

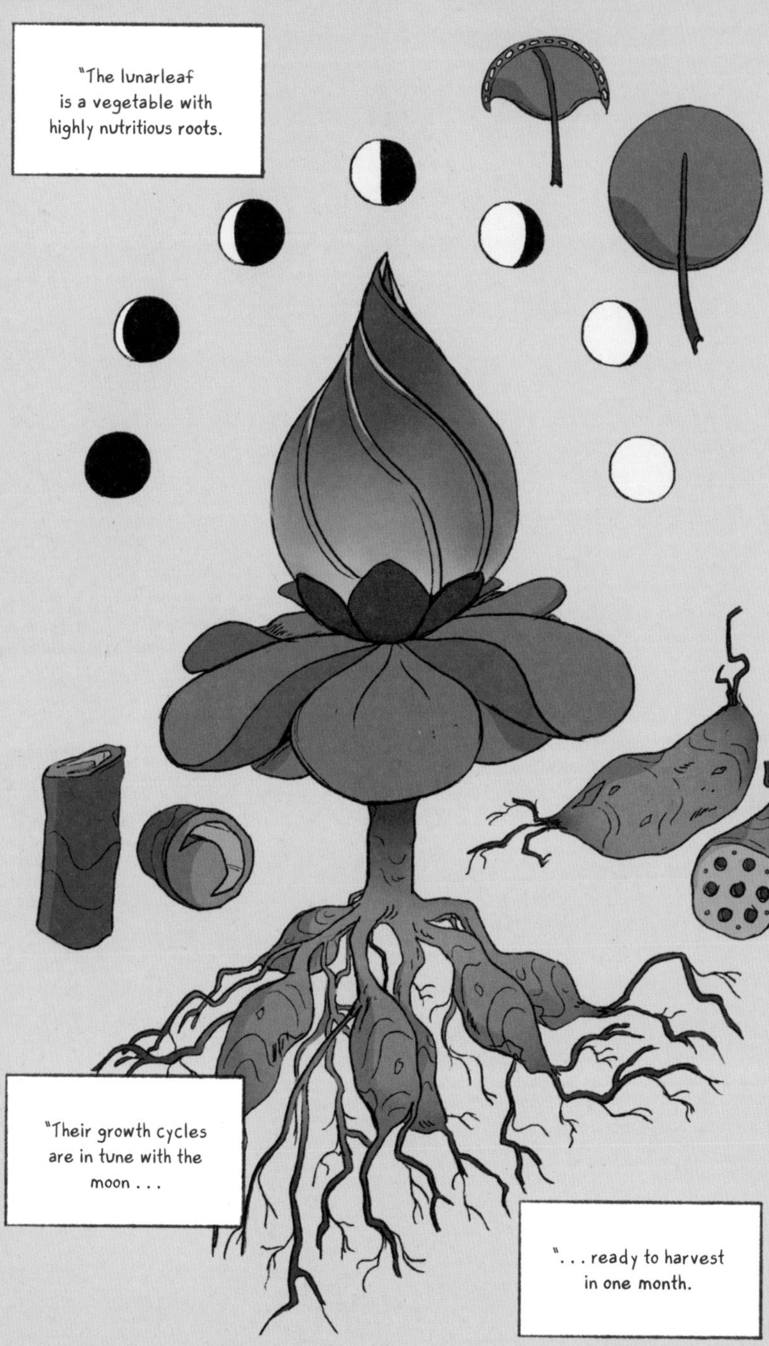
"The lunarleaf is a vegetable with highly nutritious roots.
"Their growth cycles are in tune with the moon . . .
". . . ready to harvest in one month.

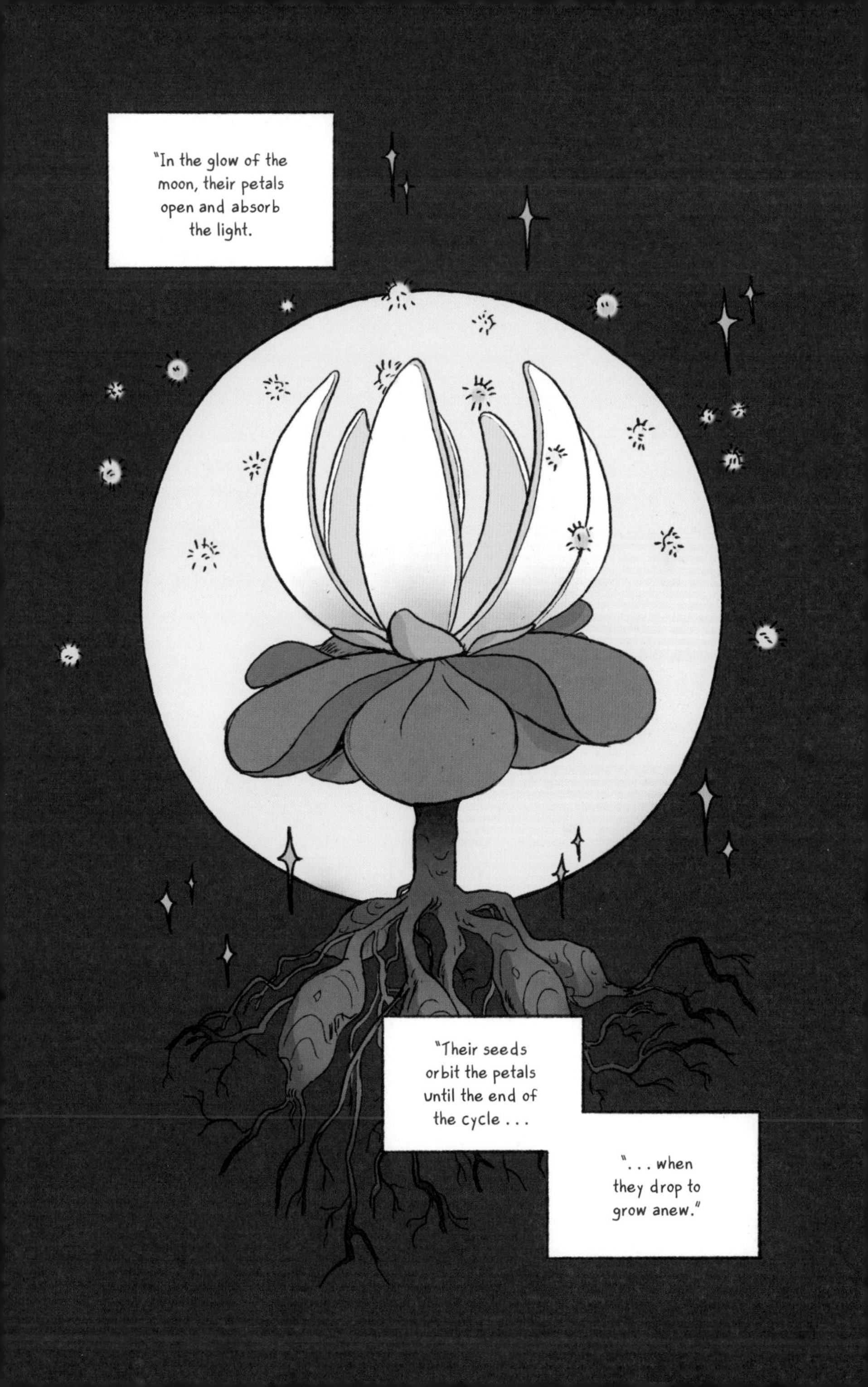
"In the glow of the moon, their petals open and absorb the light.
"Their seeds orbit the petals until the end of the cycle . . .
". . . when they drop to grow anew."

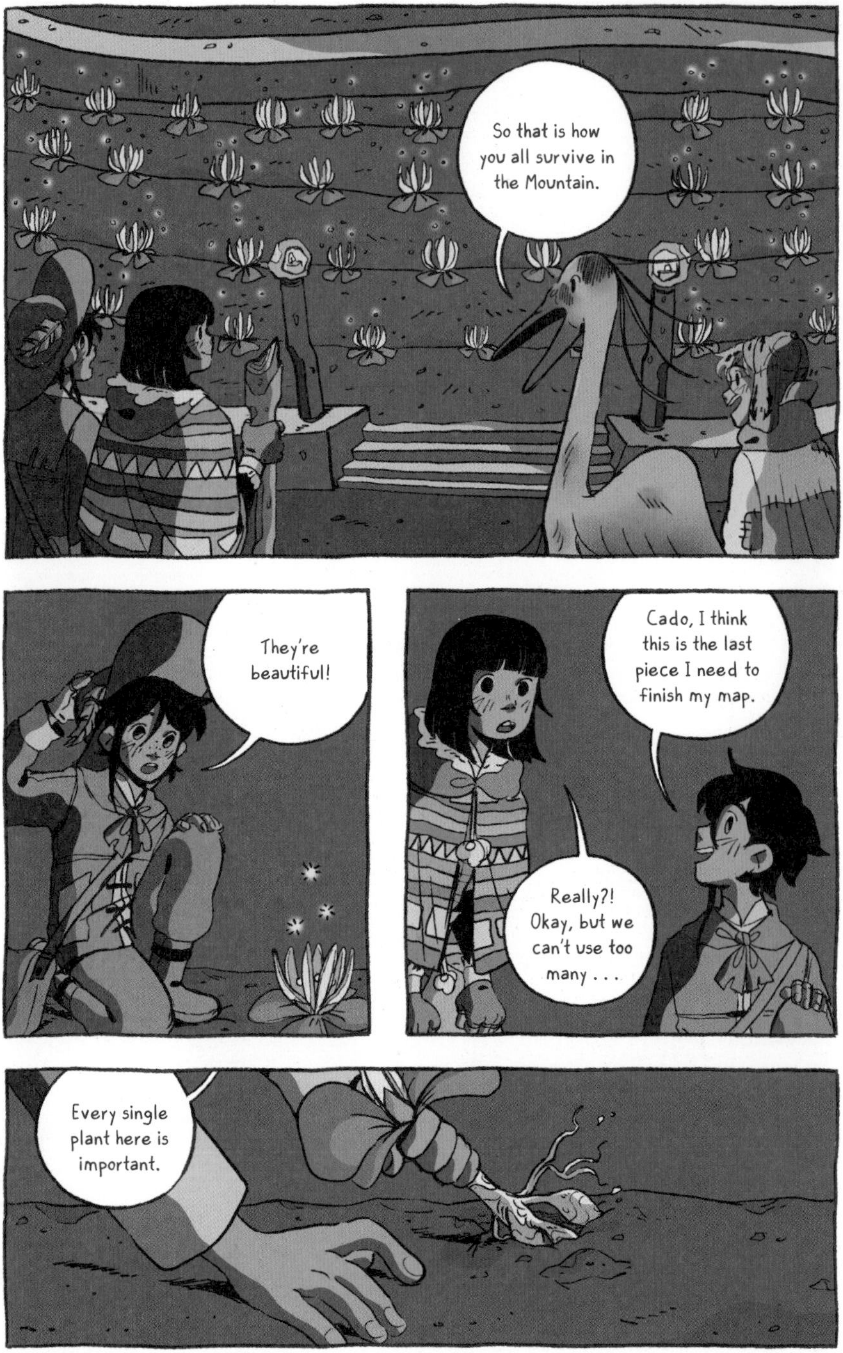
So that is how you all survive in the Mountain.
They're beautiful!
Cado, I think this is the last piece I need to finish my map.
Really?! Okay, but we can't use too many . . .
Every single plant here is important.

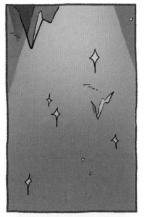

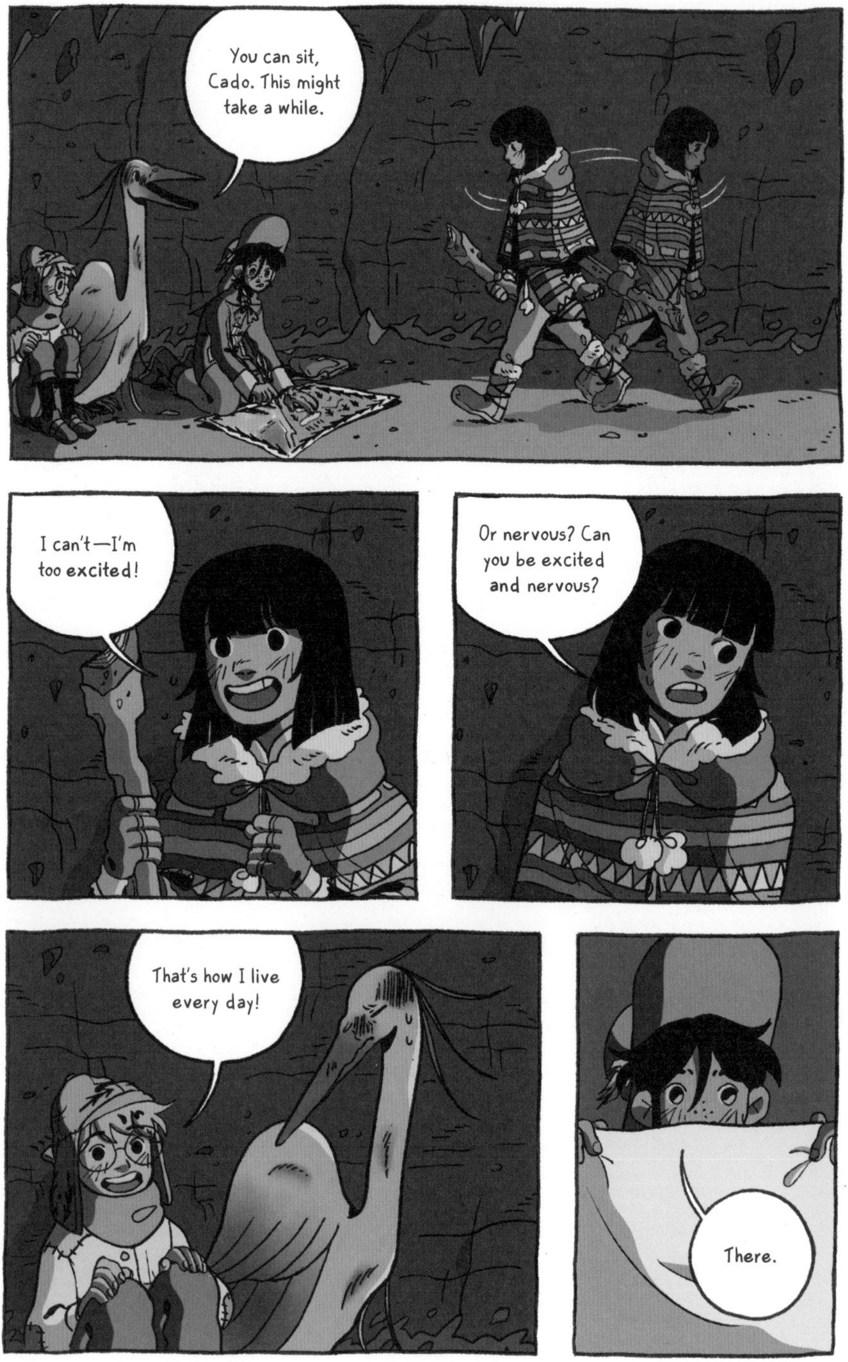
You can sit, Cado. This might take a while.
I can't—I'm too excited!
Or nervous? Can you be excited and nervous?
That's how I live every day!
There.

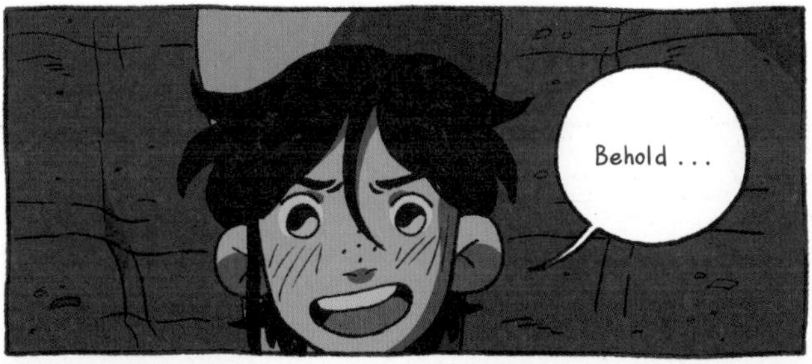
Behold . . .

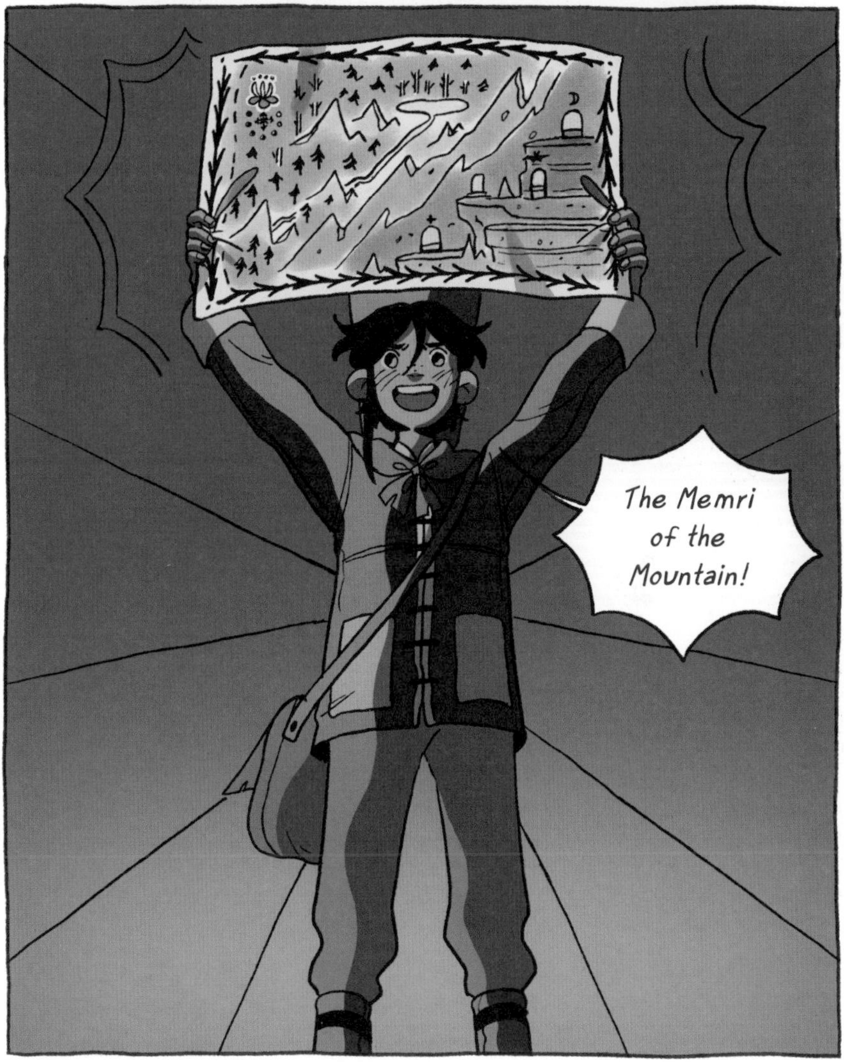
The Memri of the Mountain!

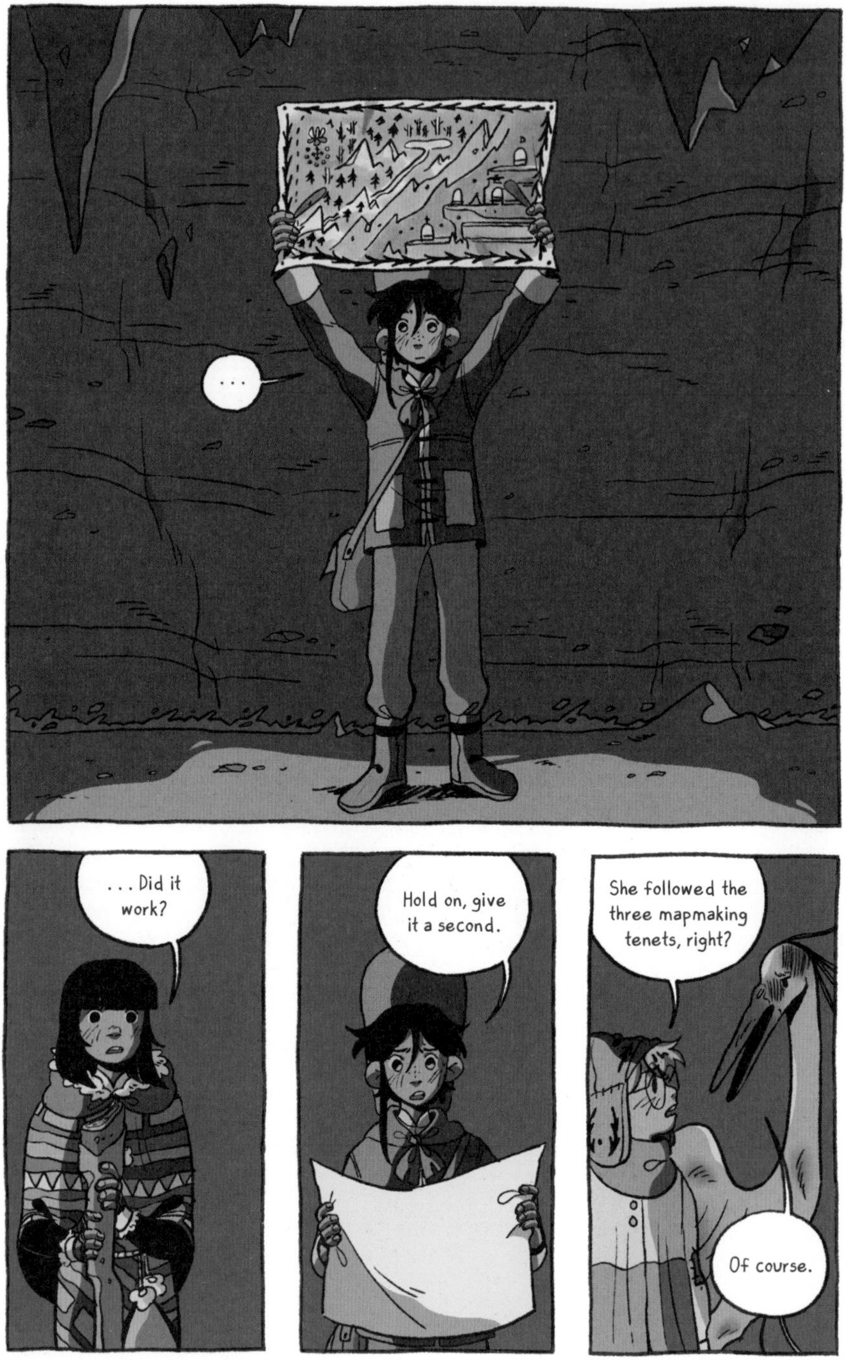

. . .
. . . Did it work?
Hold on, give it a second.
She followed the three mapmaking tenets, right?
Of course.

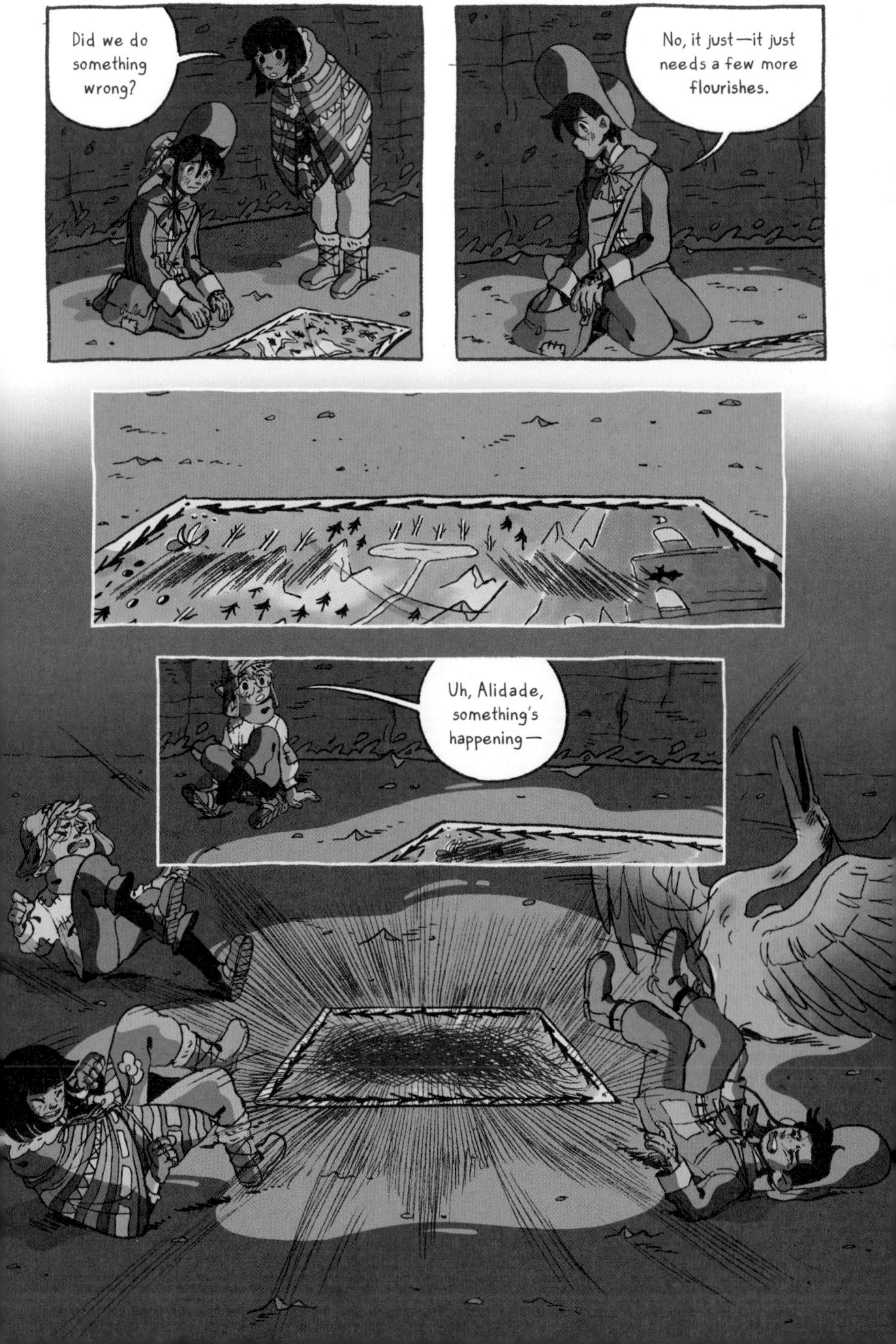
Did we do something wrong?
No, it just—it just needs a few more flourishes.
Uh, Alidade, something's happening—

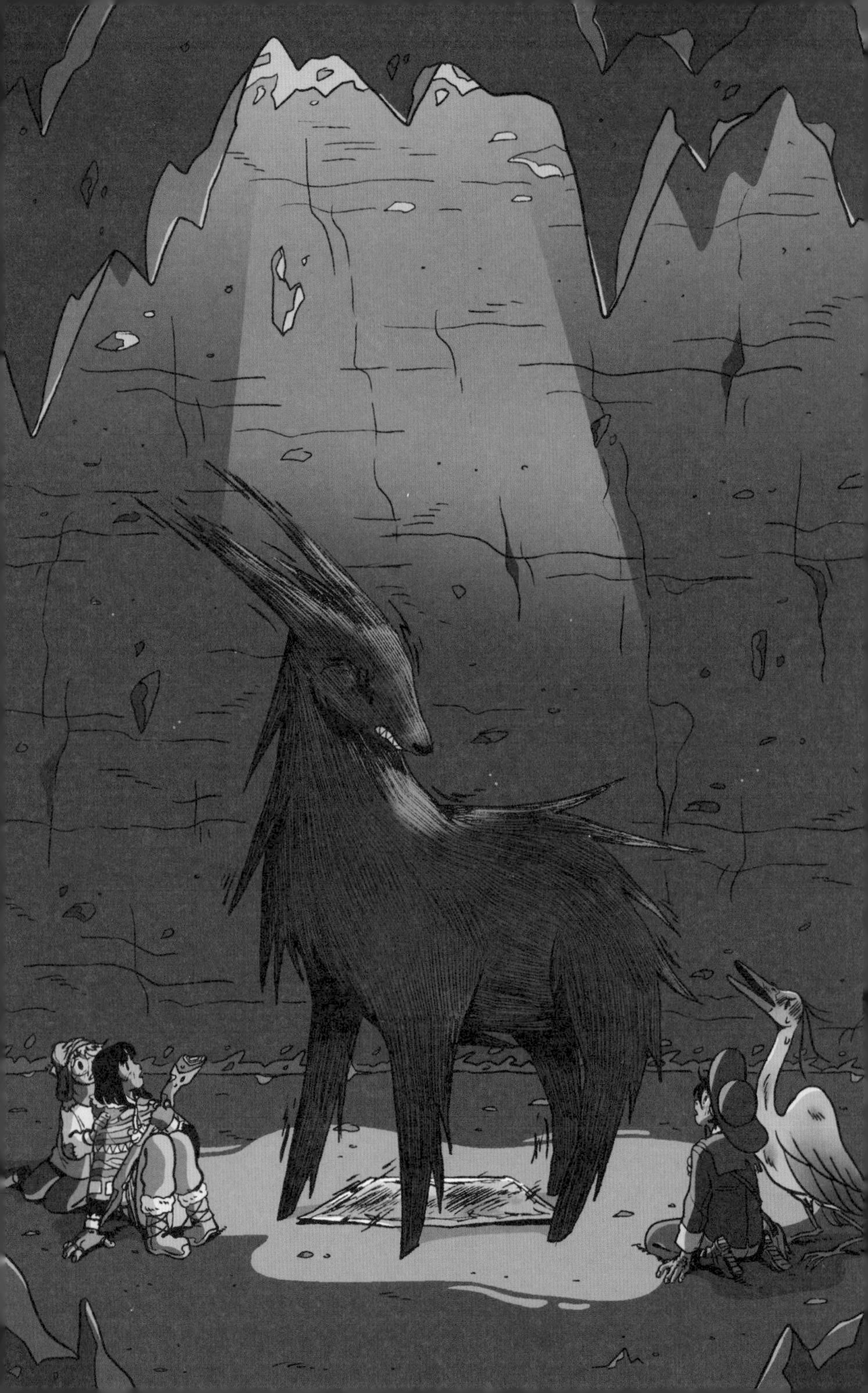

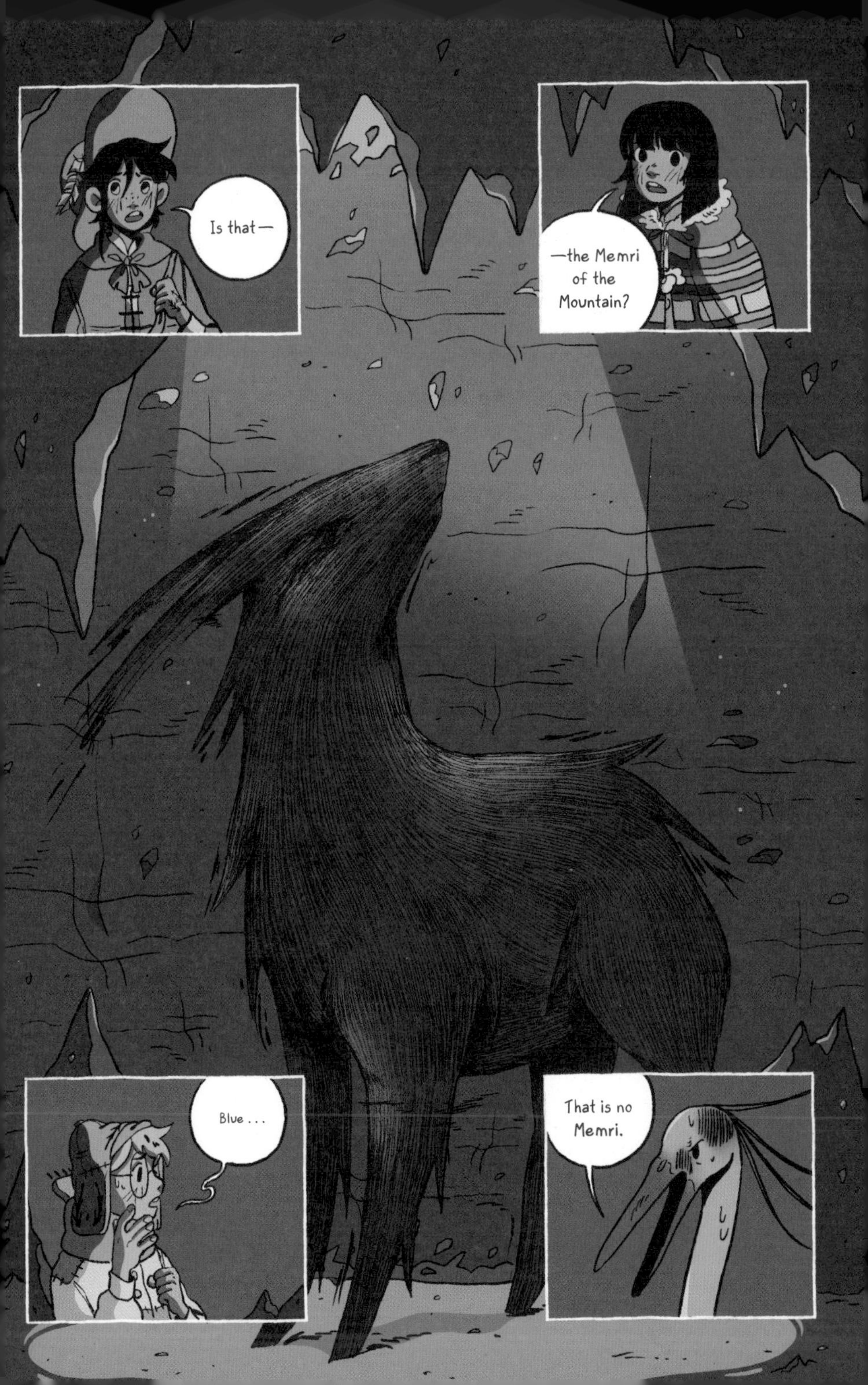
Is that—
—the Memri of the Mountain?
Blue . . .
That is no Memri.

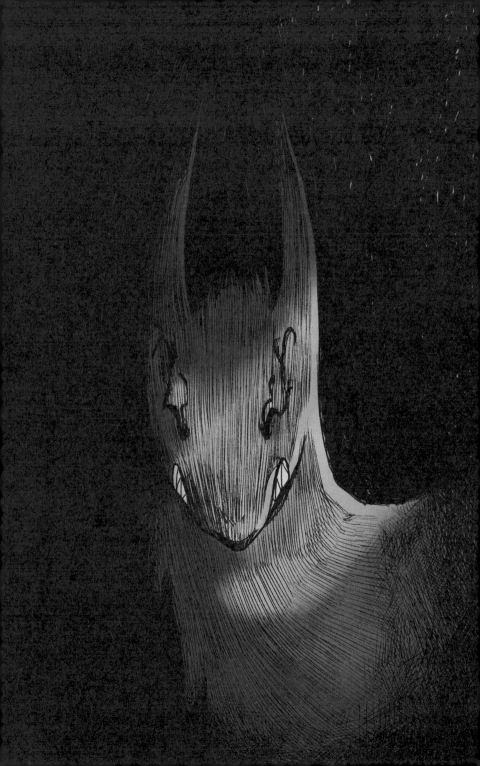

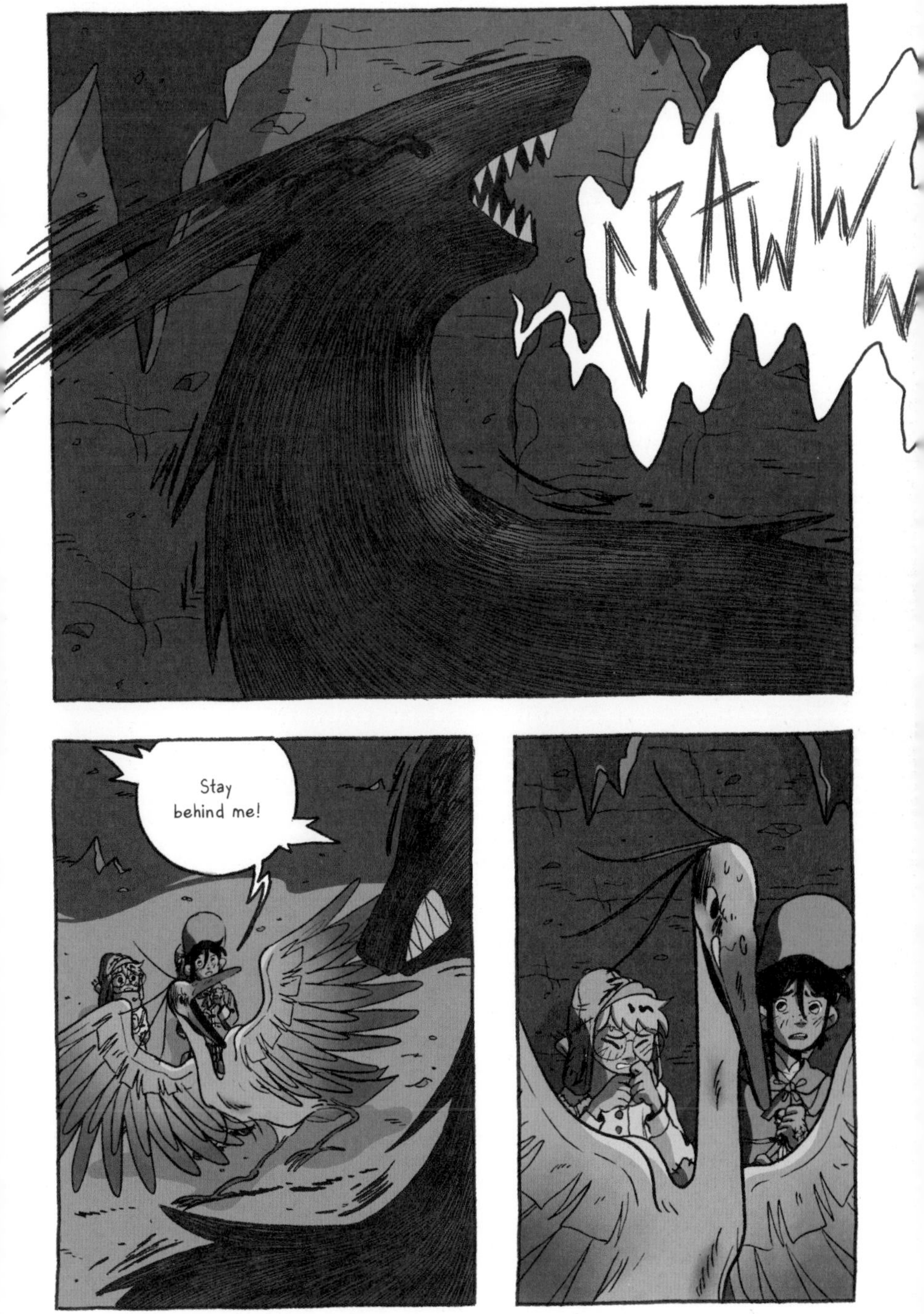
CRAWWW
Stay behind me!

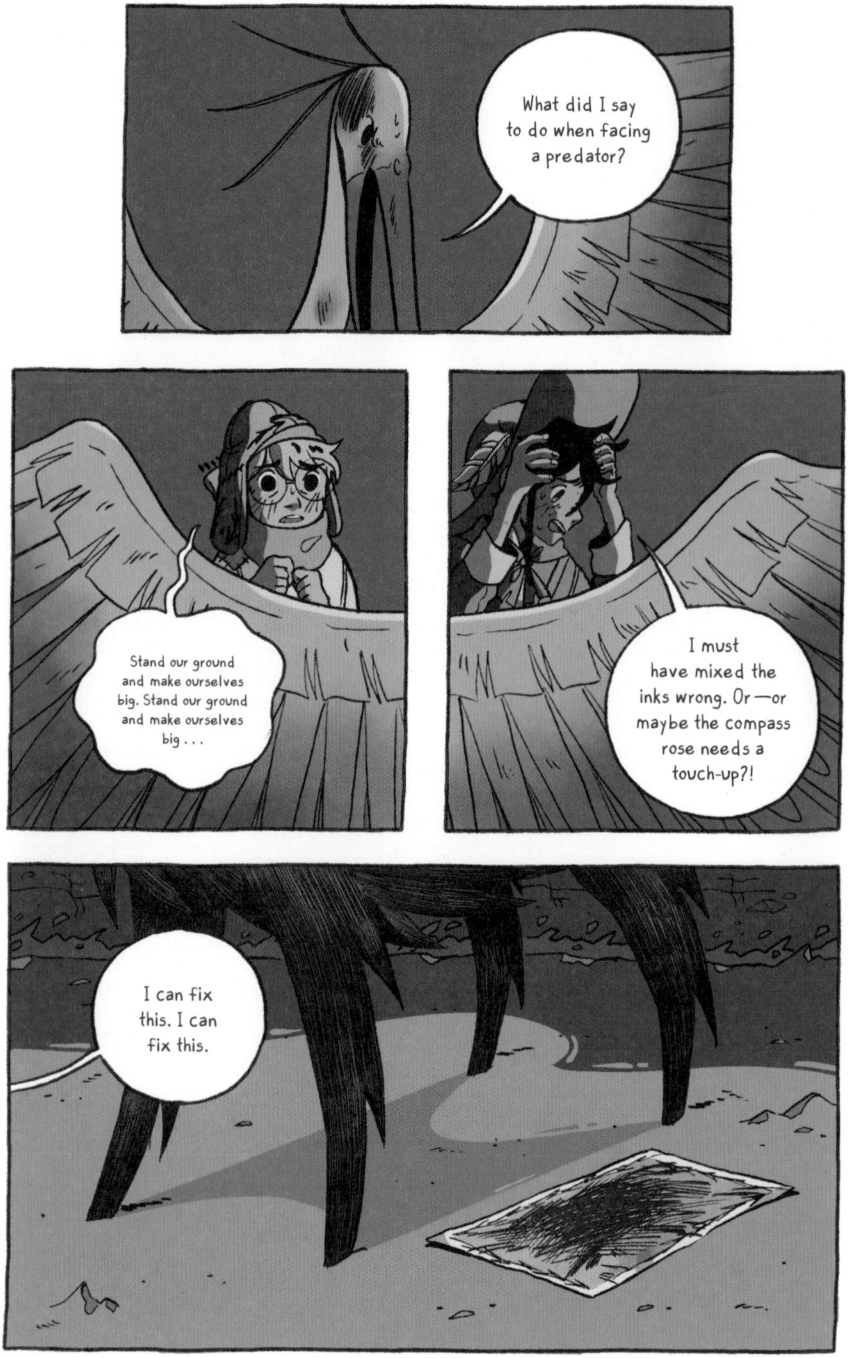
What did I say to do when facing a predator?
Stand our ground and make ourselves big. Stand our ground and make ourselves big . . .
I must have mixed the inks wrong. Or—or maybe the compass rose needs a touch-up?!
I can fix this. I can fix this.

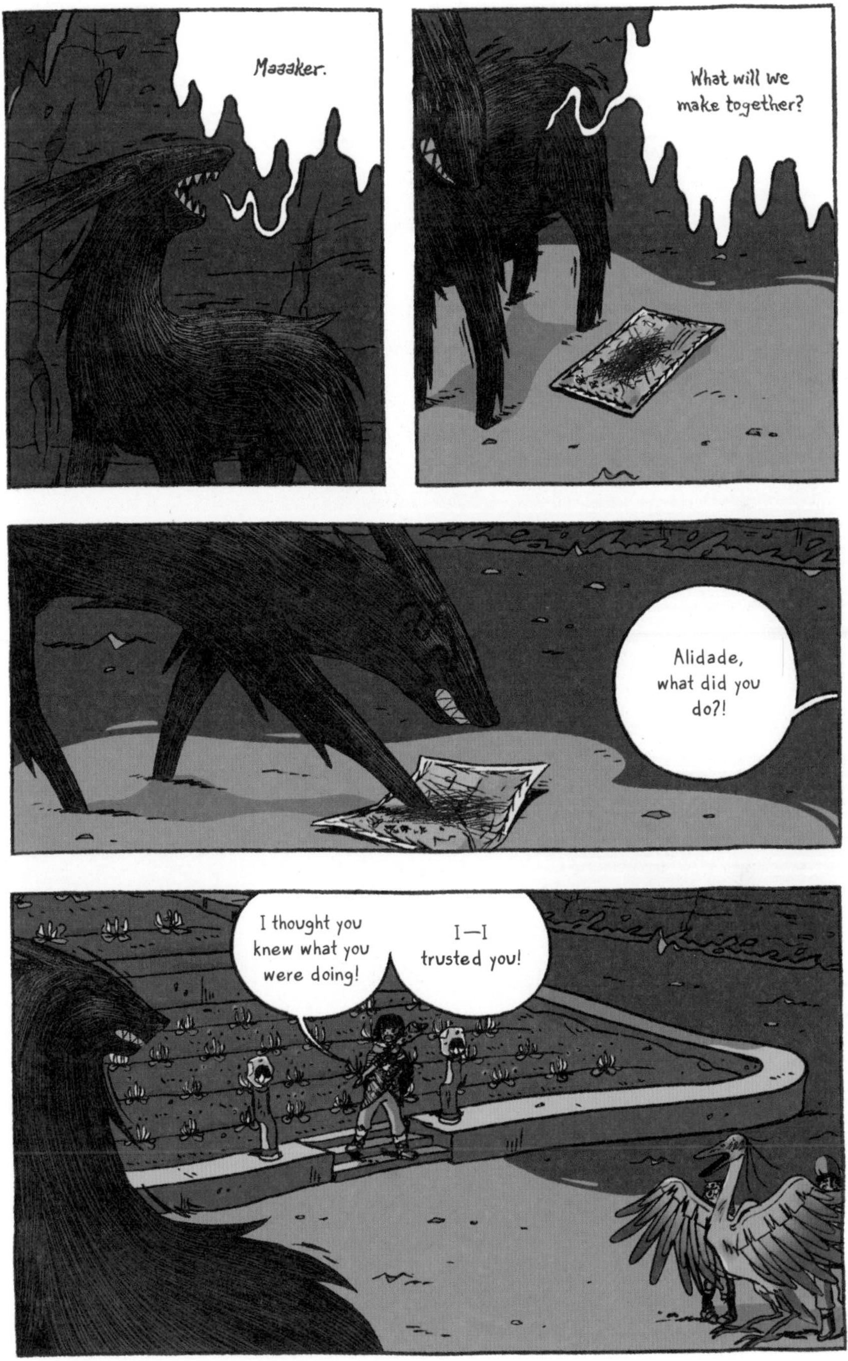
Maaaker.
What will we make together?
Alidade, what did you do?!
I thought you knew what you were doing!
I—I trusted you!

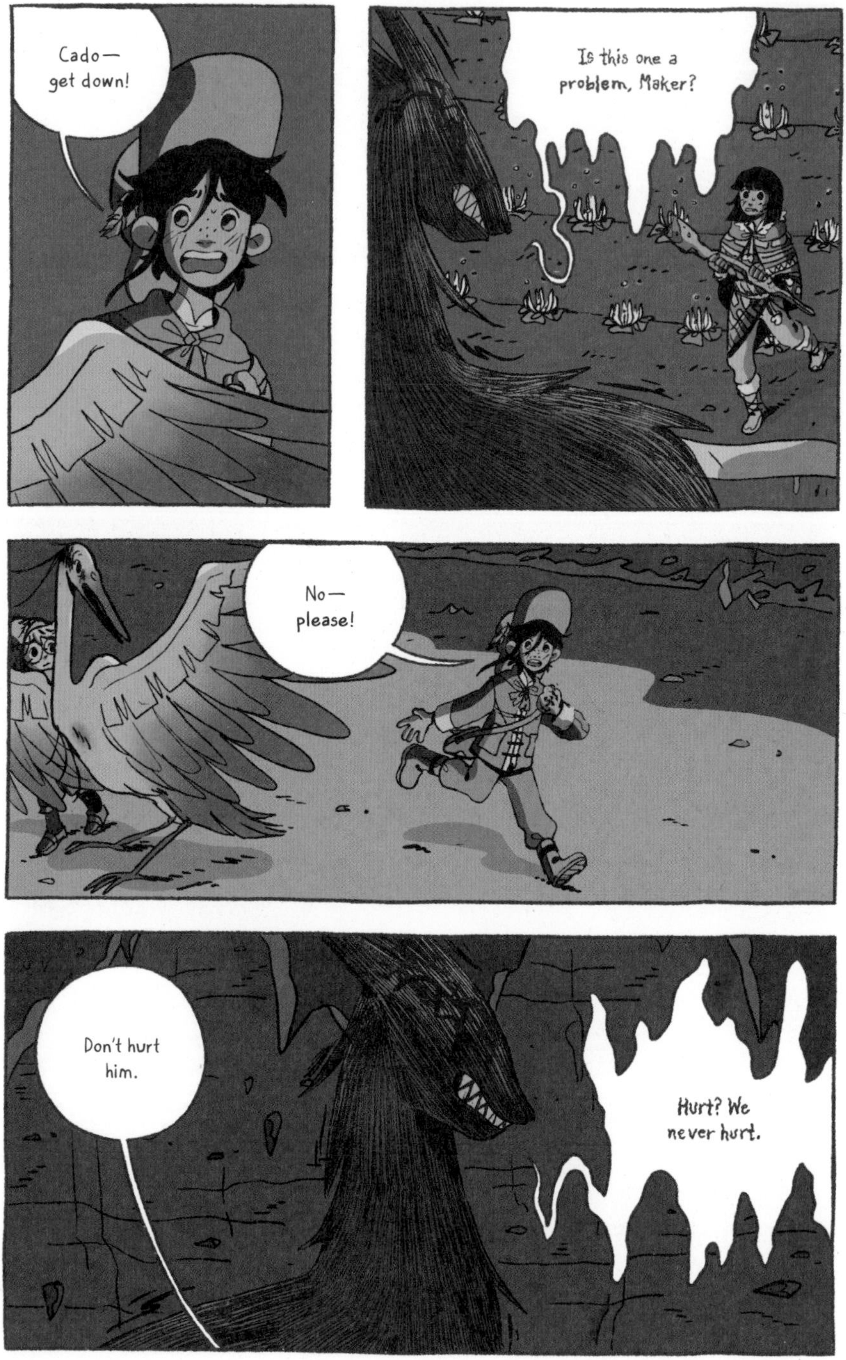
Cado—
get down!
Is this one a
problem, Maker?
No—
please!
Don't hurt
him.
Hurt? We
never hurt.

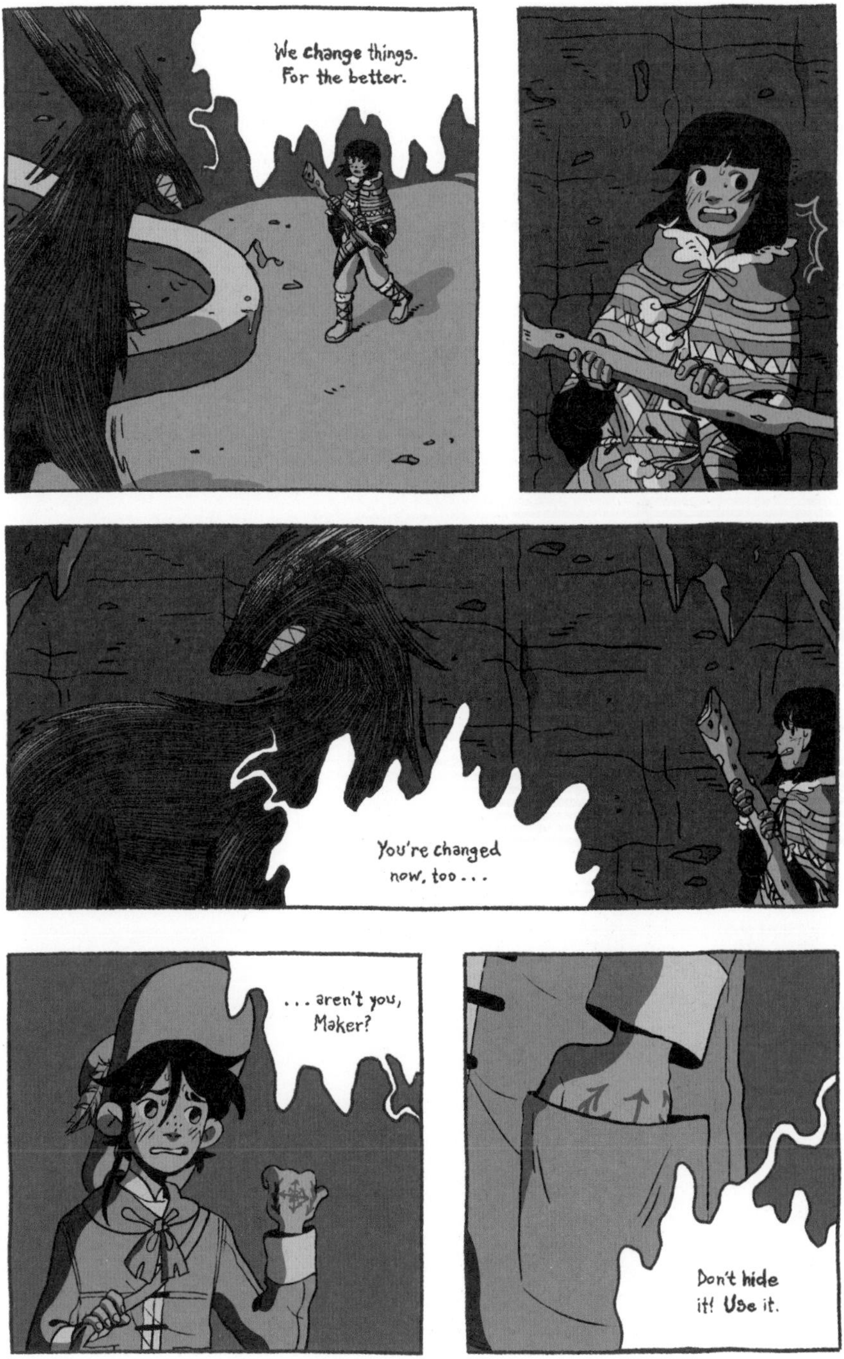
We change things.
For the better.
You're changed
now, too...
...aren't you,
Maker?
Don't hide
it! Use it.

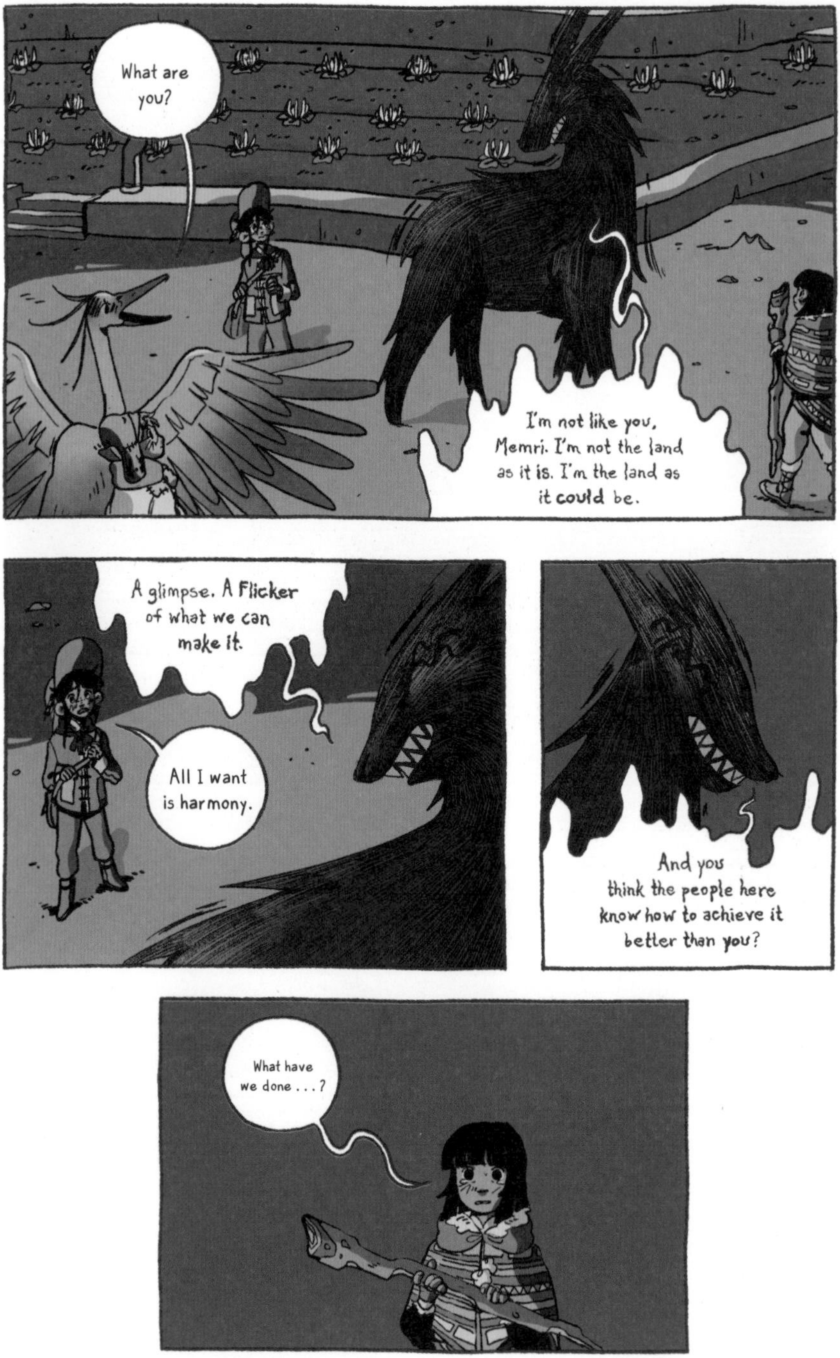
What are you?
I'm not like you, Memri. I'm not the land as it is. I'm the land as it could be.
A glimpse. A flicker of what we can make it.
All I want is harmony.
And you think the people here know how to achieve it better than you?
What have we done . . . ?

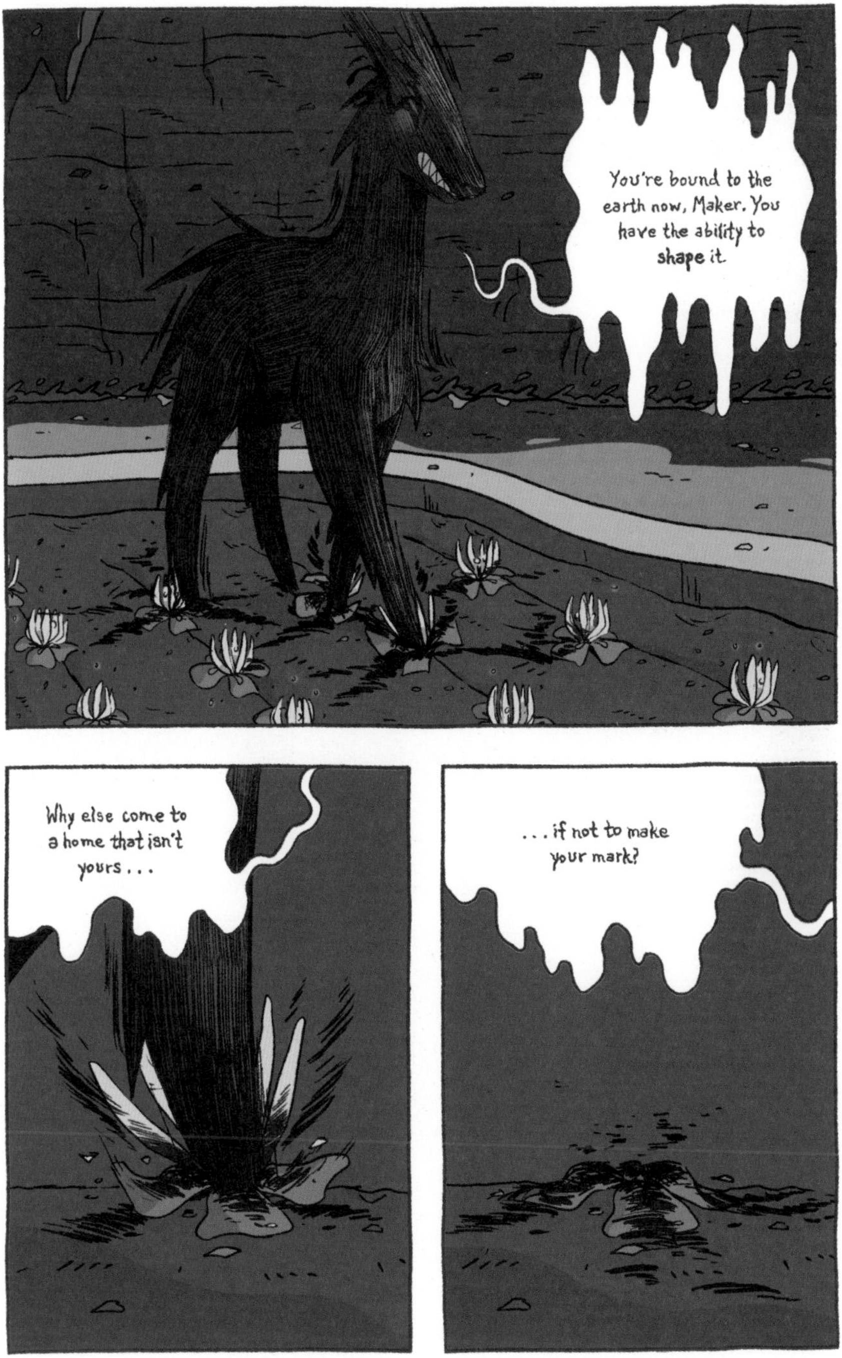
You're bound to the earth now, Maker. You have the ability to shape it.
Why else come to a home that isn't yours . . .
. . . if not to make your mark?

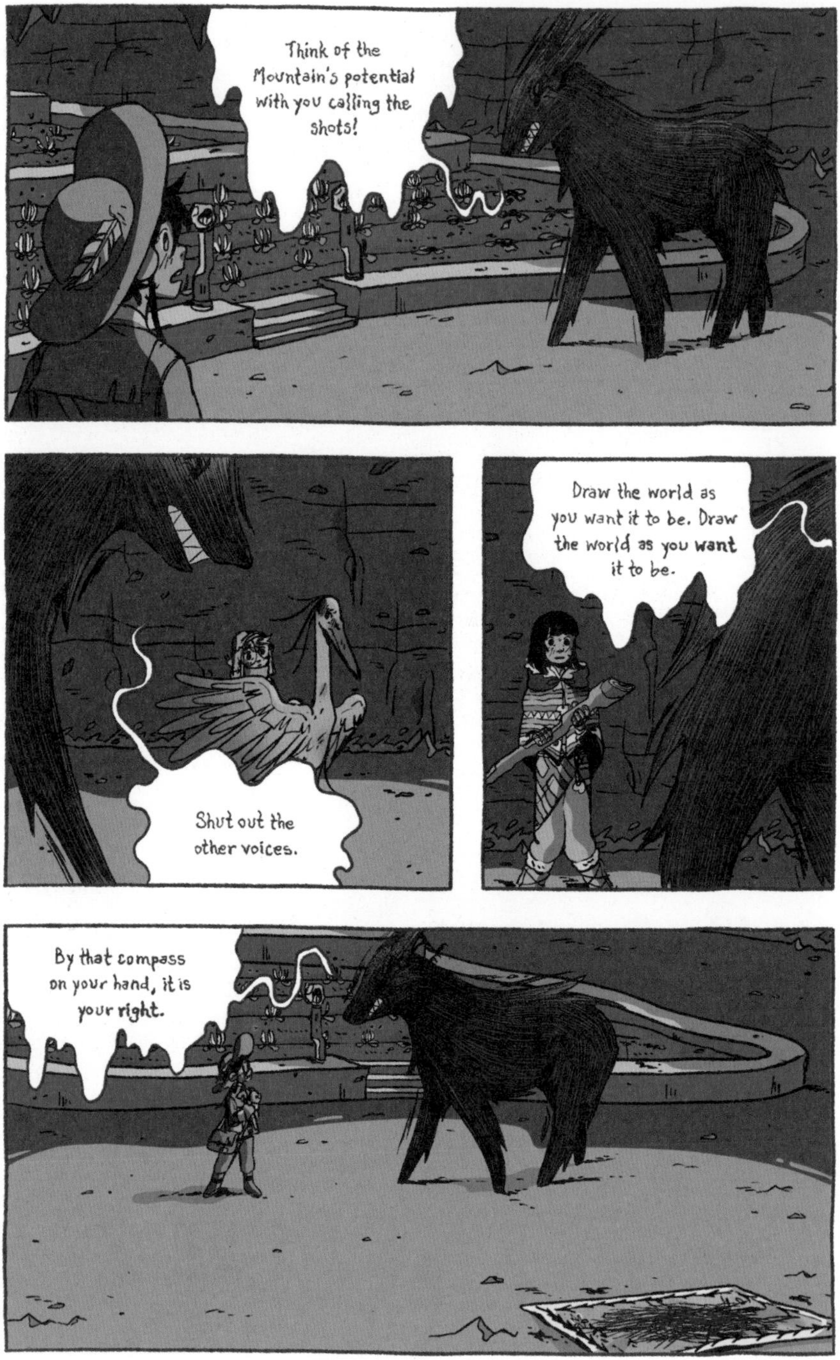
Think of the Mountain's potential with you calling the shots!
Shut out the other voices.
Draw the world as you want it to be. Draw the world as you want it to be.
By that compass on your hand, it is your right.

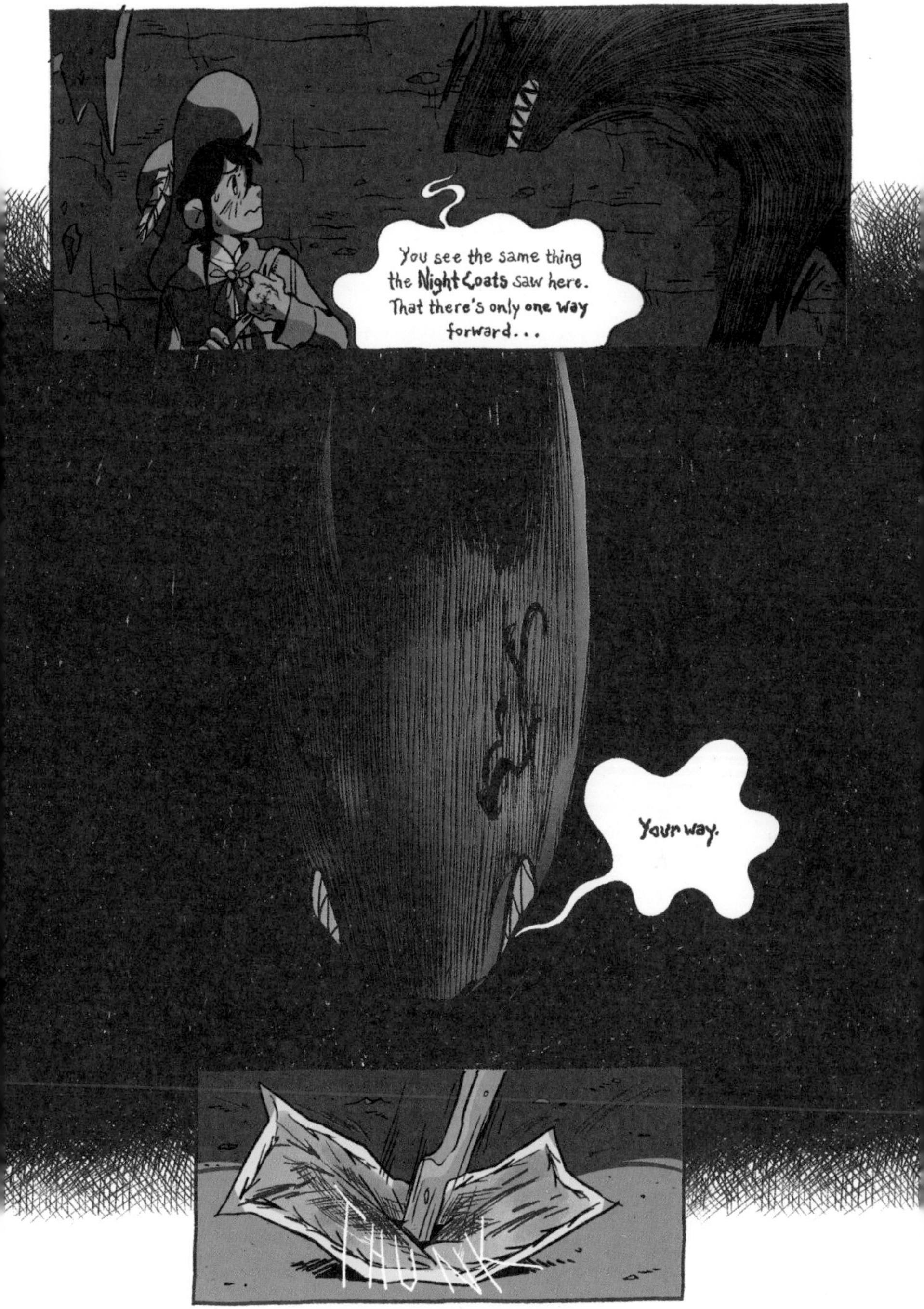

You see the same thing the Night Coats saw here. That there's only one way forward...
Your way.
THUNK

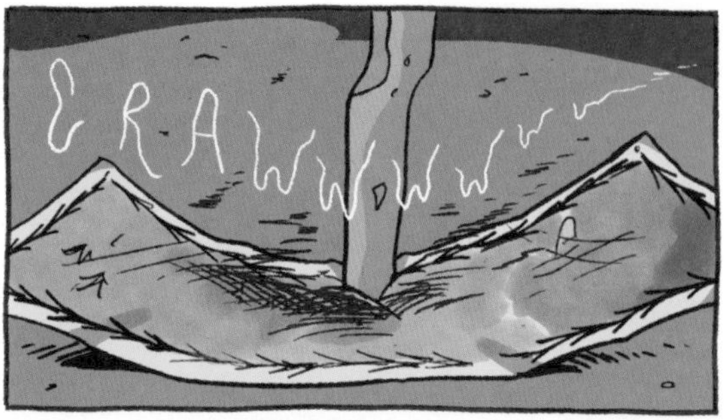
CRAWWWWWWWW

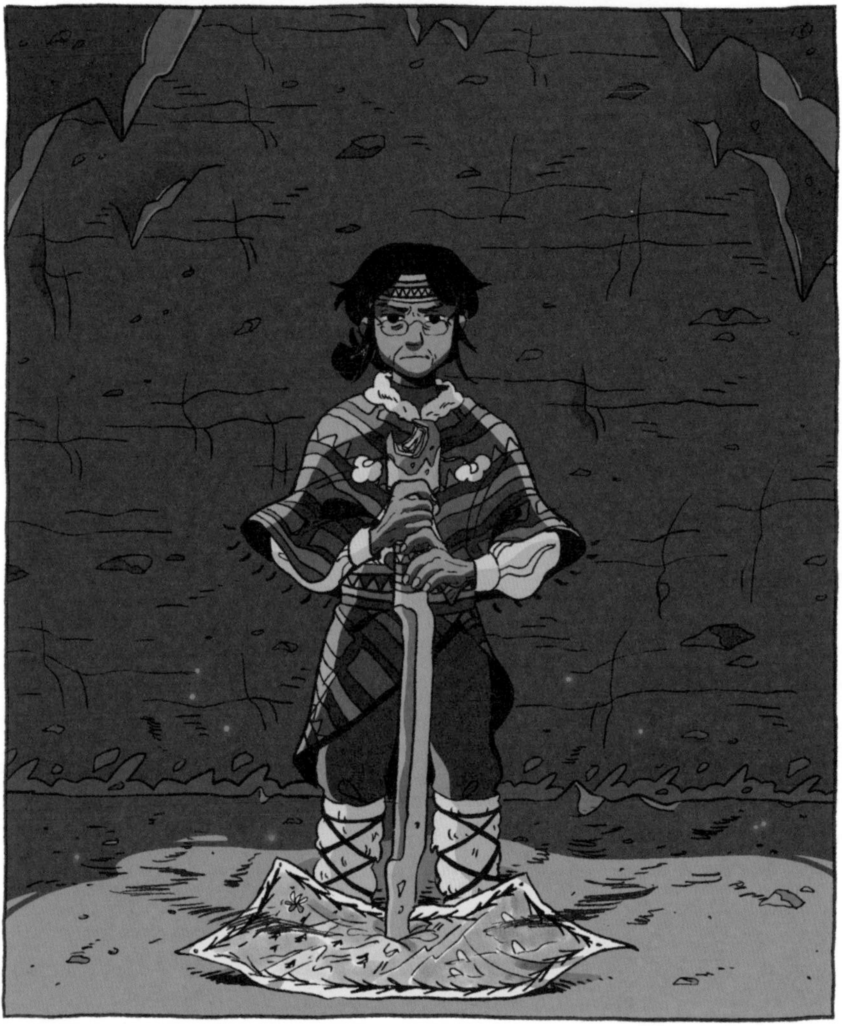

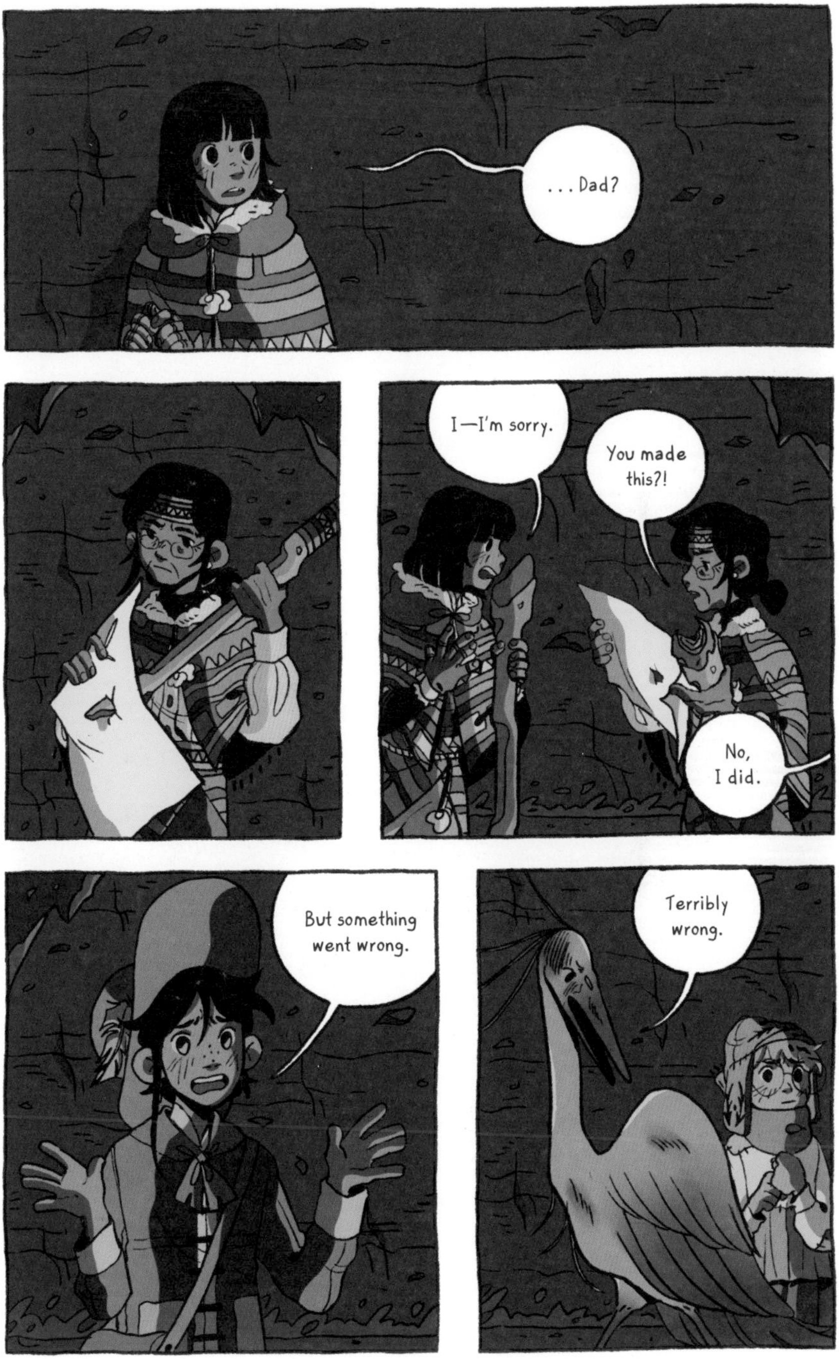
...Dad?
I—I'm sorry.
You made this?!
No, I did.
But something went wrong.
Terribly wrong.

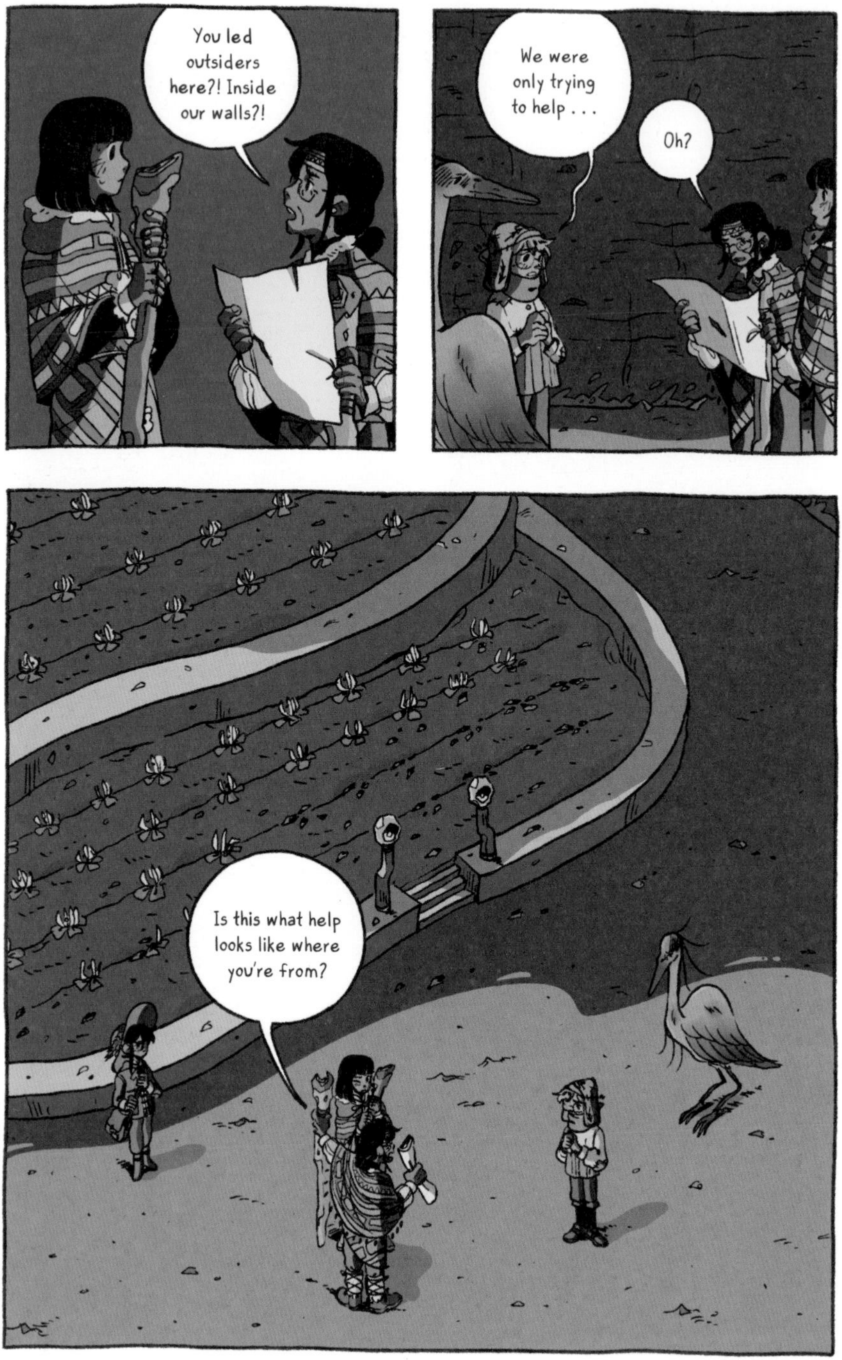
You led outsiders here?! Inside our walls?!
We were only trying to help . . .
Oh?
Is this what help looks like where you're from?

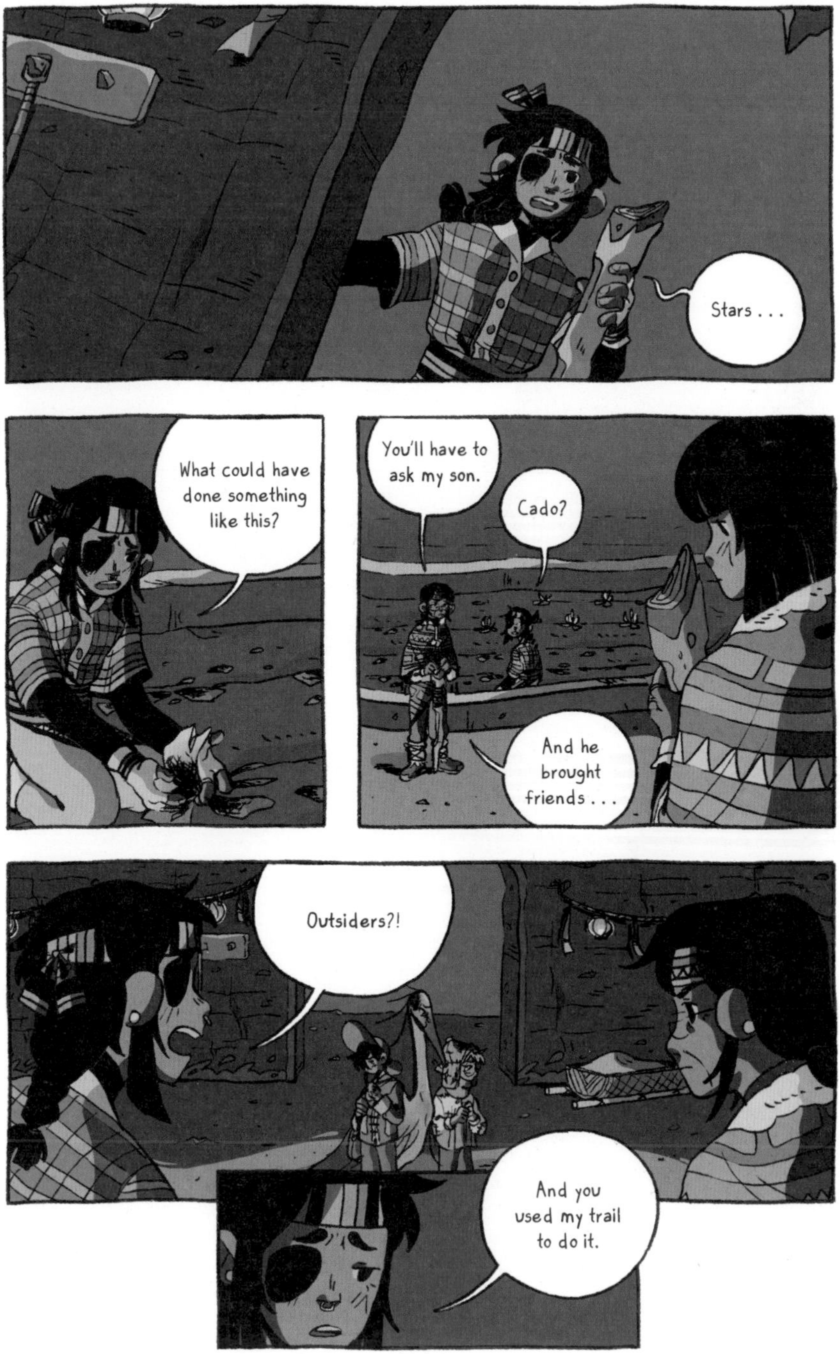
Stars . . .
What could have done something like this?
You'll have to ask my son.
Cado?
And he brought friends . . .
Outsiders?!
And you used my trail to do it.

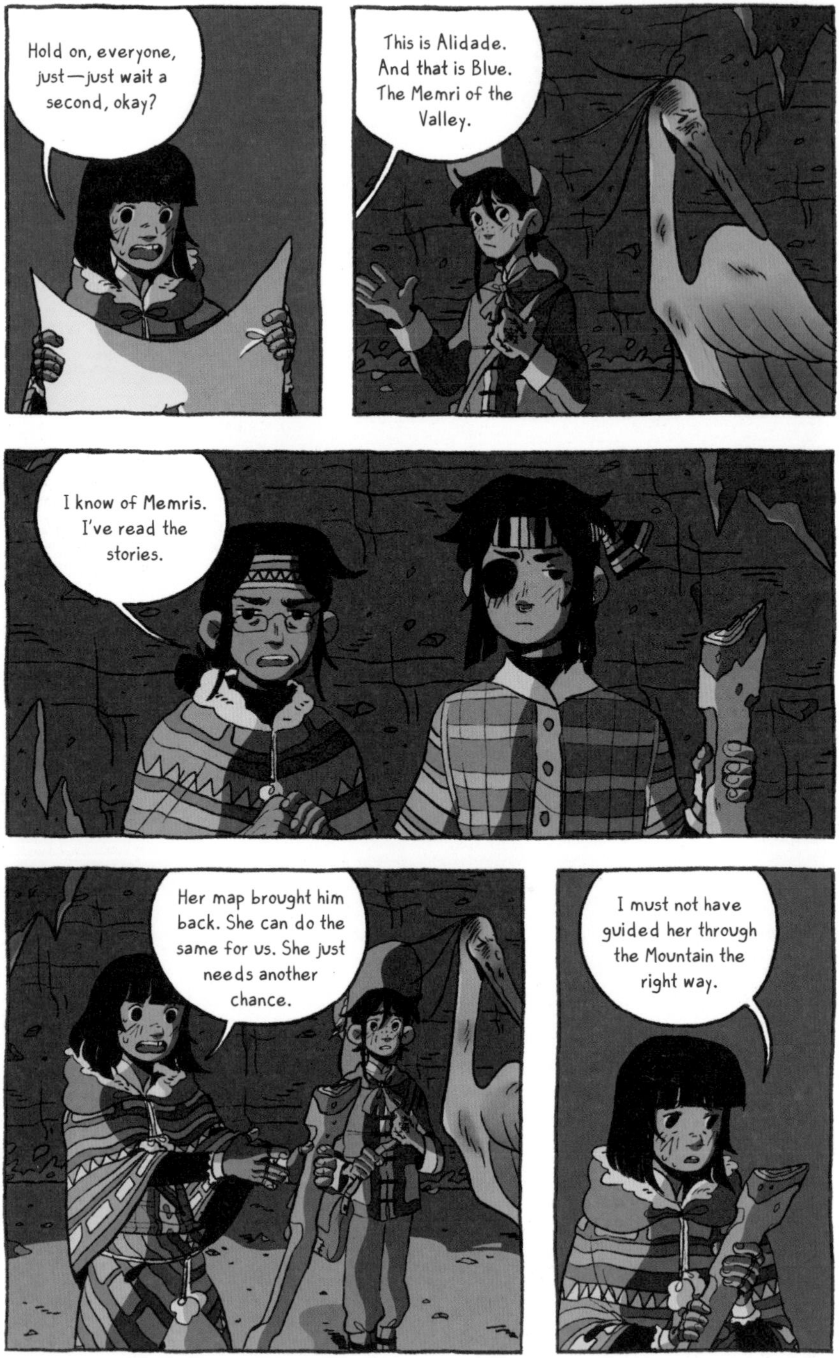
Hold on, everyone, just—just wait a second, okay?
This is Alidade. And that is Blue. The Memri of the Valley.
I know of Memris. I've read the stories.
Her map brought him back. She can do the same for us. She just needs another chance.
I must not have guided her through the Mountain the right way.

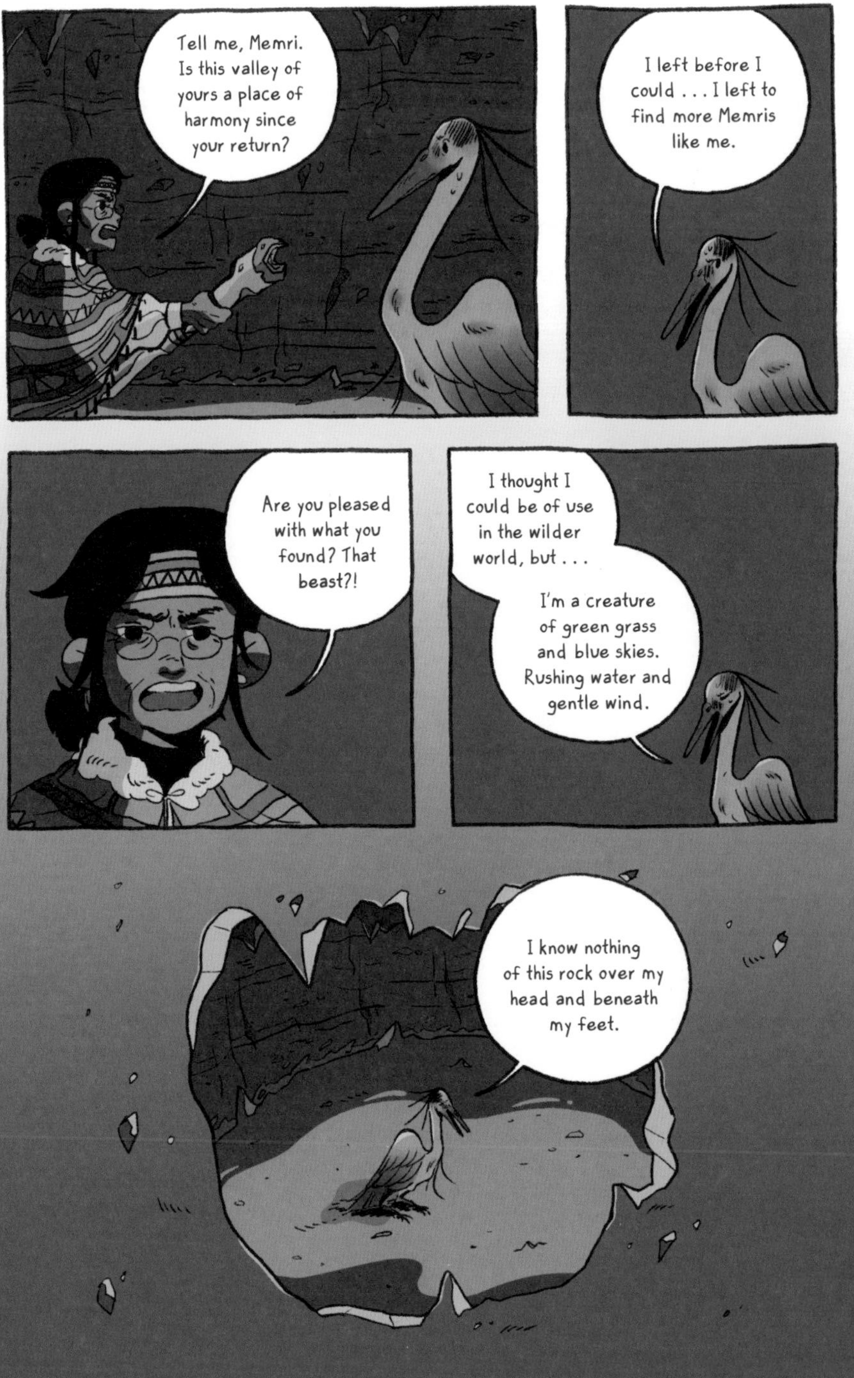
Tell me, Memri. Is this valley of yours a place of harmony since your return?
I left before I could . . . I left to find more Memris like me.
Are you pleased with what you found? That beast?!
I thought I could be of use in the wilder world, but . . .
I'm a creature of green grass and blue skies. Rushing water and gentle wind.
I know nothing of this rock over my head and beneath my feet.

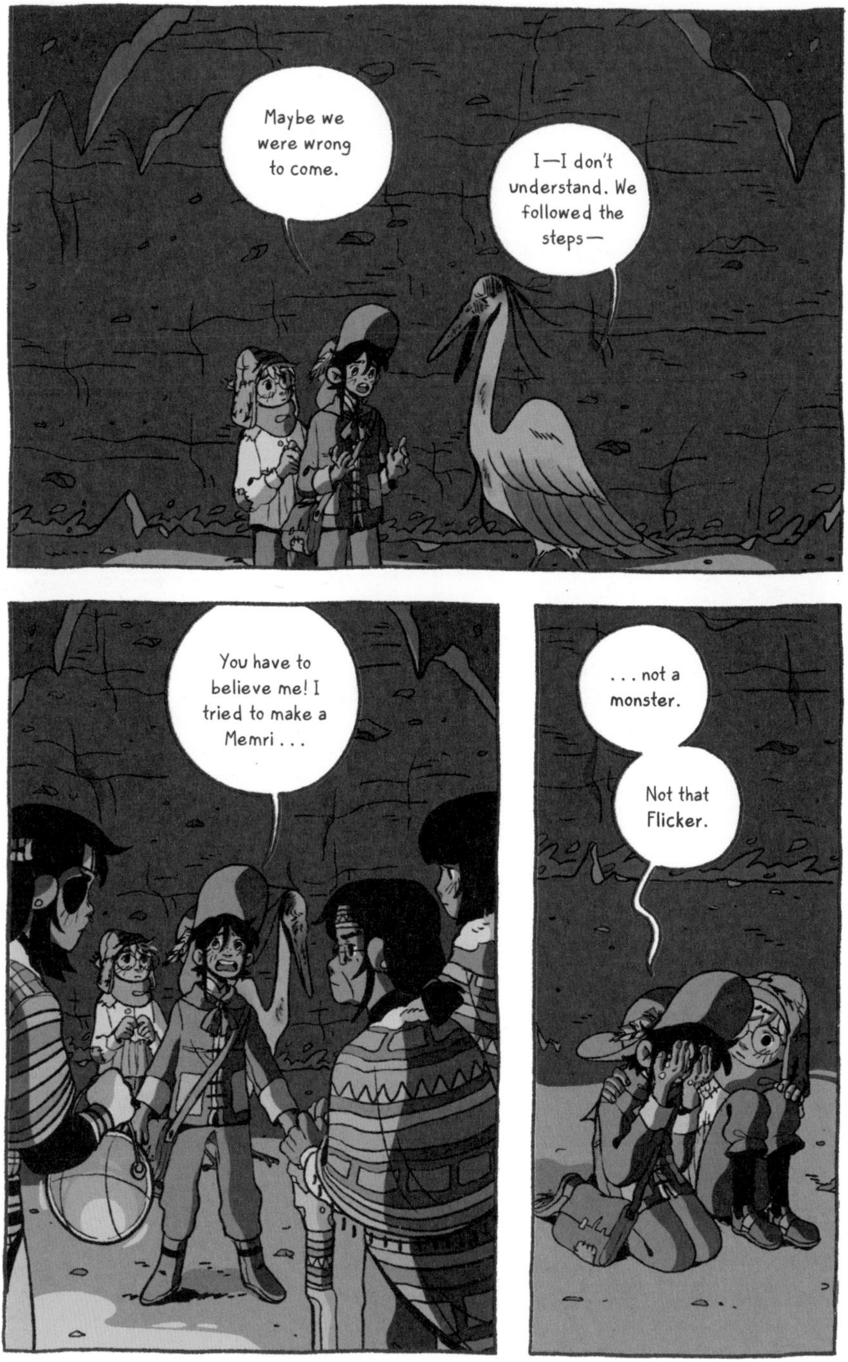
Maybe we were wrong to come.
I—I don't understand. We followed the steps—
You have to believe me! I tried to make a Memri . . .
. . . not a monster.
Not that Flicker.

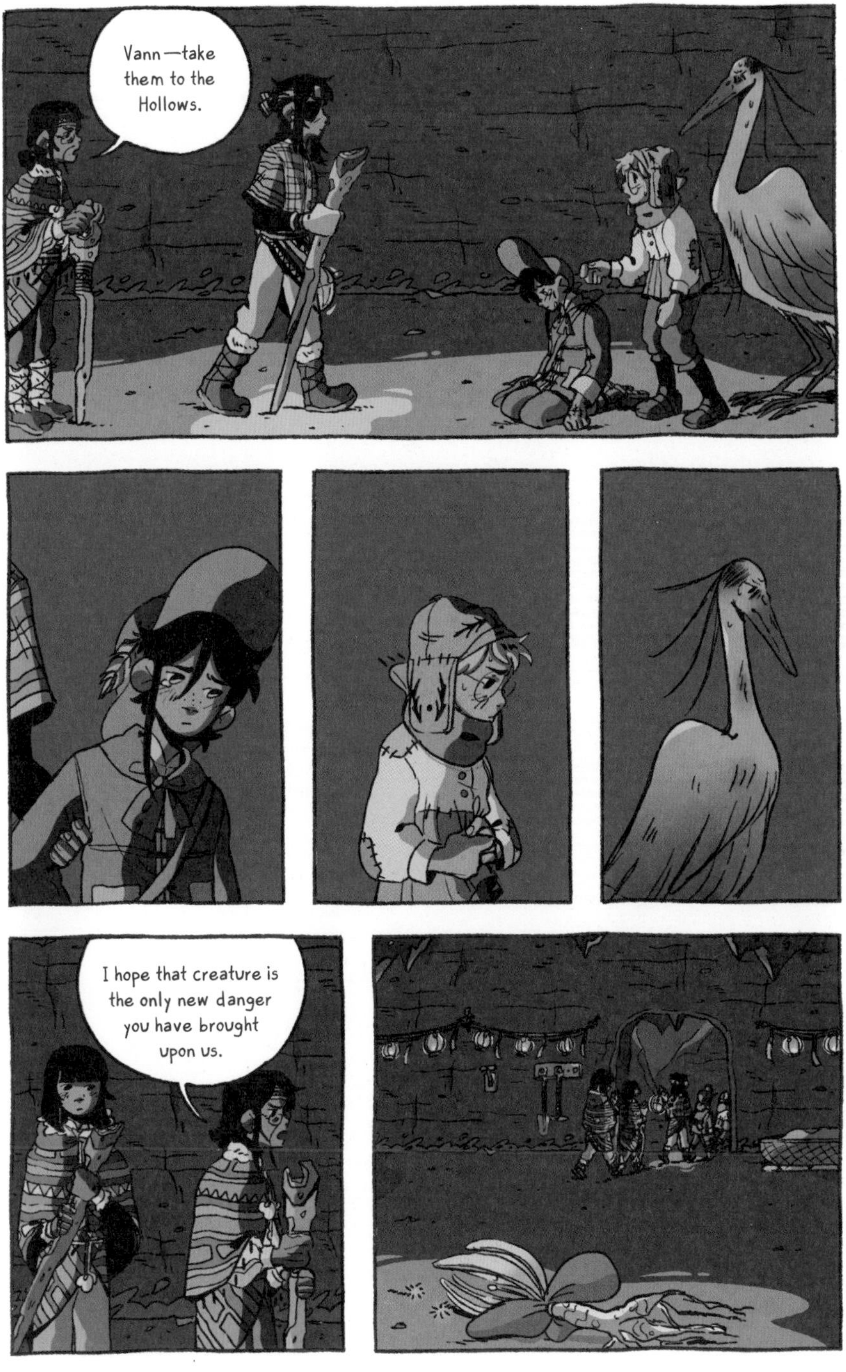

Vann—take them to the Hollows.
I hope that creature is the only new danger you have brought upon us.

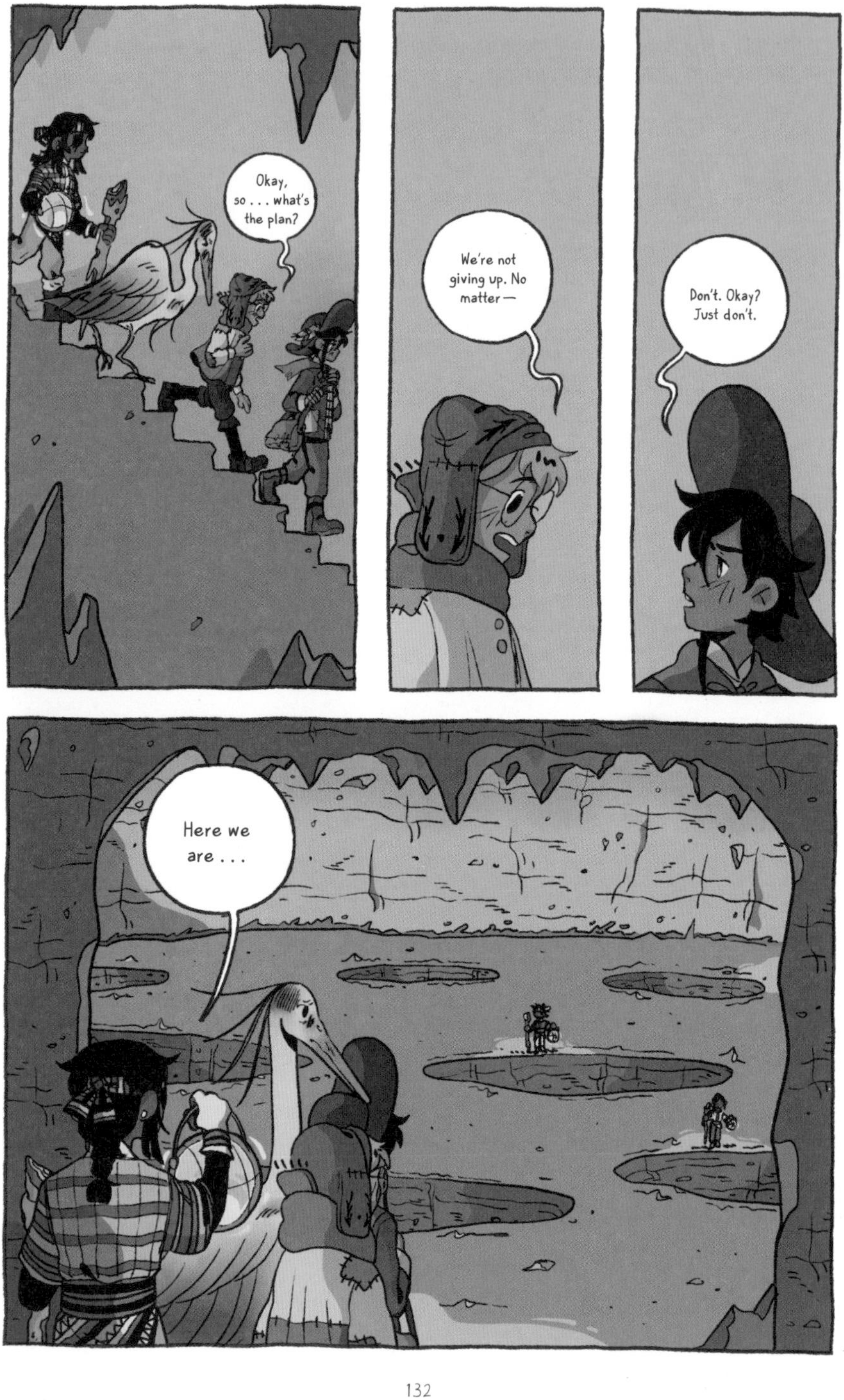
Okay, so . . . what's the plan?
We're not giving up. No matter—
Don't. Okay? Just don't.
Here we are . . .

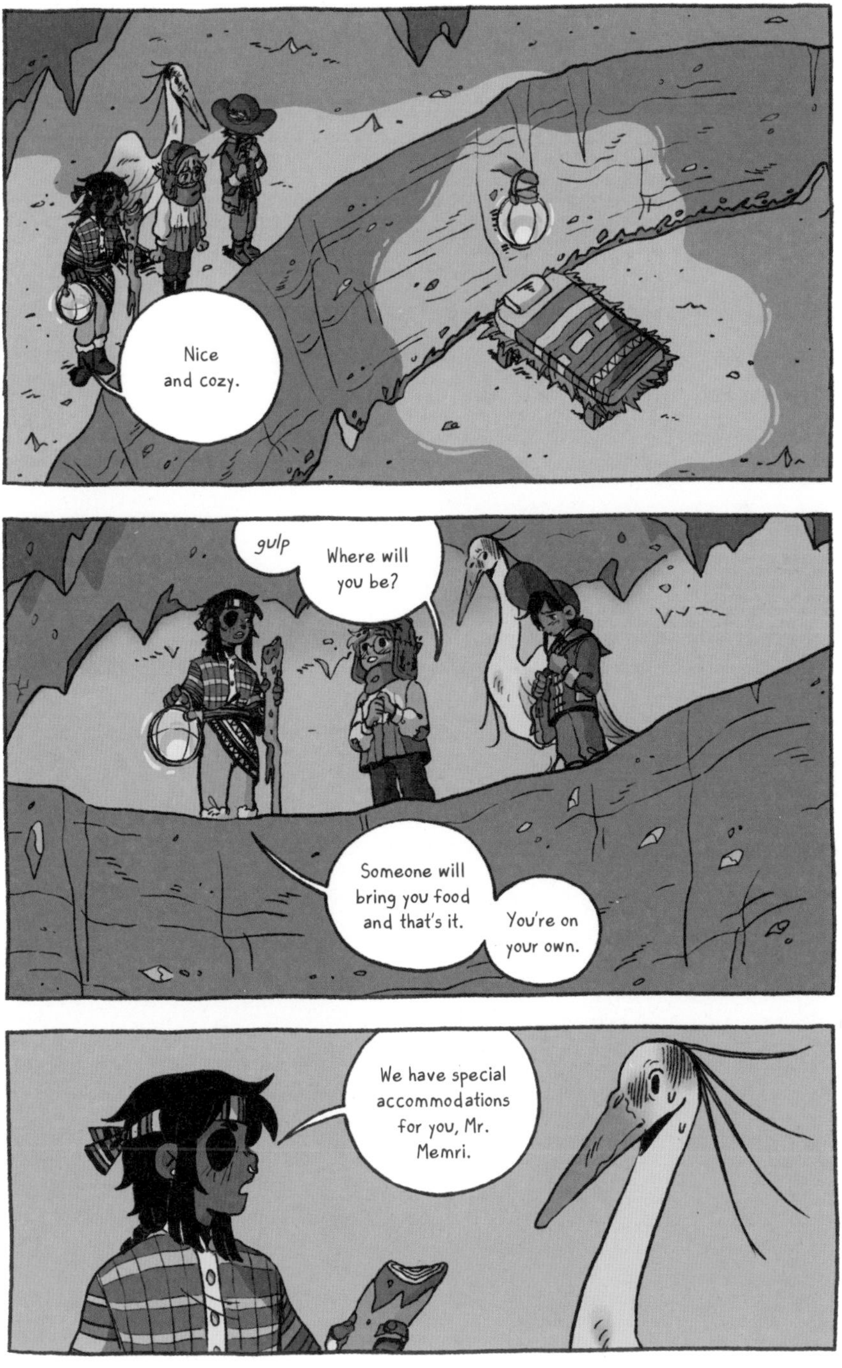
Nice and cozy.
gulp
Where will you be?
Someone will bring you food and that's it.
You're on your own.
We have special accommodations for you, Mr. Memri.

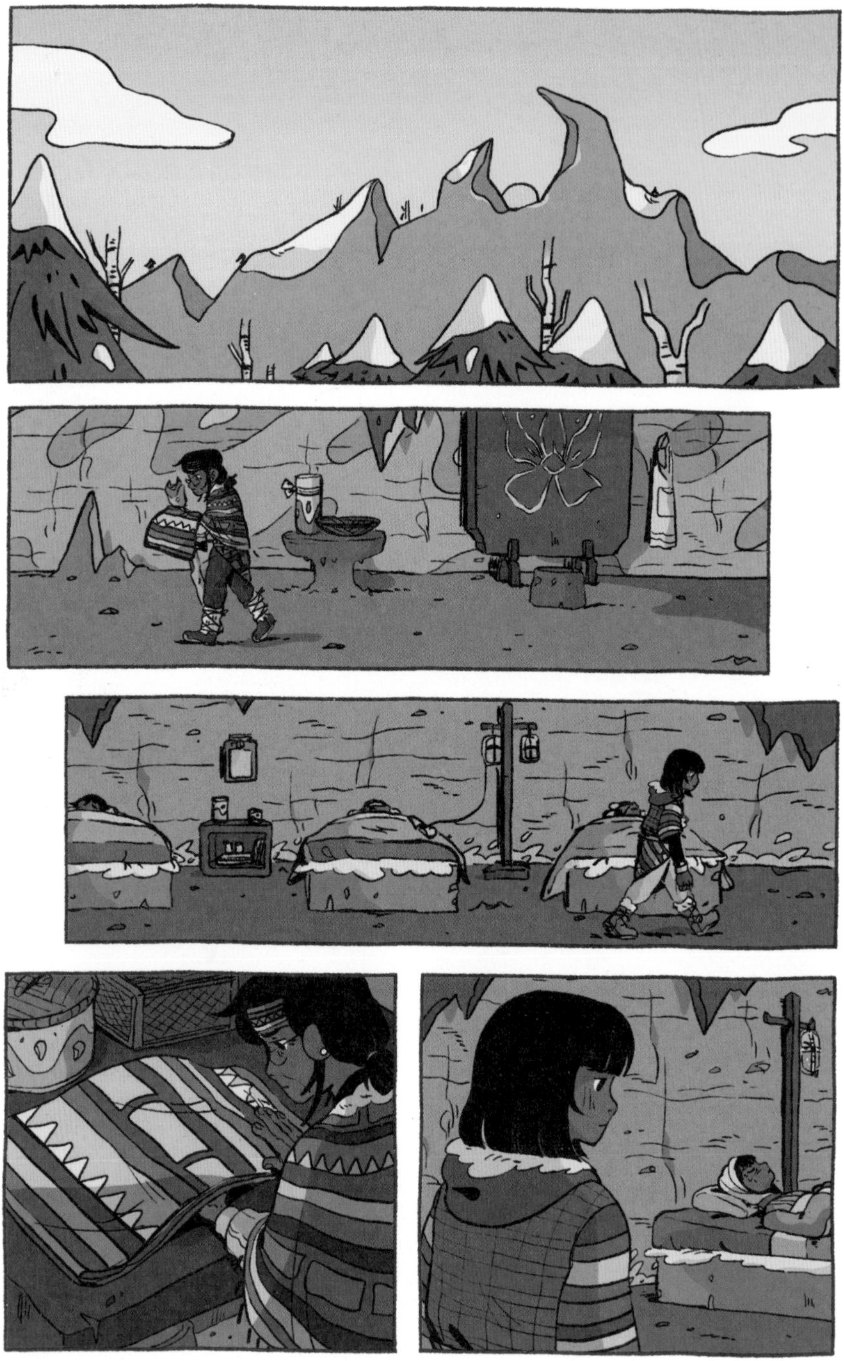

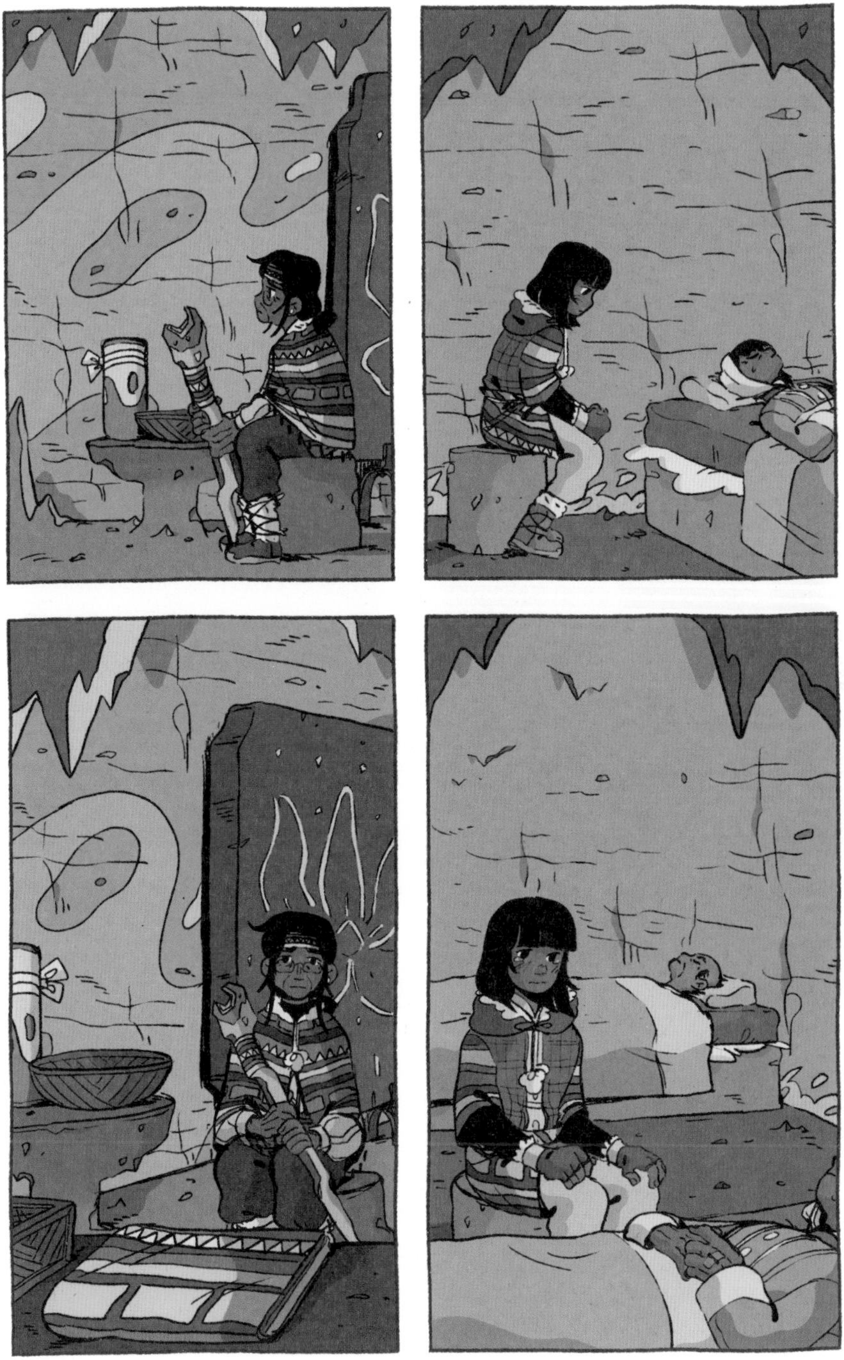

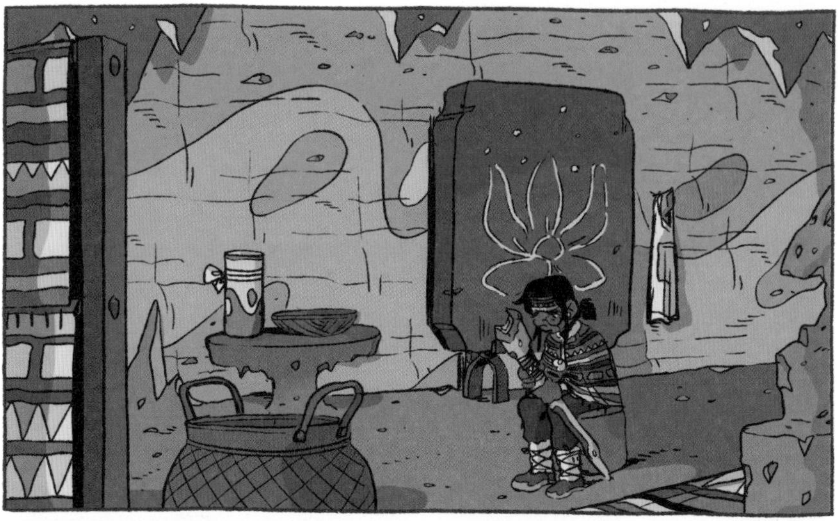

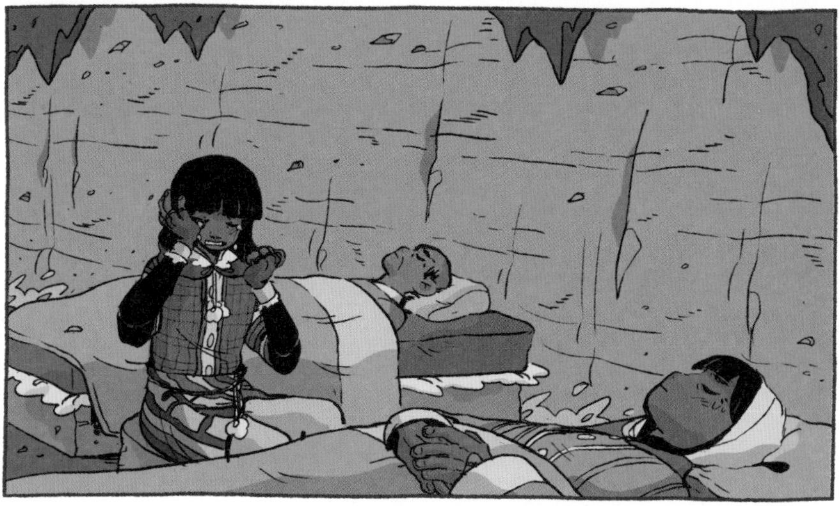

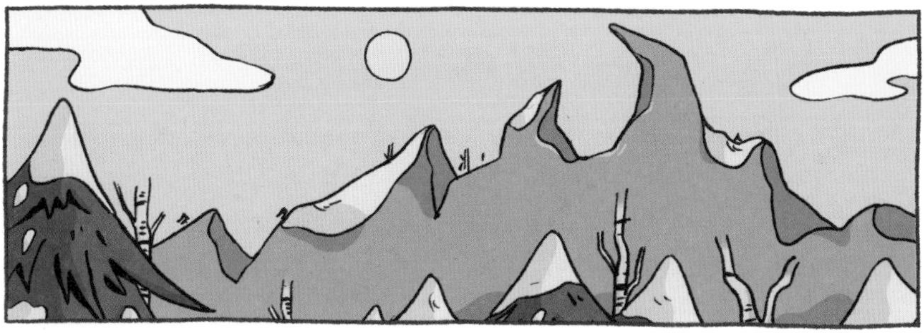

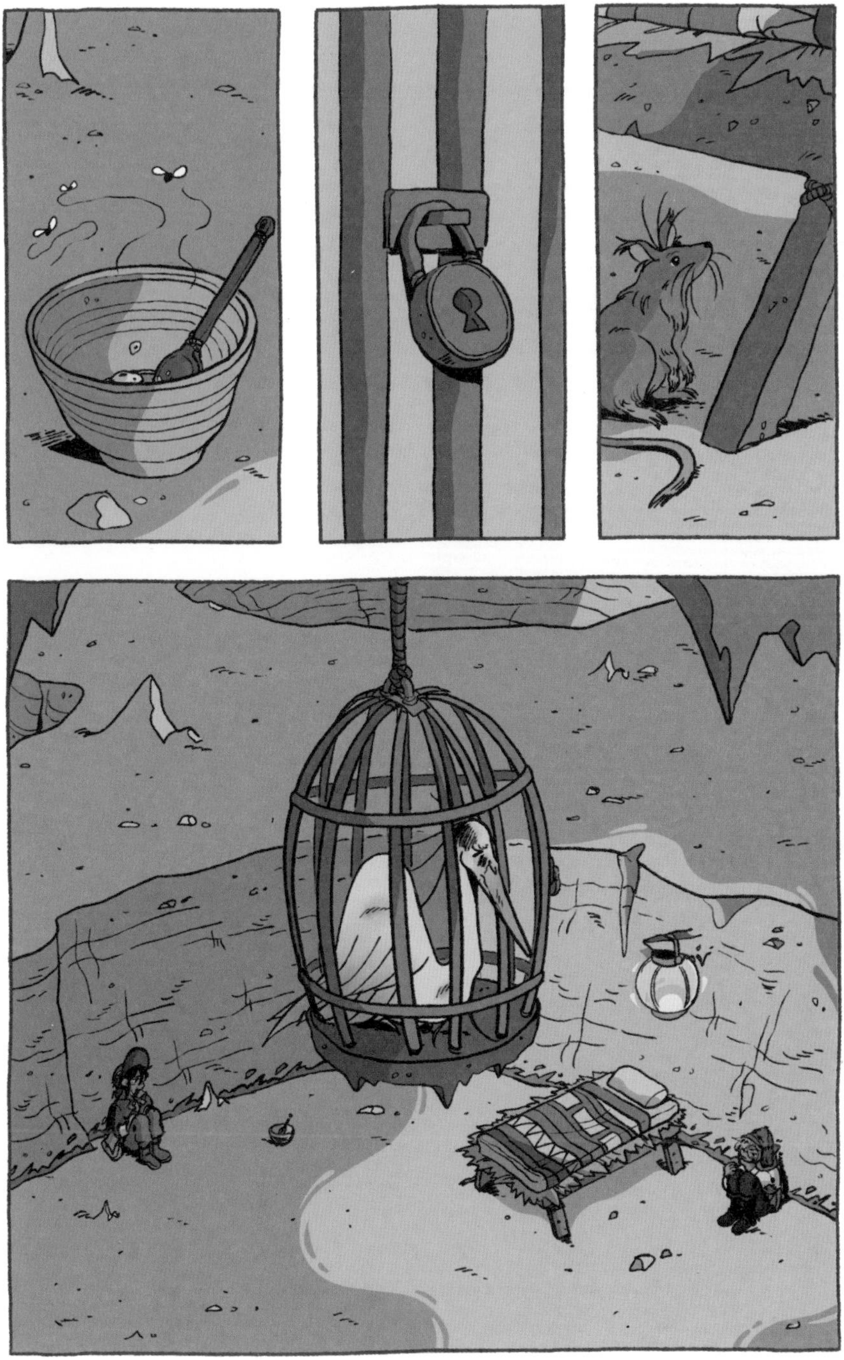

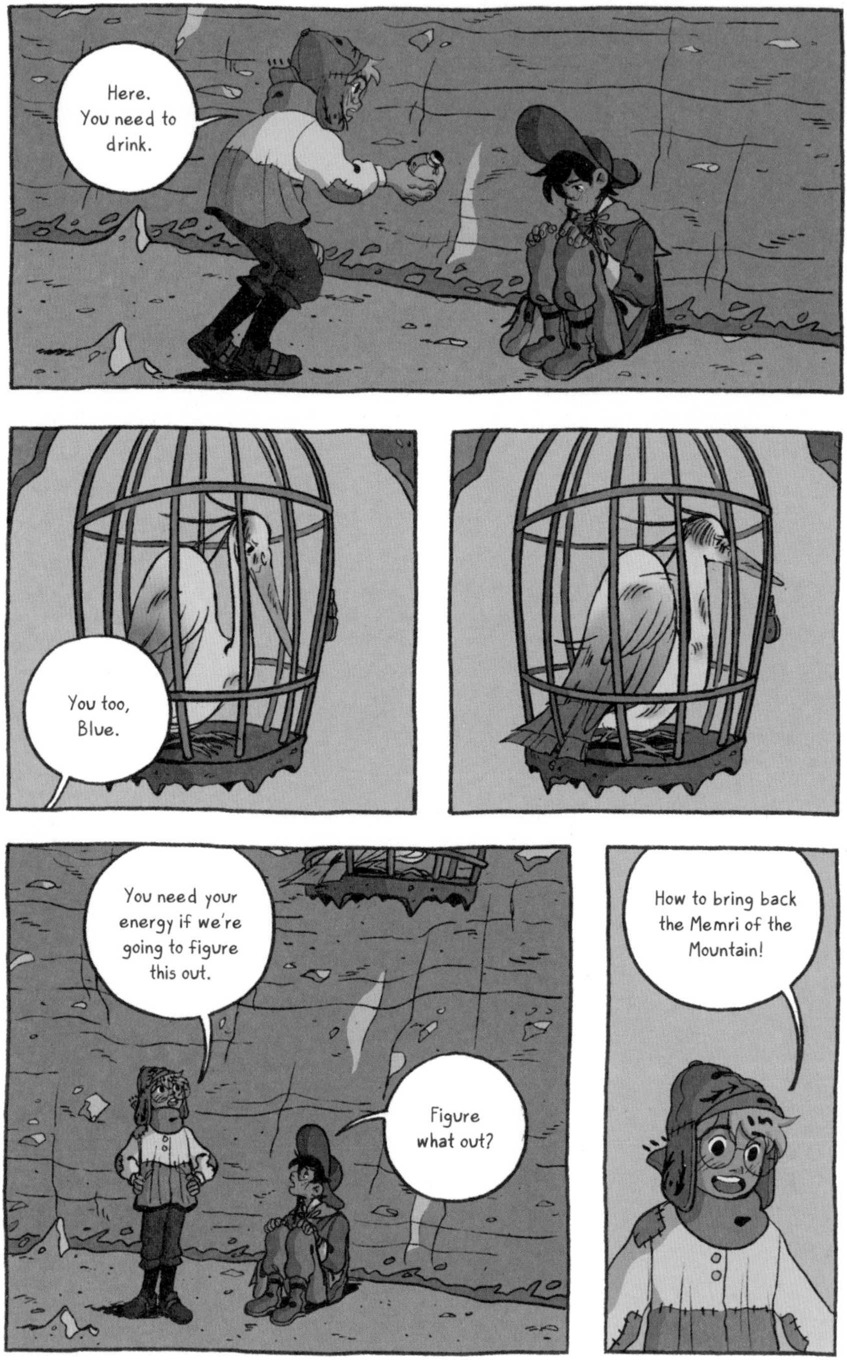
Here. You need to drink.
You too, Blue.
You need your energy if we're going to figure this out.
Figure what out?
How to bring back the Memri of the Mountain!

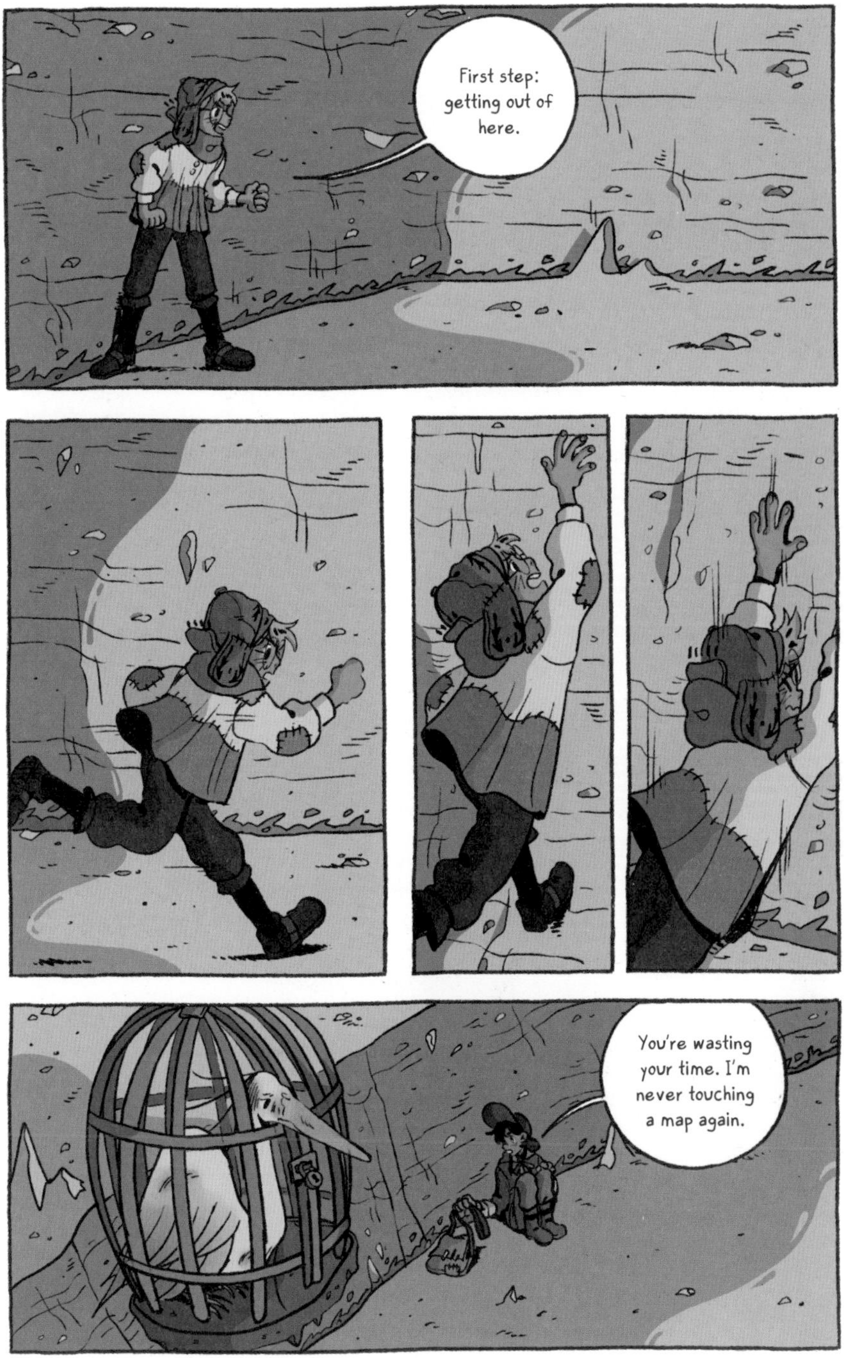
First step: getting out of here.
You're wasting your time. I'm never touching a map again.

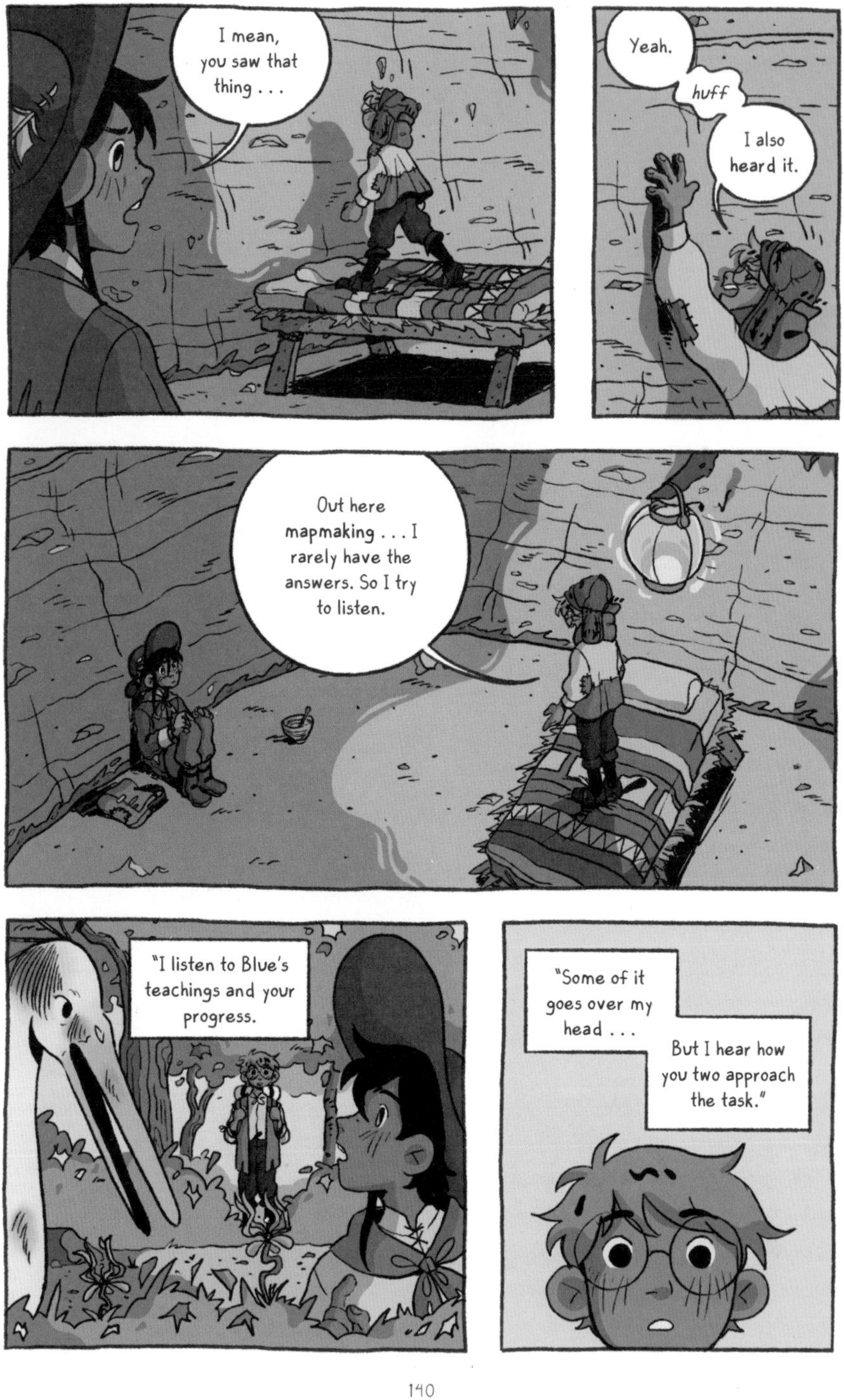
I mean, you saw that thing . . .
Yeah.
huff
I also heard it.
Out here mapmaking . . . I rarely have the answers. So I try to listen.
"I listen to Blue's teachings and your progress.
"Some of it goes over my head . . .
But I hear how you two approach the task."

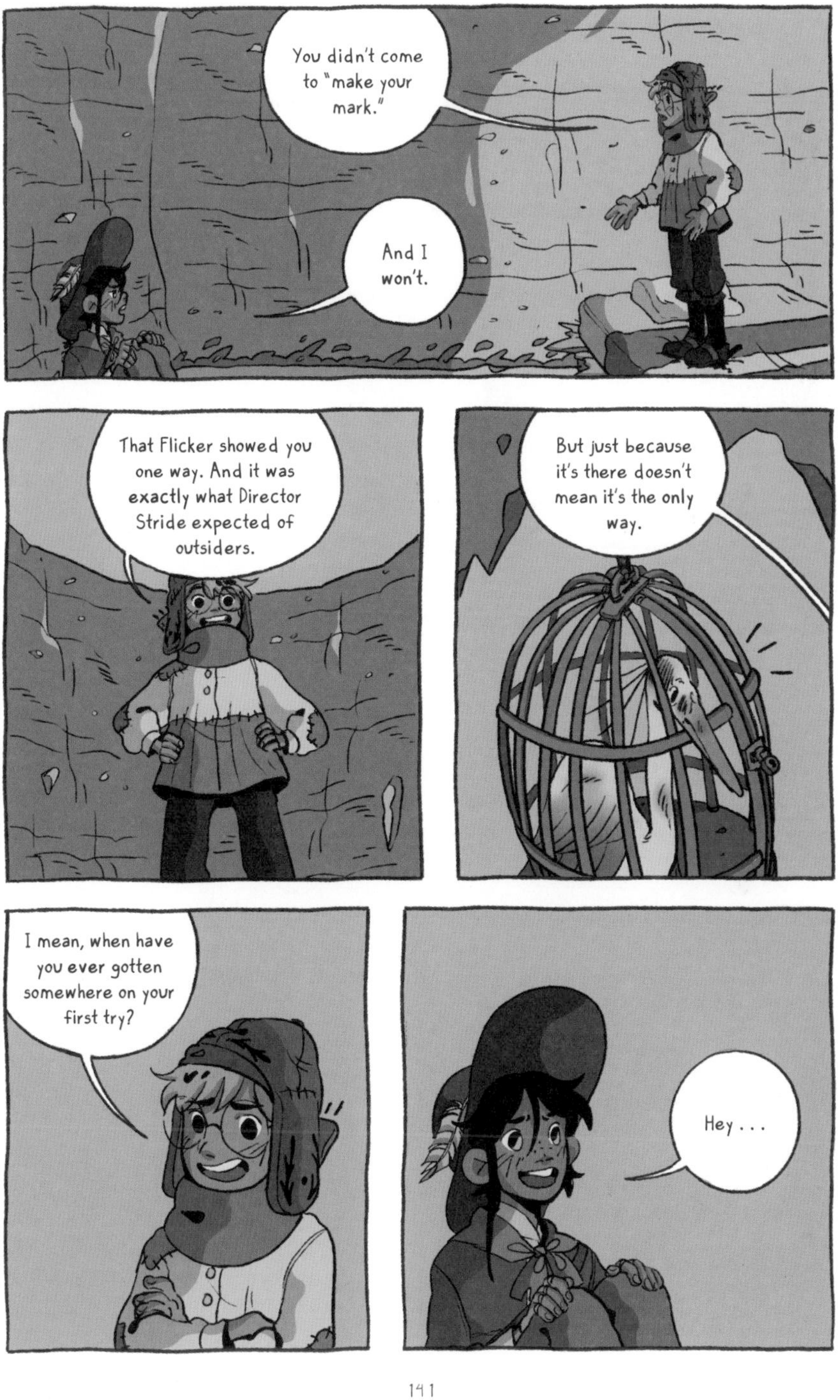
You didn't come to "make your mark."
And I won't.
That Flicker showed you one way. And it was exactly what Director Stride expected of outsiders.
But just because it's there doesn't mean it's the only way.
I mean, when have you ever gotten somewhere on your first try?
Hey . . .

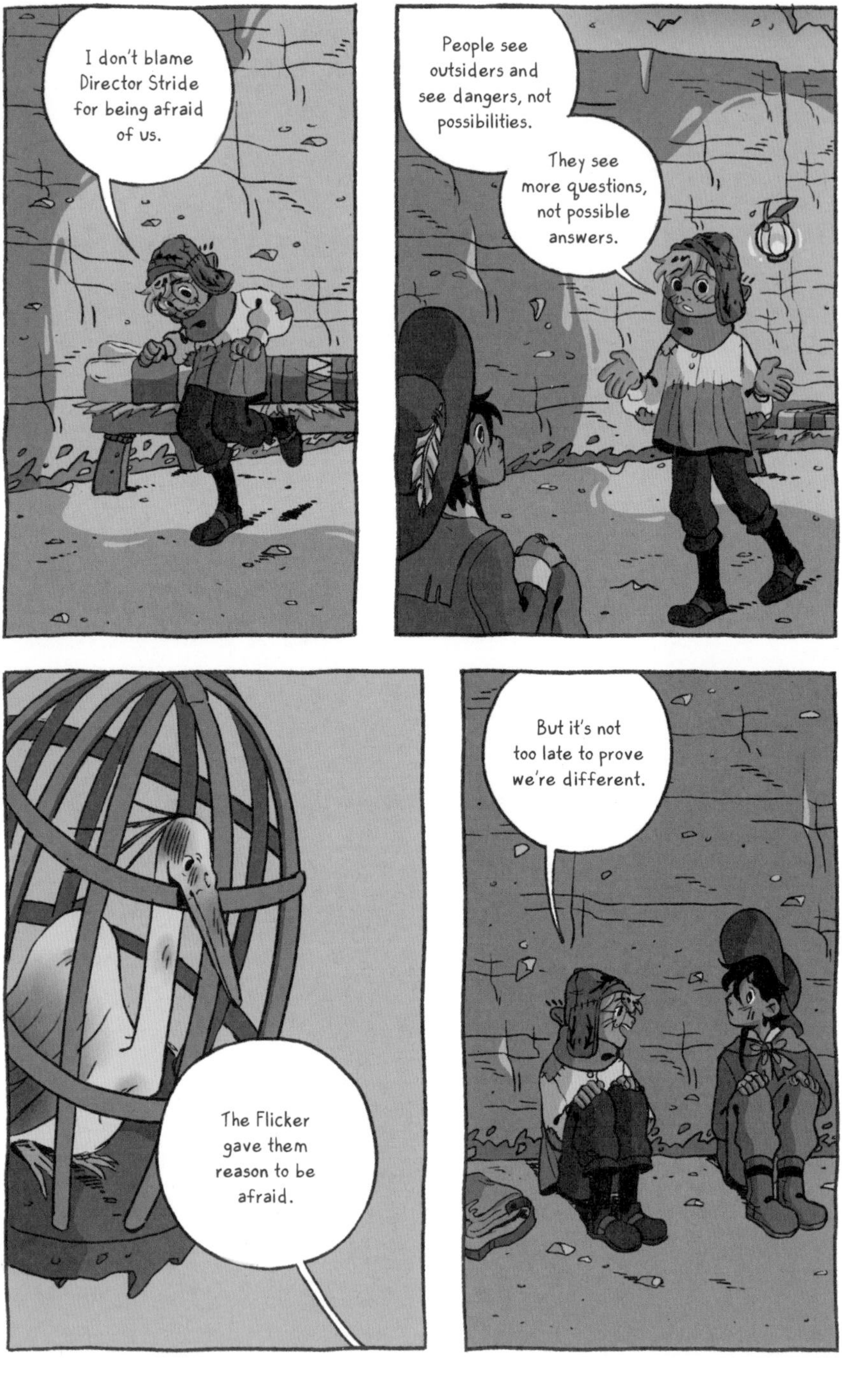
I don't blame Director Stride for being afraid of us.
People see outsiders and see dangers, not possibilities.
They see more questions, not possible answers.
The Flicker gave them reason to be afraid.
But it's not too late to prove we're different.

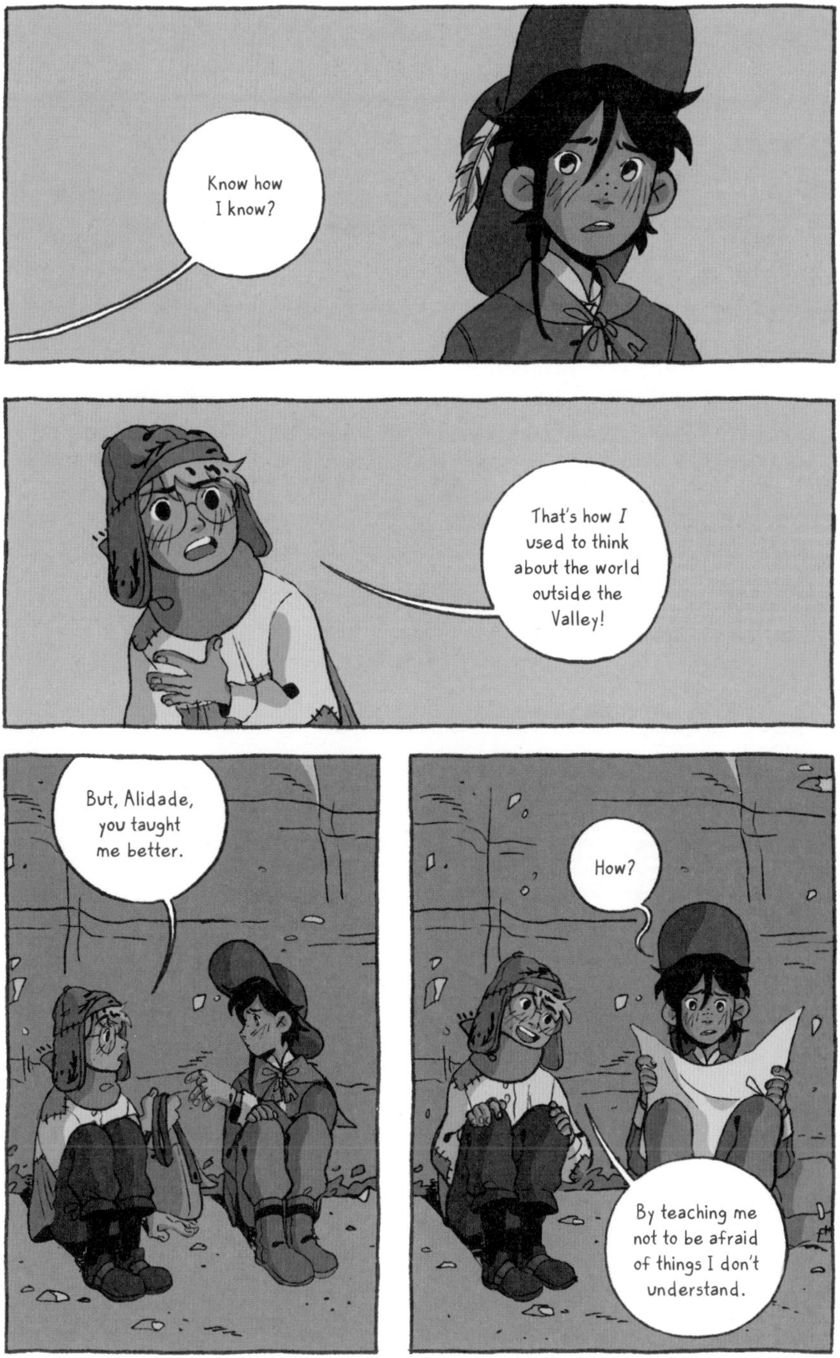
Know how I know?
That's how *I* used to think about the world outside the Valley!
But, Alidade, you taught me better.
How?
By teaching me not to be afraid of things I don't understand.

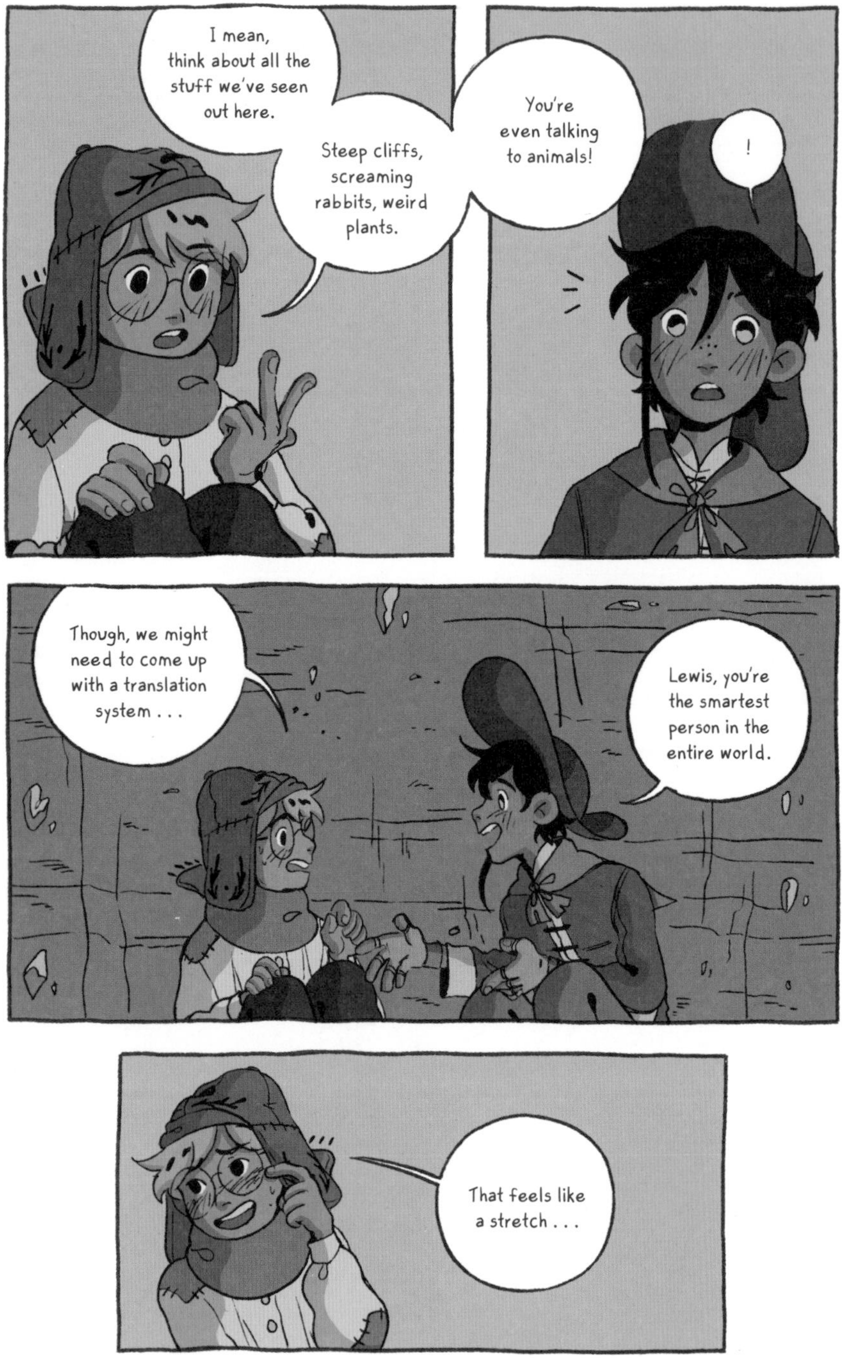
I mean, think about all the stuff we've seen out here.
Steep cliffs, screaming rabbits, weird plants.
You're even talking to animals!
!
Though, we might need to come up with a translation system . . .
Lewis, you're the smartest person in the entire world.
That feels like a stretch . . .

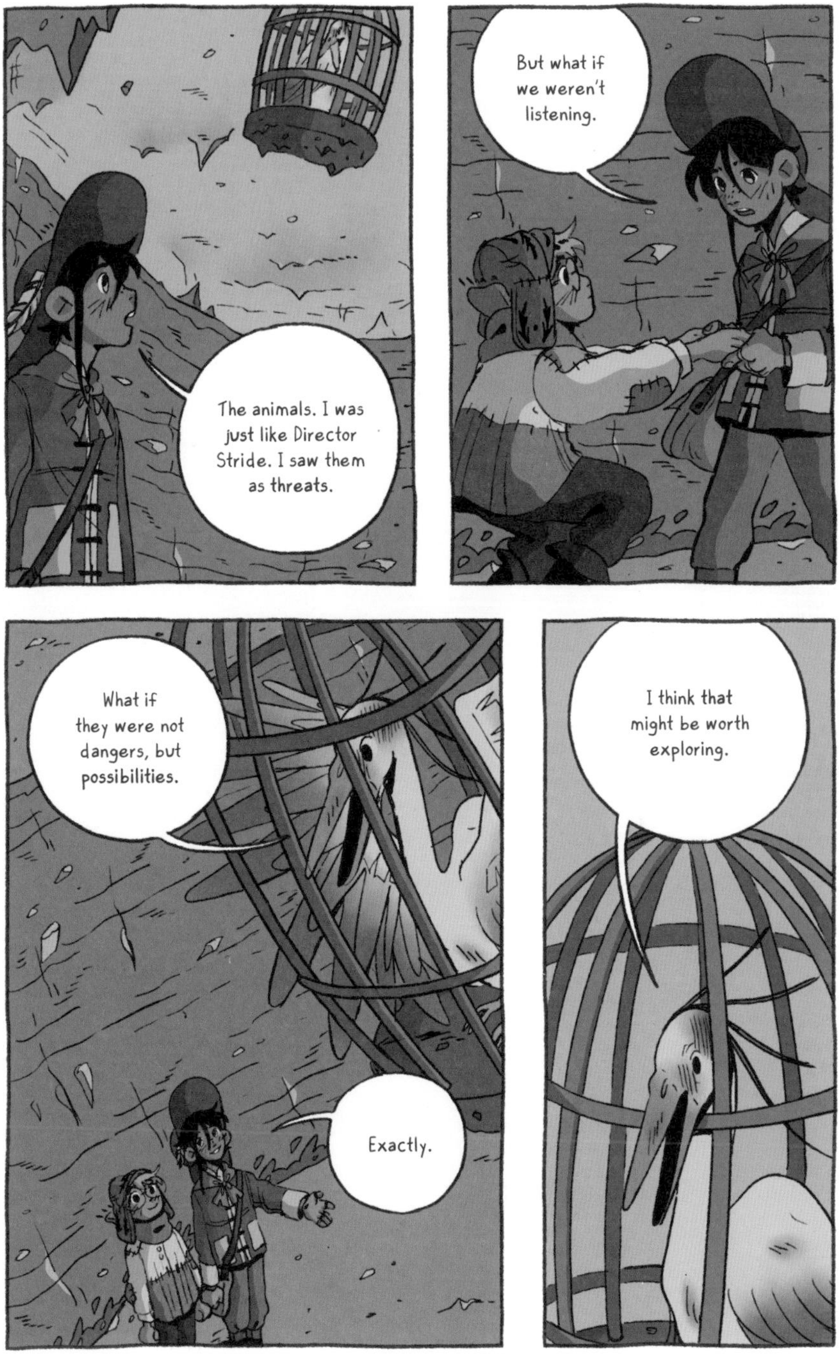
The animals. I was just like Director Stride. I saw them as threats.
But what if we weren't listening.
What if they were not dangers, but possibilities.
Exactly.
I think that might be worth exploring.

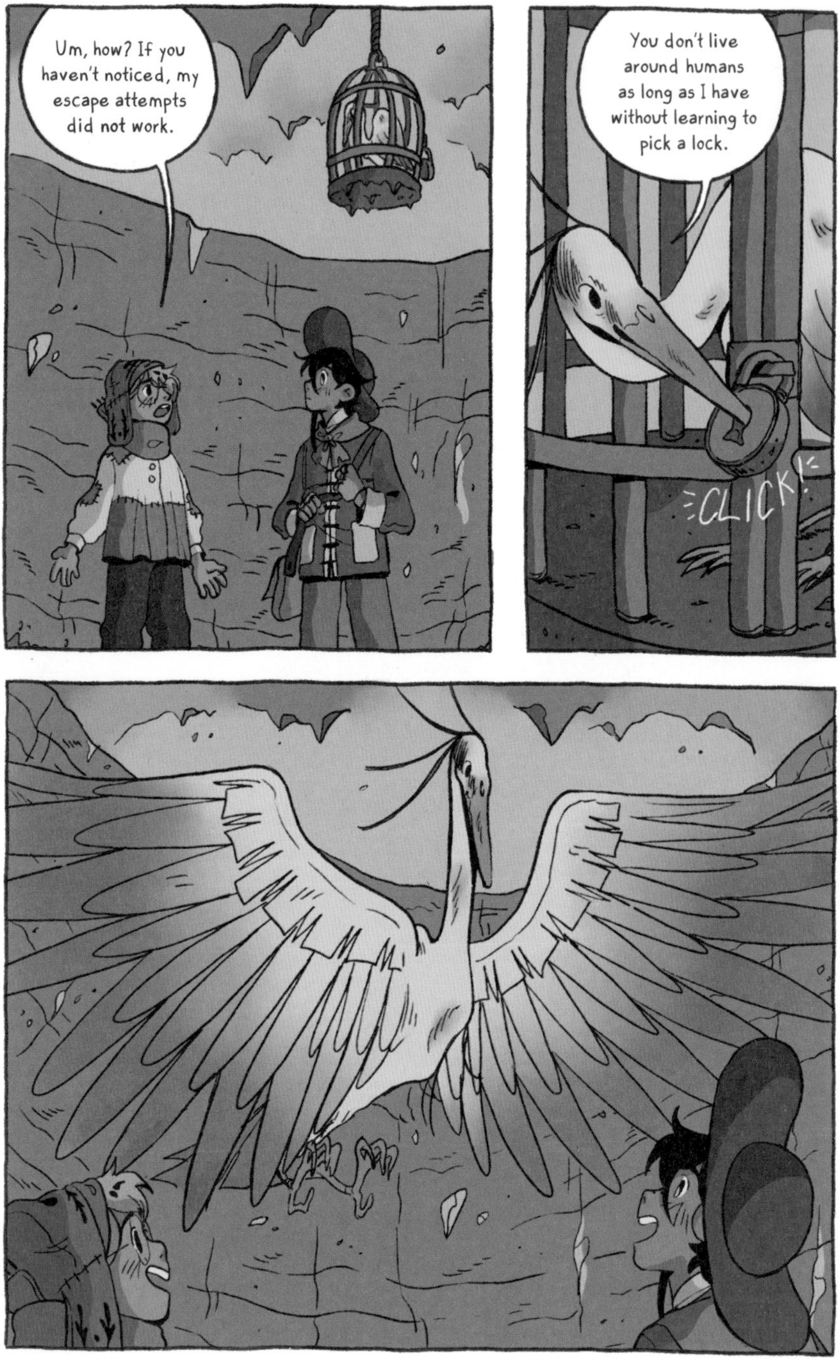
Um, how? If you haven't noticed, my escape attempts did not work.
You don't live around humans as long as I have without learning to pick a lock.
CLICK!

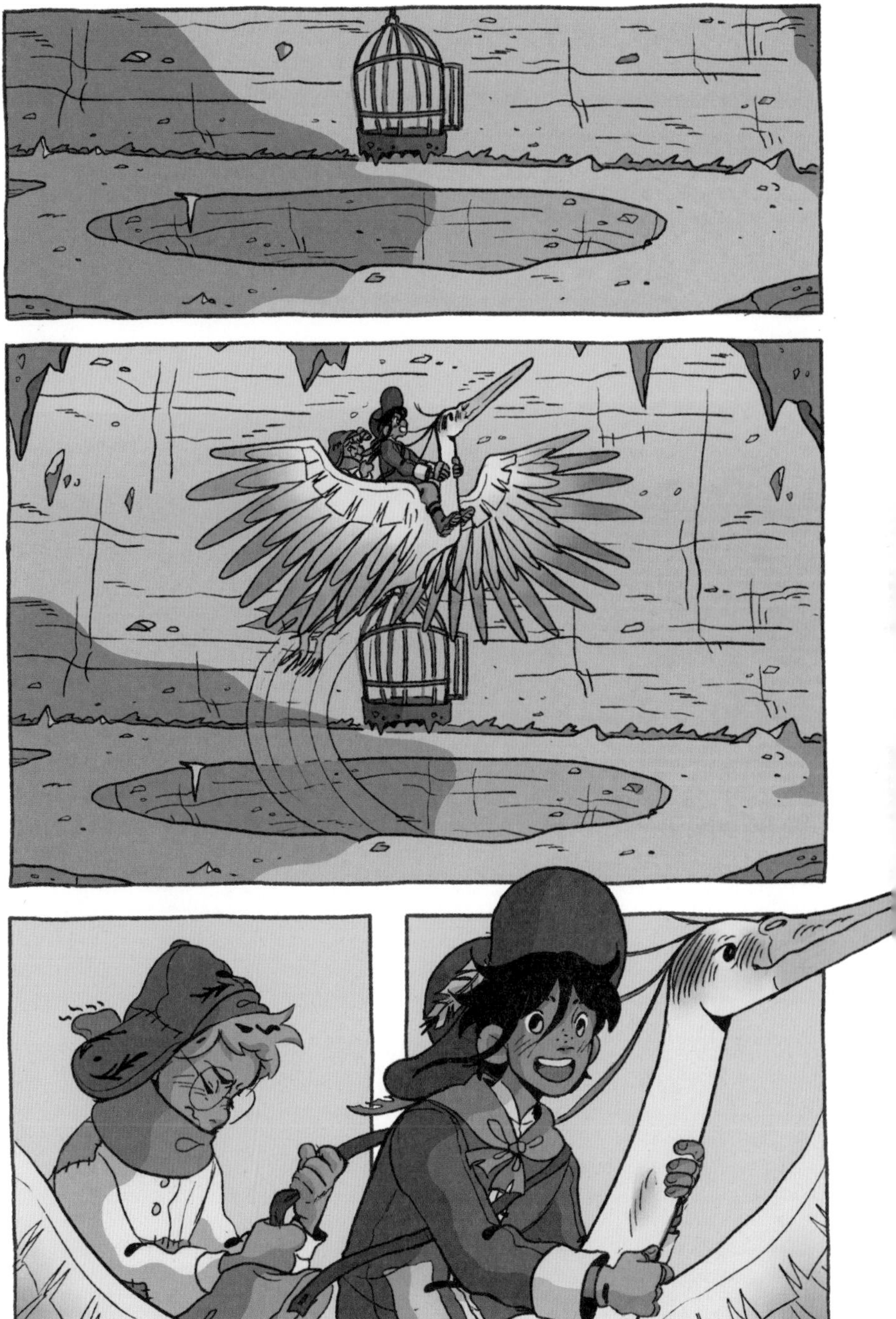

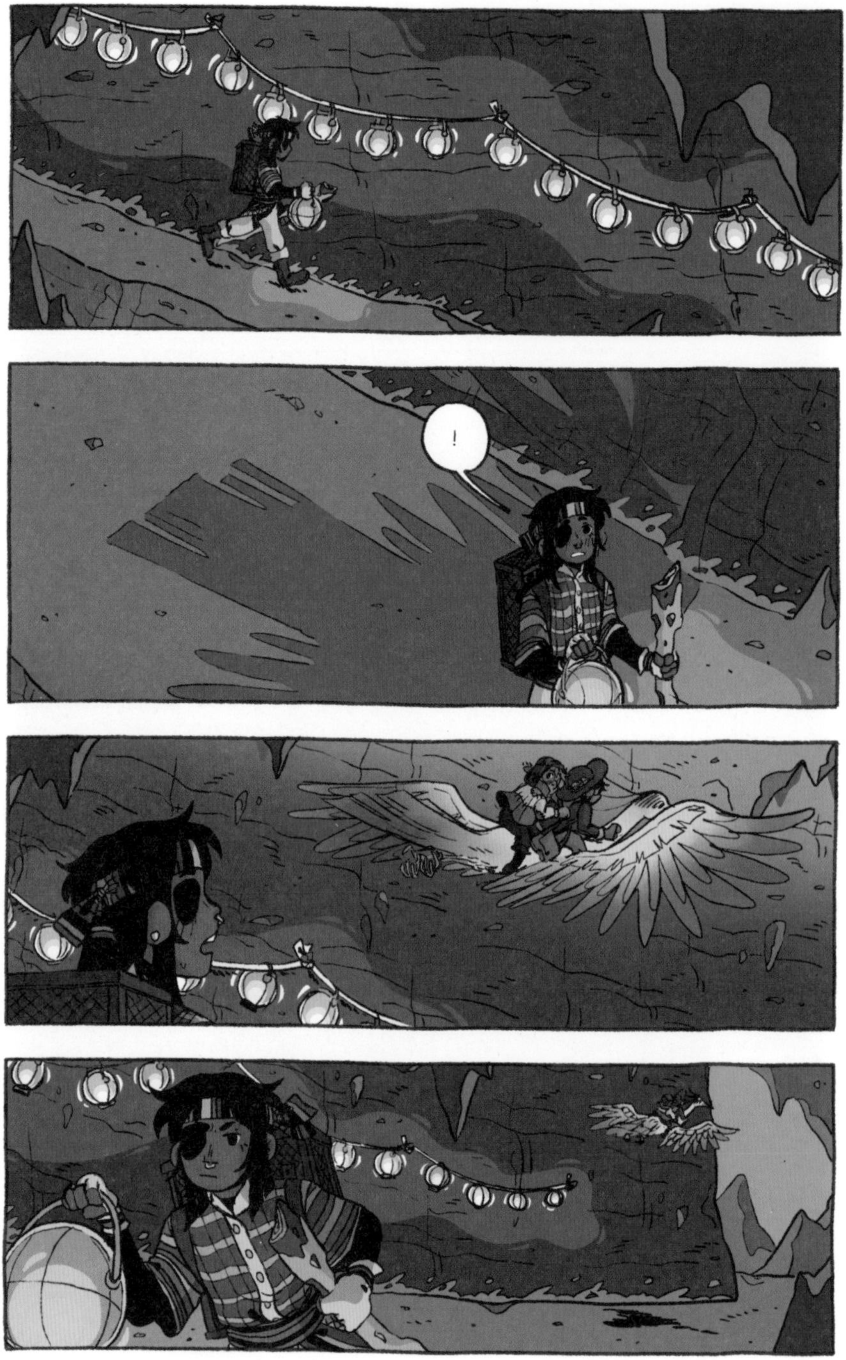
!

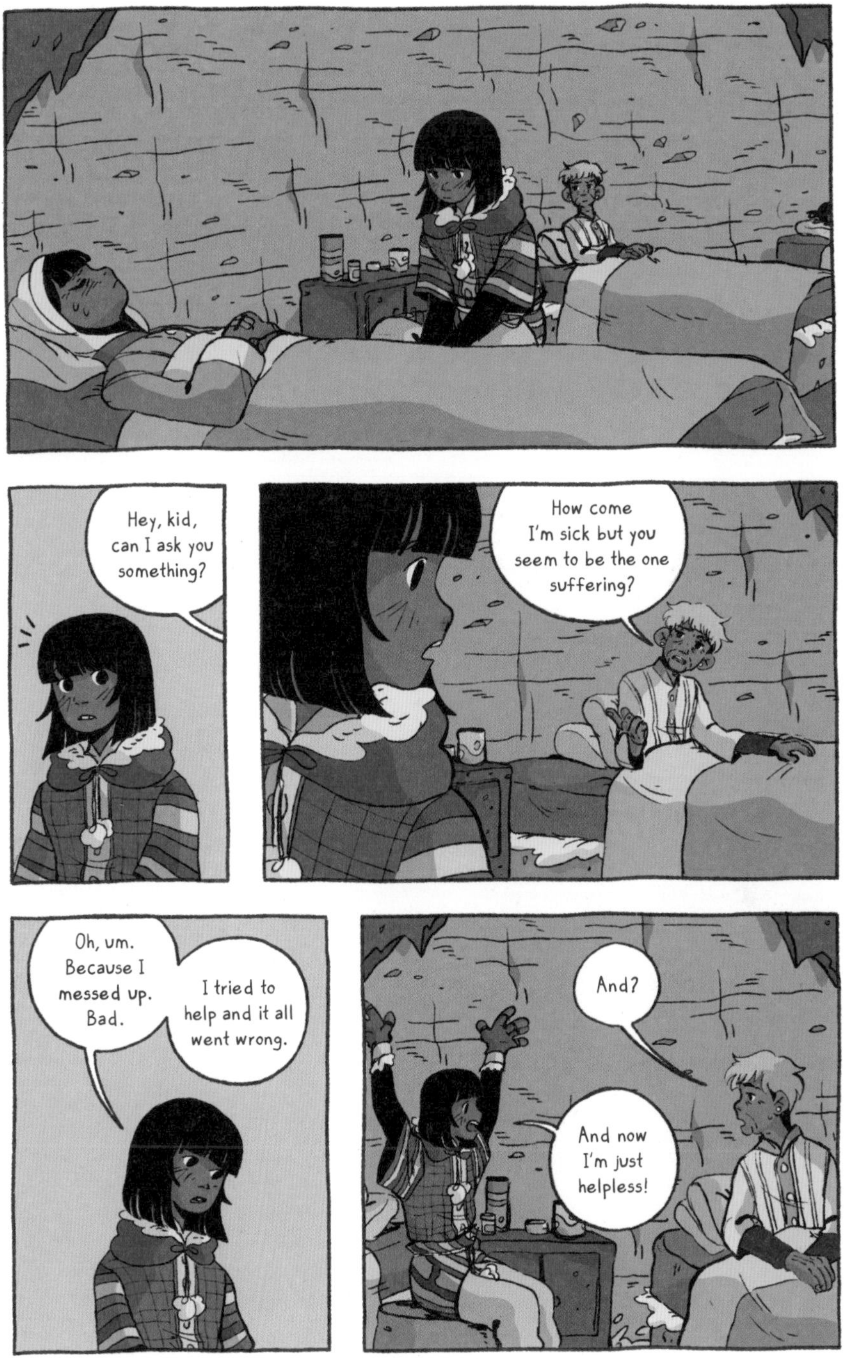
Hey, kid, can I ask you something?
How come I'm sick but you seem to be the one suffering?
Oh, um. Because I messed up. Bad.
I tried to help and it all went wrong.
And?
And now I'm just helpless!

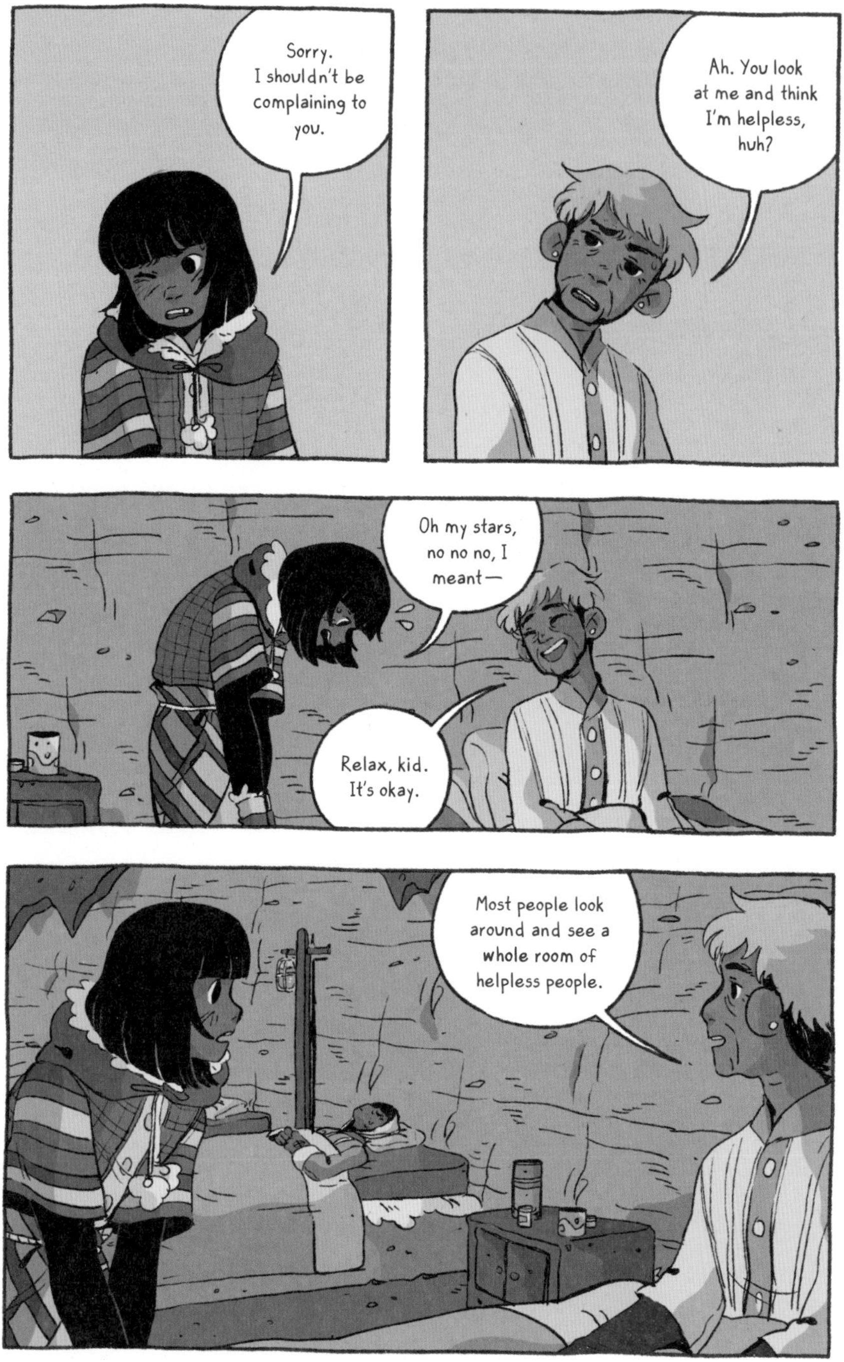
Sorry. I shouldn't be complaining to you.
Ah. You look at me and think I'm helpless, huh?
Oh my stars, no no no, I meant—
Relax, kid. It's okay.
Most people look around and see a whole room of helpless people.

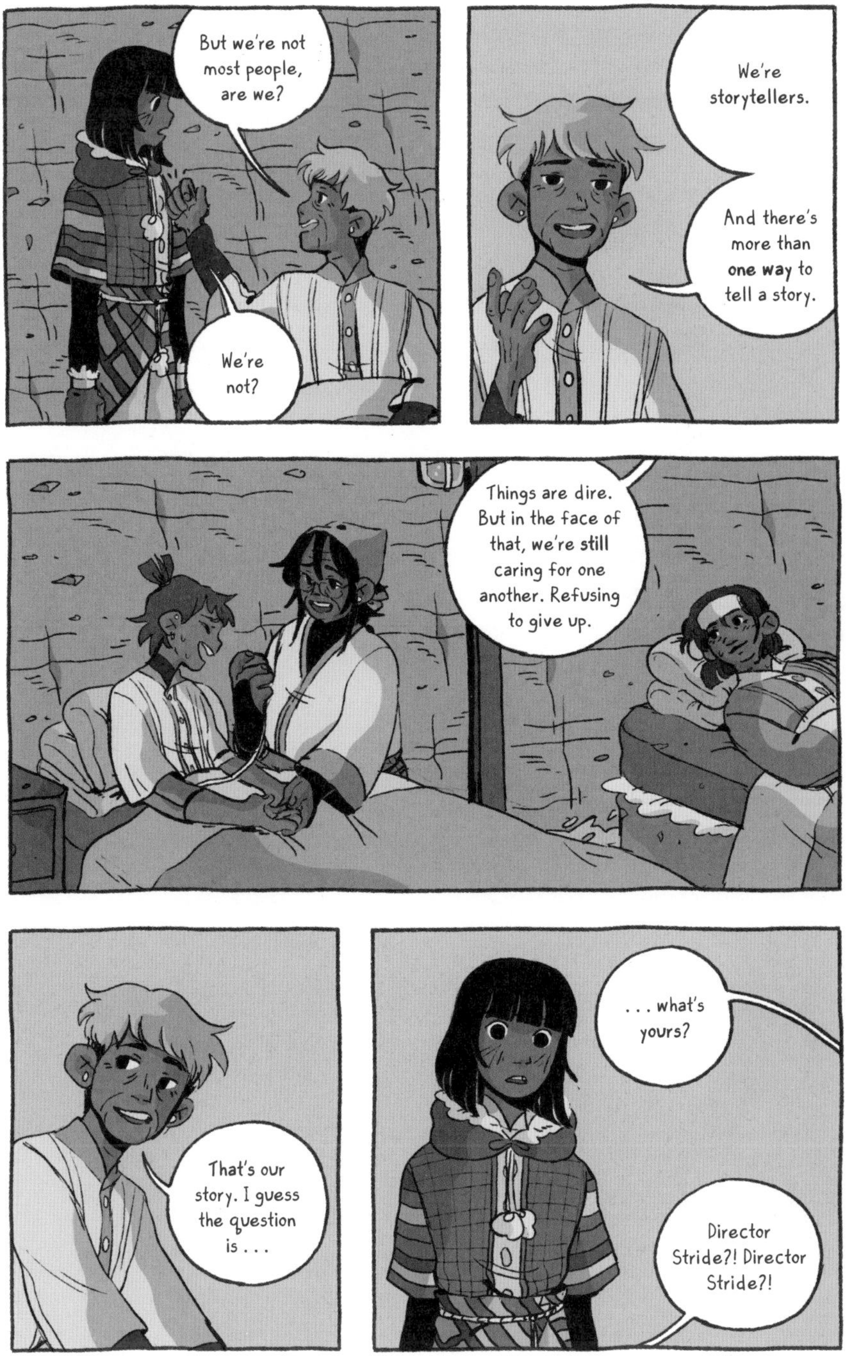
But we're not most people, are we?
We're not?
We're storytellers.
And there's more than **one way** to tell a story.
Things are dire. But in the face of that, we're **still** caring for one another. Refusing to give up.
That's our story. I guess the question is . . .
. . . what's yours?
Director Stride?! Director Stride?!

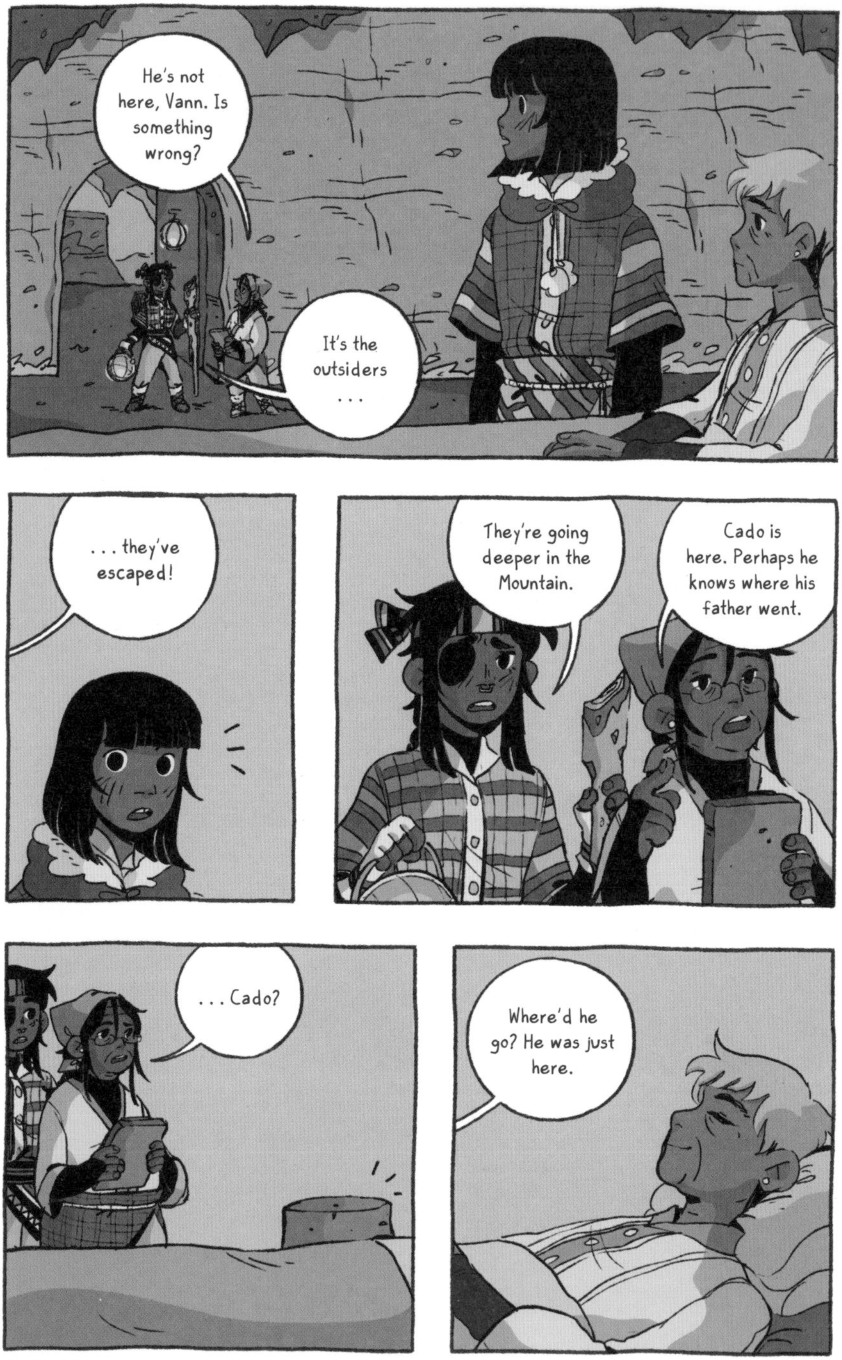
He's not here, Vann. Is something wrong?
It's the outsiders . . .
. . . they've escaped!
They're going deeper in the Mountain.
Cado is here. Perhaps he knows where his father went.
. . . Cado?
Where'd he go? He was just here.

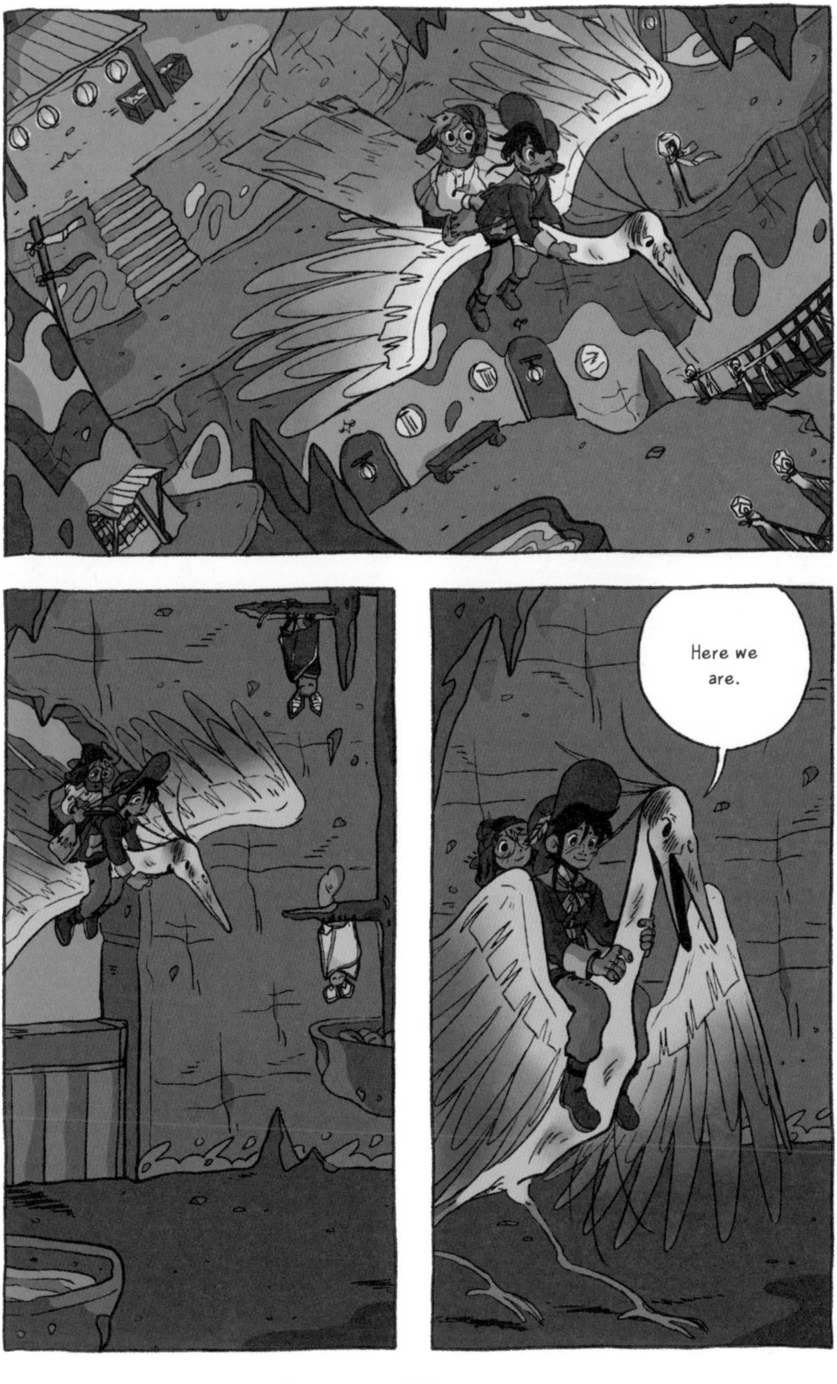
Here we are.

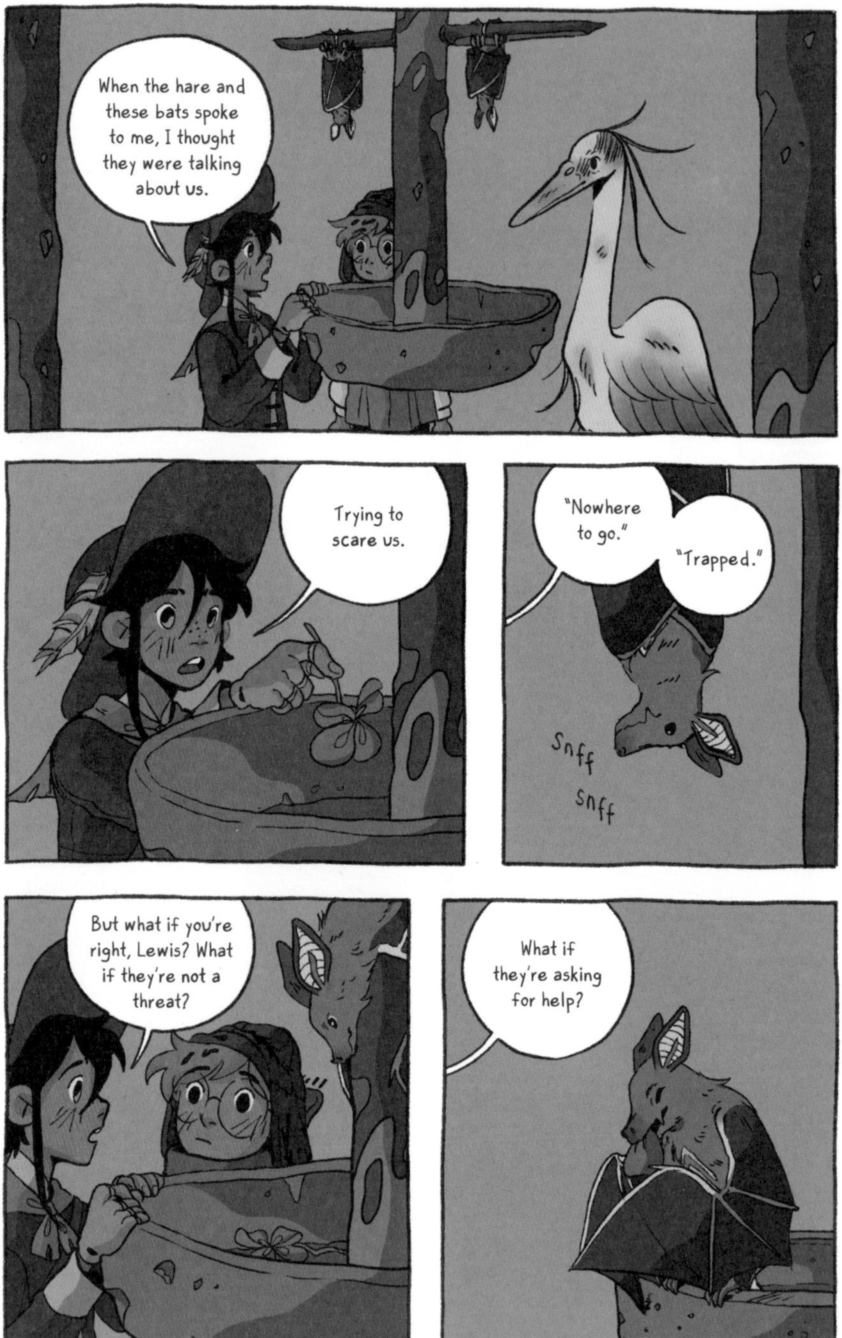
When the hare and these bats spoke to me, I thought they were talking about us.
Trying to scare us.
"Nowhere to go."
"Trapped."
Snff
snff
But what if you're right, Lewis? What if they're not a threat?
What if they're asking for help?

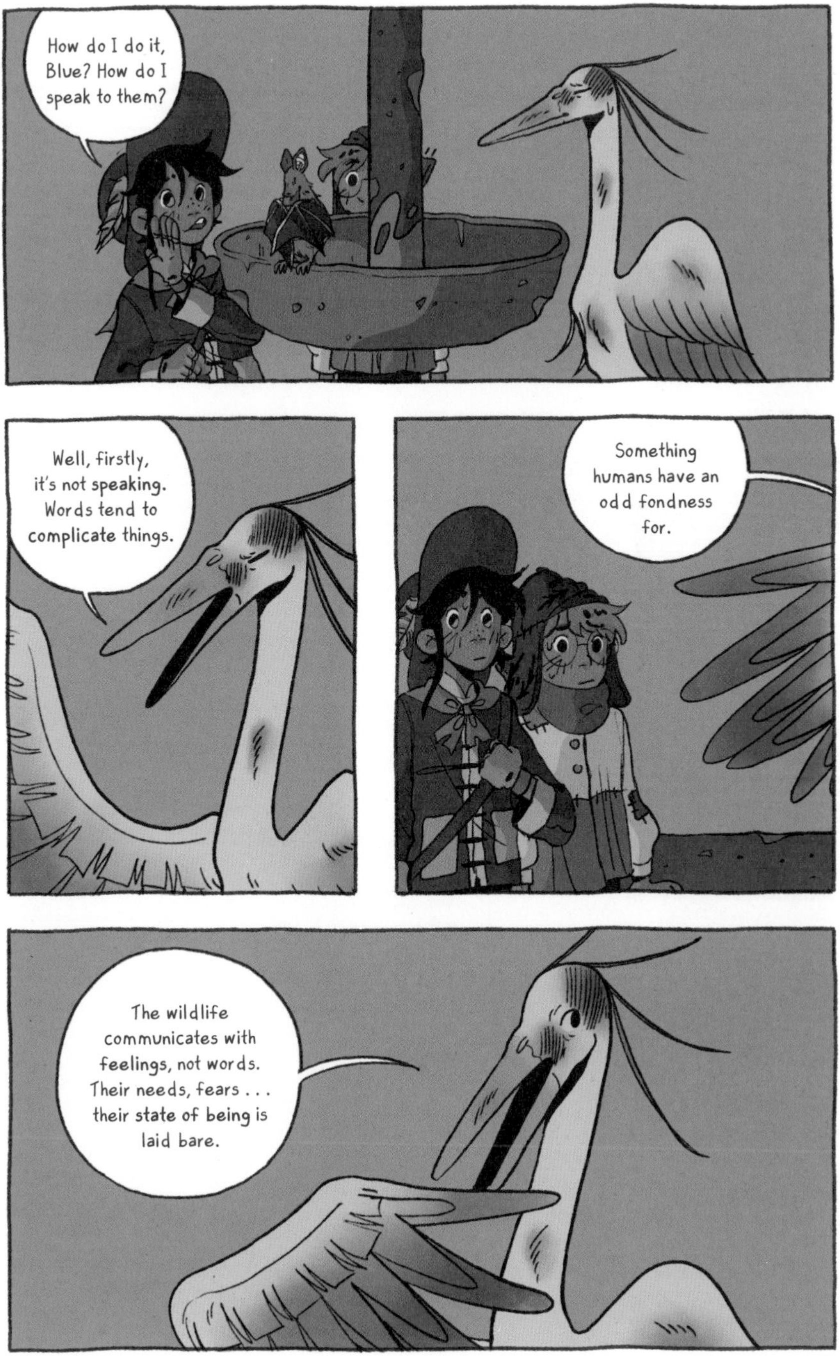
How do I do it, Blue? How do I speak to them?
Well, firstly, it's not speaking. Words tend to complicate things.
Something humans have an odd fondness for.
The wildlife communicates with feelings, not words. Their needs, fears . . . their state of being is laid bare.

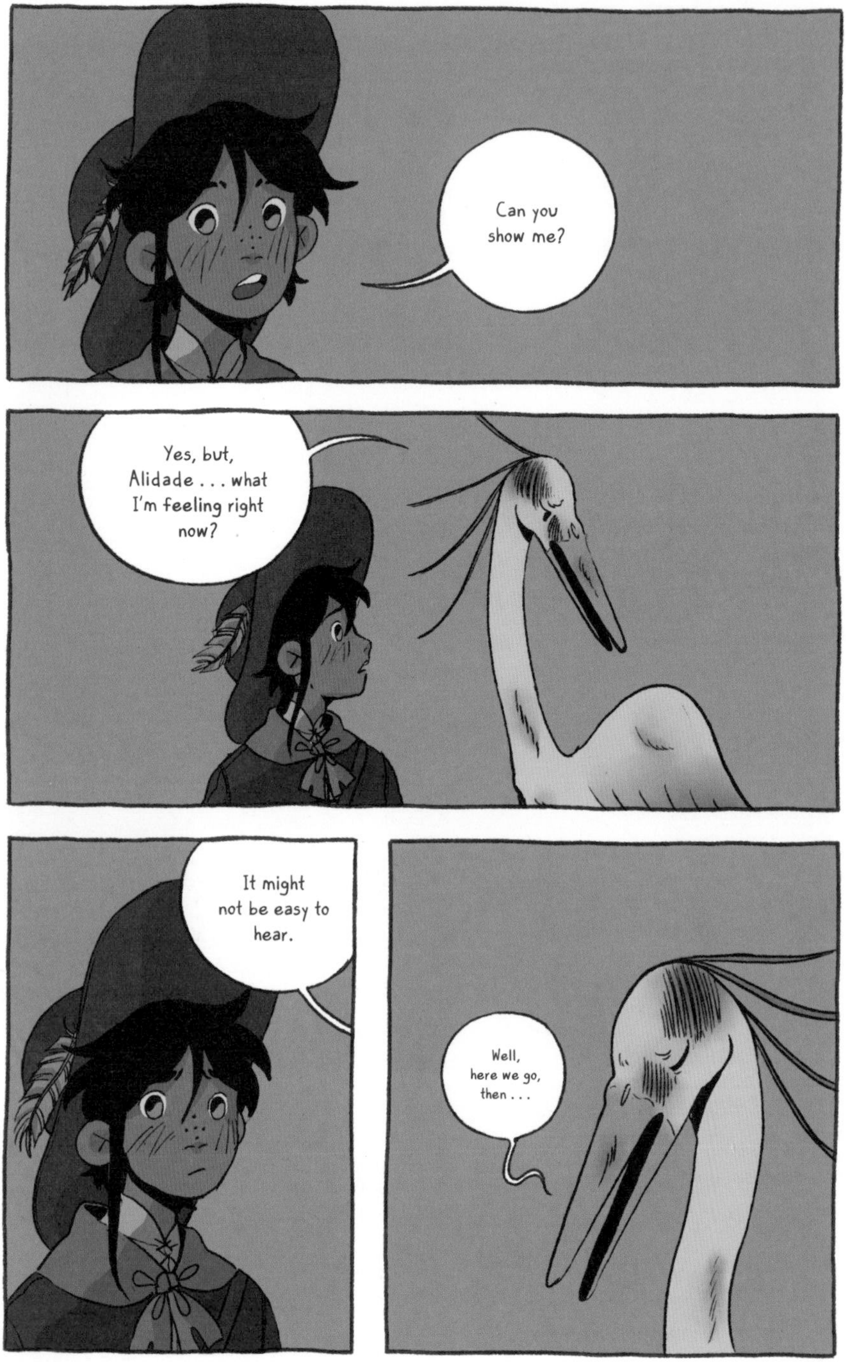
Can you show me?
Yes, but, Alidade . . . what I'm feeling right now?
It might not be easy to hear.
Well, here we go, then . . .

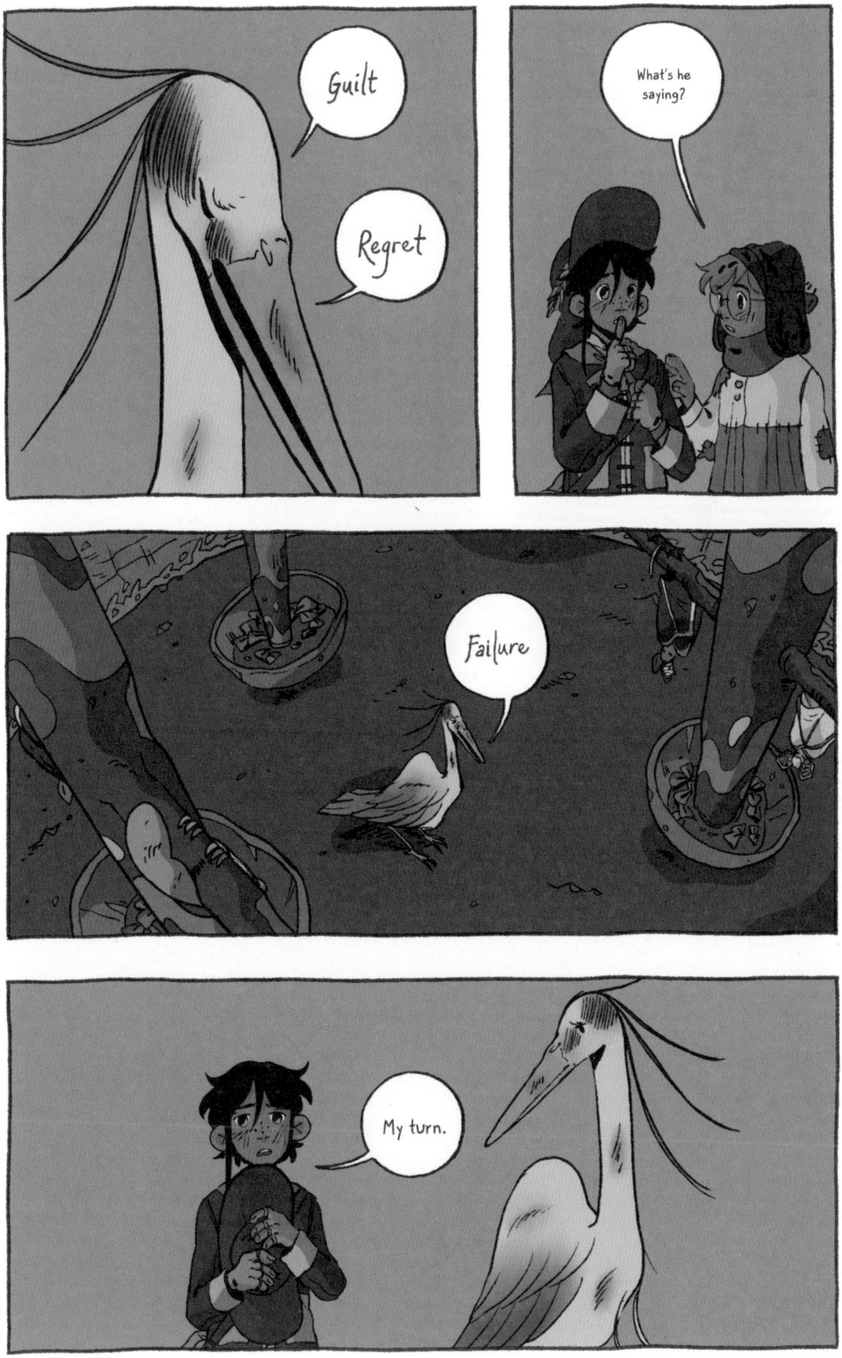
Guilt
Regret
What's he saying?
Failure
My turn.

Ashamed

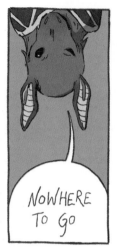

NOWHERE TO GO

Hopeful

TRAPPED

Lost

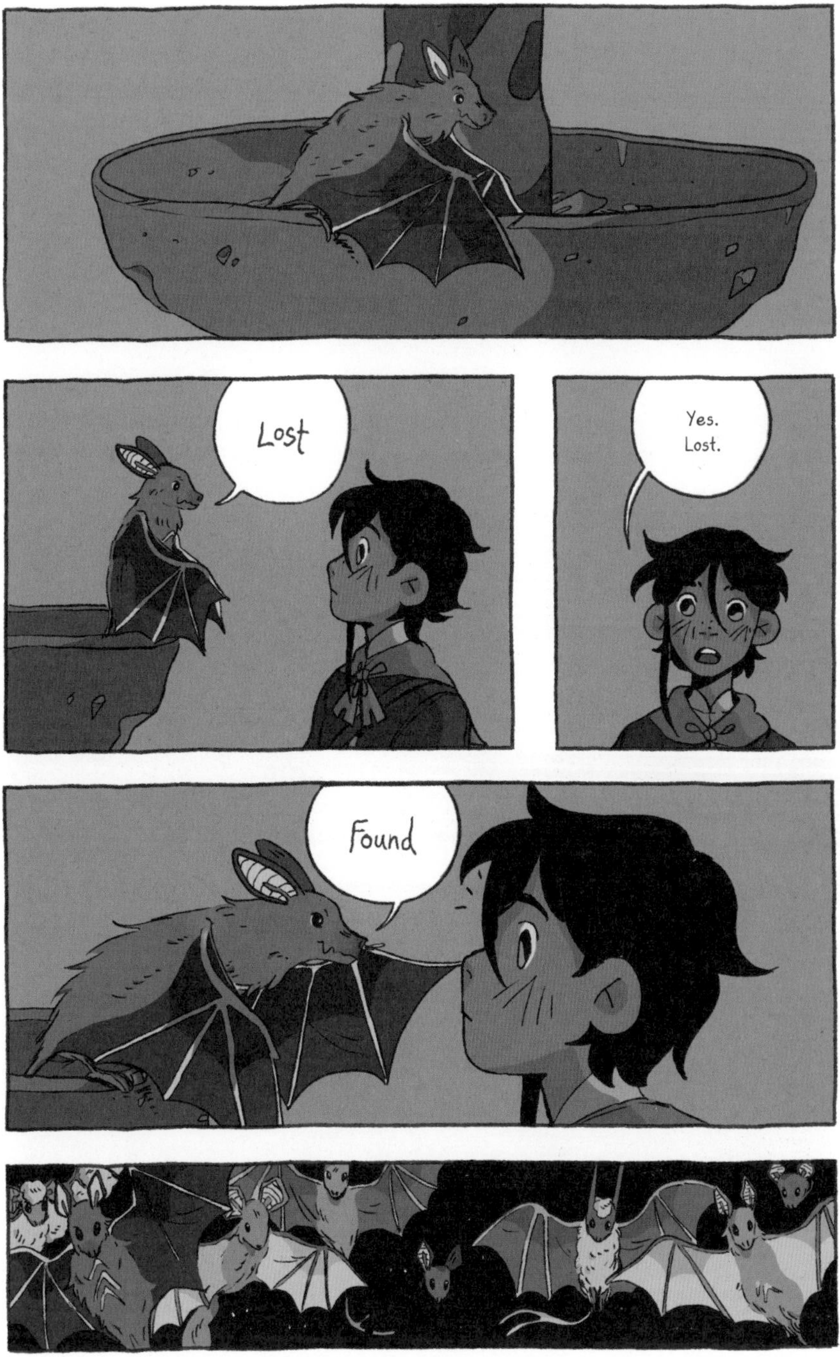
Lost
Yes.
Lost.
Found

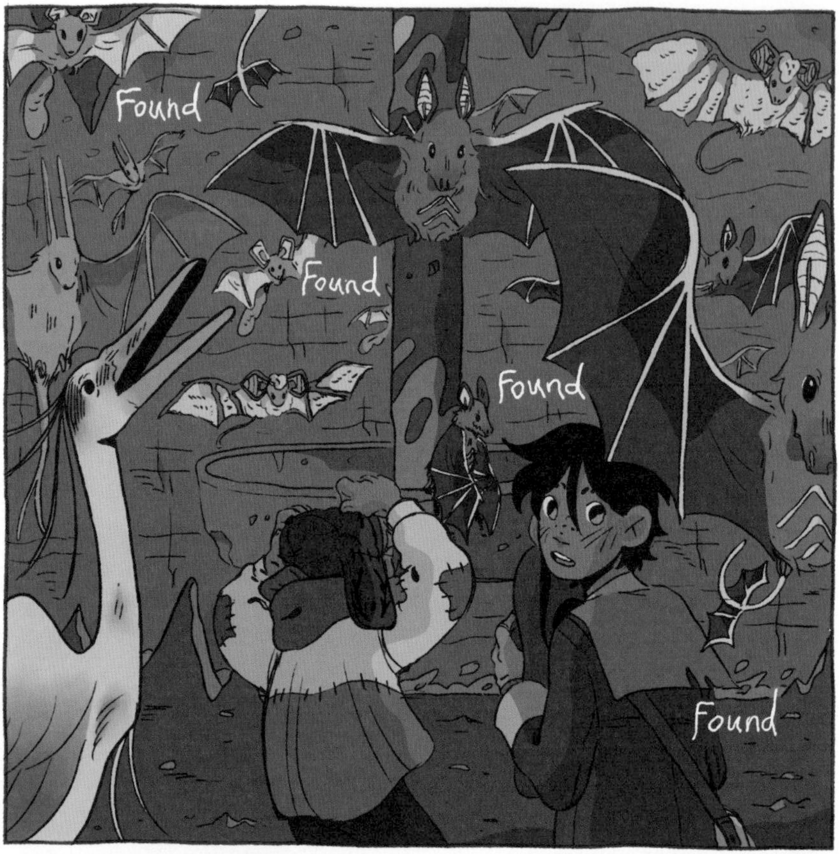
Found
Found
Found
Found

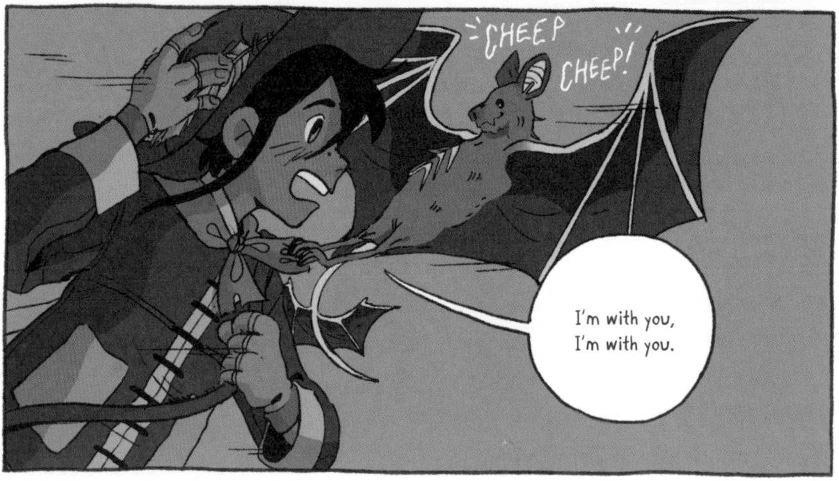
CHEEP
CHEEP!
I'm with you,
I'm with you.

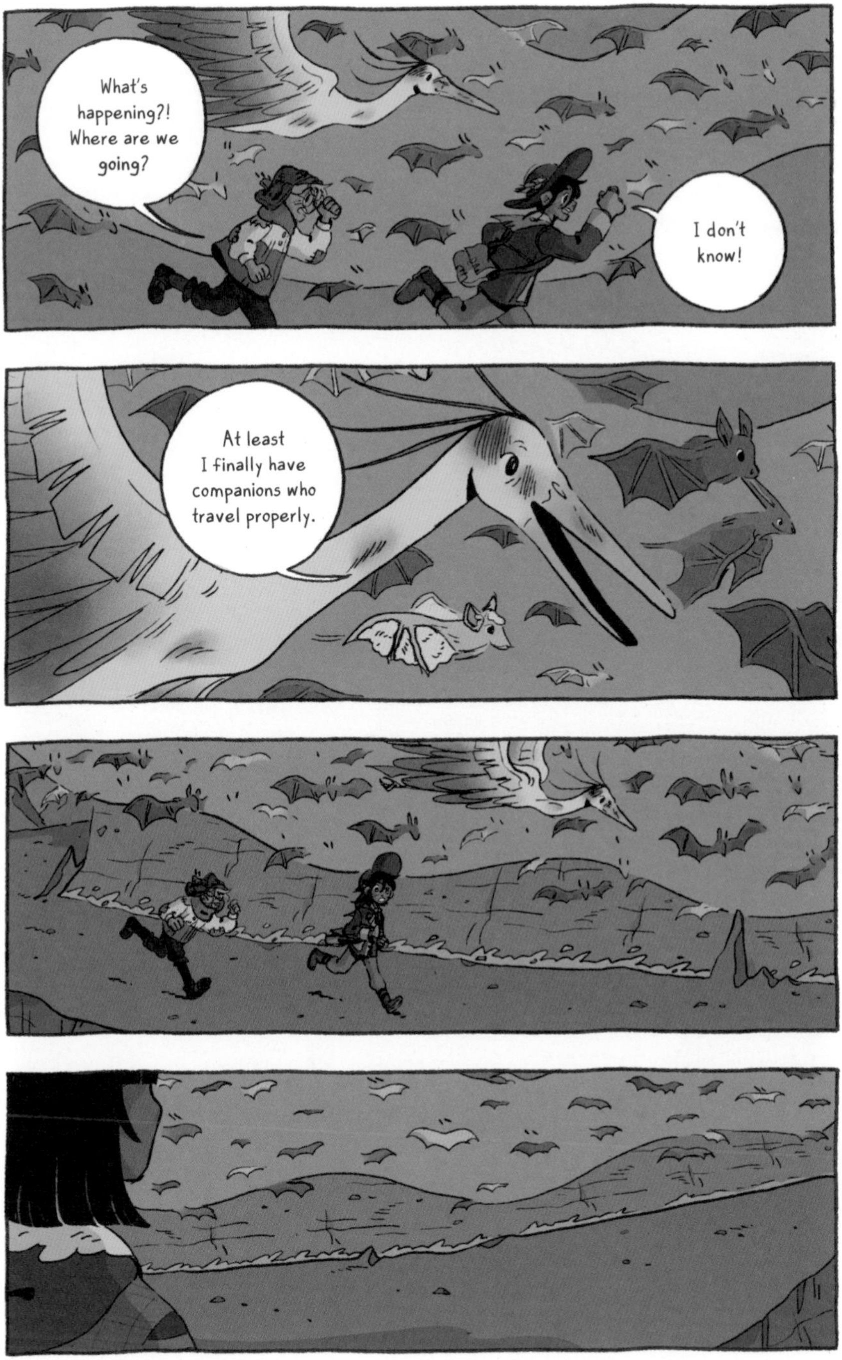
What's happening?! Where are we going?
I don't know!
At least I finally have companions who travel properly.

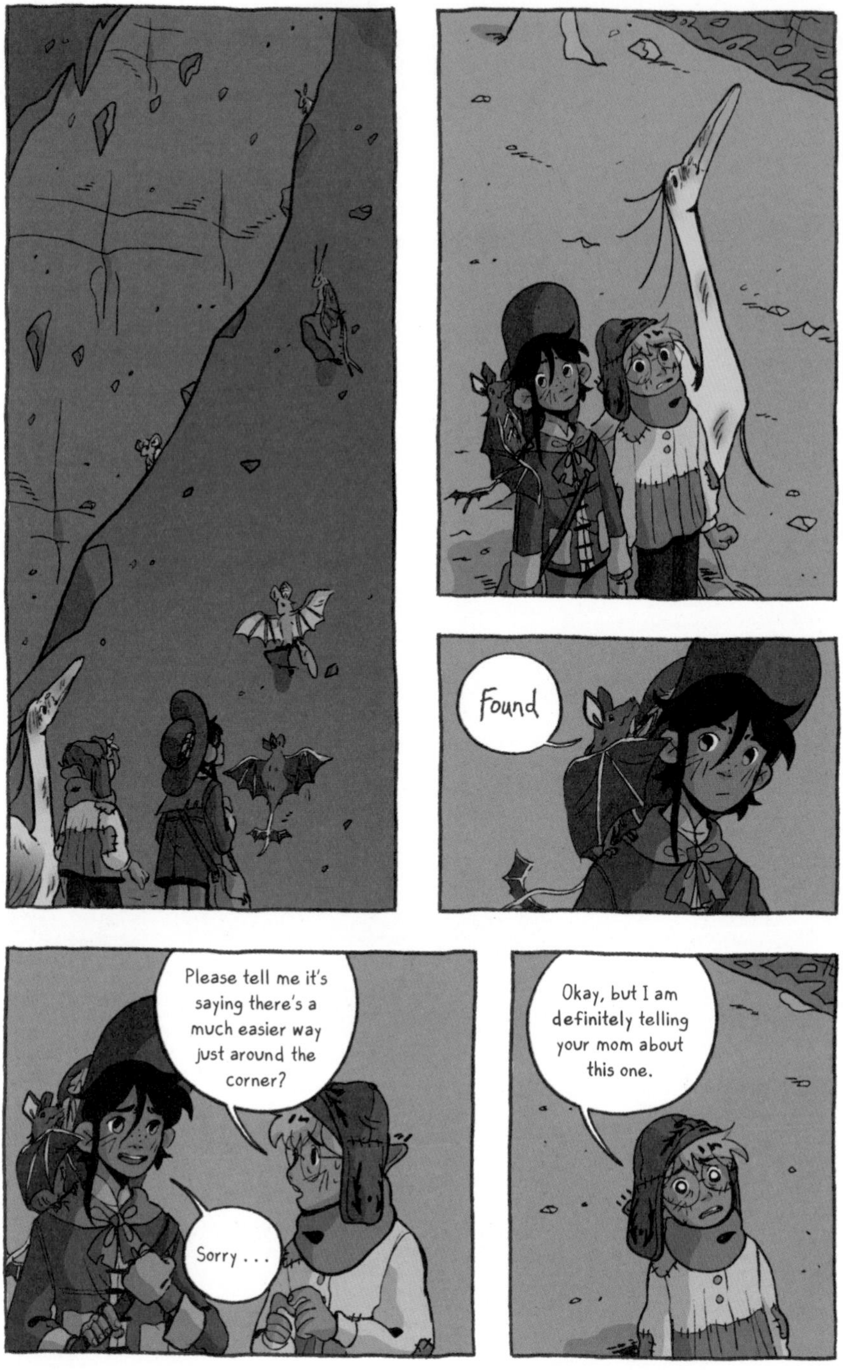
Found
Please tell me it's saying there's a much easier way just around the corner?
Sorry . . .
Okay, but I am definitely telling your mom about this one.

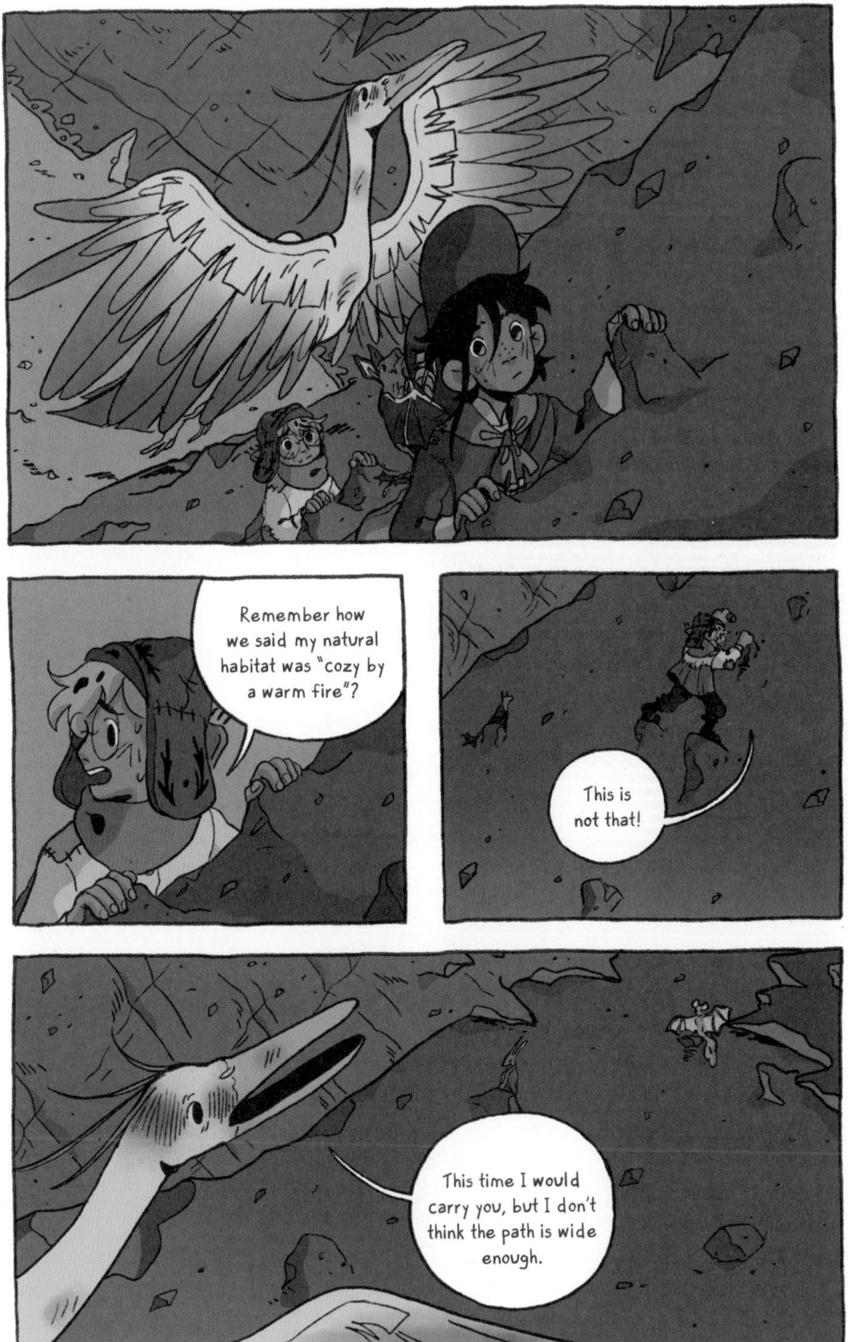
Remember how we said my natural habitat was "cozy by a warm fire"?
This is not that!
This time I would carry you, but I don't think the path is wide enough.

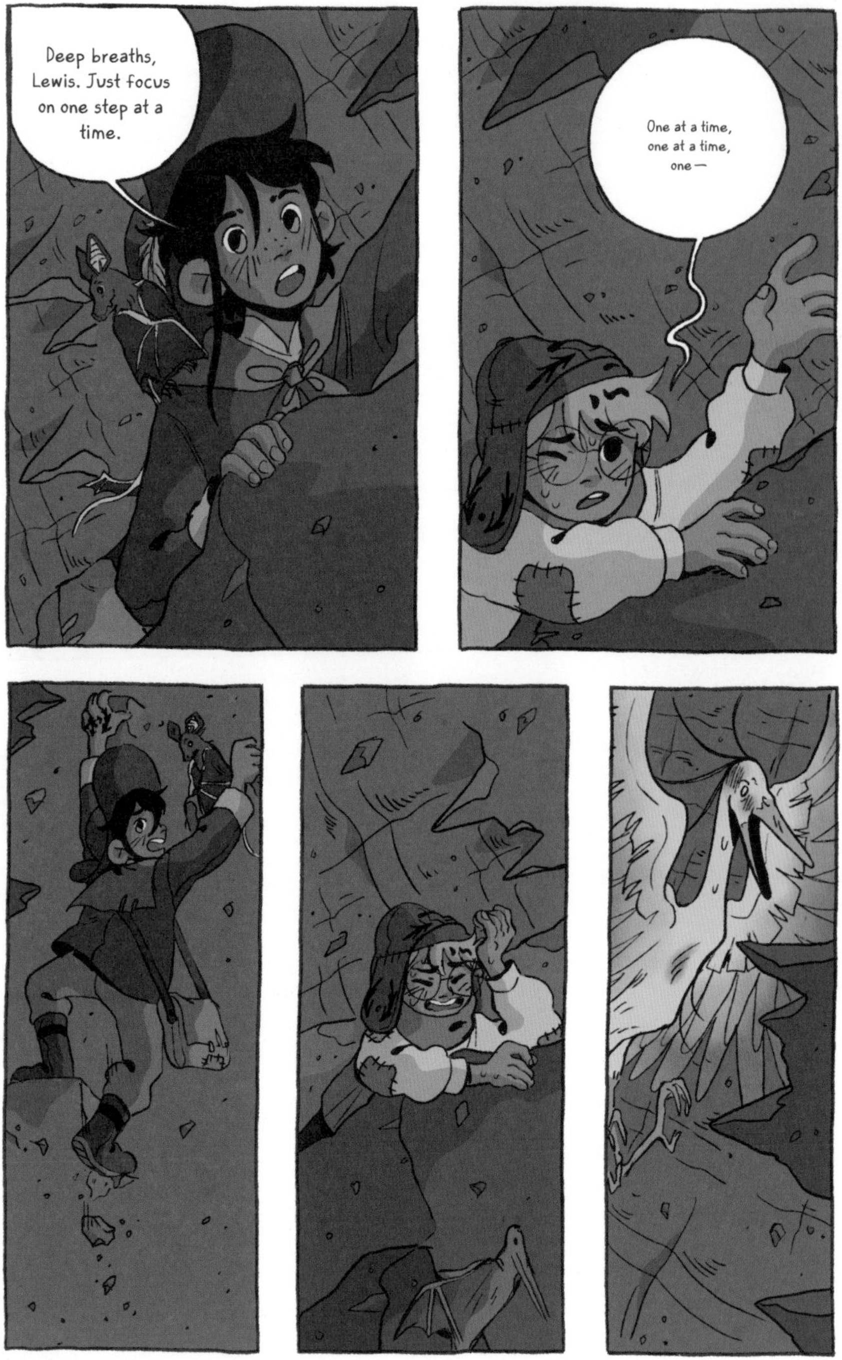
Deep breaths, Lewis. Just focus on one step at a time.
One at a time, one at a time, one—

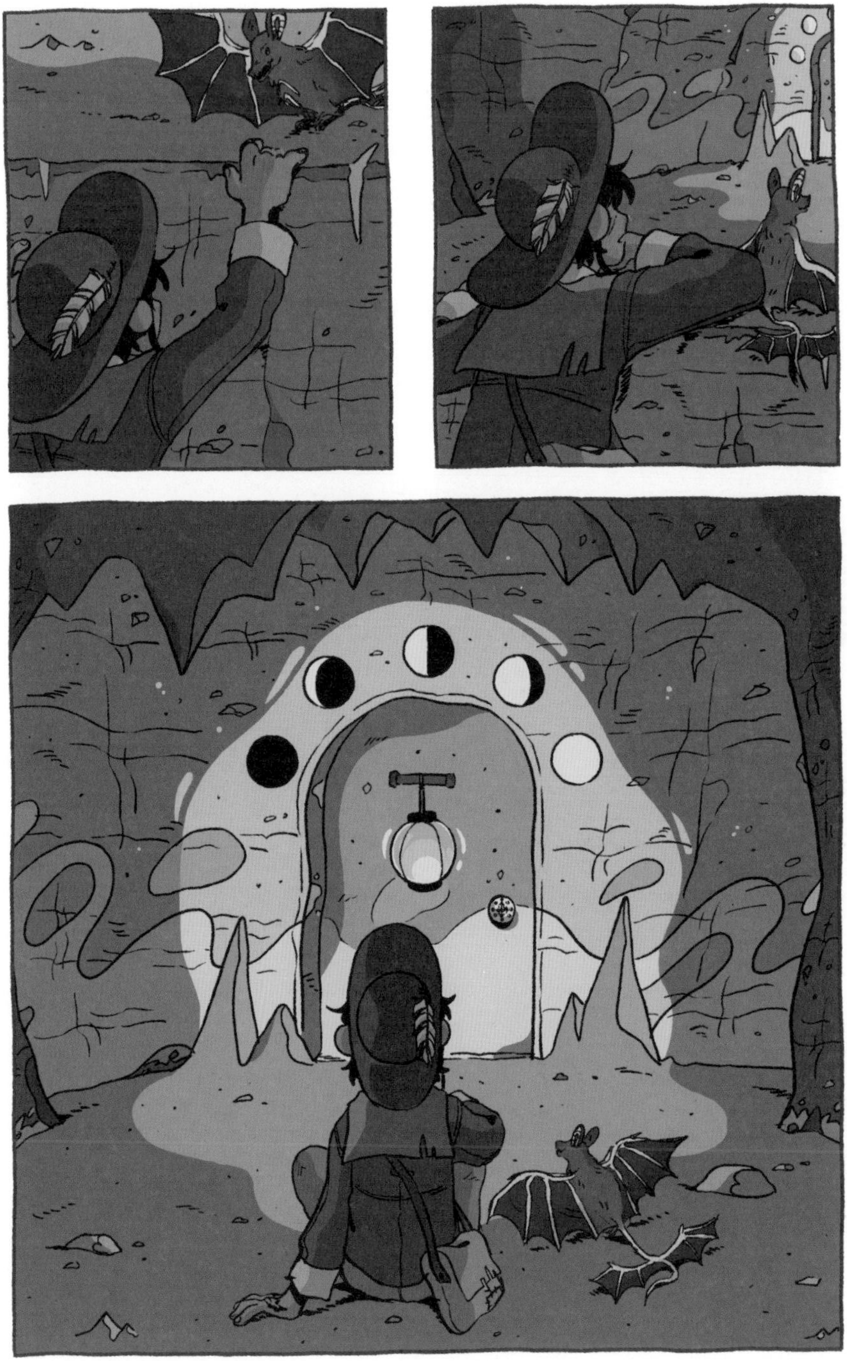

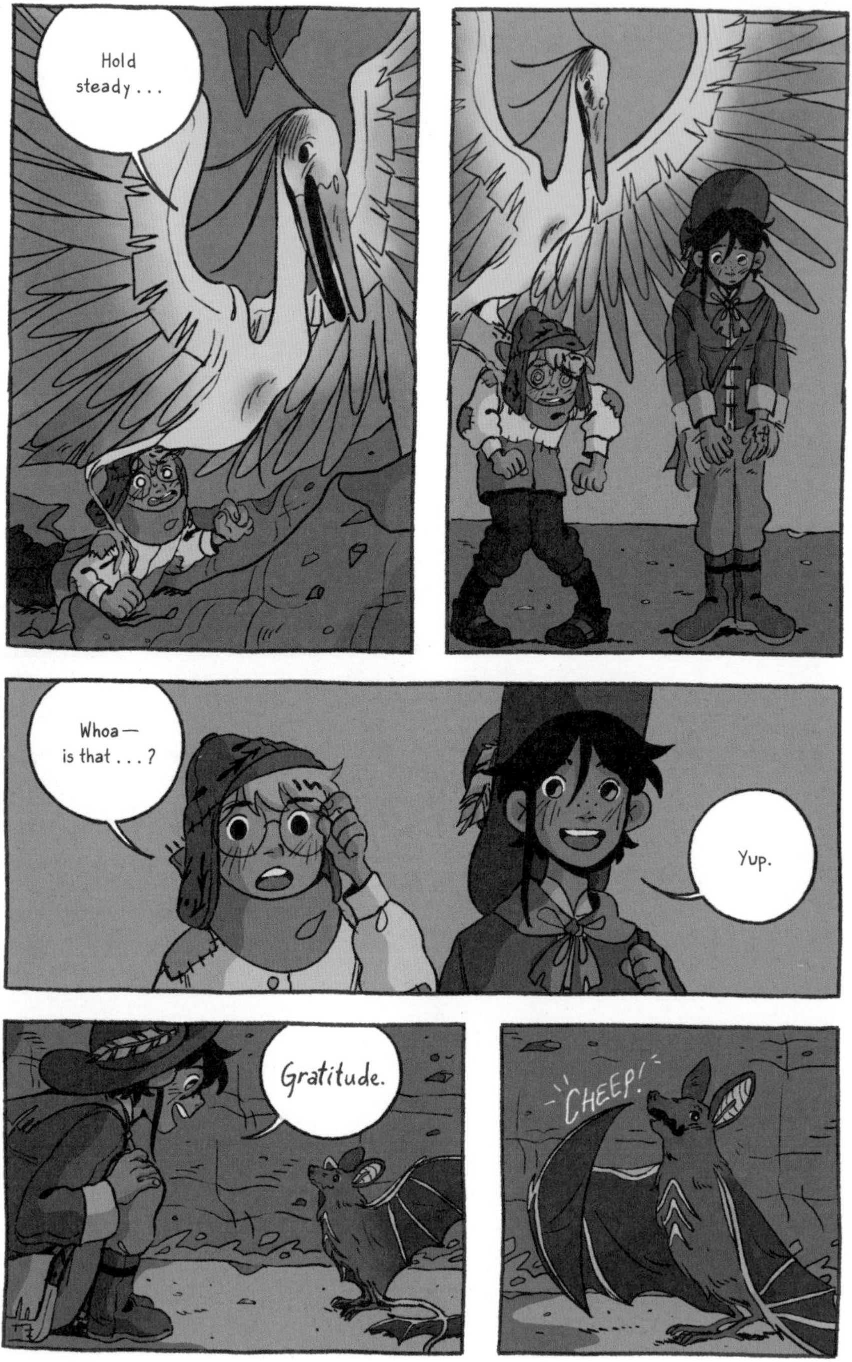
Hold steady . . .
Whoa— is that . . . ?
Yup.
Gratitude.
CHEEP!

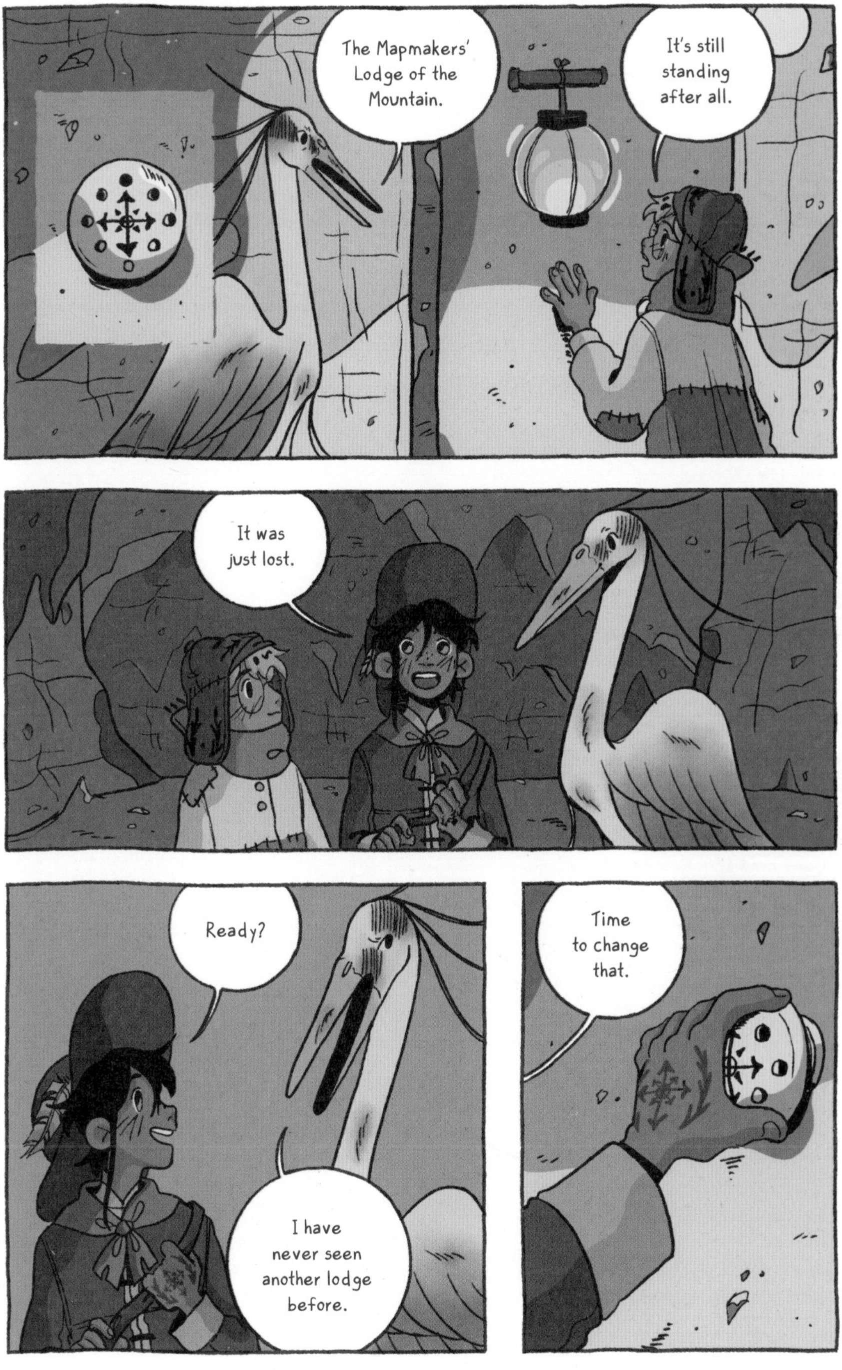
The Mapmakers' Lodge of the Mountain.
It's still standing after all.
It was just lost.
Ready?
I have never seen another lodge before.
Time to change that.

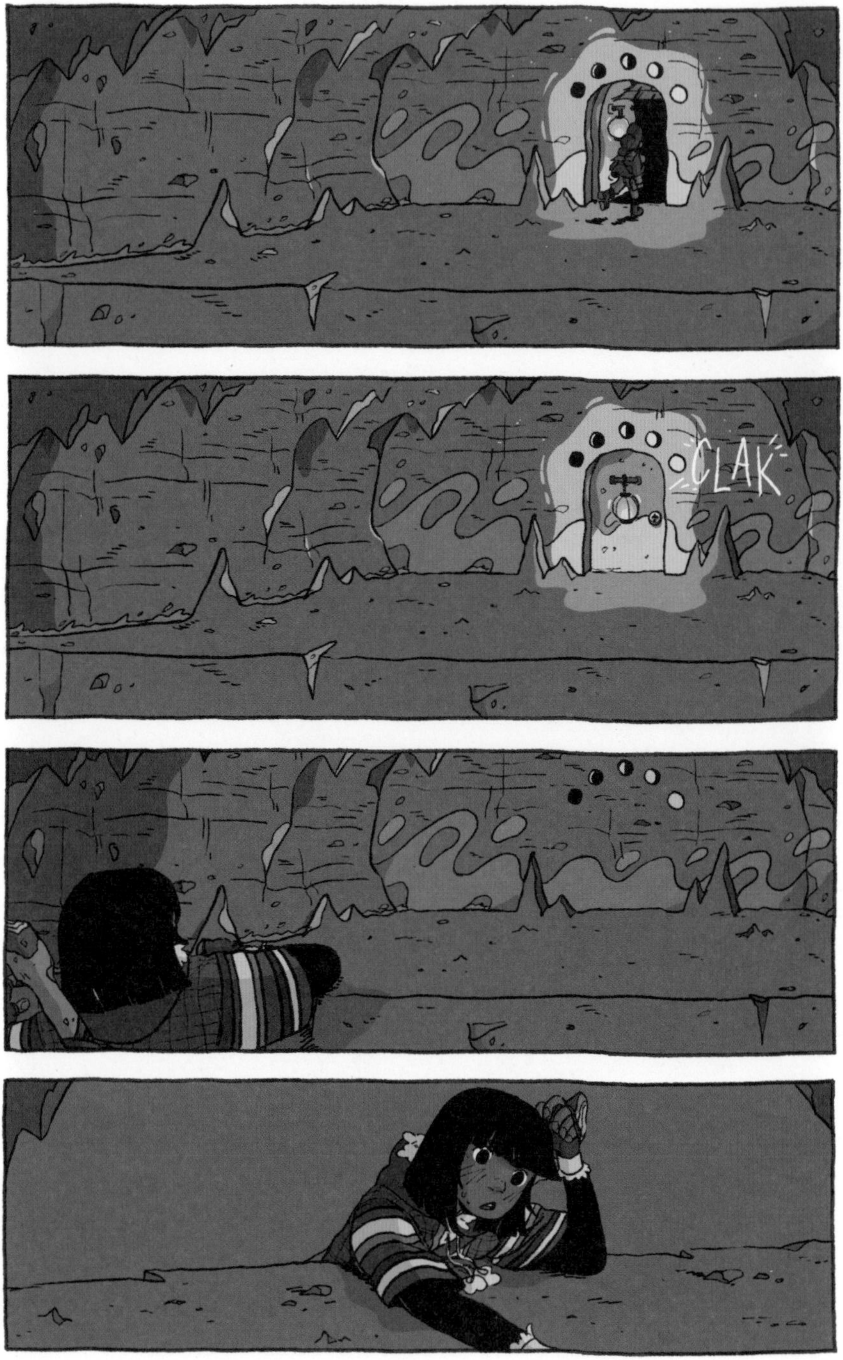
CLAK

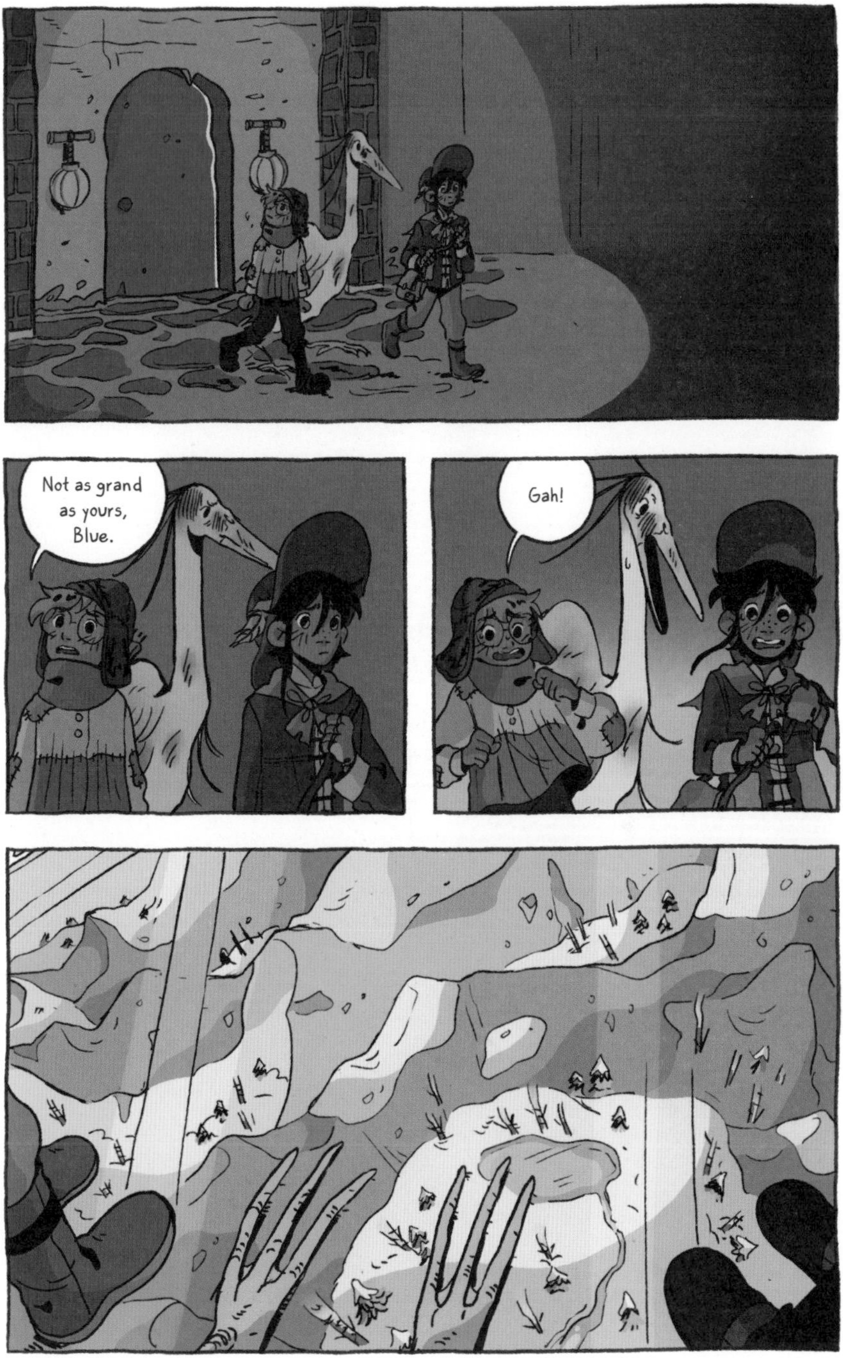
Not as grand as yours, Blue.
Gah!

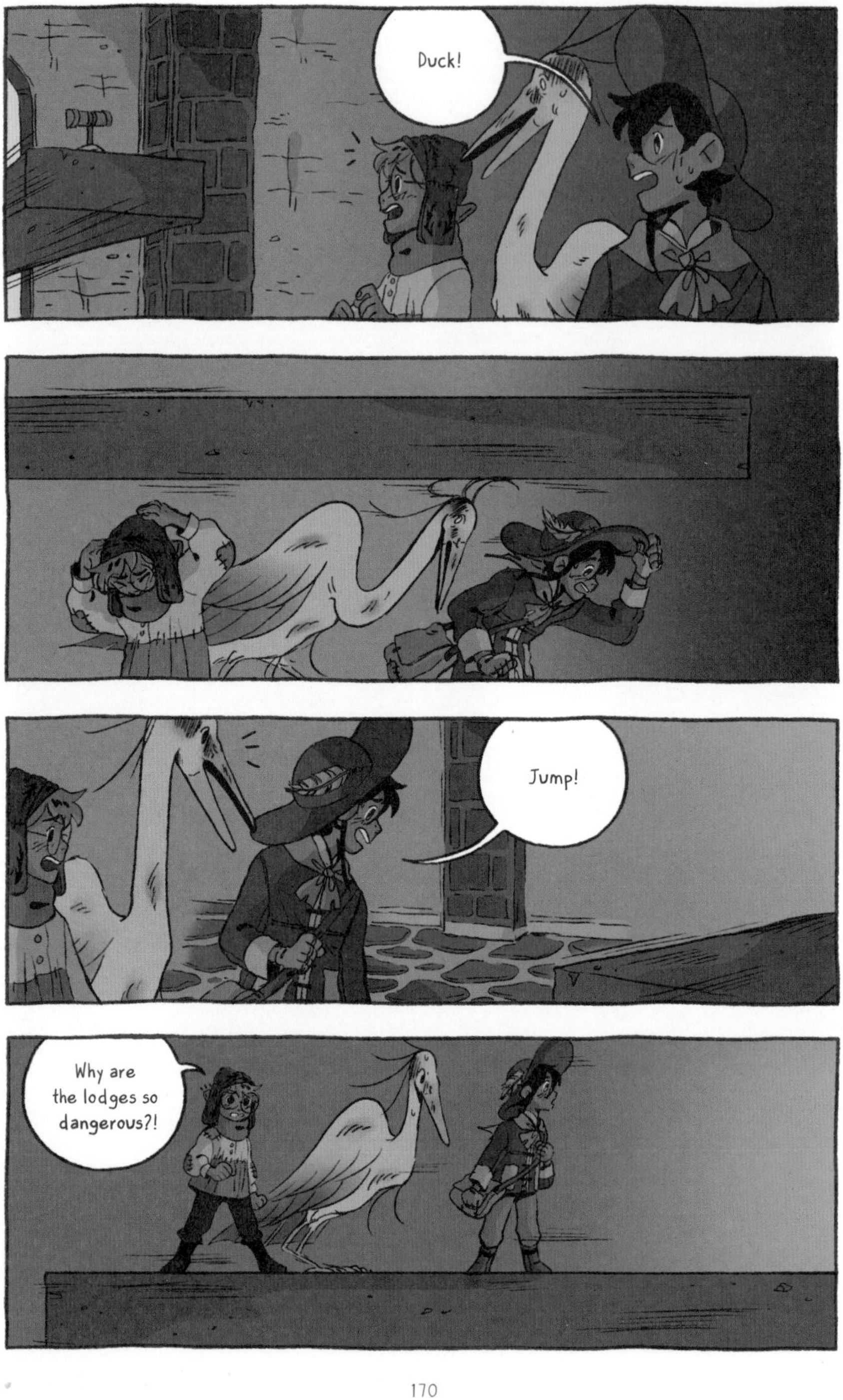
Duck!
Jump!
Why are the lodges so dangerous?!

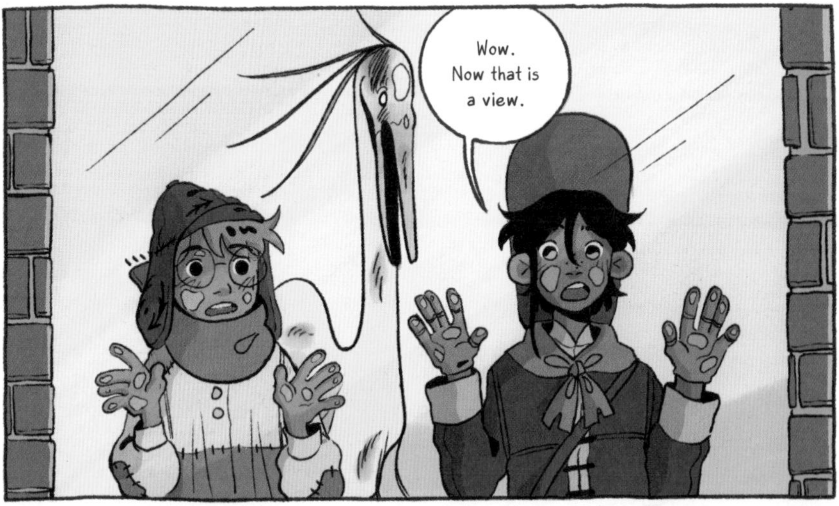
Wow.
Now that is
a view.

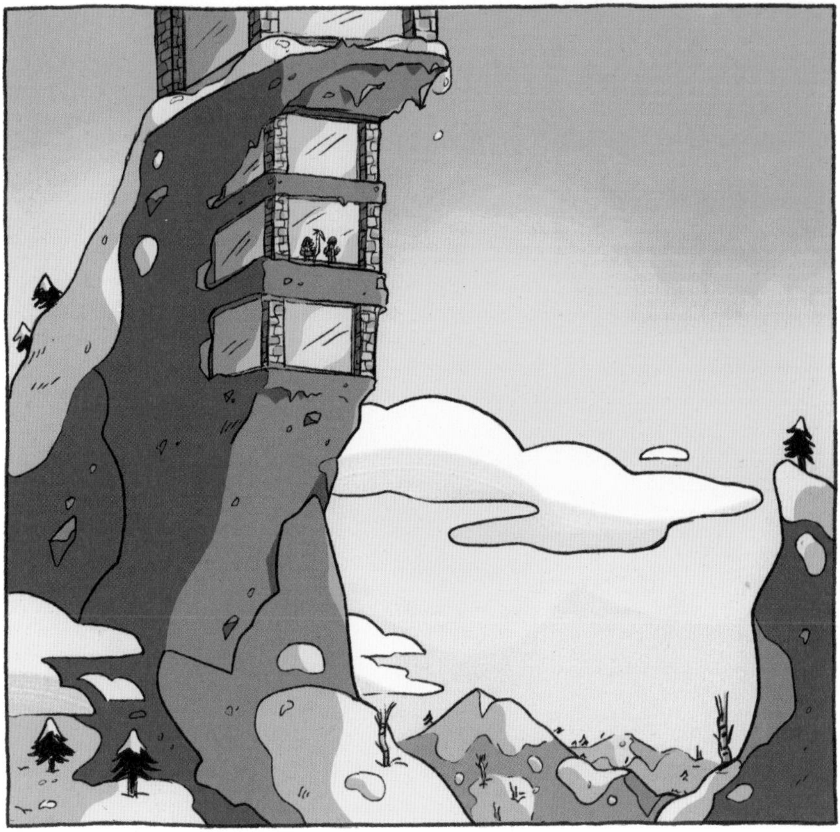

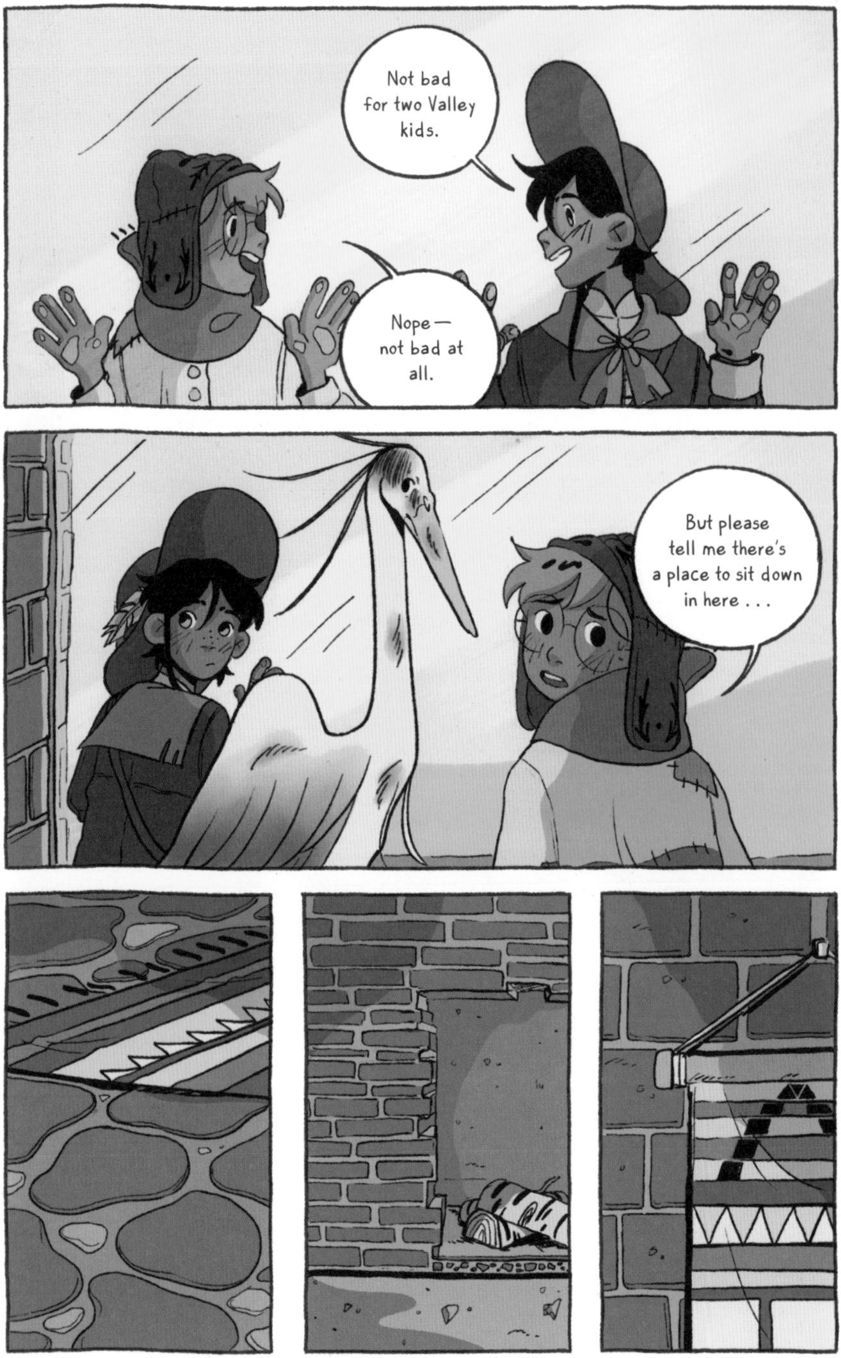
Not bad for two Valley kids.
Nope— not bad at all.
But please tell me there's a place to sit down in here . . .

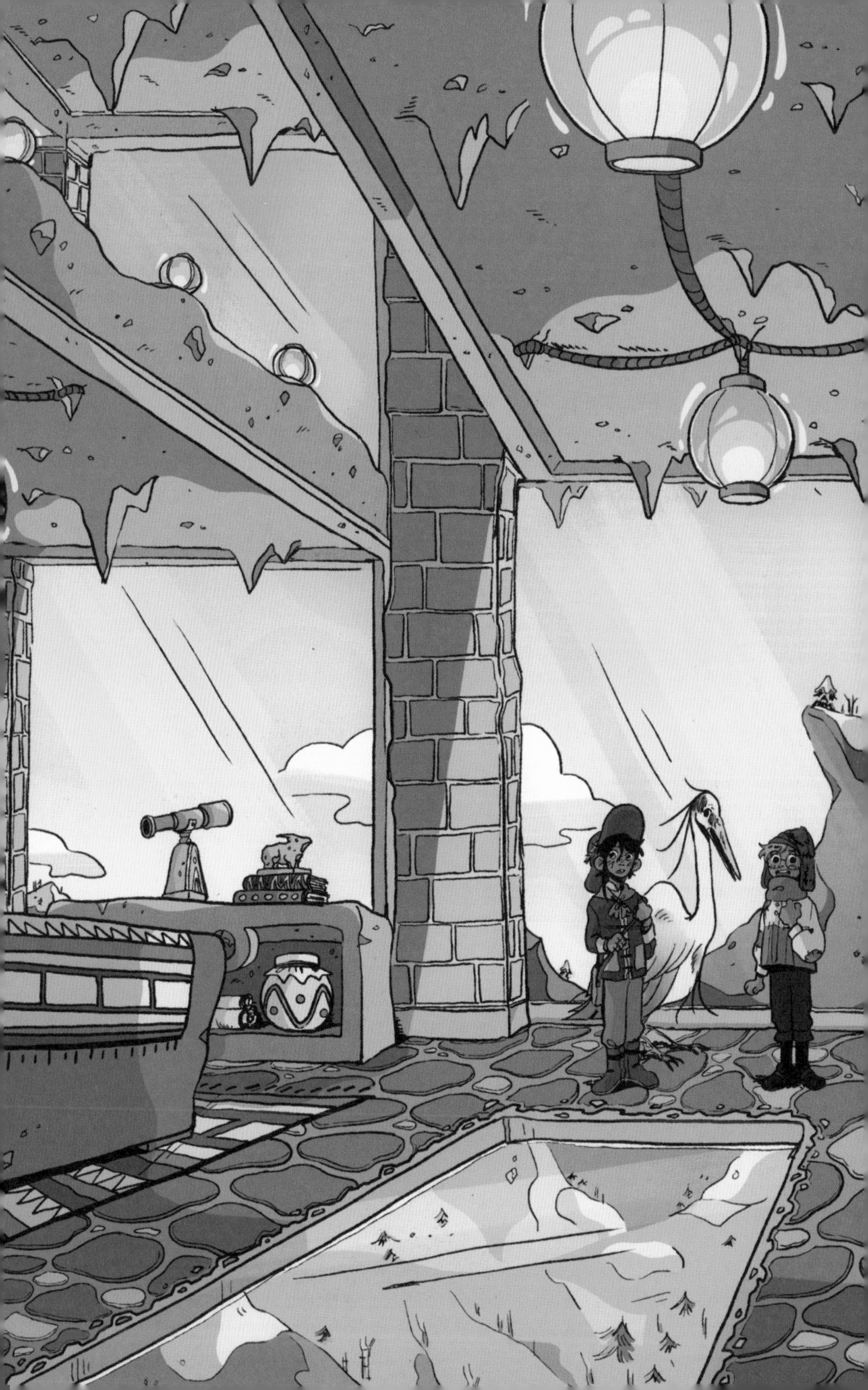

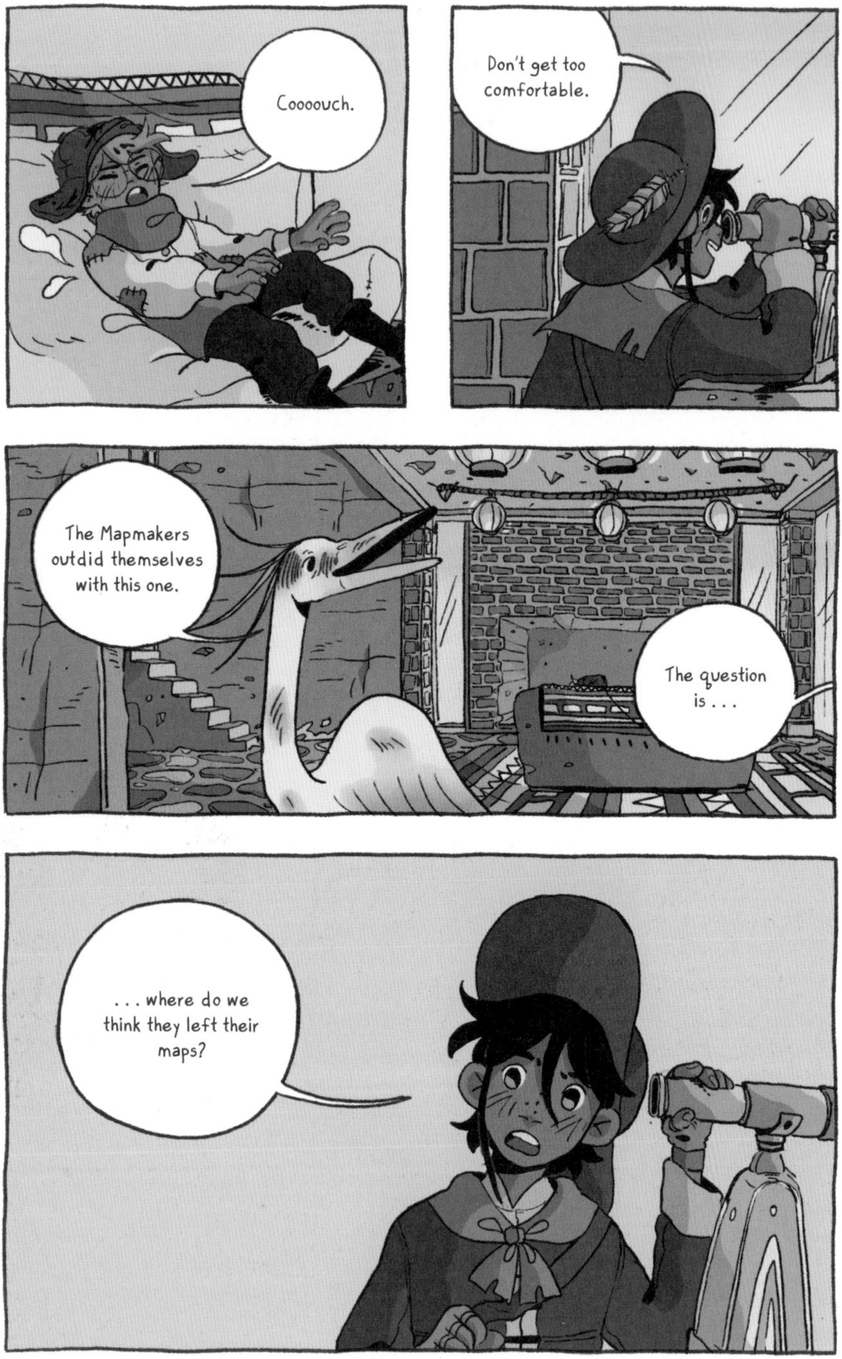
Cooooouch.
Don't get too comfortable.
The Mapmakers outdid themselves with this one.
The question is . . .
. . . where do we think they left their maps?

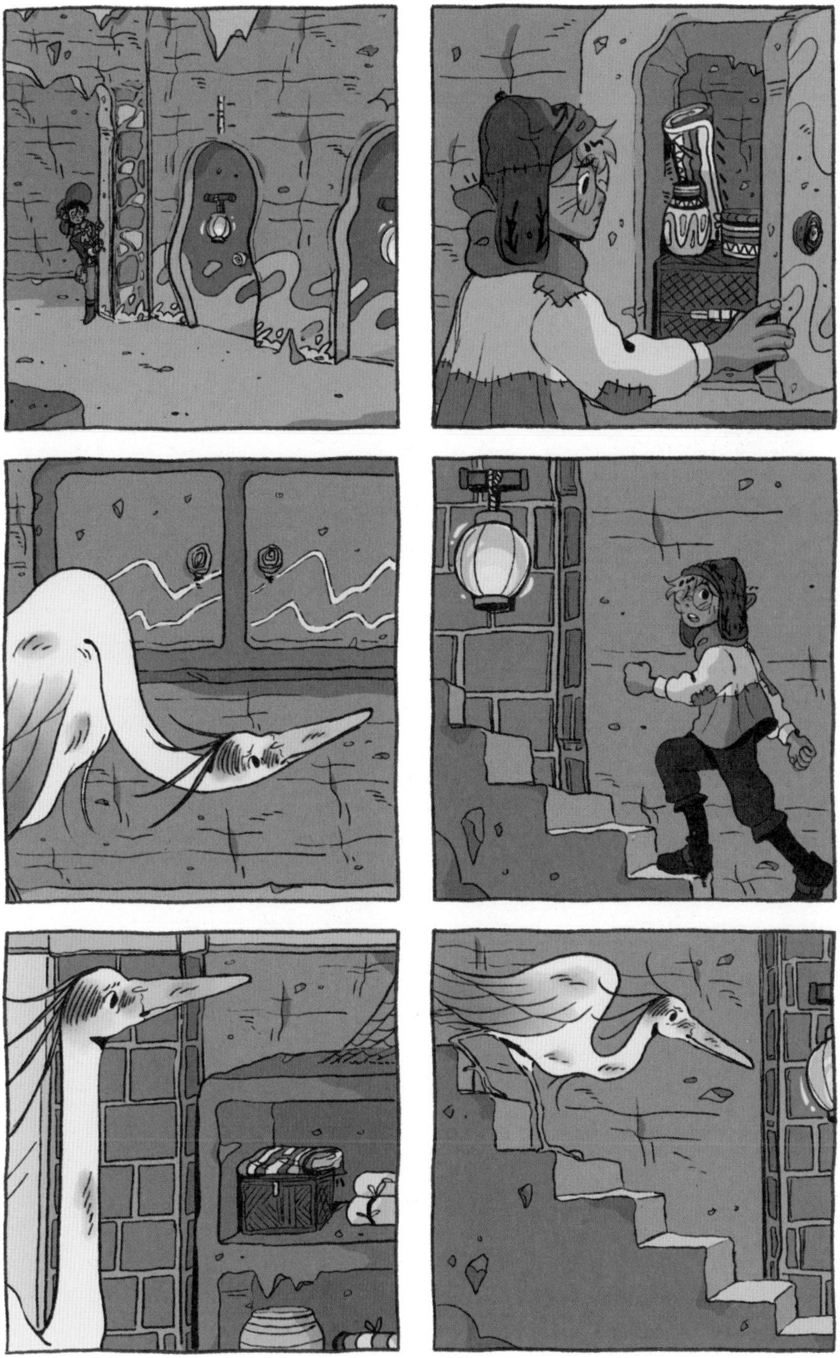

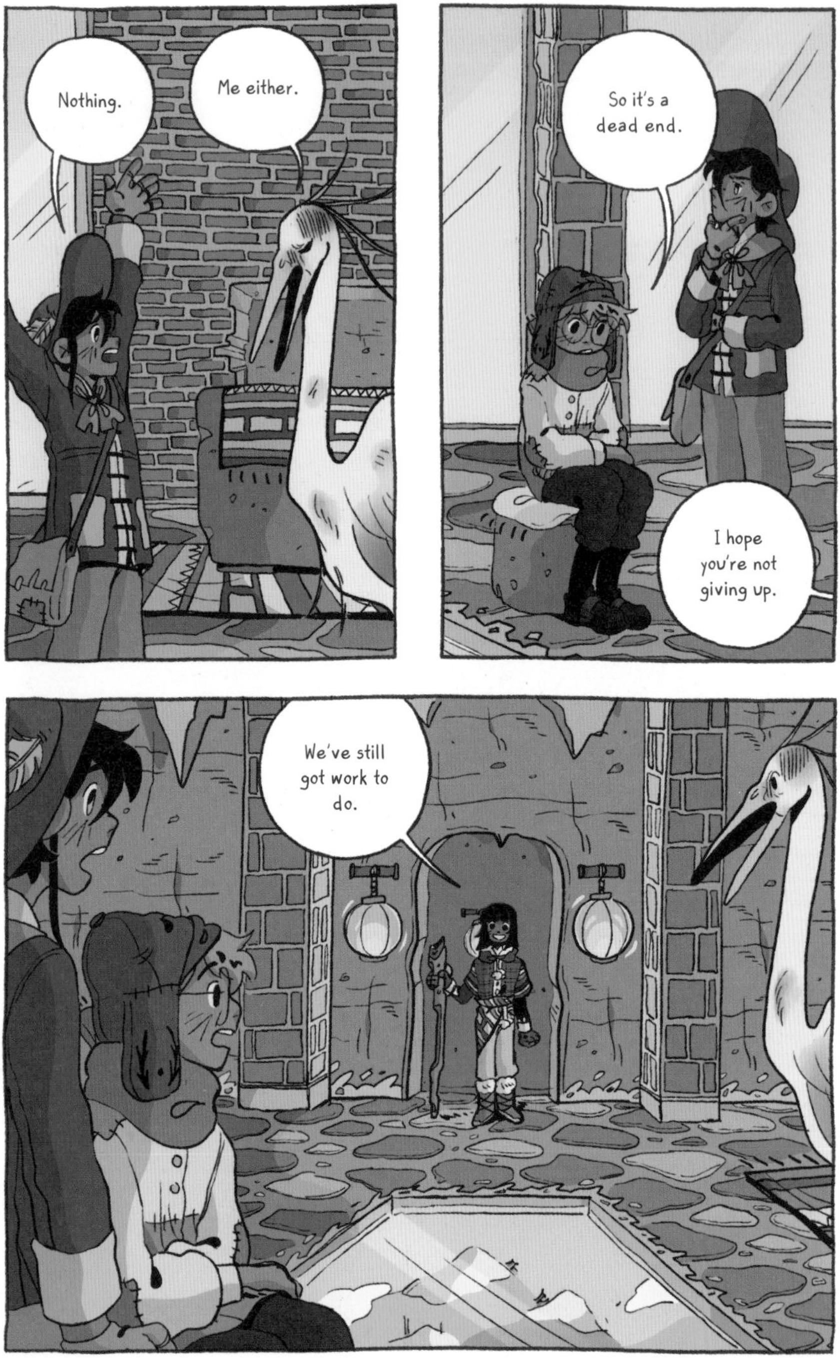
Nothing.
Me either.
So it's a dead end.
I hope you're not giving up.
We've still got work to do.

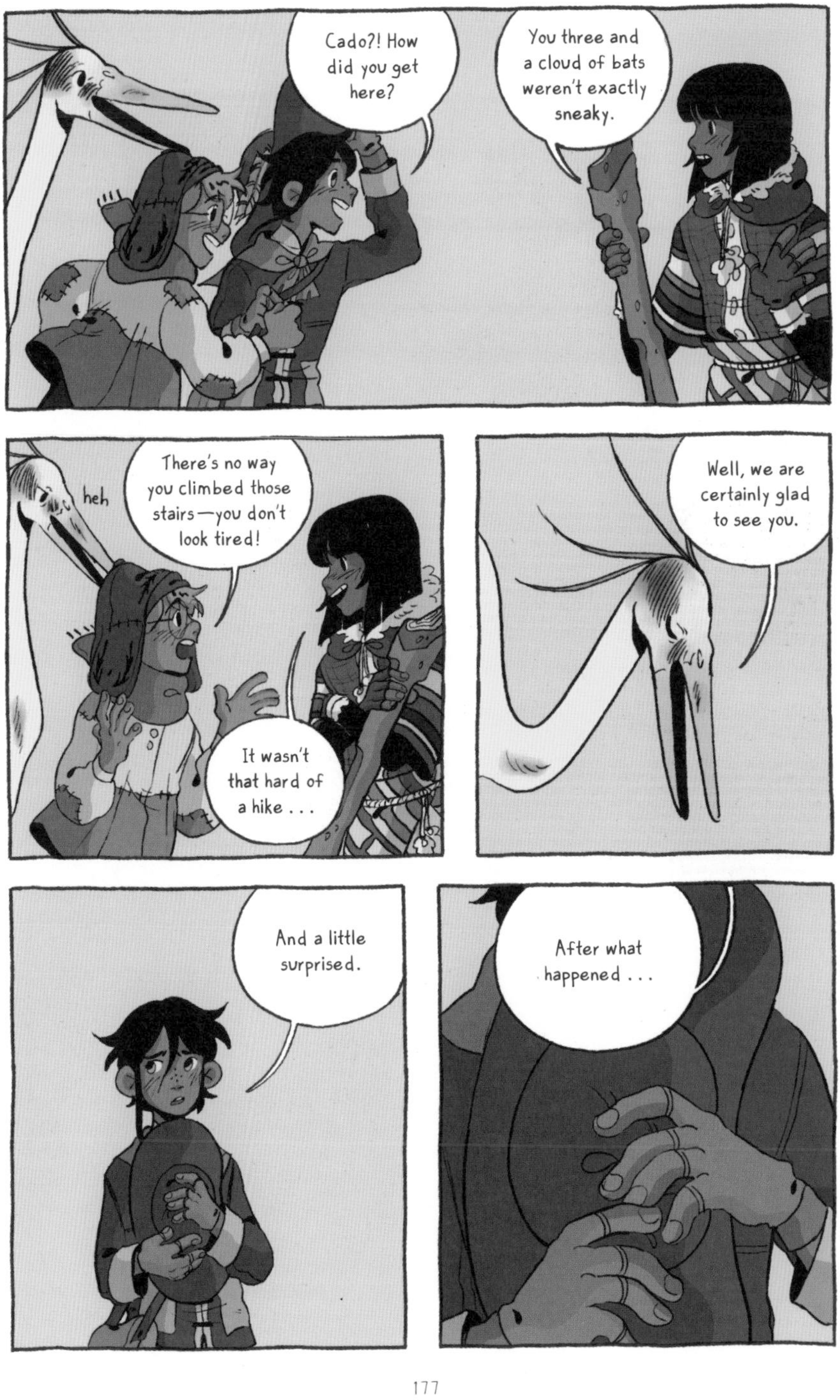
Cado?! How did you get here?
You three and a cloud of bats weren't exactly sneaky.
heh
There's no way you climbed those stairs—you don't look tired!
It wasn't that hard of a hike . . .
Well, we are certainly glad to see you.
And a little surprised.
After what happened . . .

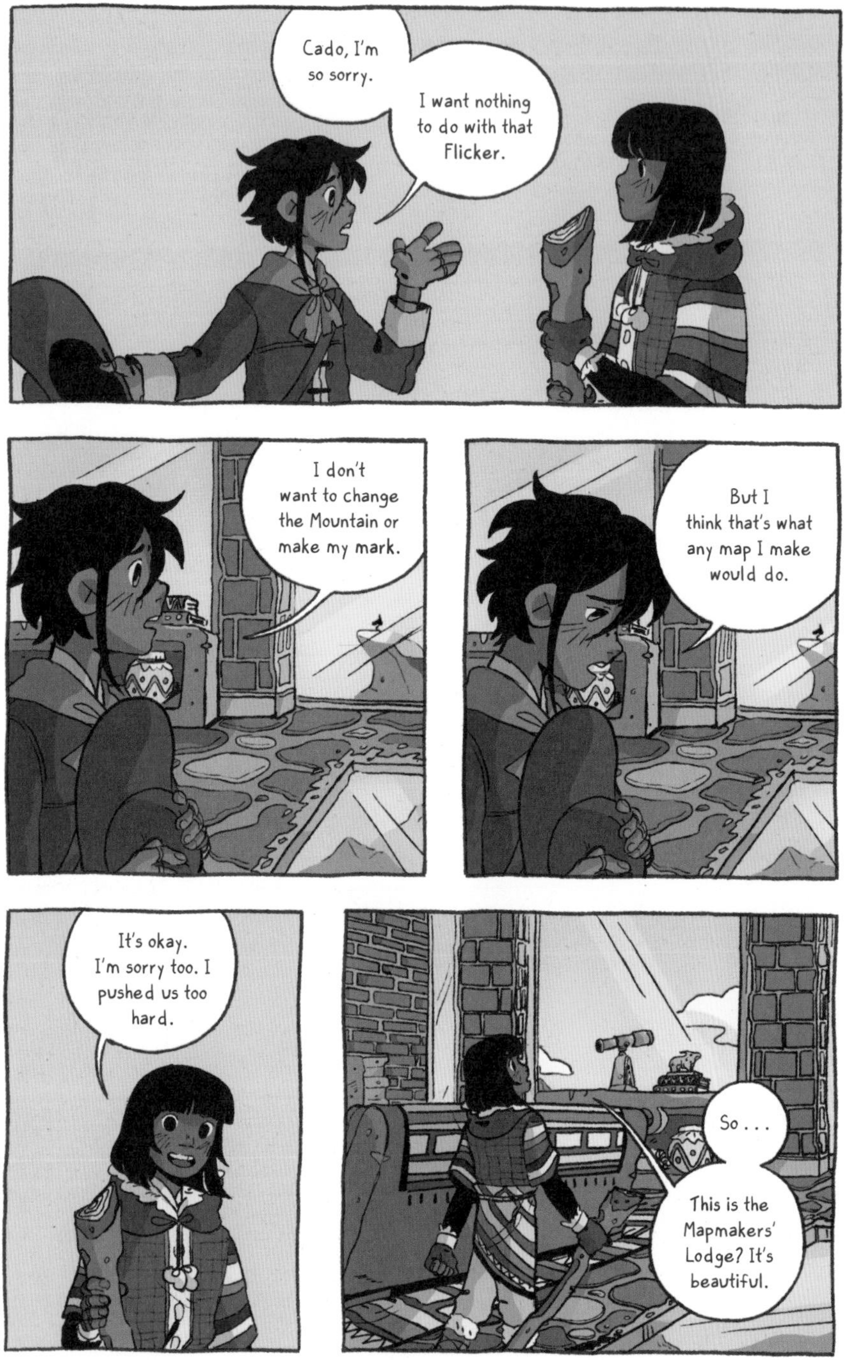

Cado, I'm so sorry.
I want nothing to do with that Flicker.
I don't want to change the Mountain or make my mark.
But I think that's what any map I make would do.
It's okay. I'm sorry too. I pushed us too hard.
So . . .
This is the Mapmakers' Lodge? It's beautiful.

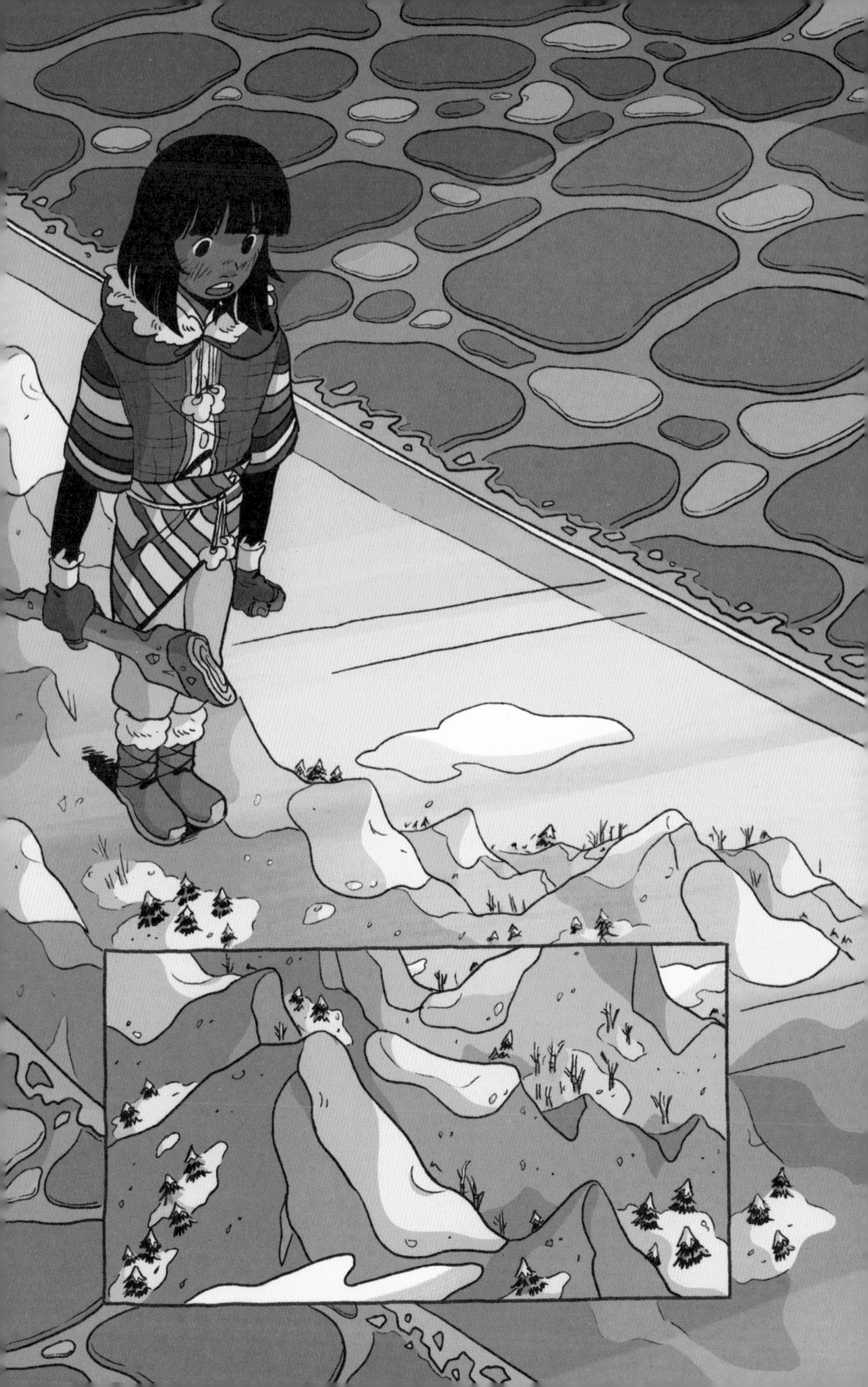

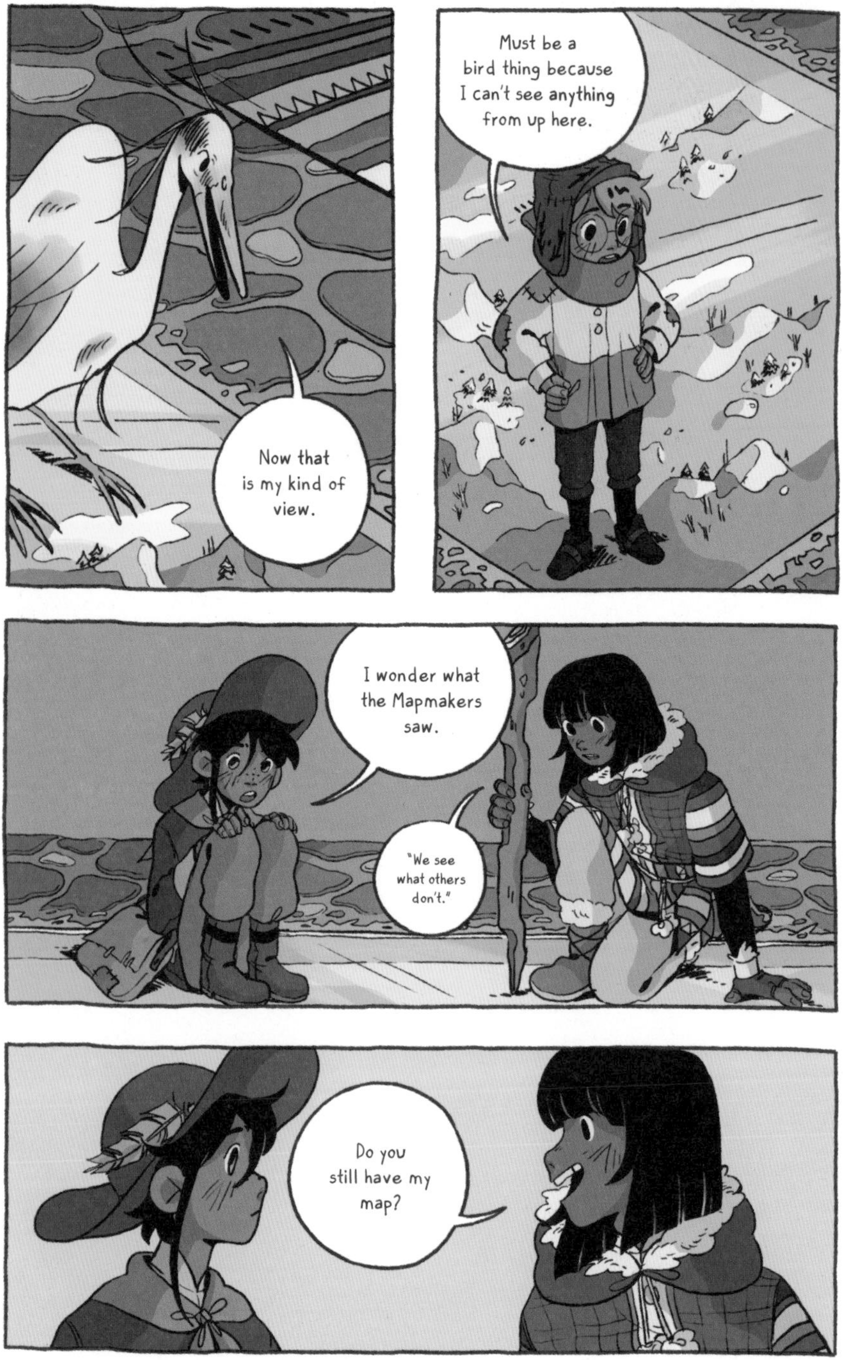
Now that is my kind of view.
Must be a bird thing because I can't see anything from up here.
I wonder what the Mapmakers saw.
"We see what others don't."
Do you still have my map?

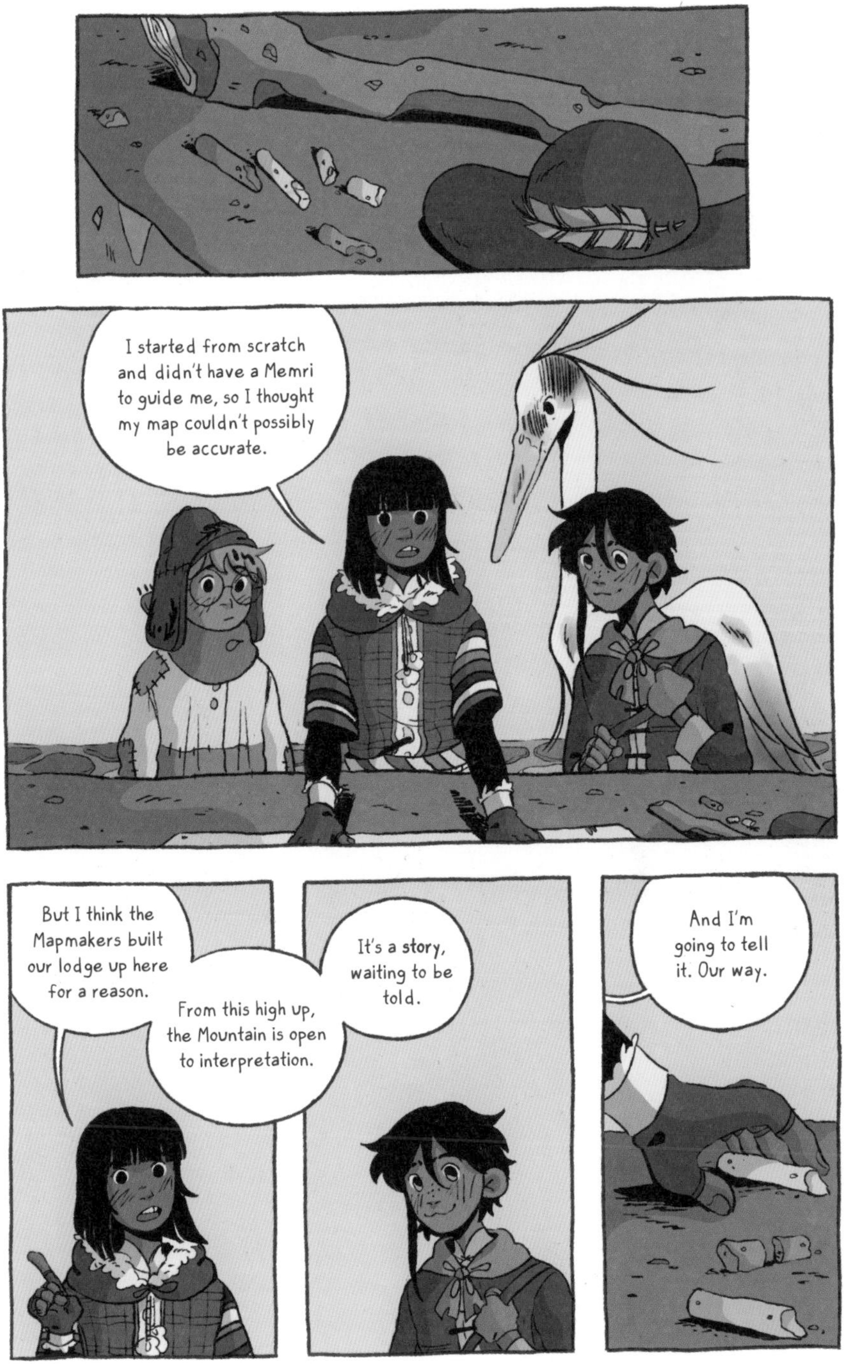
I started from scratch and didn't have a Memri to guide me, so I thought my map couldn't possibly be accurate.
But I think the Mapmakers built our lodge up here for a reason.
From this high up, the Mountain is open to interpretation.
It's a story, waiting to be told.
And I'm going to tell it. Our way.

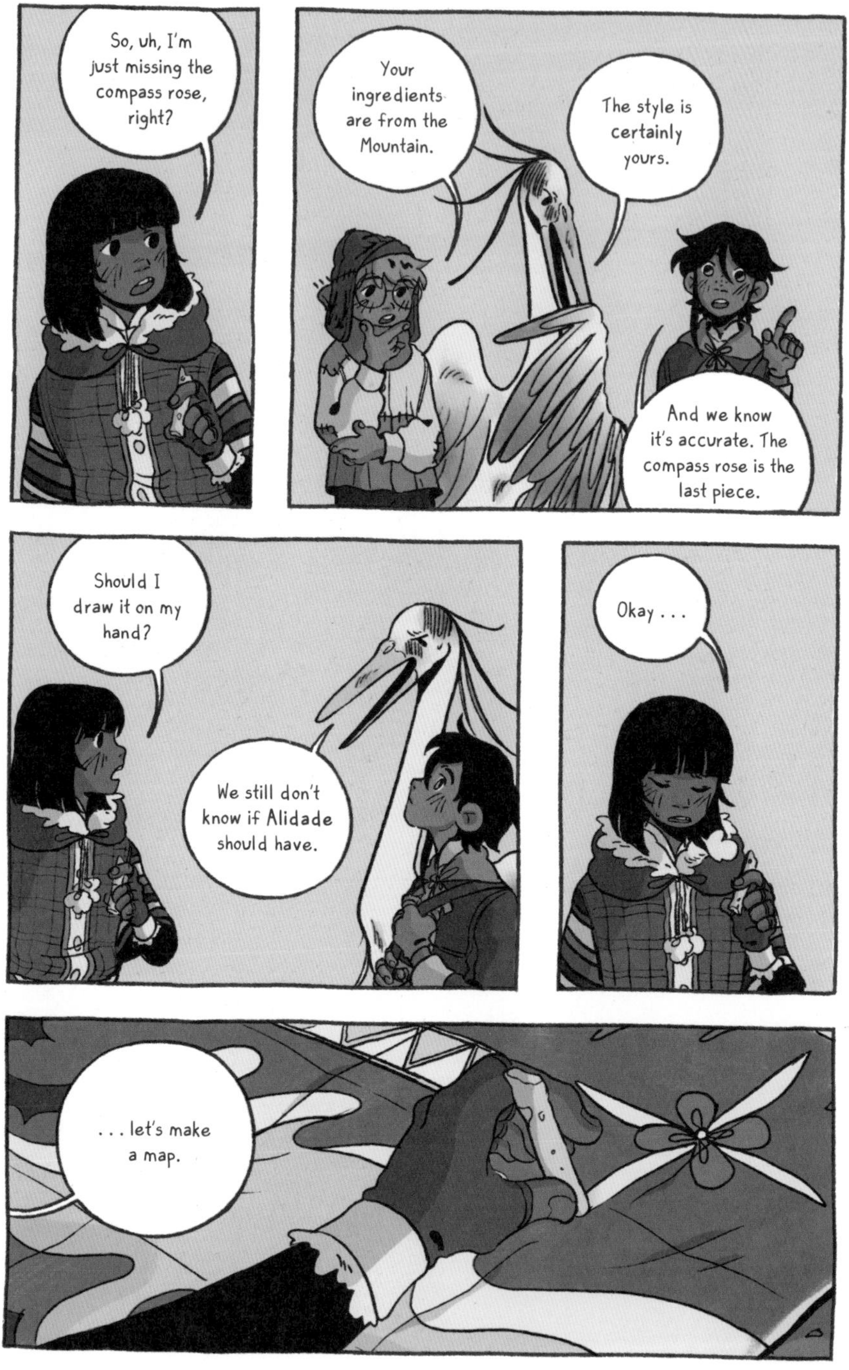
So, uh, I'm just missing the compass rose, right?
Your ingredients are from the Mountain.
The style is certainly yours.
And we know it's accurate. The compass rose is the last piece.
Should I draw it on my hand?
We still don't know if Alidade should have.
Okay . . .
. . . let's make a map.

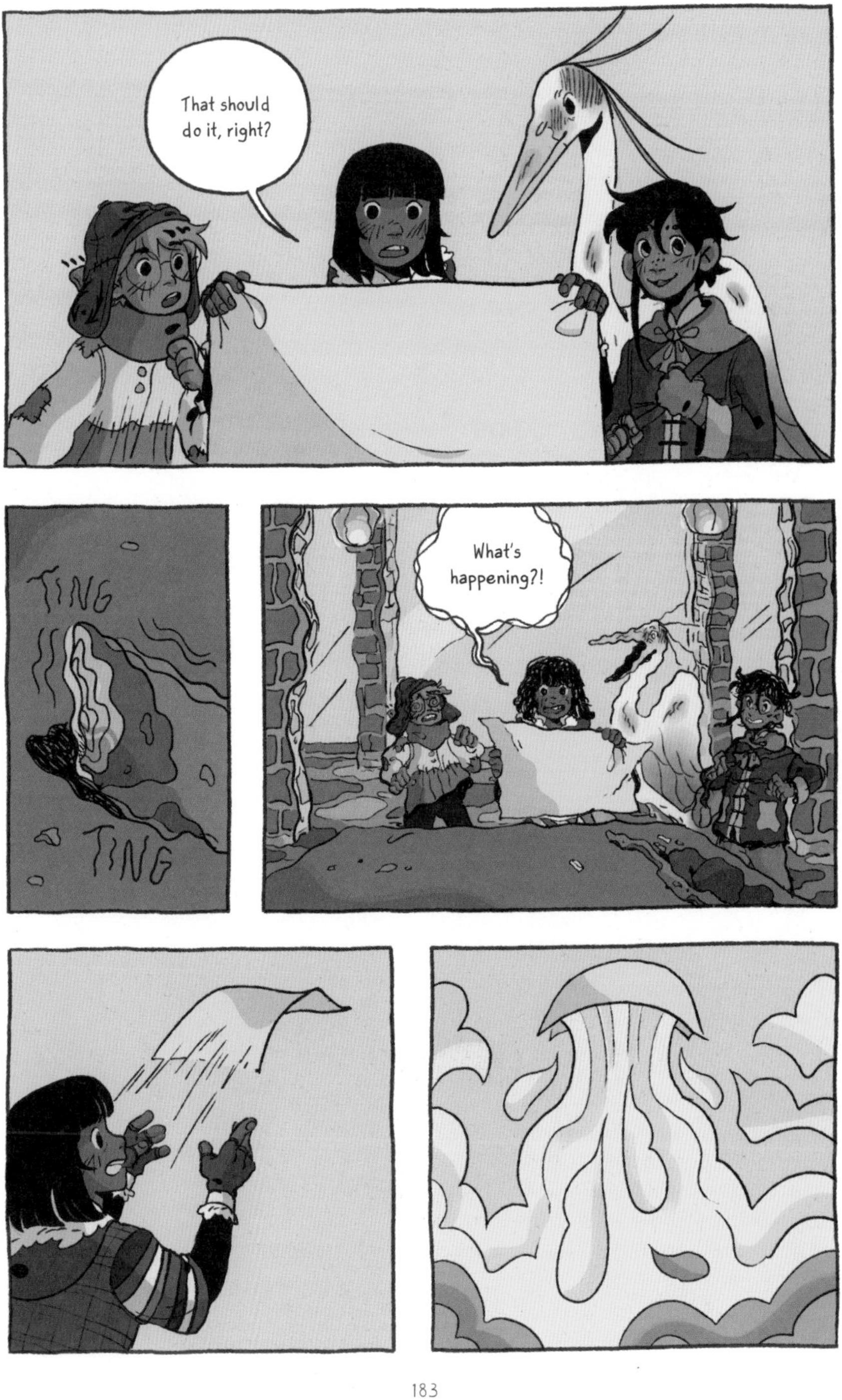
That should do it, right?
TING
TING
What's happening?!

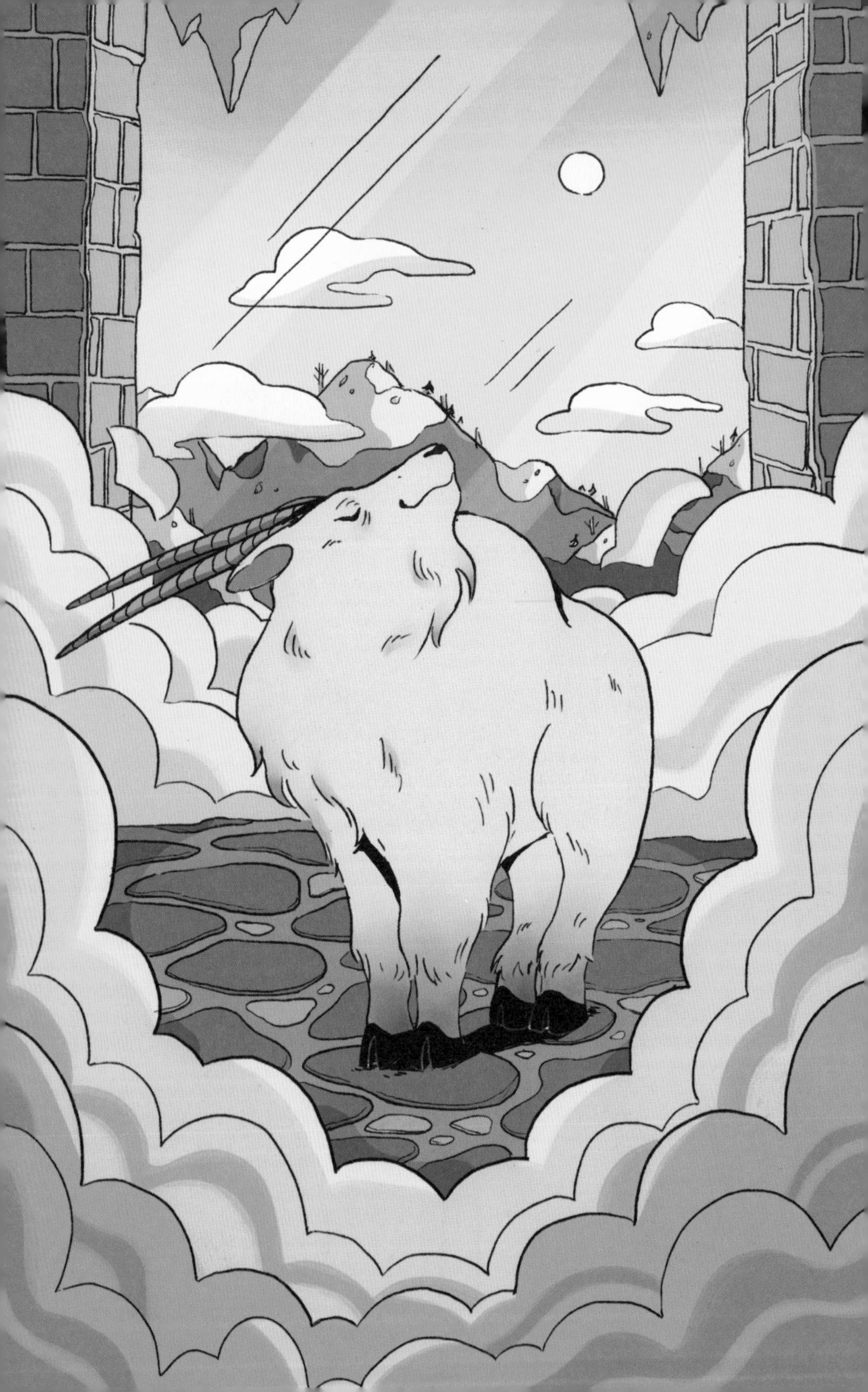

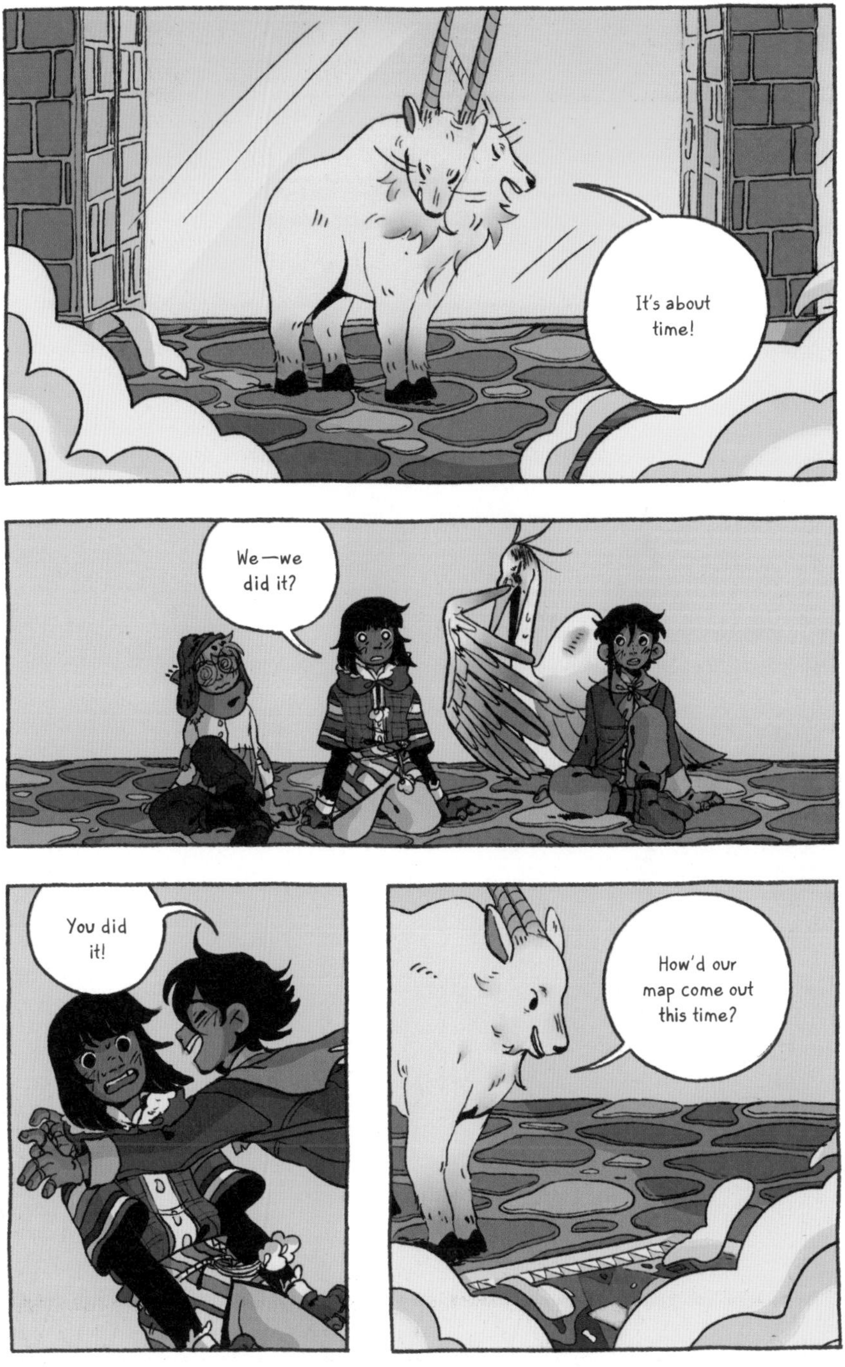
It's about time!
We—we did it?
You did it!
How'd our map come out this time?

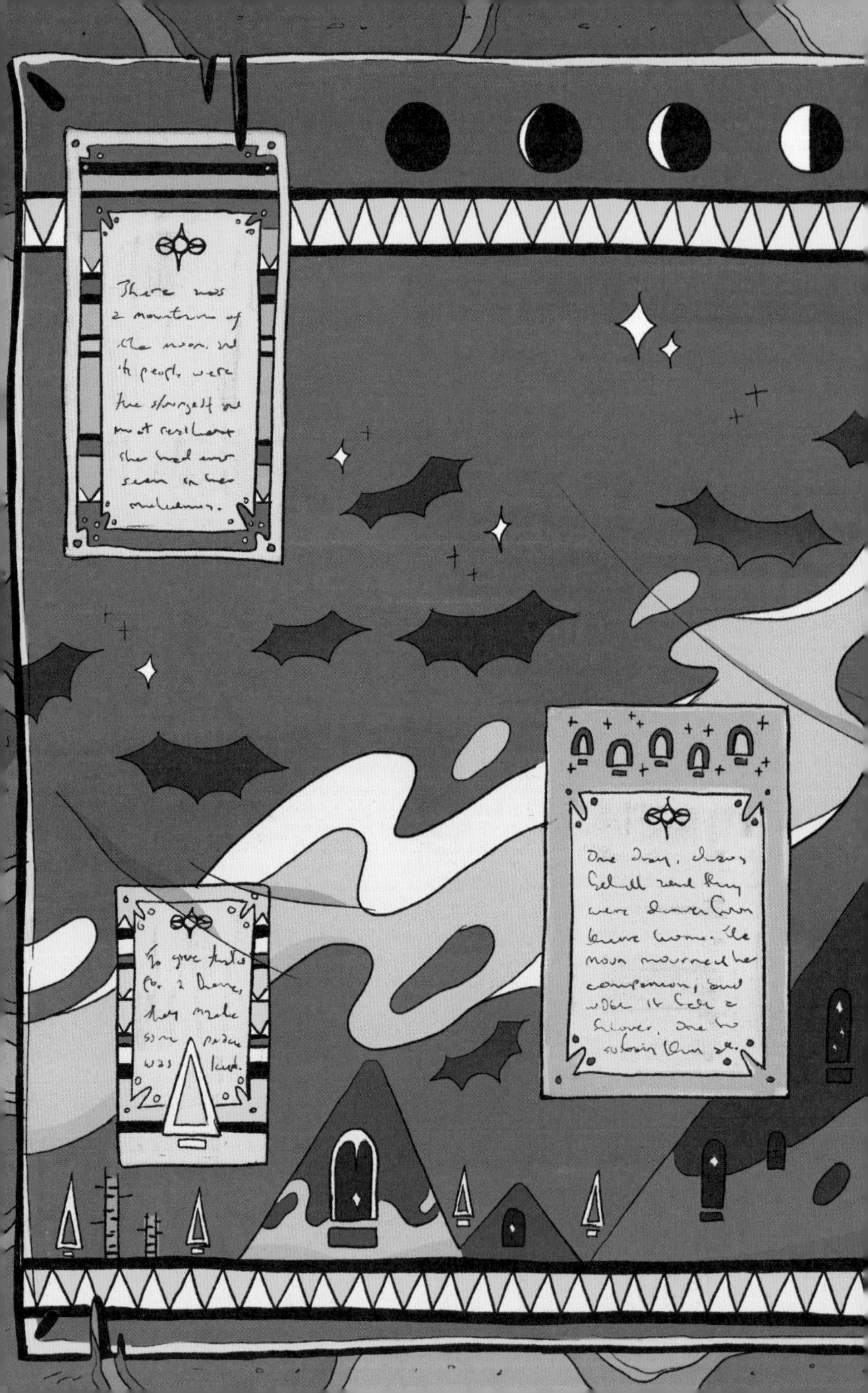
There was a mountain of the moon, and its people were the strongest and most resilient she had ever seen in her millennia.

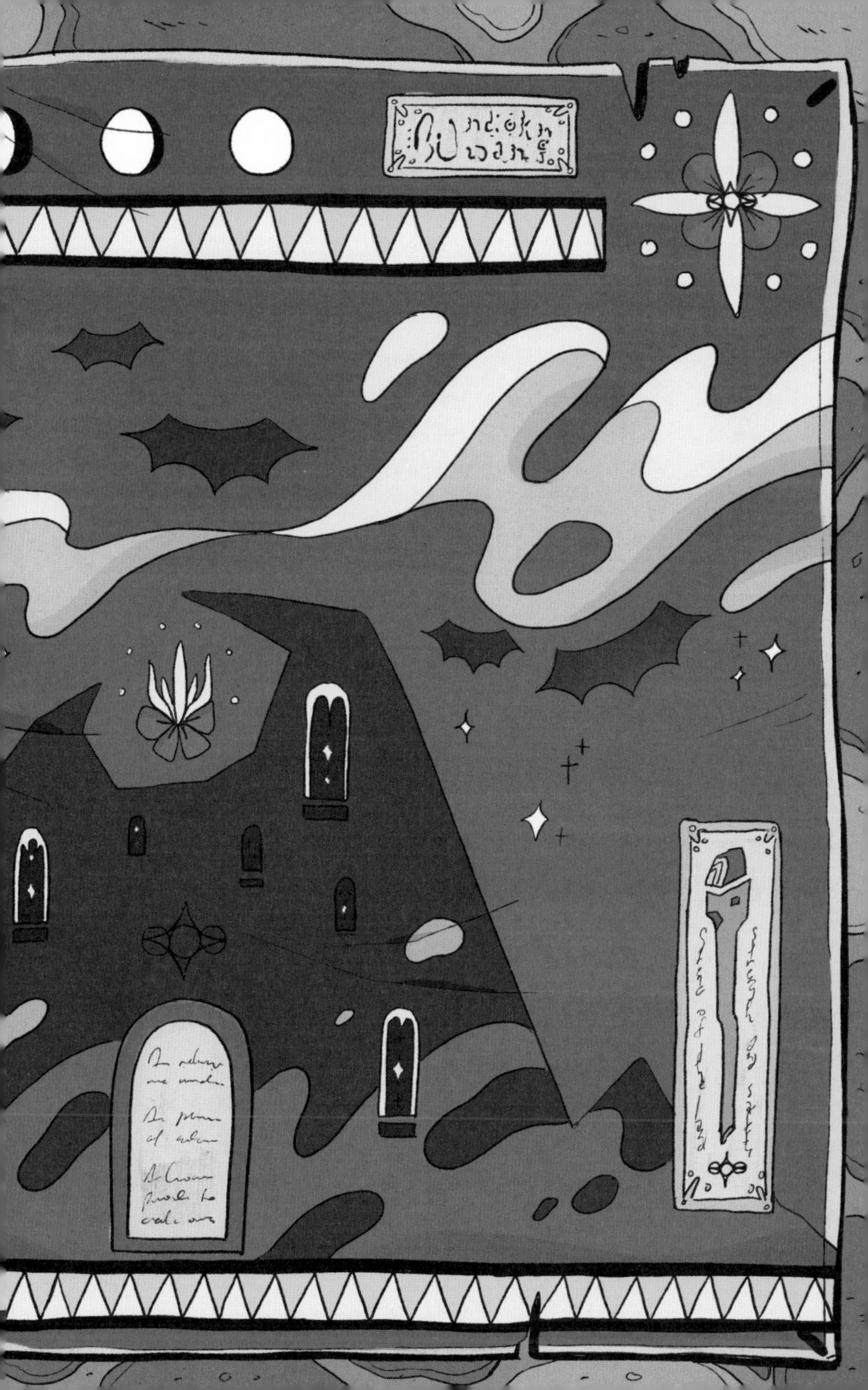

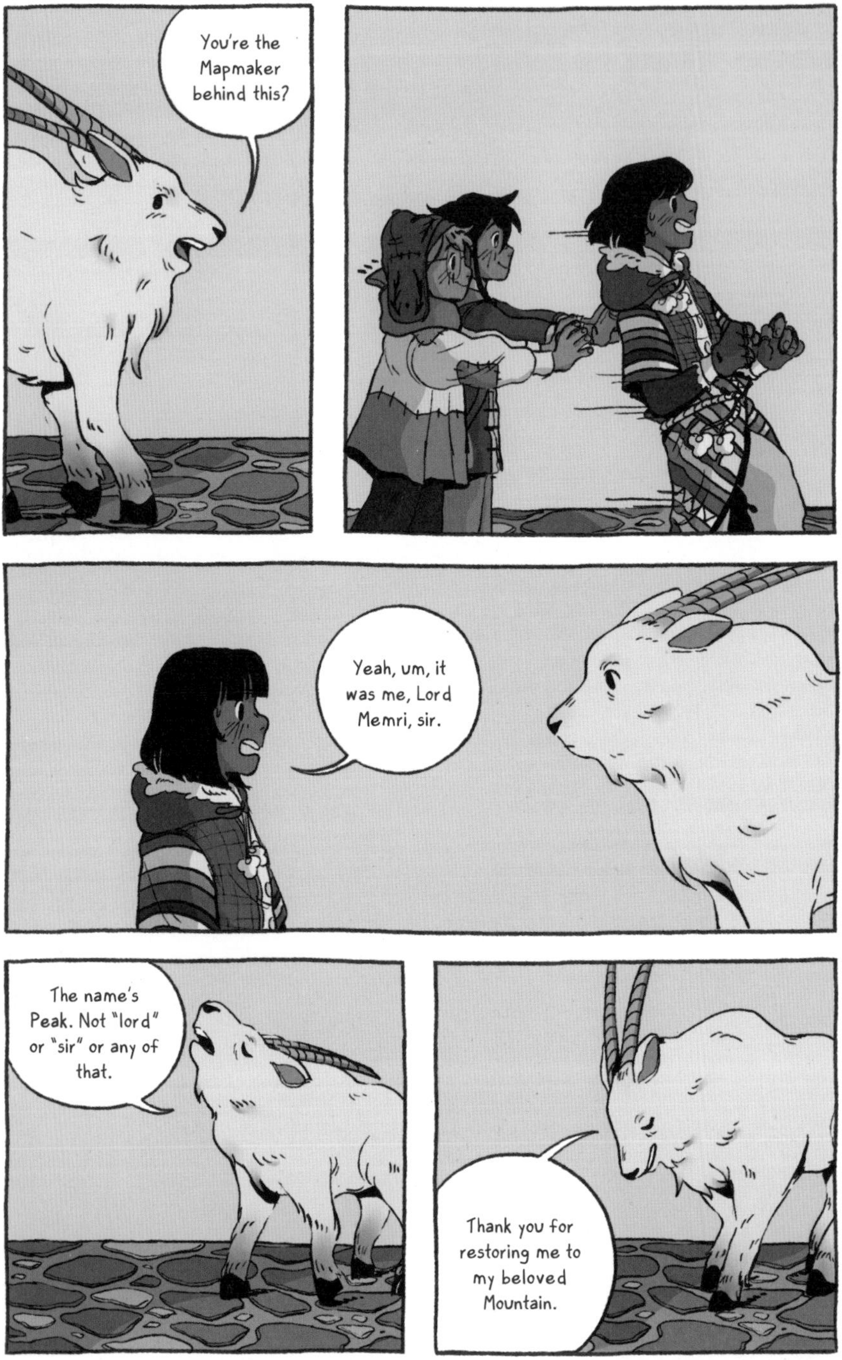
You're the Mapmaker behind this?
Yeah, um, it was me, Lord Memri, sir.
The name's Peak. Not "lord" or "sir" or any of that.
Thank you for restoring me to my beloved Mountain.

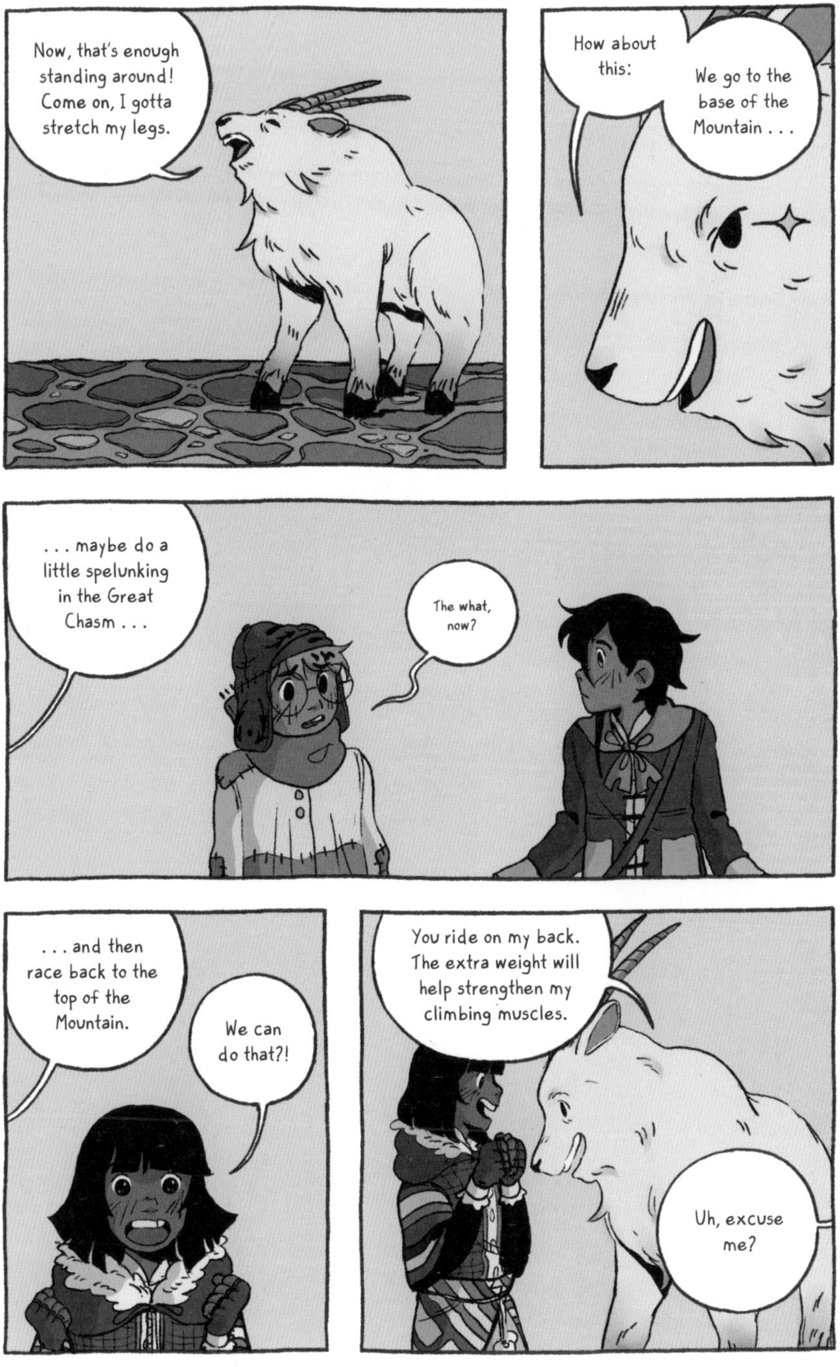
Now, that's enough standing around! Come on, I gotta stretch my legs.
How about this:
We go to the base of the Mountain . . .
. . . maybe do a little spelunking in the Great Chasm . . .
The what, now?
. . . and then race back to the top of the Mountain.
We can do that?!
You ride on my back. The extra weight will help strengthen my climbing muscles.
Uh, excuse me?

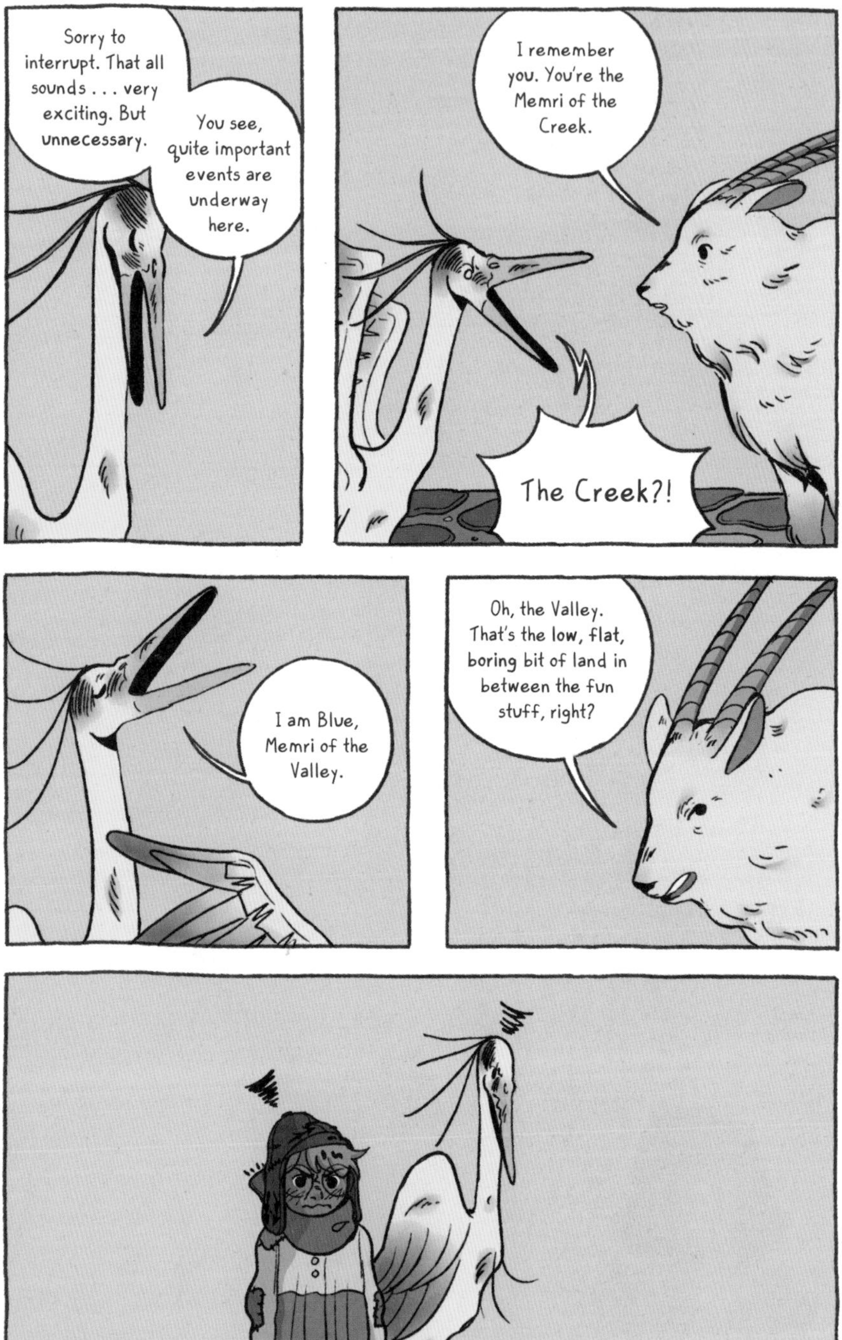

Sorry to interrupt. That all sounds . . . very exciting. But unnecessary.
You see, quite important events are underway here.
I remember you. You're the Memri of the Creek.
The Creek?!
I am Blue, Memri of the Valley.
Oh, the Valley. That's the low, flat, boring bit of land in between the fun stuff, right?

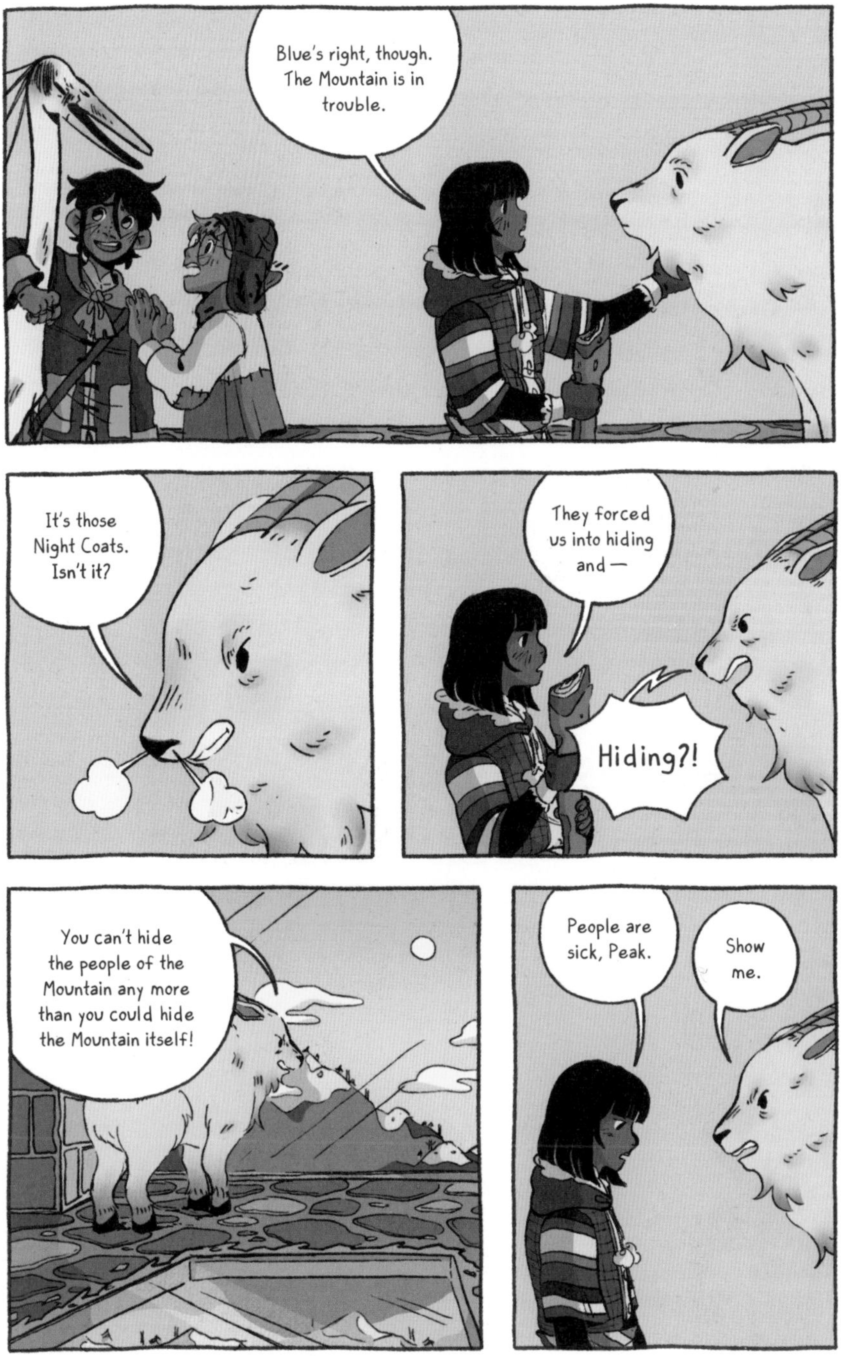
Blue's right, though. The Mountain is in trouble.
It's those Night Coats. Isn't it?
They forced us into hiding and —
Hiding?!
You can't hide the people of the Mountain any more than you could hide the Mountain itself!
People are sick, Peak.
Show me.

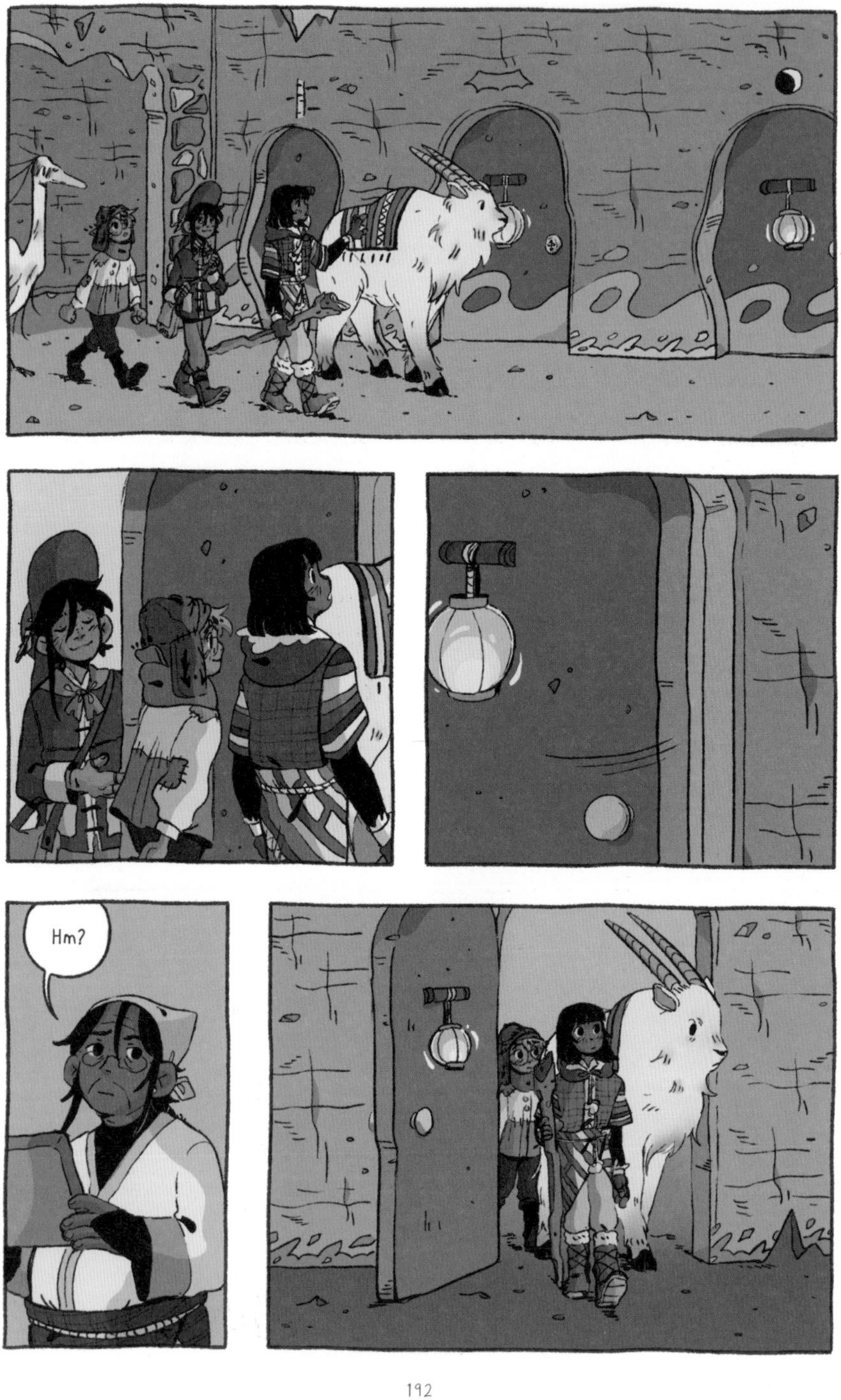
Hm?

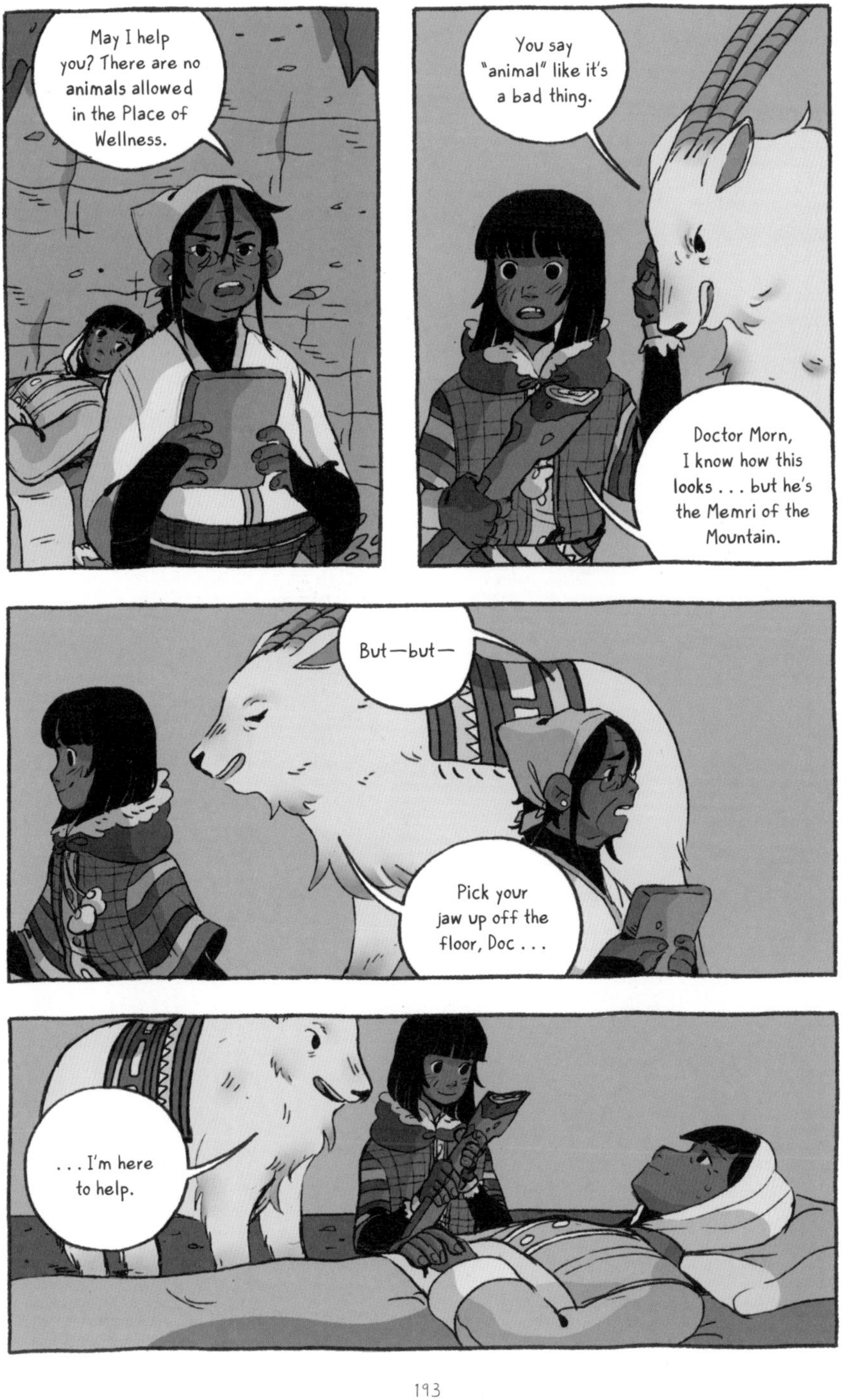
May I help you? There are no animals allowed in the Place of Wellness.
You say "animal" like it's a bad thing.
Doctor Morn, I know how this looks . . . but he's the Memri of the Mountain.
But—but—
Pick your jaw up off the floor, Doc . . .
. . . I'm here to help.

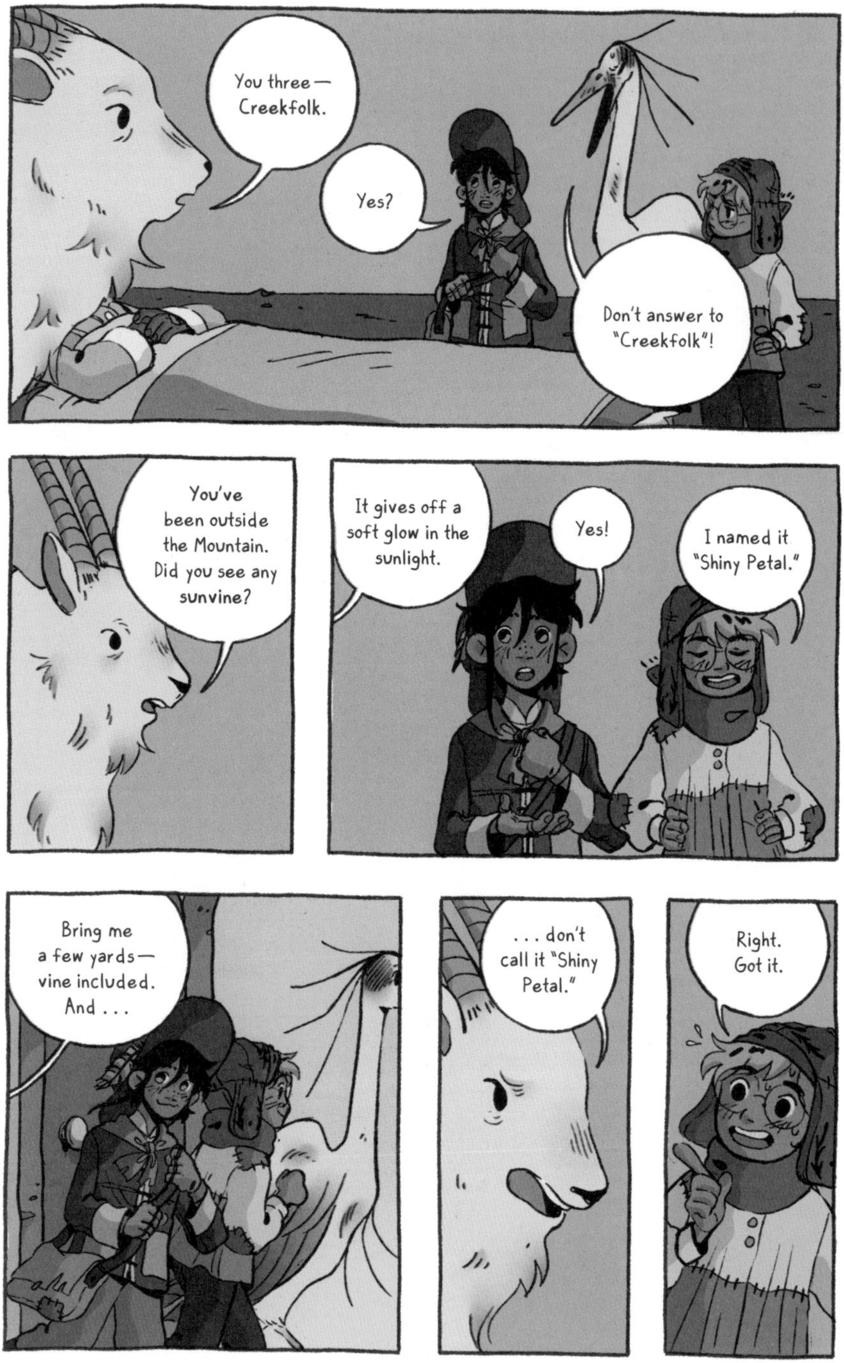
You three— Creekfolk.
Yes?
Don't answer to "Creekfolk"!
You've been outside the Mountain. Did you see any sunvine?
It gives off a soft glow in the sunlight.
Yes!
I named it "Shiny Petal."
Bring me a few yards— vine included. And . . .
. . . don't call it "Shiny Petal."
Right. Got it.

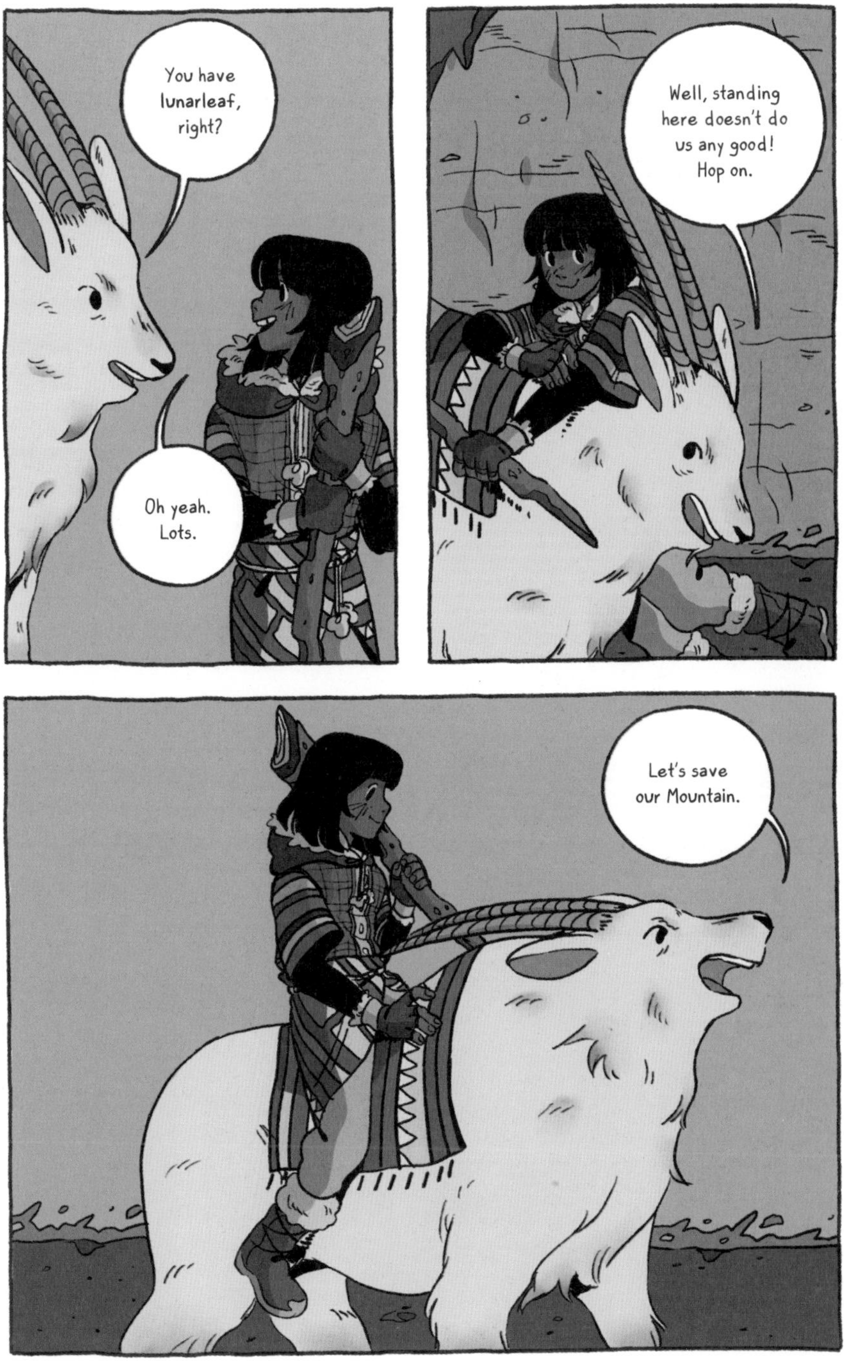
You have lunarleaf, right?
Oh yeah. Lots.
Well, standing here doesn't do us any good! Hop on.
Let's save our Mountain.

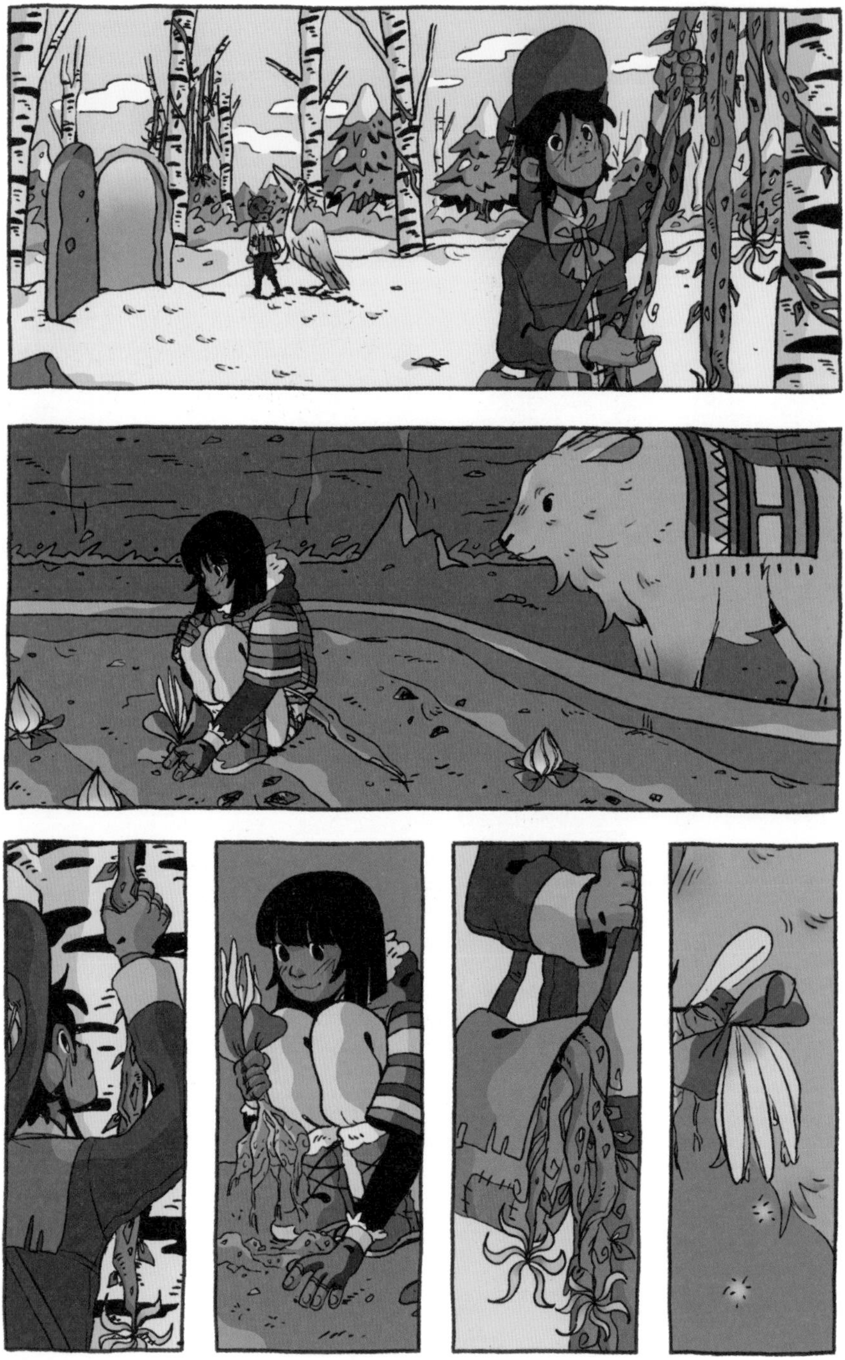

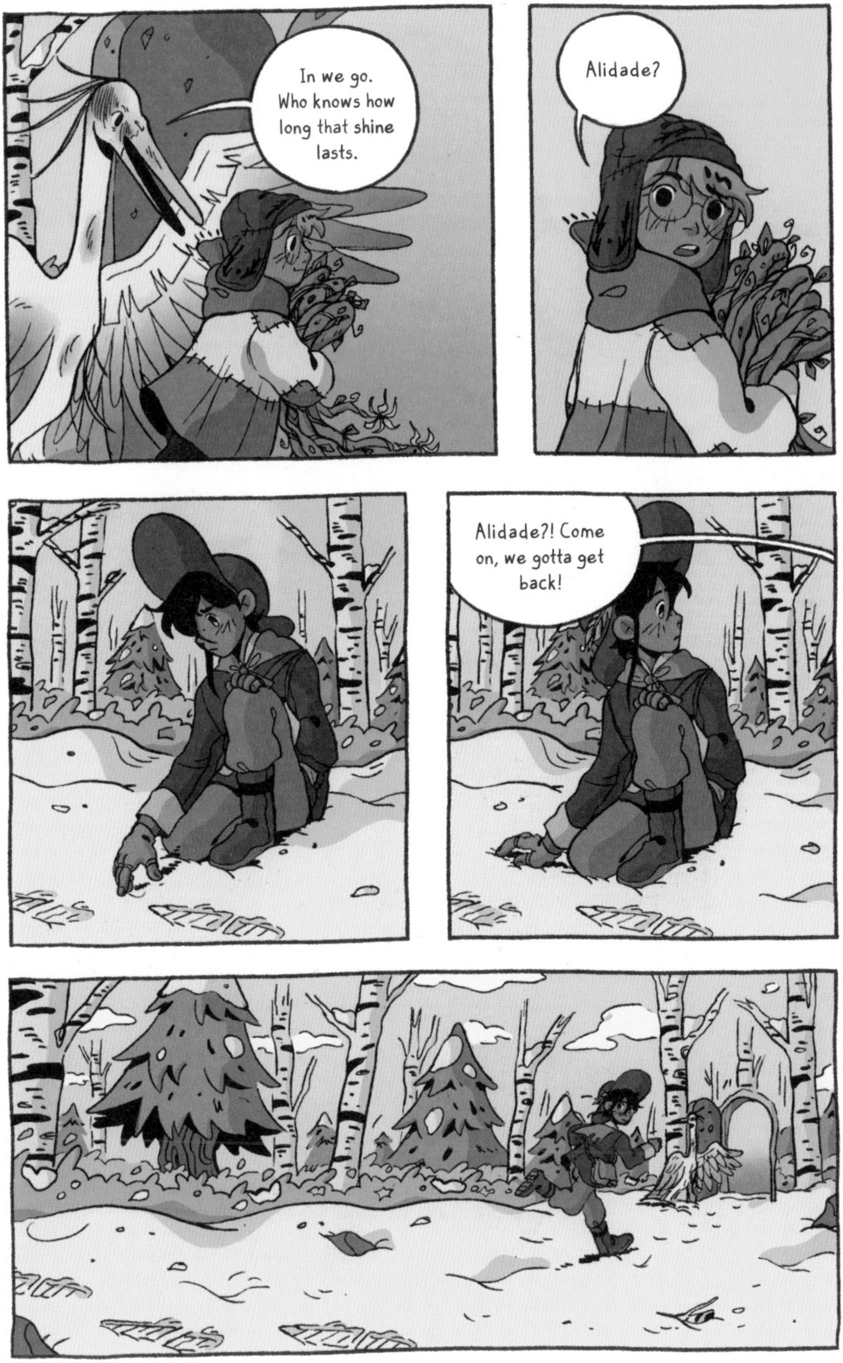
In we go. Who knows how long that shine lasts.
Alidade?
Alidade?! Come on, we gotta get back!

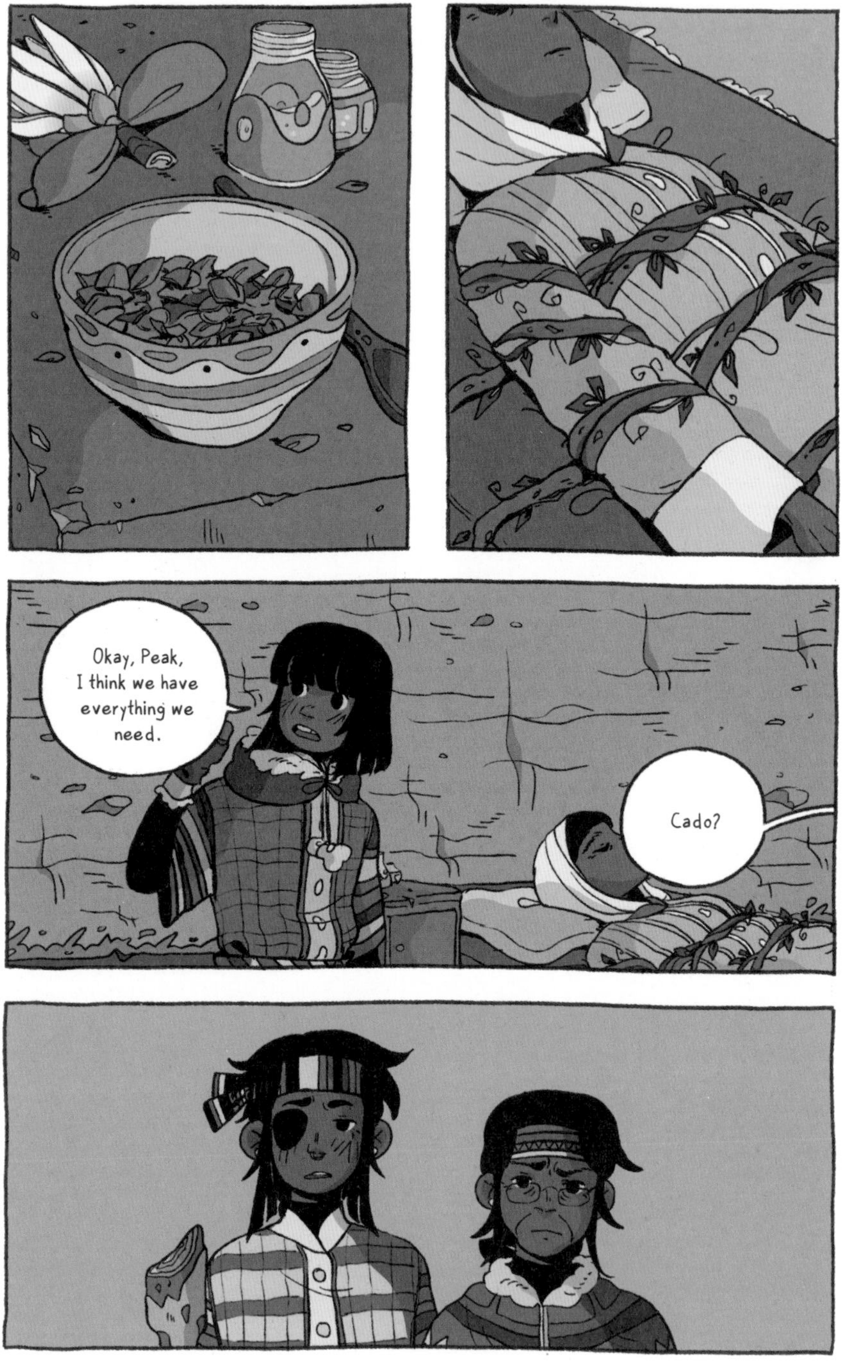
Okay, Peak, I think we have everything we need.
Cado?

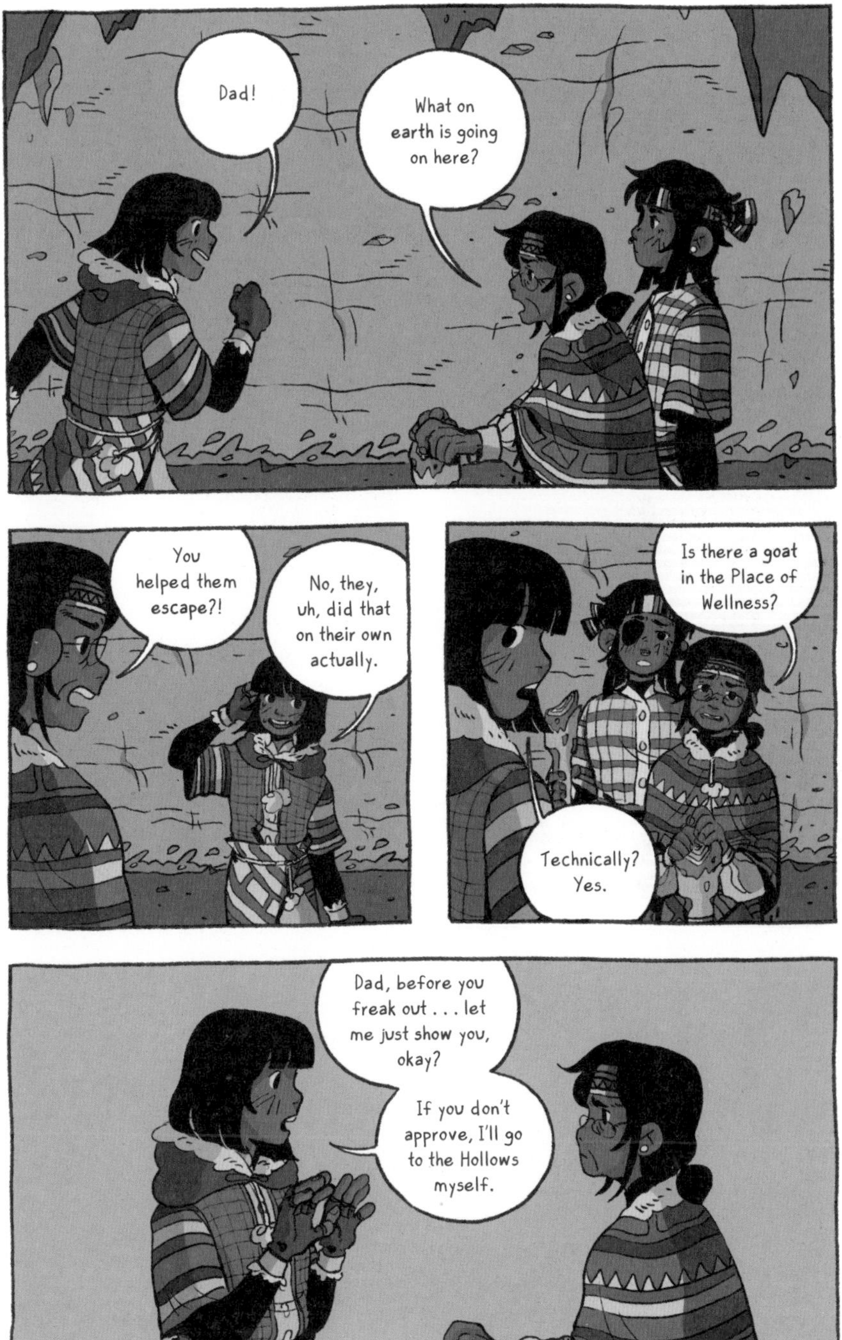

Dad!
What on earth is going on here?
You helped them escape?!
No, they, uh, did that on their own actually.
Is there a goat in the Place of Wellness?
Technically? Yes.
Dad, before you freak out . . . let me just show you, okay?
If you don't approve, I'll go to the Hollows myself.

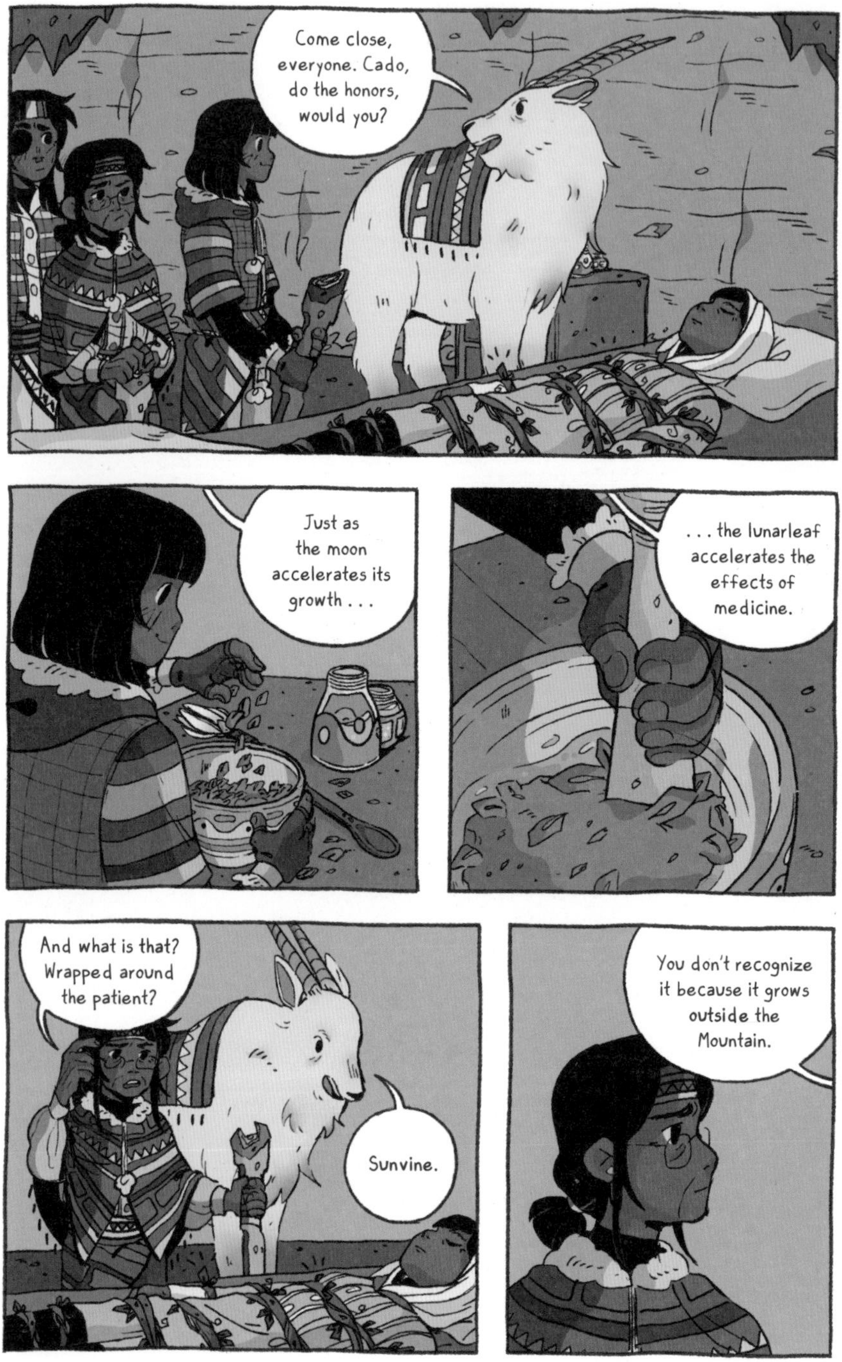

Come close, everyone. Cado, do the honors, would you?
Just as the moon accelerates its growth . . .
. . . the lunarleaf accelerates the effects of medicine.
And what is that? Wrapped around the patient?
Sunvine.
You don't recognize it because it grows outside the Mountain.

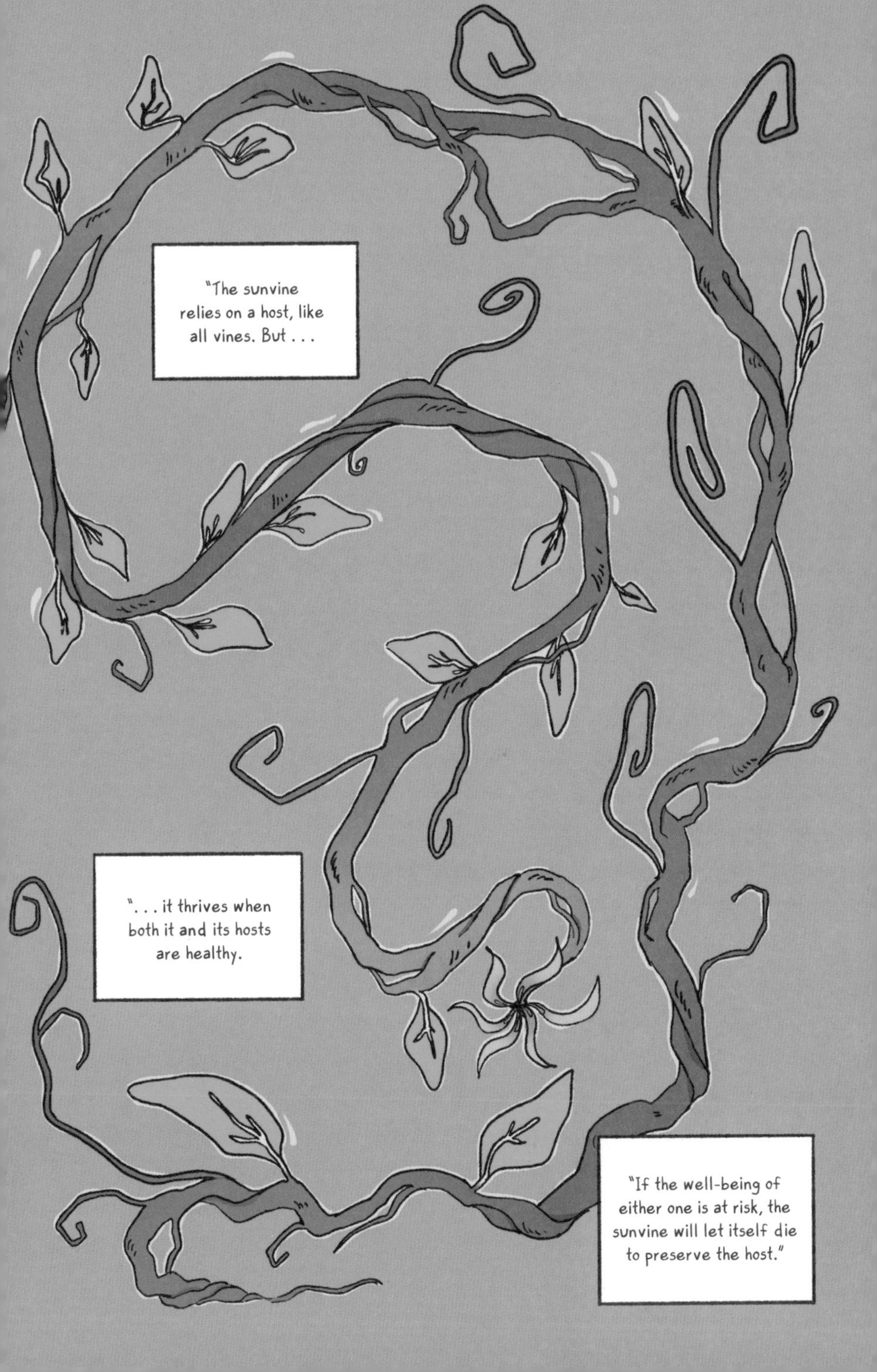
"The sunvine relies on a host, like all vines. But . . .
". . . it thrives when both it and its hosts are healthy.
"If the well-being of either one is at risk, the sunvine will let itself die to preserve the host."

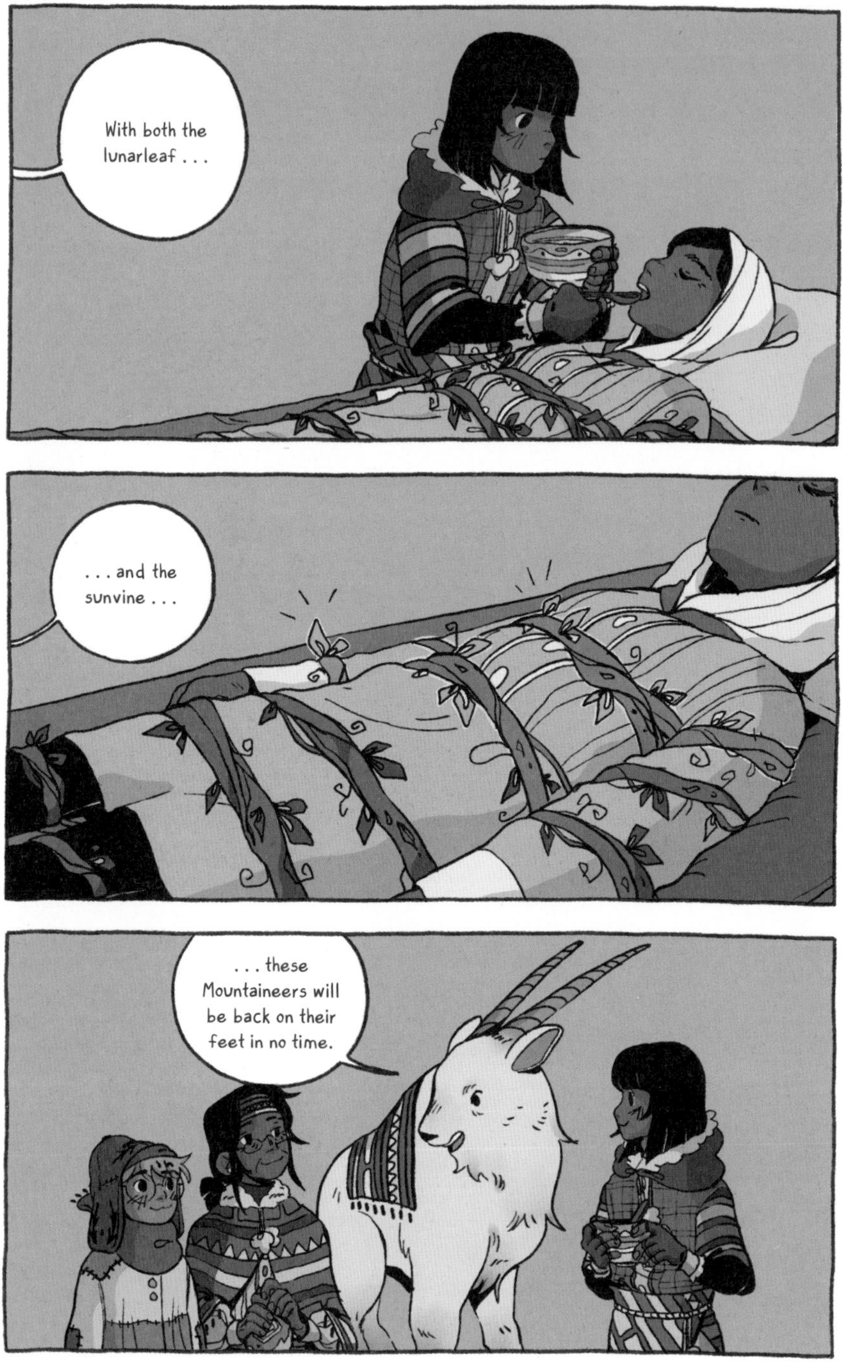
With both the lunarleaf . . .
. . . and the sunvine . . .
. . . these Mountaineers will be back on their feet in no time.

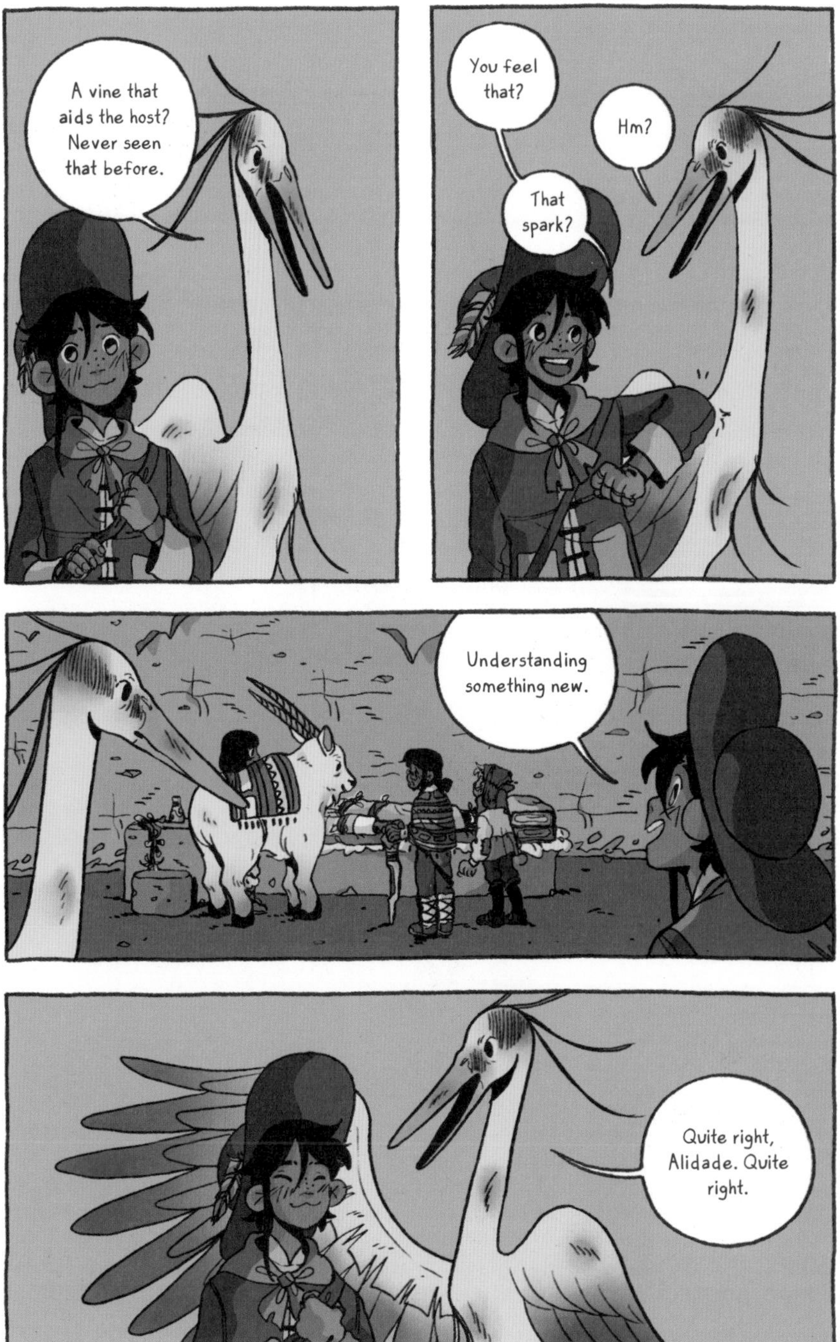
A vine that aids the host? Never seen that before.
You feel that?
Hm?
That spark?
Understanding something new.
Quite right, Alidade. Quite right.

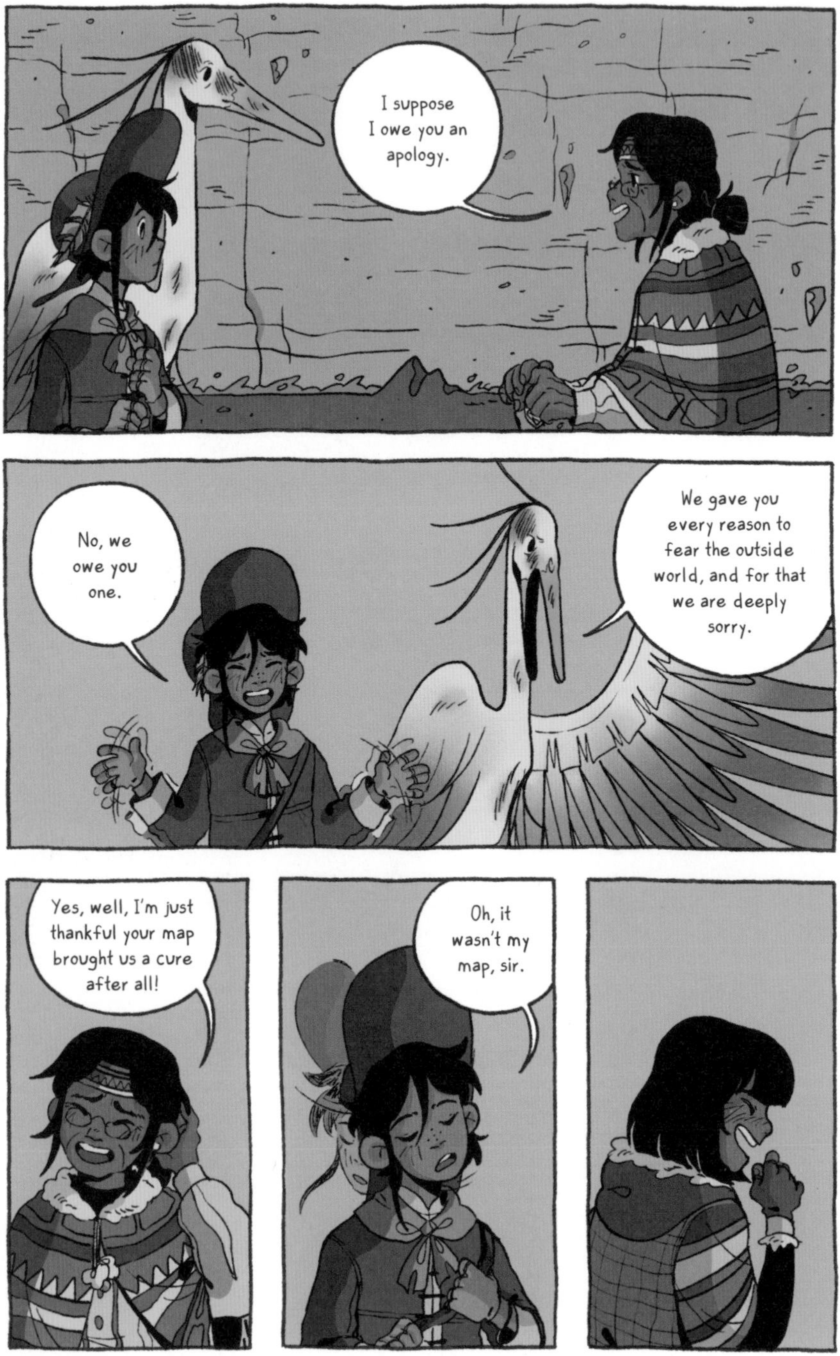
I suppose I owe you an apology.
No, we owe you one.
We gave you every reason to fear the outside world, and for that we are deeply sorry.
Yes, well, I'm just thankful your map brought us a cure after all!
Oh, it wasn't my map, sir.

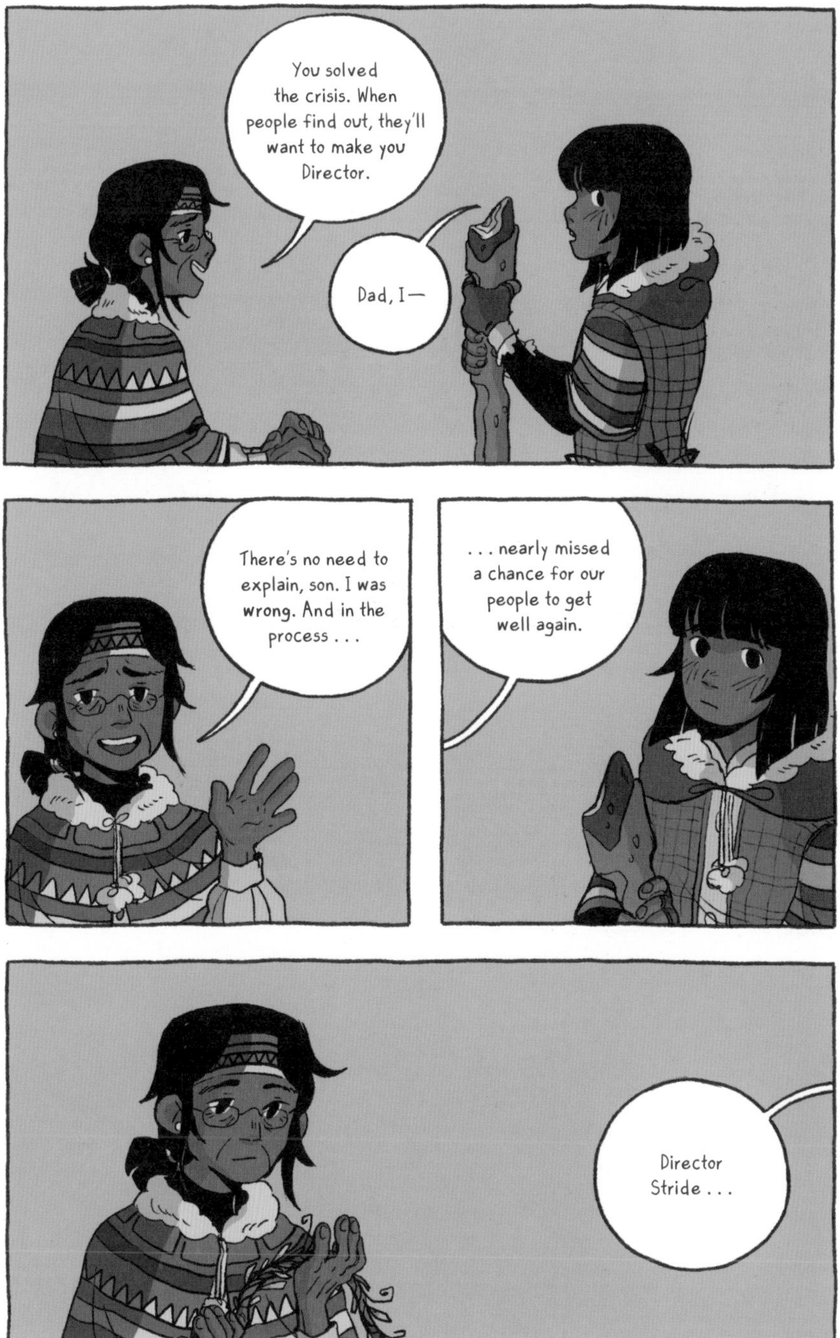
You solved the crisis. When people find out, they'll want to make you Director.
Dad, I—
There's no need to explain, son. I was wrong. And in the process . . .
. . . nearly missed a chance for our people to get well again.
Director Stride . . .

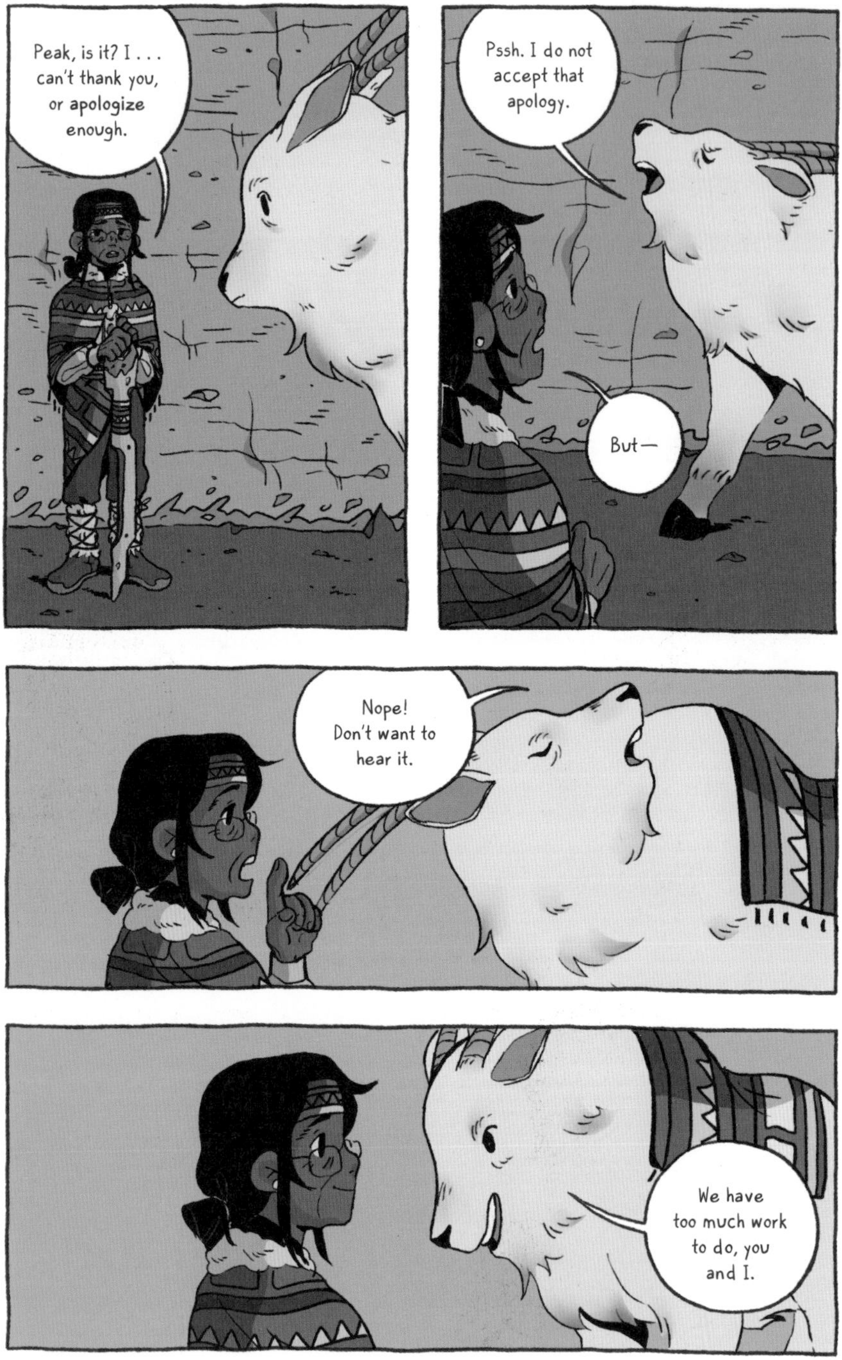
Peak, is it? I . . . can't thank you, or apologize enough.
Pssh. I do not accept that apology.
But—
Nope! Don't want to hear it.
We have too much work to do, you and I.

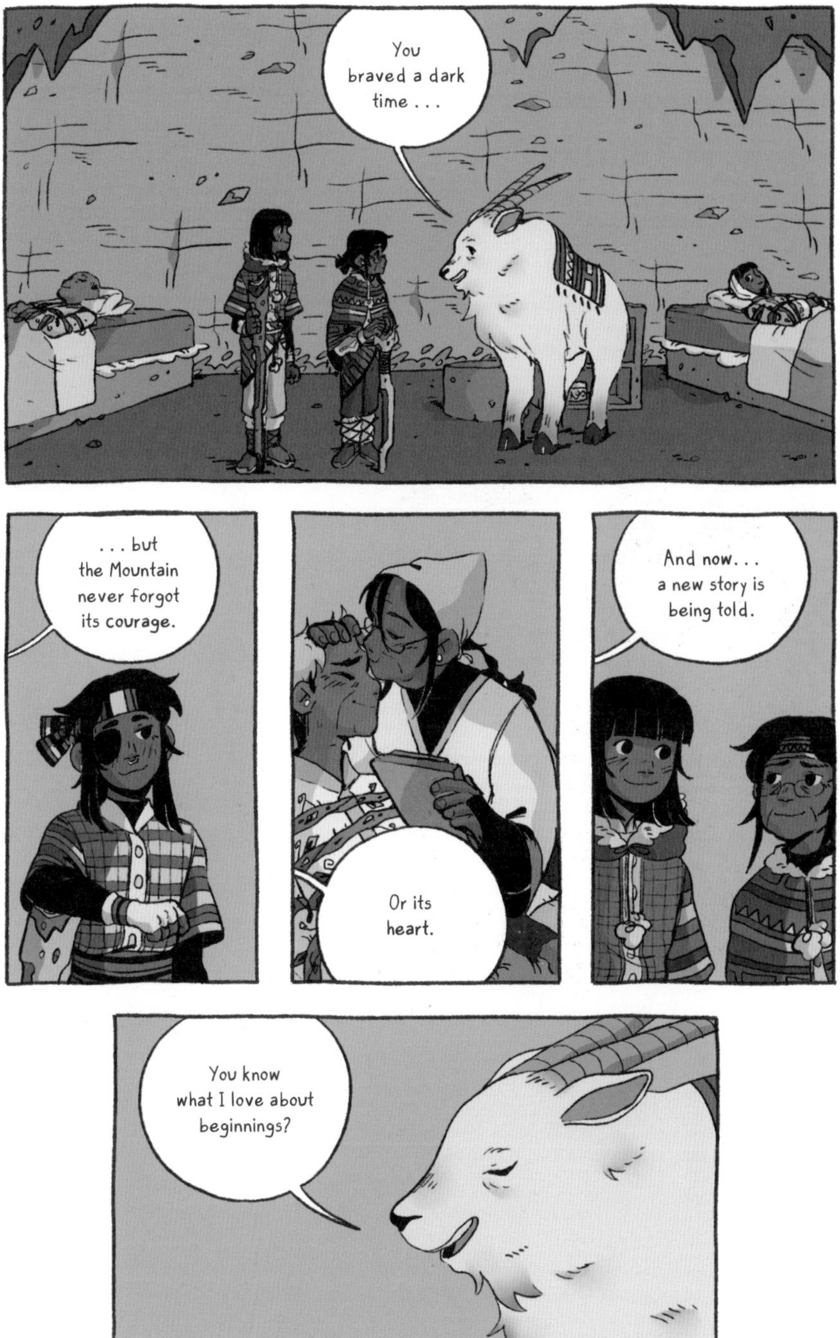
You braved a dark time . . .
. . . but the Mountain never forgot its courage.
Or its heart.
And now. . . a new story is being told.
You know what I love about beginnings?

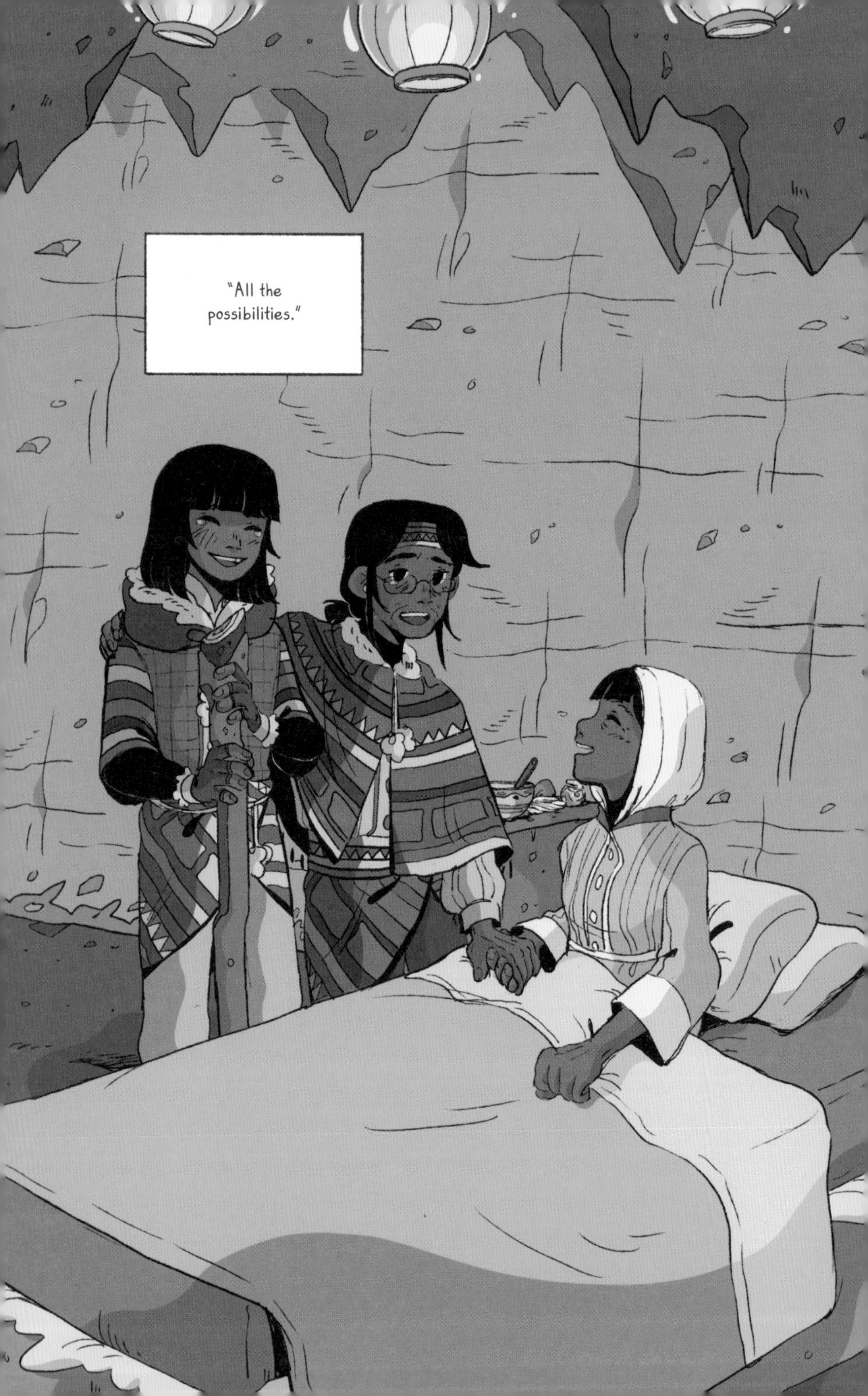
"All the possibilities."

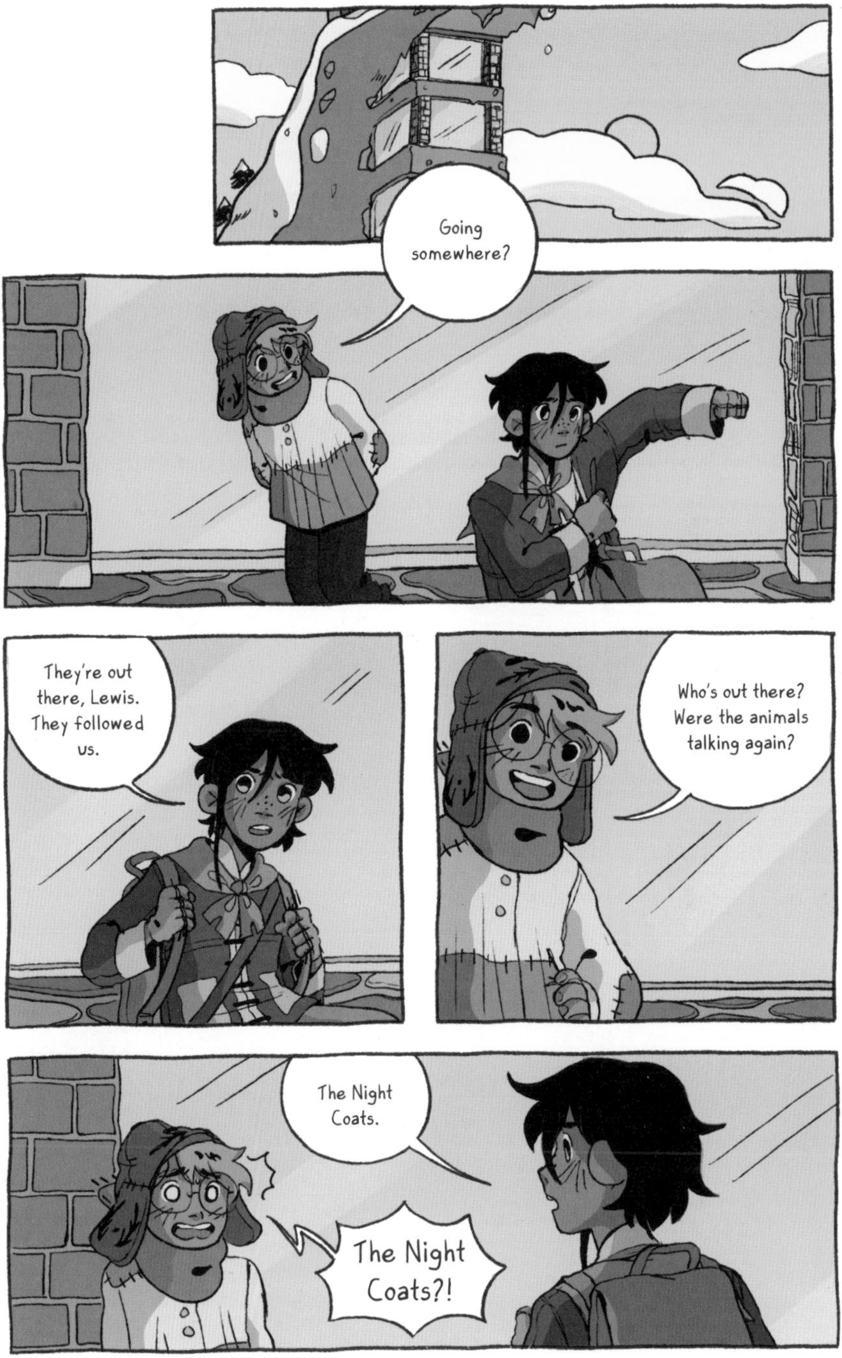

Going somewhere?
They're out there, Lewis. They followed us.
Who's out there? Were the animals talking again?
The Night Coats.
The Night Coats?!

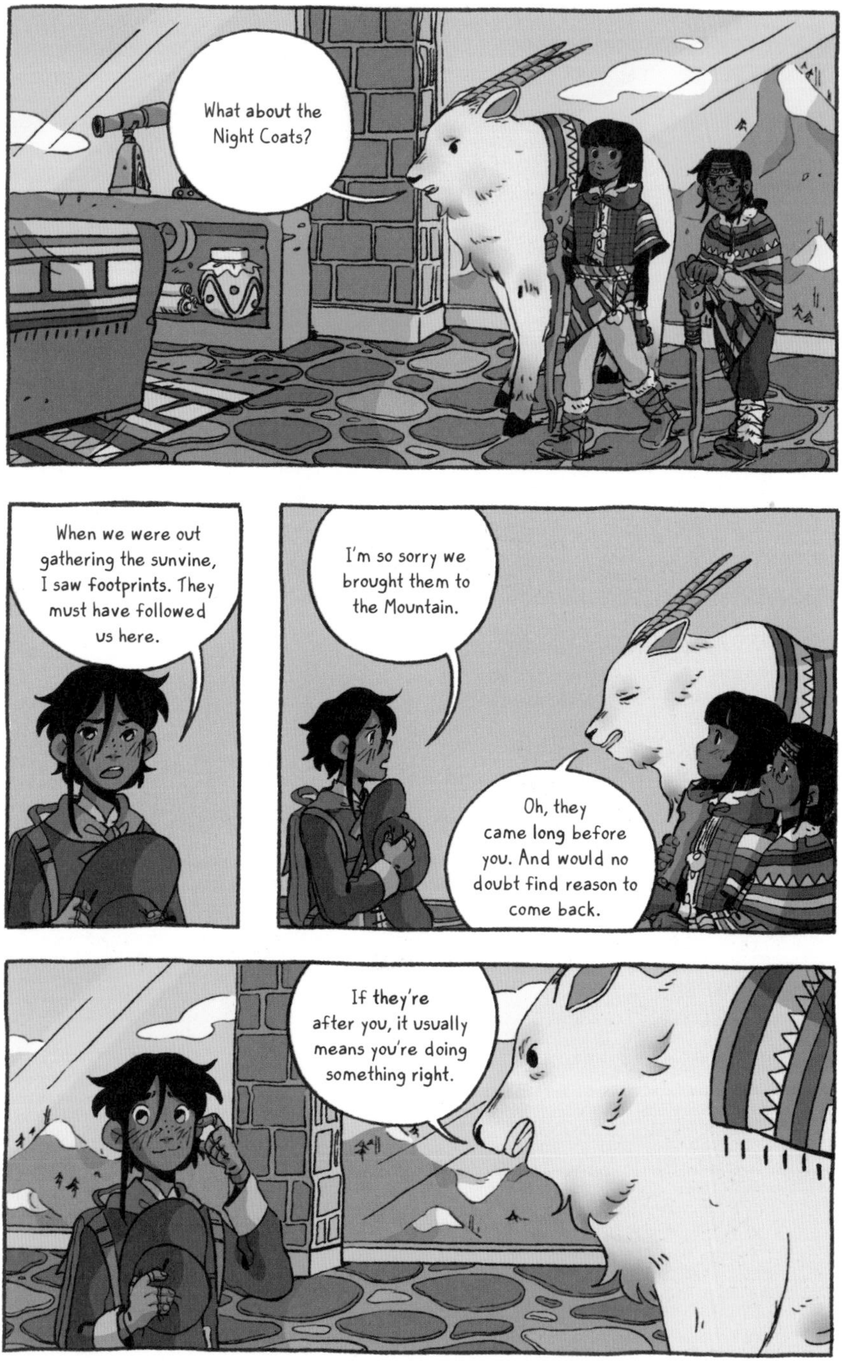
What about the Night Coats?
When we were out gathering the sunvine, I saw footprints. They must have followed us here.
I'm so sorry we brought them to the Mountain.
Oh, they came long before you. And would no doubt find reason to come back.
If they're after you, it usually means you're doing something right.

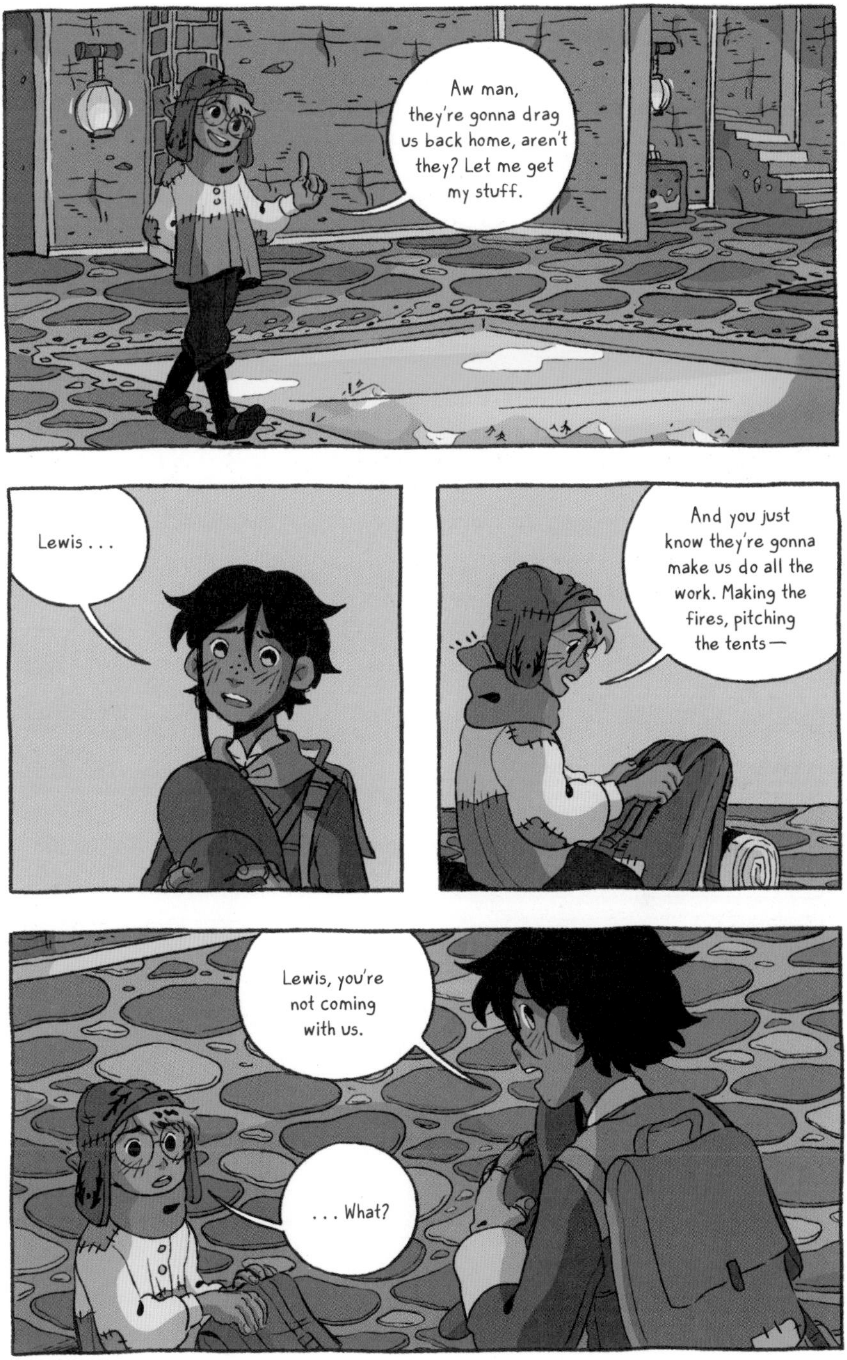
Aw man, they're gonna drag us back home, aren't they? Let me get my stuff.
Lewis . . .
And you just know they're gonna make us do all the work. Making the fires, pitching the tents—
Lewis, you're not coming with us.
. . . What?

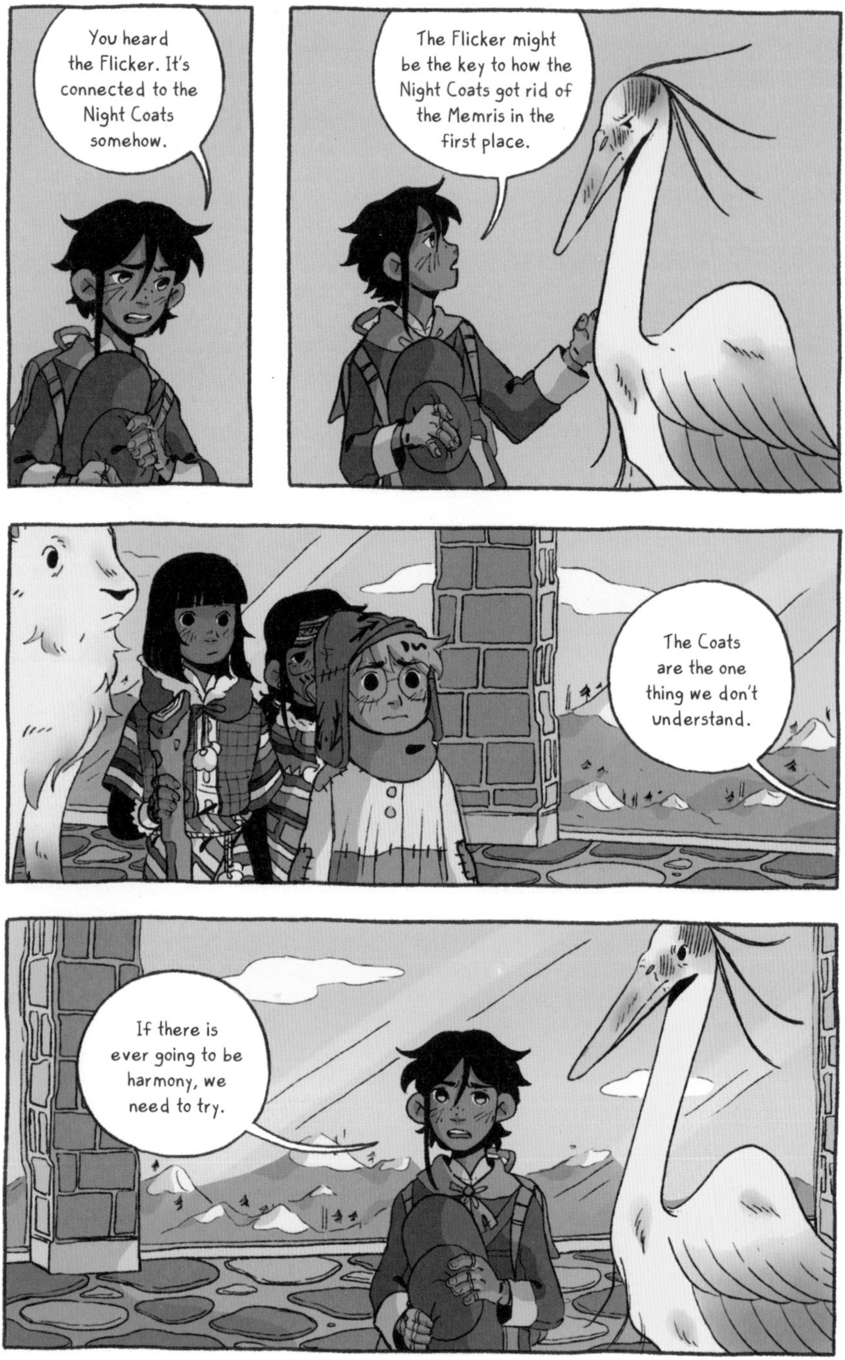
You heard the Flicker. It's connected to the Night Coats somehow.
The Flicker might be the key to how the Night Coats got rid of the Memris in the first place.
The Coats are the one thing we don't understand.
If there is ever going to be harmony, we need to try.

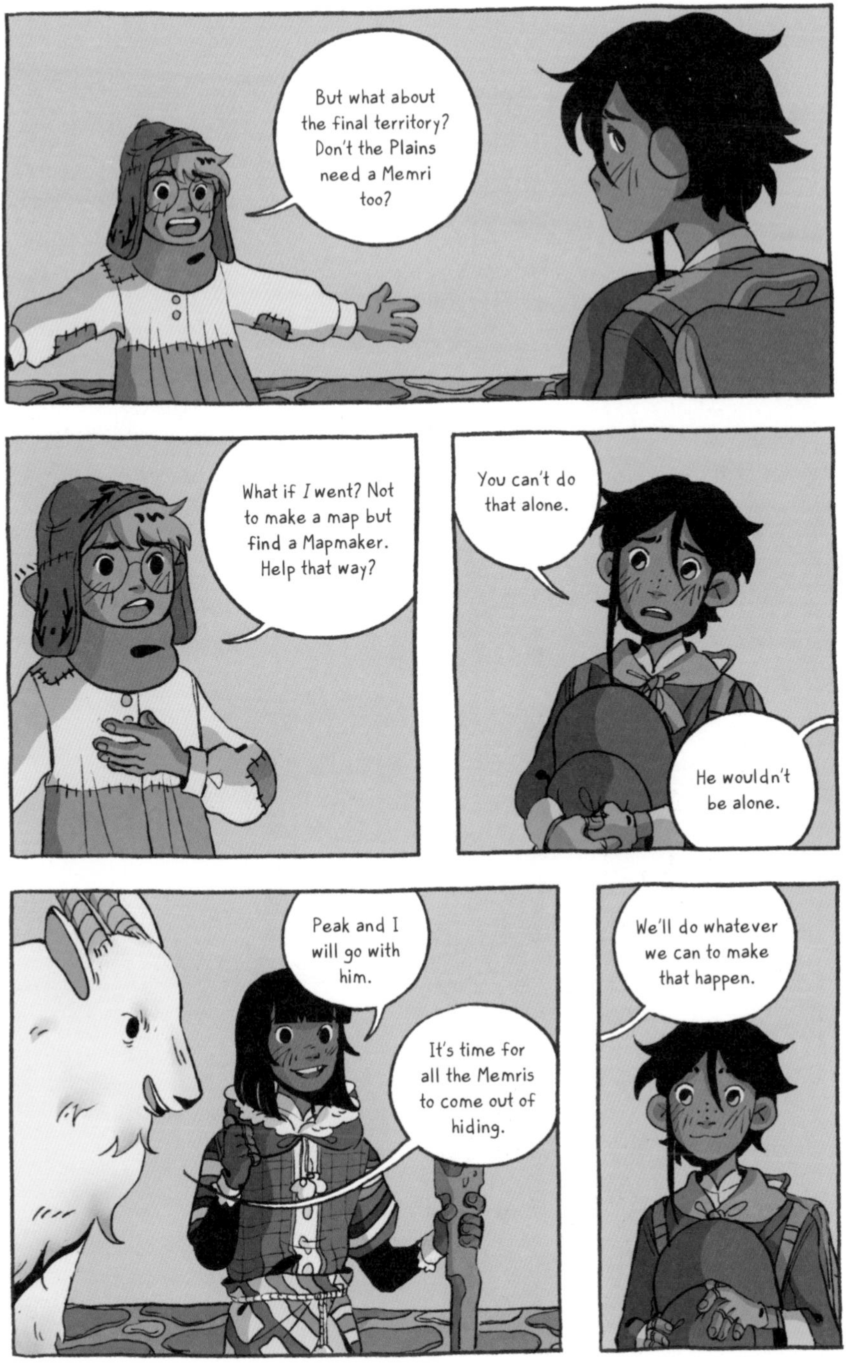
But what about the final territory? Don't the Plains need a Memri too?
What if *I* went? Not to make a map but find a Mapmaker. Help that way?
You can't do that alone.
He wouldn't be alone.
Peak and I will go with him.
It's time for all the Memris to come out of hiding.
We'll do whatever we can to make that happen.

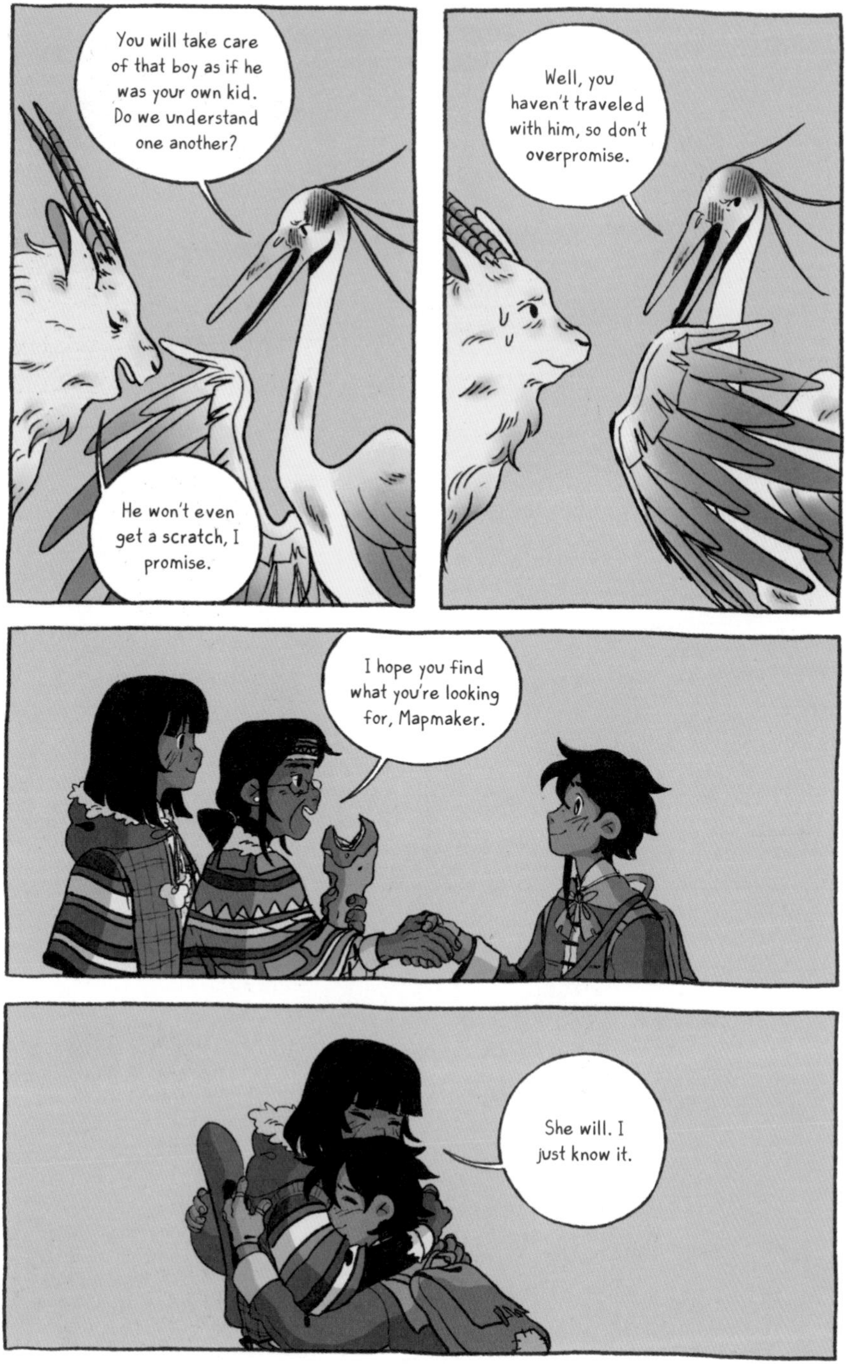
You will take care of that boy as if he was your own kid. Do we understand one another?
He won't even get a scratch, I promise.
Well, you haven't traveled with him, so don't overpromise.
I hope you find what you're looking for, Mapmaker.
She will. I just know it.

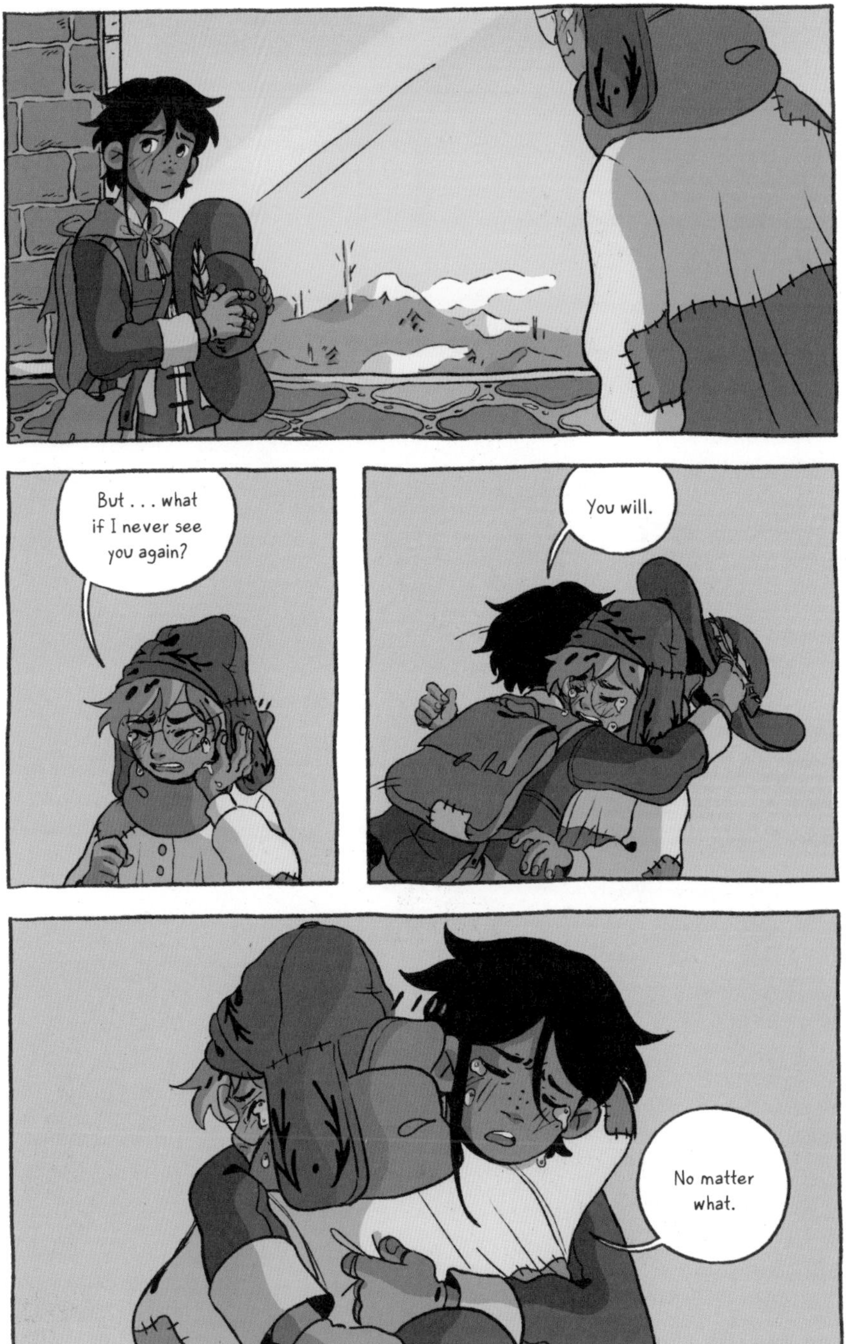
But . . . what if I never see you again?
You will.
No matter what.

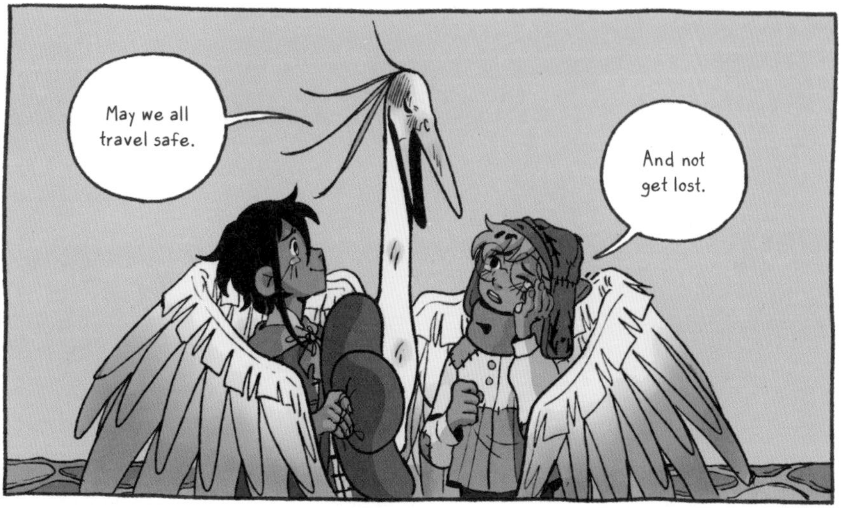
May we all travel safe.
And not get lost.

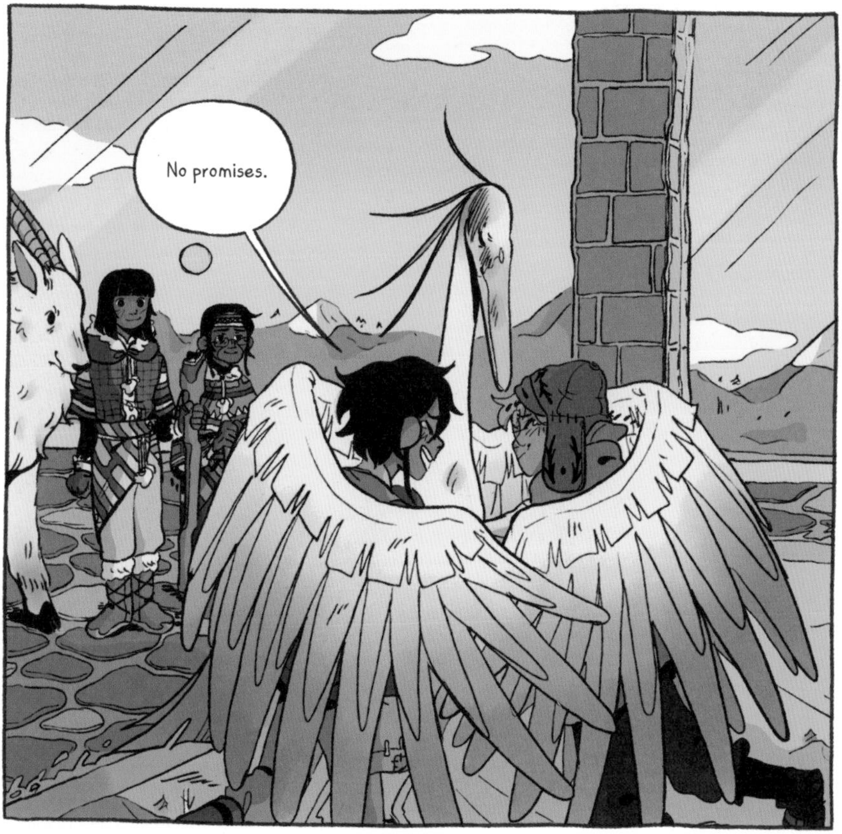
No promises.

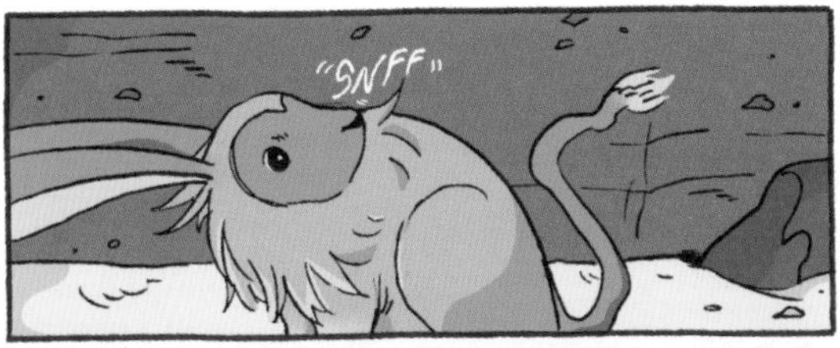
"SNFF"

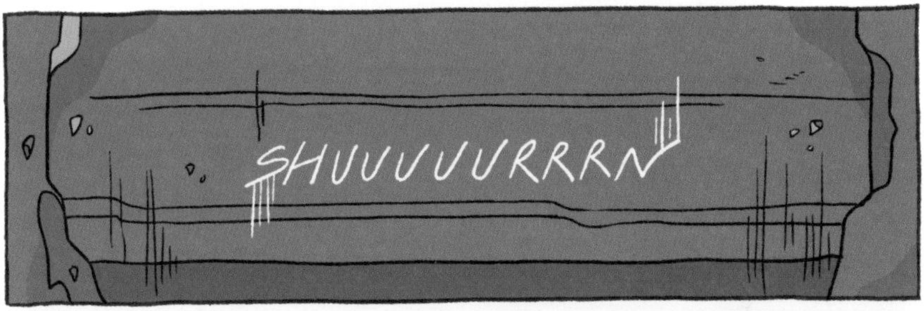
SHUUUUUURRRRN

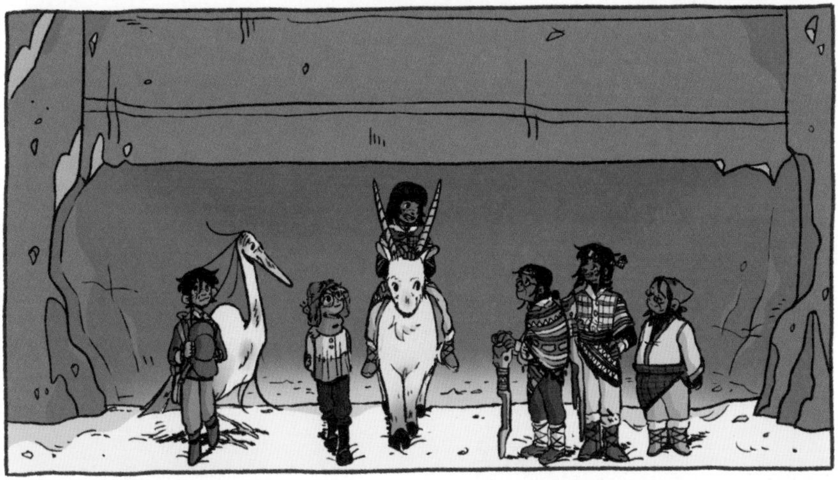

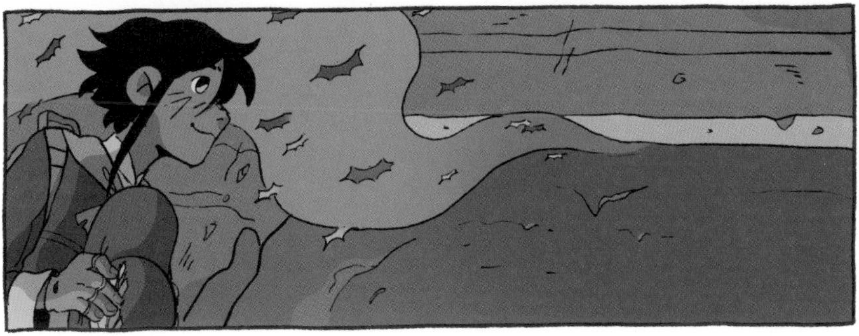

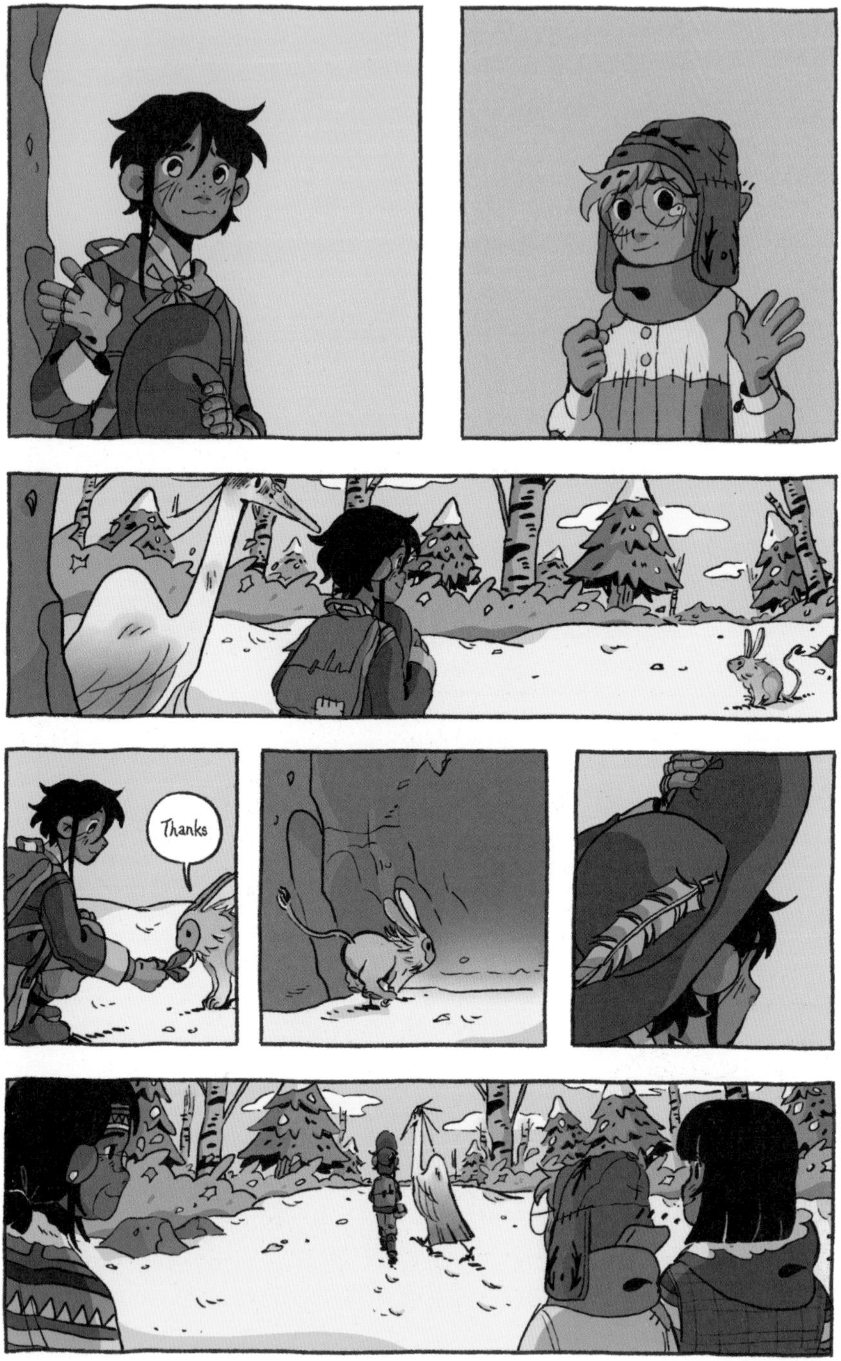
Thanks

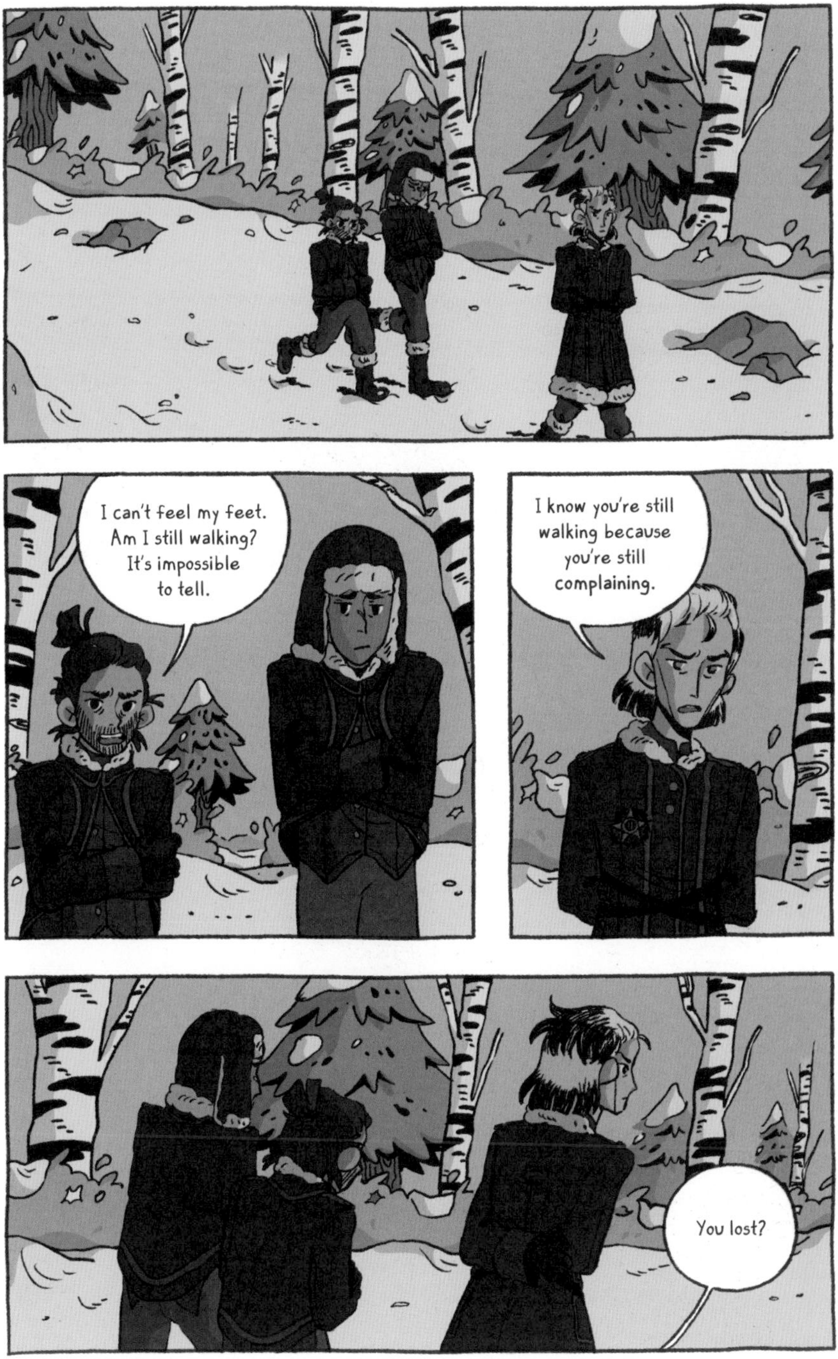
I can't feel my feet. Am I still walking? It's impossible to tell.
I know you're still walking because you're still complaining.
You lost?

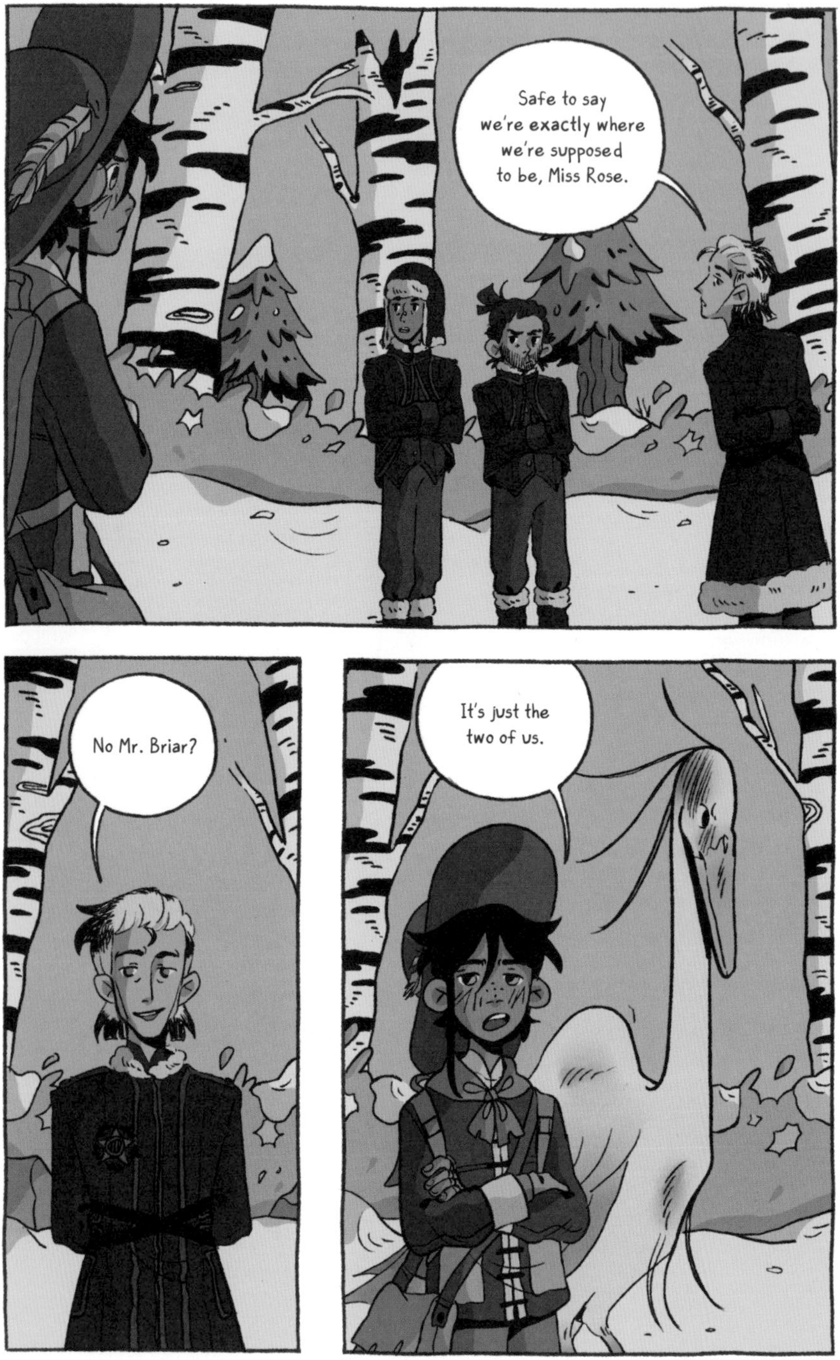
Safe to say we're exactly where we're supposed to be, Miss Rose.
No Mr. Briar?
It's just the two of us.

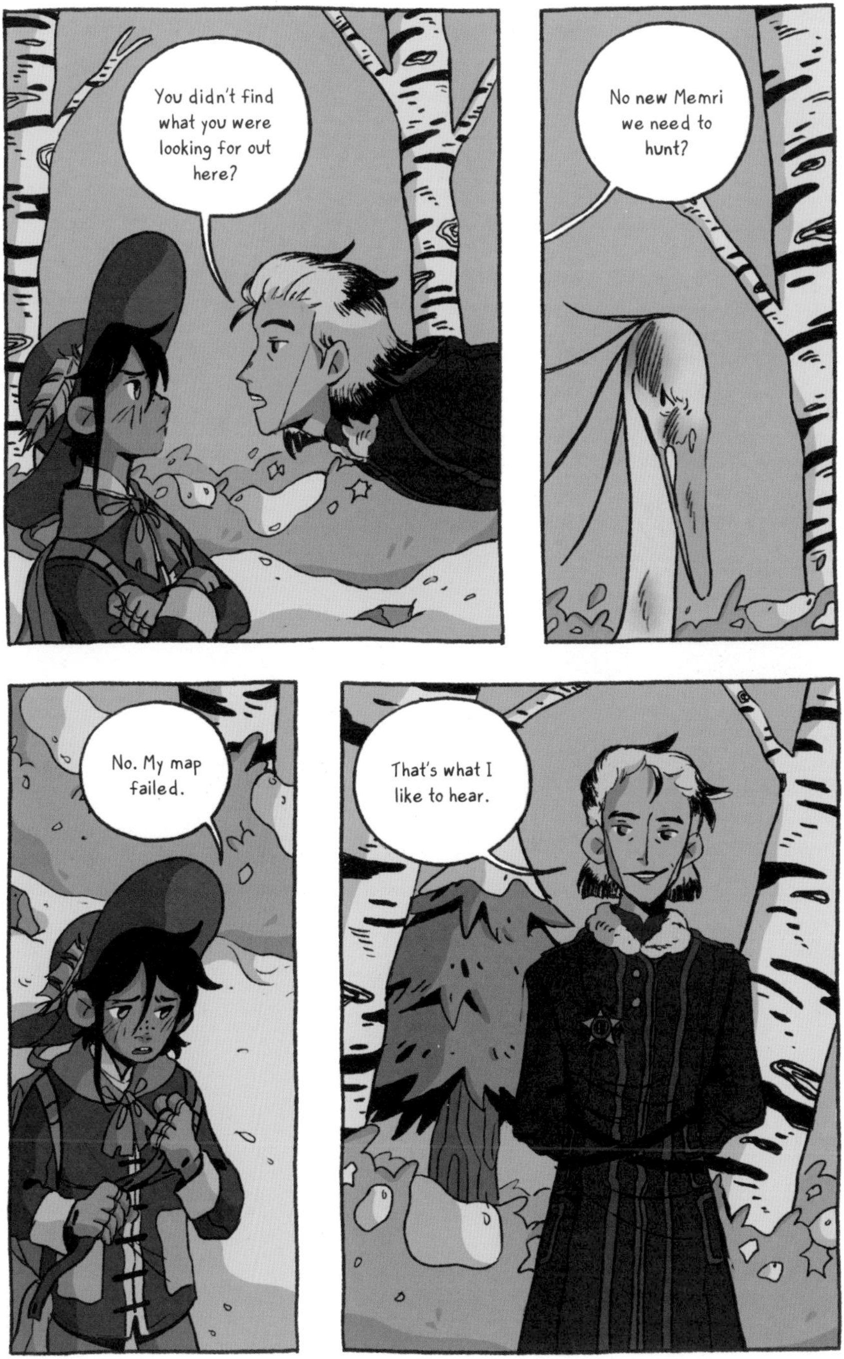
You didn't find what you were looking for out here?
No new Memri we need to hunt?
No. My map failed.
That's what I like to hear.

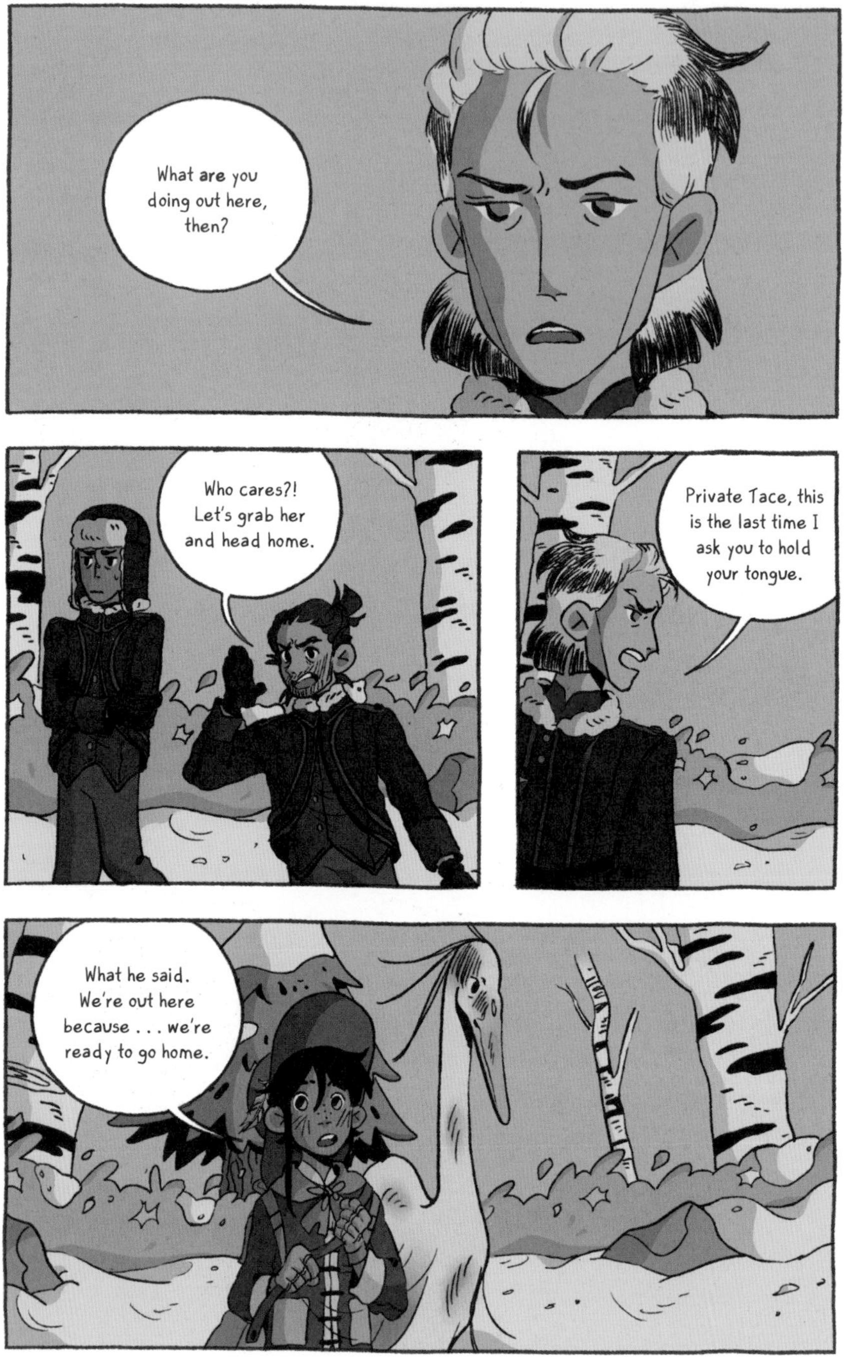
What are you doing out here, then?
Who cares?! Let's grab her and head home.
Private Tace, this is the last time I ask you to hold your tongue.
What he said. We're out here because . . . we're ready to go home.

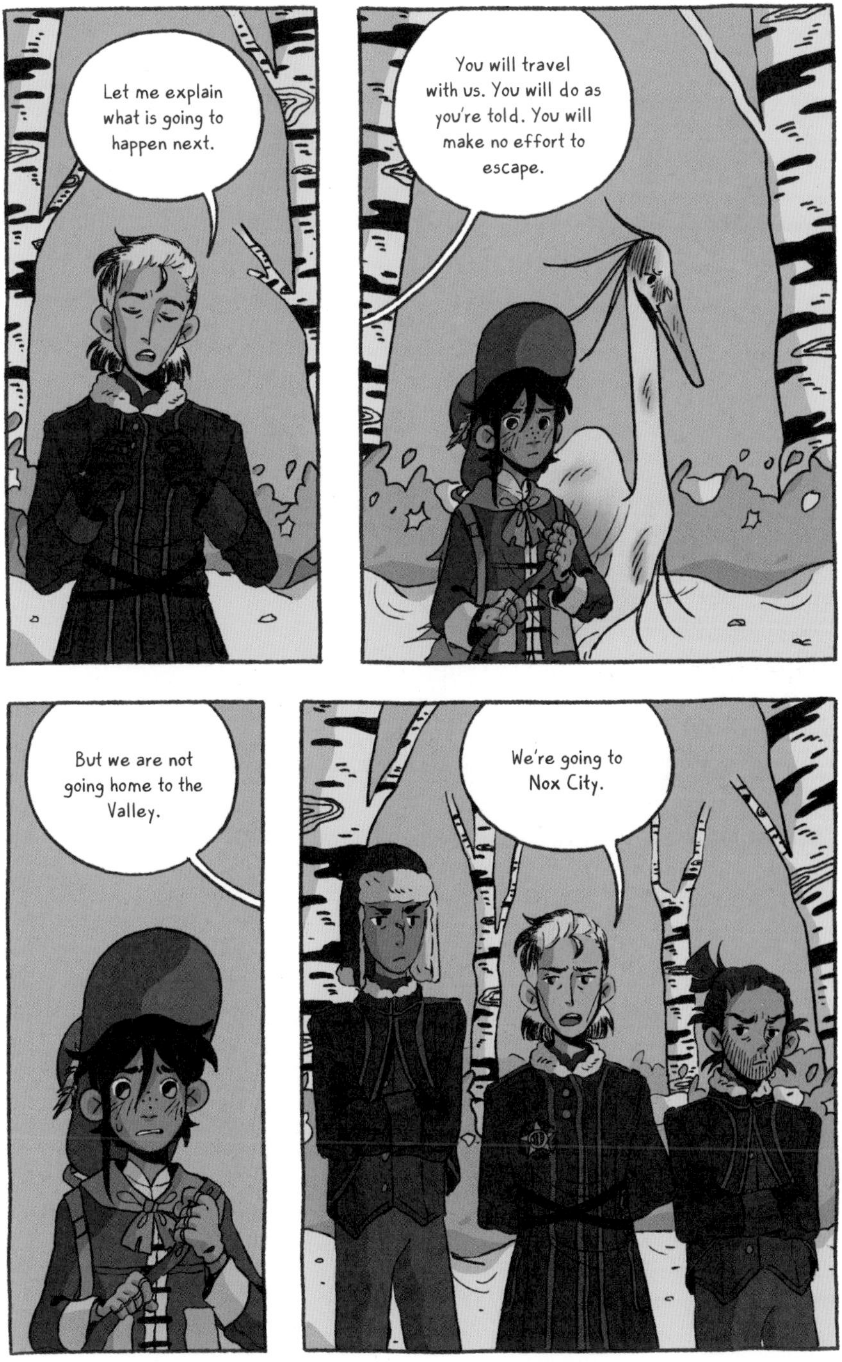
Let me explain what is going to happen next.
You will travel with us. You will do as you're told. You will make no effort to escape.
But we are not going home to the Valley.
We're going to Nox City.

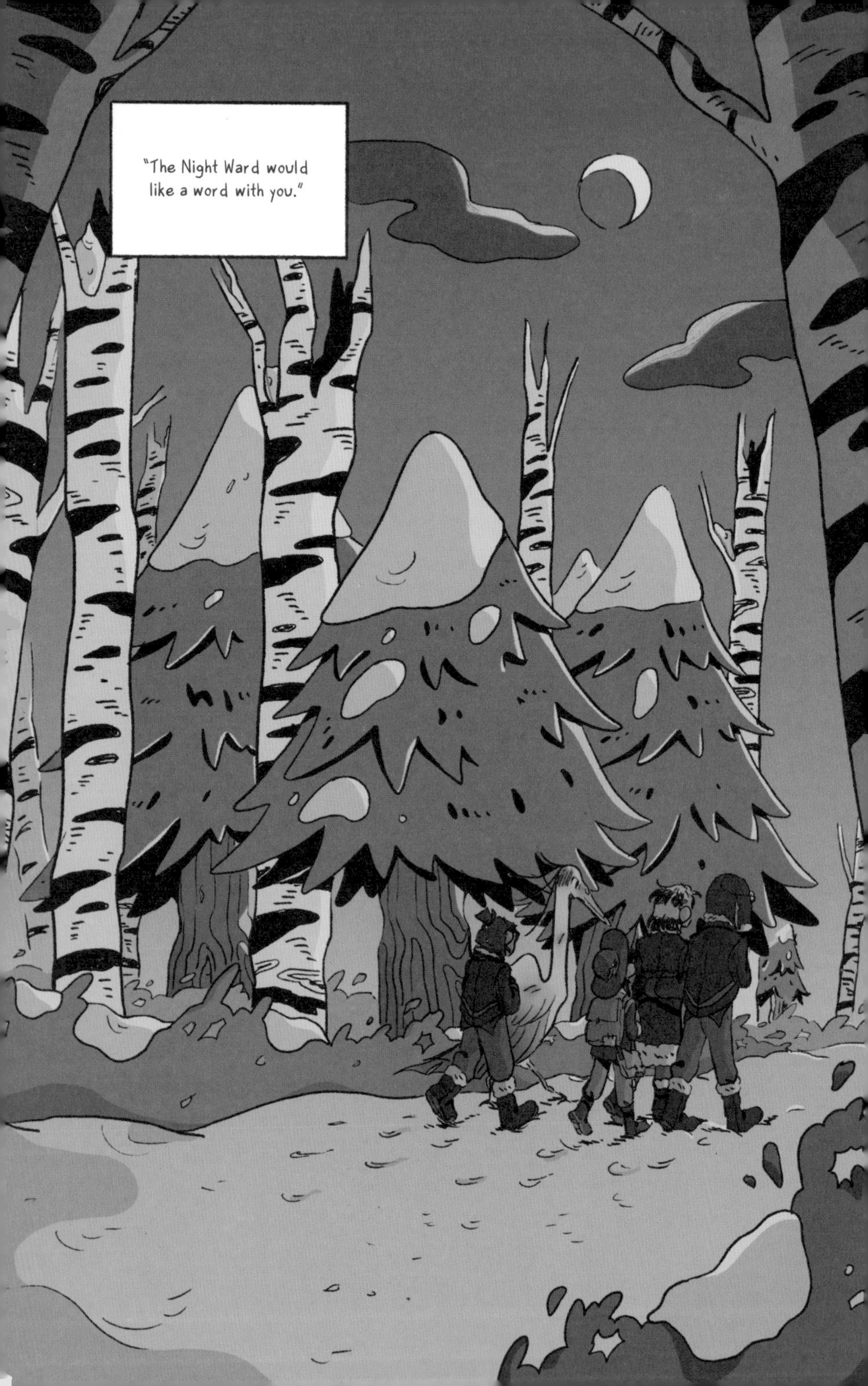
"The Night Ward would like a word with you."

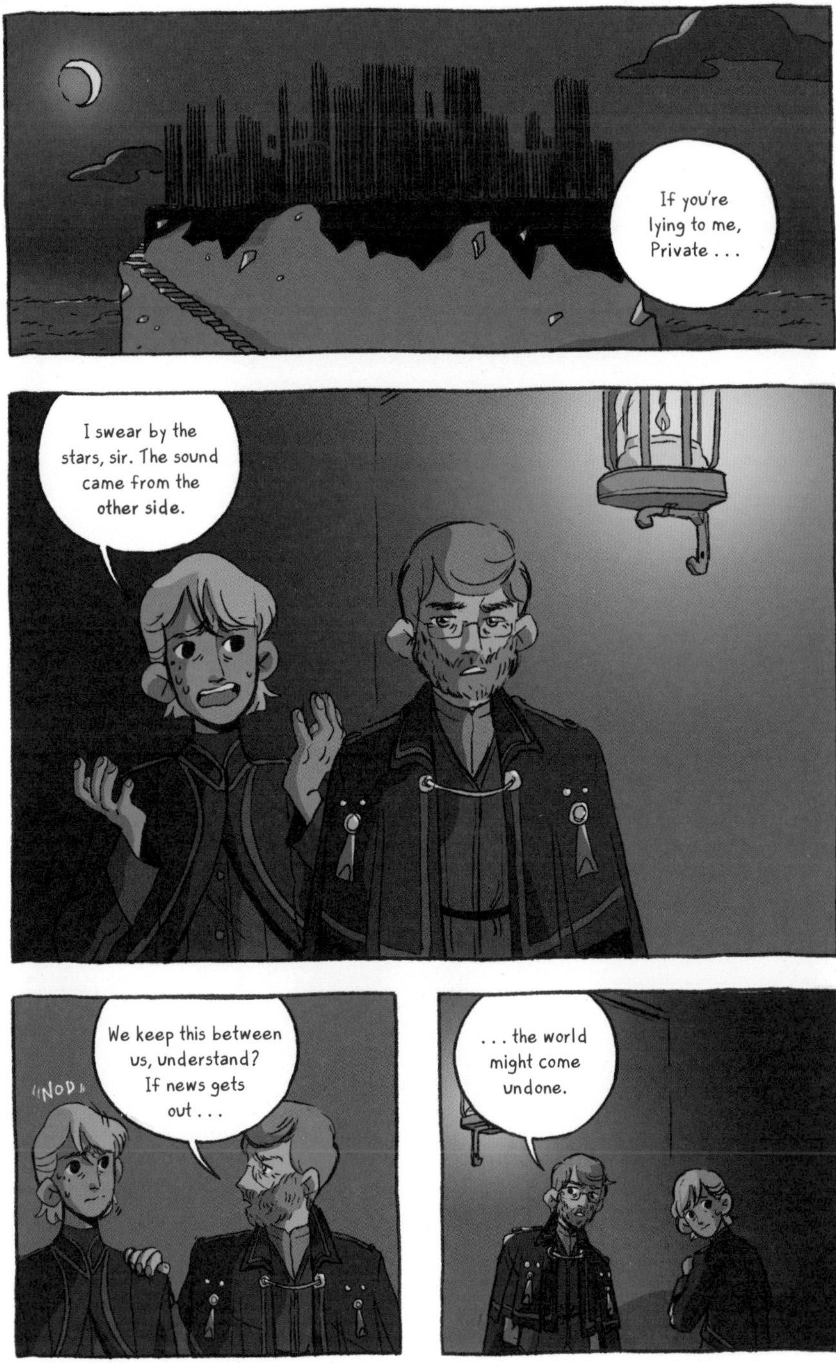
If you're lying to me, Private . . .
I swear by the stars, sir. The sound came from the other side.
"NOD"
We keep this between us, understand? If news gets out . . .
. . . the world might come undone.

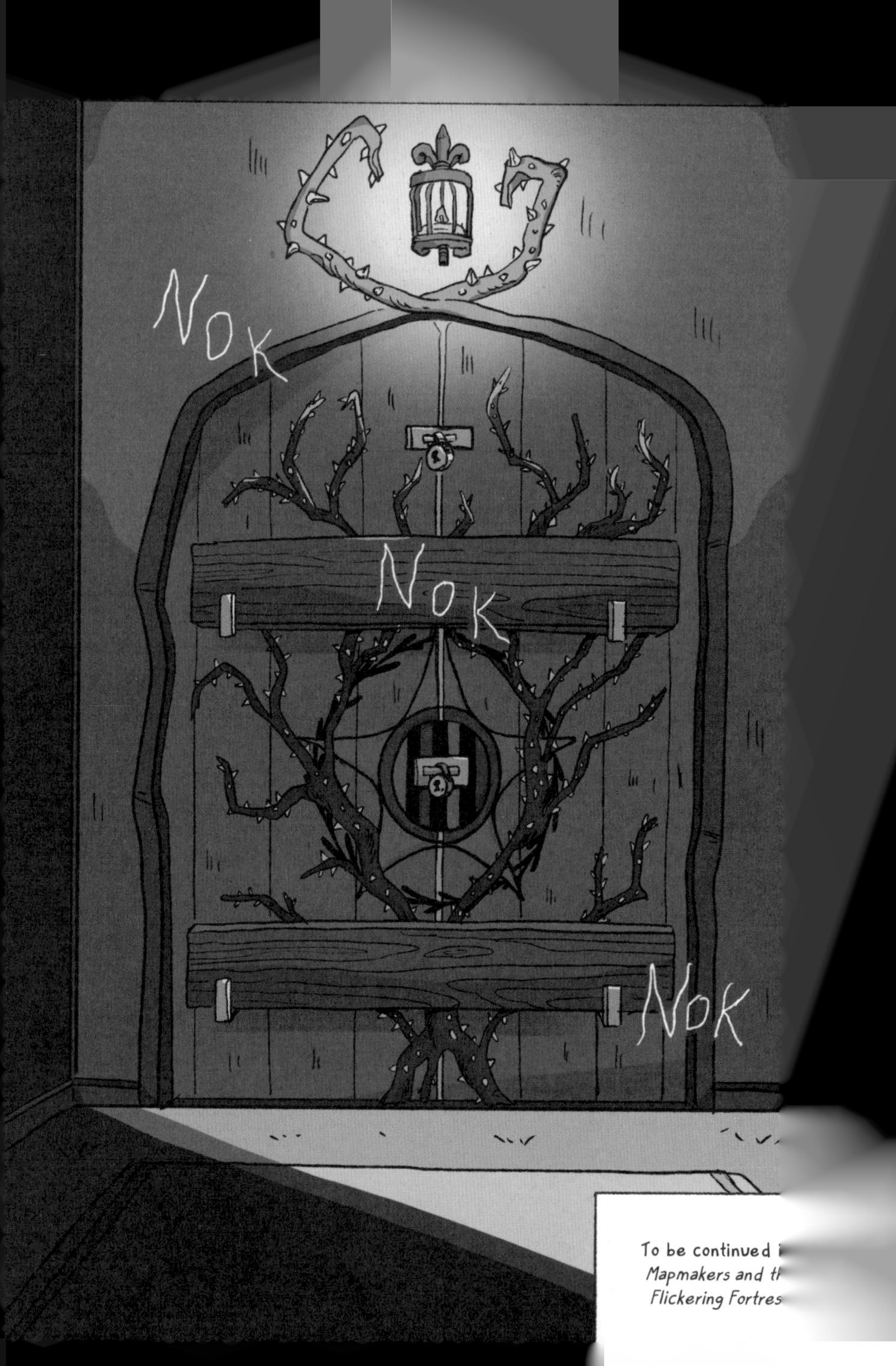
NOK
NOK
NOK
To be continued
Mapmakers and
Flickering

Lewis? You ready to go?
What's taking that boy so long?
READY.
No way I'm getting cold this time.
We're going to the Plains. You know it's going to be hot, right?
It's what?
This is what happens when I travel without Alidade . . .
Oh, relax, breaking a sweat is good for you!

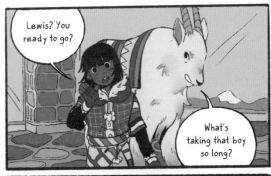

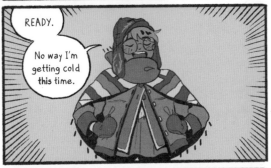

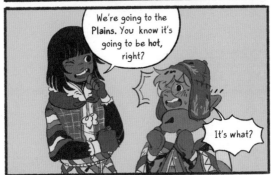

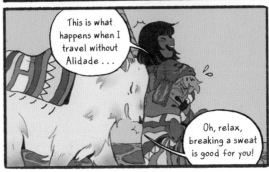

sounds like rOOOOOAAh!

## Howler-Hare

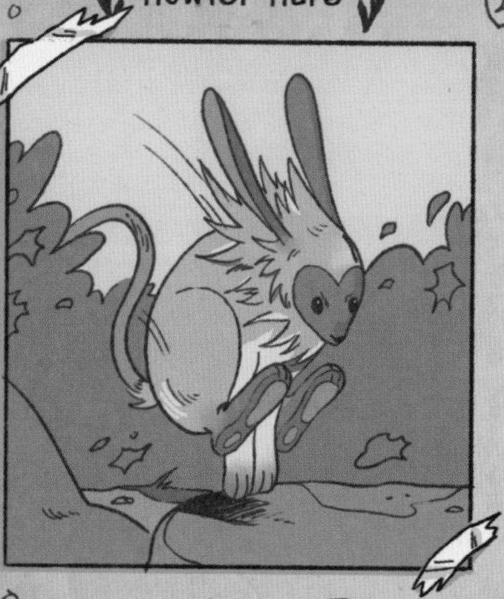

Bigggg tuft of tail fur!! (it fell off don't worry)

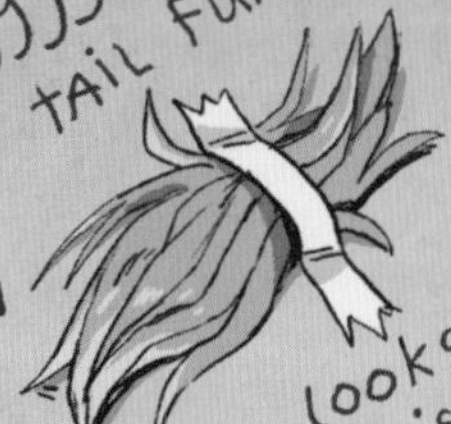

looks soft but is sort of rough...

A rabbit with a distinctive mane and large hind legs. But you'll hear them way before you see any of those details. With their mighty howl, they can pretend to be bigger beasts and scare off predators (and travelers).

Personality: Their bark is worse than their bite.

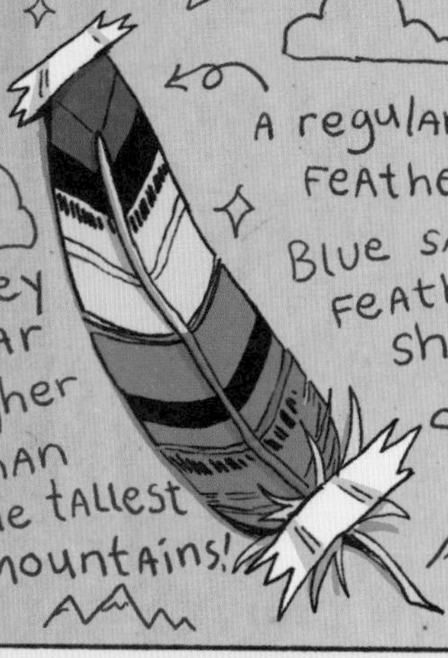

A regular feather

Blue said the streamer feather never gets shed

they soar higher than the tallest mountains!

## Northern Streamer (AKA the Super Mega Hawk)

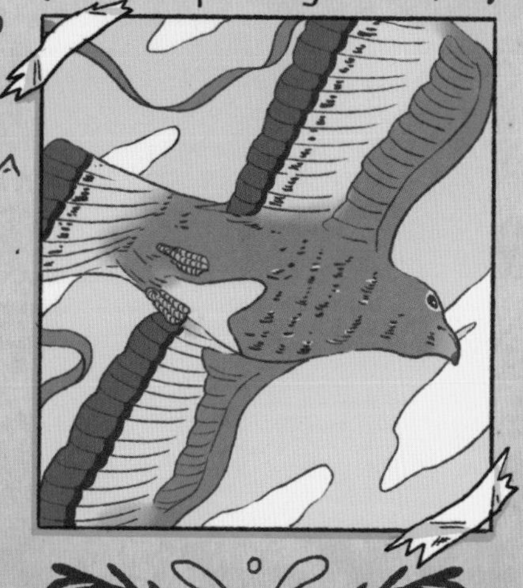

You can spot this bird of prey from ground level thanks to its long, trailing wing tips. But the only way to get a good look is by traveling to the highest of heights. (It's worth it!)

**Personality:** Lewis noted that they're "dignified." He did not explain further . . .

**Call:** A sharp, screaming ***cree-eeee-trah.***

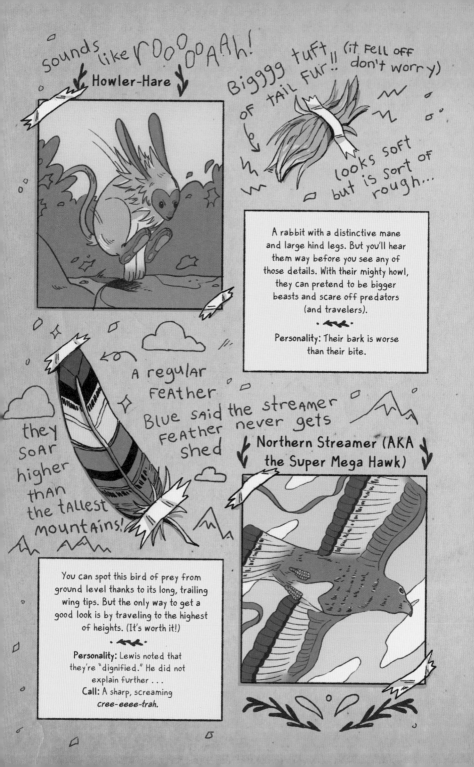

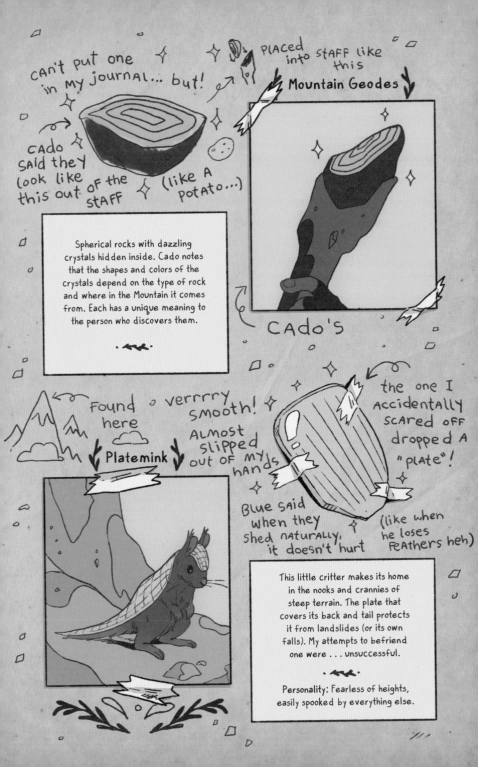

can't put one in my journal... but!

CADO said they look like this out of the STAFF (like A POTATO...)

PLACED into STAFF like this

**Mountain Geodes**

Spherical rocks with dazzling crystals hidden inside. Cado notes that the shapes and colors of the crystals depend on the type of rock and where in the Mountain it comes from. Each has a unique meaning to the person who discovers them.

CADO'S

Found here

verrrry smooth!

ALMOST slipped out of MY hands

**Platemink**

the one I ACCIDENTALLY SCARED OFF dropped A "PLATE"!

Blue said when they shed NATURALLY, it doesn't hurt (like when he loses FEATHERS heh)

This little critter makes its home in the nooks and crannies of steep terrain. The plate that covers its back and tail protects it from landslides (or its own falls). My attempts to befriend one were . . . unsuccessful.

Personality: Fearless of heights, easily spooked by everything else.

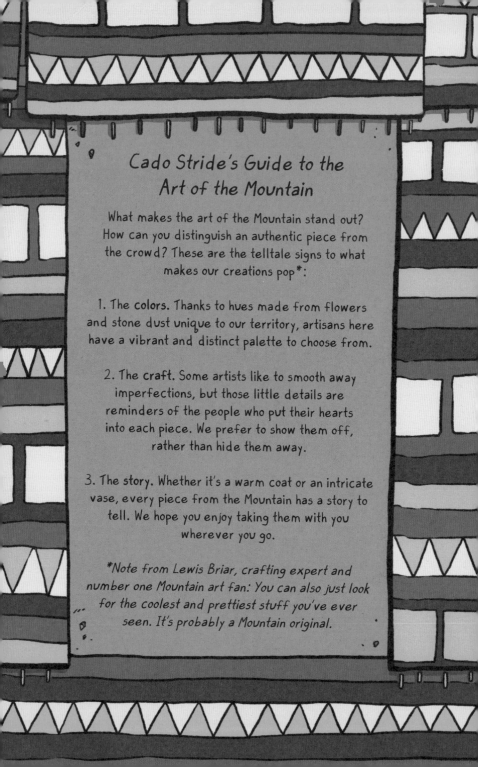

# Cado Stride's Guide to the Art of the Mountain

What makes the art of the Mountain stand out? How can you distinguish an authentic piece from the crowd? These are the telltale signs to what makes our creations pop*:

1. The colors. Thanks to hues made from flowers and stone dust unique to our territory, artisans here have a vibrant and distinct palette to choose from.

2. The craft. Some artists like to smooth away imperfections, but those little details are reminders of the people who put their hearts into each piece. We prefer to show them off, rather than hide them away.

3. The story. Whether it's a warm coat or an intricate vase, every piece from the Mountain has a story to tell. We hope you enjoy taking them with you wherever you go.

*Note from Lewis Briar, crafting expert and number one Mountain art fan: You can also just look for the coolest and prettiest stuff you've ever seen. It's probably a Mountain original.

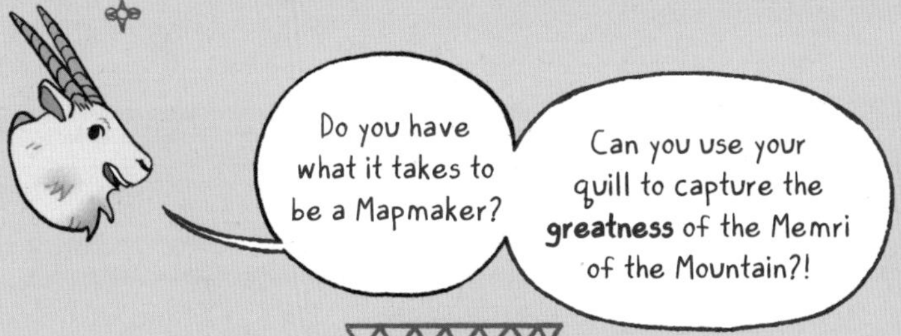
Do you have what it takes to be a Mapmaker?
Can you use your quill to capture the **greatness** of the Memri of the Mountain?!

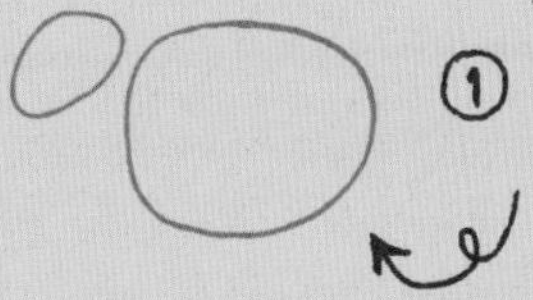

(1) First! A strong base shape. The key word here is "strong."

(2) Next, powerful legs fit for scaling any height! And horns, sharp and mighty.

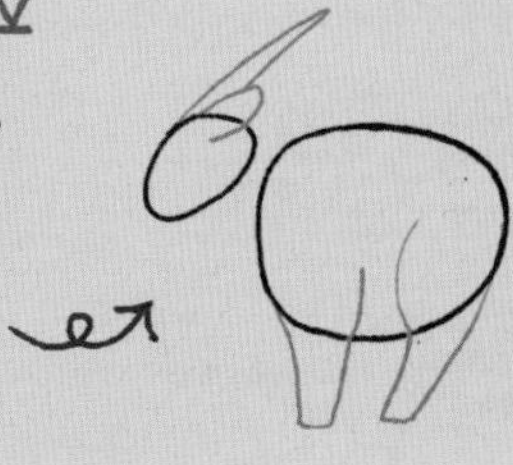

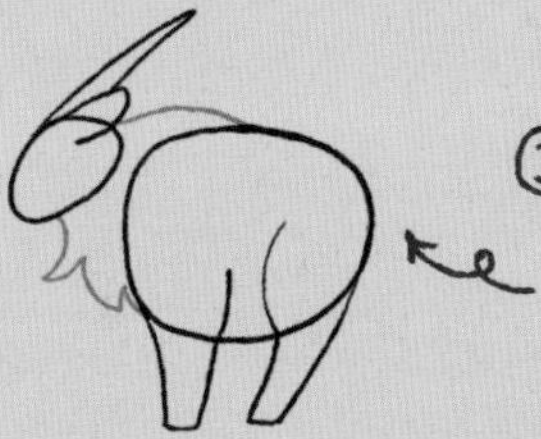

(3) Then you refine it with **muscles**! You can never have too many muscles.

(4) Finally, add in details and erase the guidelines. And there you have it! The **greatest** Memri of all.

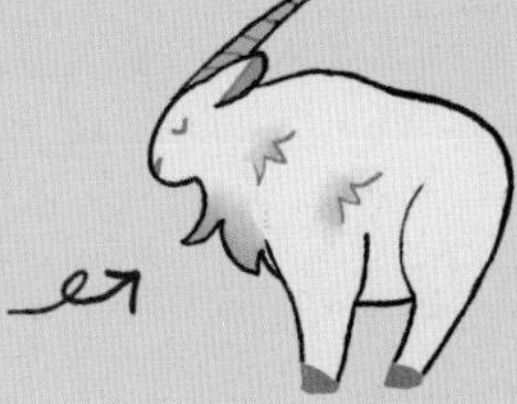

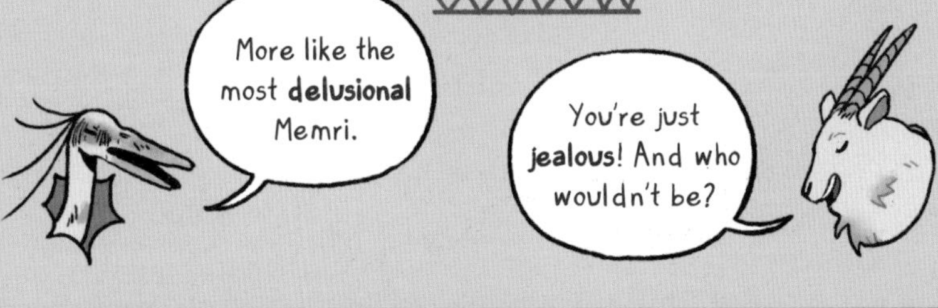
More like the most **delusional** Memri.
You're just **jealous**! And who wouldn't be?

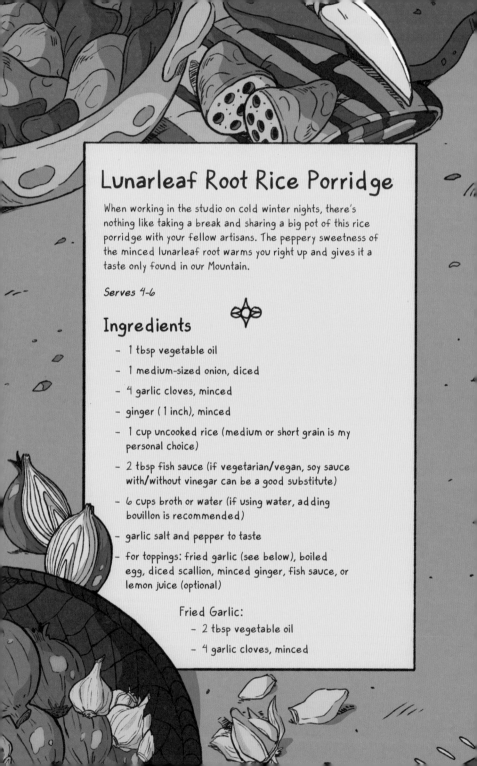

# Lunarleaf Root Rice Porridge

When working in the studio on cold winter nights, there's nothing like taking a break and sharing a big pot of this rice porridge with your fellow artisans. The peppery sweetness of the minced lunarleaf root warms you right up and gives it a taste only found in our Mountain.

*Serves 4-6*

## Ingredients

- 1 tbsp vegetable oil

- 1 medium-sized onion, diced

- 4 garlic cloves, minced

- ginger (1 inch), minced

- 1 cup uncooked rice (medium or short grain is my personal choice)

- 2 tbsp fish sauce (if vegetarian/vegan, soy sauce with/without vinegar can be a good substitute)

- 6 cups broth or water (if using water, adding bouillon is recommended)

- garlic salt and pepper to taste

- for toppings: fried garlic (see below), boiled egg, diced scallion, minced ginger, fish sauce, or lemon juice (optional)

### Fried Garlic:
- 2 tbsp vegetable oil

- 4 garlic cloves, minced

# Directions

1. Heat the vegetable oil on medium in a large pot. Once heated, add the onion, garlic, and ginger. Sauté until the onion is softened and the mixture is fragrant.

2. Add the rice and fish sauce. Mix until all ingredients are incorporated.

3. Add the broth or water, stir well, and let the pot come to a boil.

4. Once boiling, cover the pot and reduce the heat to low. Allow the mixture to simmer for 30 minutes or until the rice is fully cooked and the mixture has thickened. Stir occasionally to prevent the rice from sticking to the bottom.

5. While the rice cooks, heat vegetable oil in a medium-sized pan on low heat to make the fried garlic.

6. Once the oil has heated up (be careful to not let it get too hot or the garlic will burn), add the minced garlic and cook on low heat until it becomes a light golden brown.

7. Remove the garlic from the pan with a skimmer and drain on a paper towel.

8. Once rice is fully cooked, serve with the toppings of your choice.

**Note:** This dish is essentially the Filipino dish lugaw, and it can be made with meat! Either cook the meat before step 1 and use rendered fat in place of or in addition to the vegetable oil, or add the meat after step 1 and sauté until almost cooked. Bonus: Bone-in meat will add extra flavor!

# Acknowledgments

Another book, another long list of wonderful folks who played an invaluable role in making it a reality. We're so grateful for Whitney, Danny, Patrick, and Cynthia, who all contributed their incredible talents to this book. To Walter Parenton for designing our logo, and to Sara Calhoun, who was one of the biggest supporters of the series from the beginning and is now officially part of the team as the colorist.

Finally, eternal thanks to all of our loved ones: Amanda's parents, sister, and the rest of their family and friends. Your support throughout the years has been and will always be irreplaceable. And to Cam's family. None of this would be possible without his girls. His favorite story is the one he gets to make each and every day with Tay, Rowe, and Taren.

The art for this book was created on the unceded lands of the Chochenyo-speaking Ohlone people.

—Cameron & Amanda

**Cameron Chittock** is the writer of the Mapmakers graphic novel series. When he's not writing, he enjoys coaching basketball, reading comics of all kinds, and exploring New England with his family.

cameronwtchittock.com
@CameronChittock

**Amanda Castillo** is a comic artist, illustrator, and storyteller from the Bay Area in California (unceded Ohlone land) who loves to tell warm and heartfelt stories, whether it be through drawings, words, or both. When not creating comics, Amanda enjoys making warm meals for loved ones, learning to tend to plants, and soaking up the summer sun.

amanda-castillo.com
@mandallin